NEVER
SEEN
AGAIN

Paul Finch is an award-winning, *Sunday Times* bestseller. He studied History at Goldsmiths before becoming a cop in the North-West of England and then followed a career in journalism and screenwriting. He lives in Lancashire, UK, with his wife Cathy and their two four-legged companions, Buck and Buddy.

NEVER SEEN AGAIN

Paul Finch

ORION

First published in Great Britain in 2022 by Orion Fiction,
an imprint of The Orion Publishing Group Ltd.,
Carmelite House, 50 Victoria Embankment
London EC4Y 0DZ

An Hachette UK Company

1 3 5 7 9 10 8 6 4 2

A CIP catalogue record for this book is
available from the British Library.

ISBN (Paperback) 978 1 4091 8404 1
ISBN (eBook) 978 1 4091 8405 8

Typeset at The Spartan Press Ltd,
Lymington, Hants

Printed and bound in Great Britain by Clays Ltd,
Elcograf S.p.A.

www.orionbooks.co.uk

For my wife, Catherine

Six years ago

Freddie didn't know why Jodie and Rick were so glum. As they pulled away from the multiplex, his head was filled with the movie's mind-blowing final images. Bond and his latest girl jumping hand-in-hand down the central section of an abandoned building. The chase along the Thames, Bond in a speedboat, Blofeld in a helicopter. At first, Freddie thought that Rick had quite liked it, his sister's fiancé muttering as they'd left the cinema about it being 'derivative of earlier 007s,' whatever that meant, 'but still a bit of fun.'

Now though, the silence filling the car was heavy.

'Everything OK, Jode?' Freddie ventured.

Jodie didn't look around from the front passenger seat. 'Everything's fine. Don't worry.'

Freddie glanced from the Audi's window. It was past ten on an October night, wind whipping the shrivelled leaves along the verges. If they were genuinely cross, it couldn't have been about the movie, and at no point this evening had he noticed them having words about anything else. Which left one possibility.

They were cross with *him*.

And yet Jodie had just said that everything was fine. Which wouldn't have been the case if Freddie had annoyed her. She was twenty-three and he was thirteen – she'd have told him off in no uncertain terms.

'*See you later,*' she'd told everyone earlier that evening, when Rick had arrived. '*We're off to see the new Bond.*'

Freddie had immediately protested, and the usual strained conversation had followed; their mother attempting to guilt-trip Jodie into taking him along, Jodie resisting more forcefully than usual. Freddie wondered about that. It wasn't as if he was a difficult kid. And he got on with Rick. Well, the guy was a bit boring – he was training to be a lawyer, and how naff did that sound? – but they ribbed each other a lot, and they both supported Ipswich Town.

But they'd been OK during the actual movie, eating popcorn and chatting...

And then it struck him.

Had Jodie and Rick been planning to do something else? Something they weren't willing to mention? Freddie couldn't believe it.

Surely they hadn't been intending to park up the way they'd used to when they were teenagers? He felt a pang of indignation. All this moodiness because he'd got in the way of *that*? Though it still didn't make sense. Not when Rick had his own flat.

They pulled up on a quiet lane, parking at the farthest end of it, a horseshoe of thick bushes, overhanging trees and mountains of dead leaves turning it into a cluttered, shadow-filled cul-de-sac. Rick switched the engine off.

Jodie turned around. 'Do you want to go for a little walk, Freddie?'

'No. It's wet.'

'It's not wet. It hasn't rained since yesterday morning.'

'It's cold then.'

Jodie looked to the front again. 'Don't you fancy some fish and chips?'

He shrugged. 'Maybe.'

'I fancy some.'

'Go and get some, then.'

'Don't be silly, Freddie!' Her tone was sharp, irritable, which surprised him. They used to play this game years ago, Freddie finding that his status as official gooseberry could be quite lucrative, though the negotiations had usually been good-natured.

'I don't see a chippie round here,' Freddie said.

Jodie readopted her patient tone. 'If you walk back along the road, there's a path through the woods on your left.'

'Through the woods?' Freddie was unhappy about that. He wasn't a baby anymore, but the thought of cutting through a wood at night on his own…

'It's not real woods,' she said. 'Just a belt of trees. Then you're on the Black Brook golf course.'

'Golf course?' Freddie was puzzled.

'You don't have to go all the way across it,' Rick said. 'If you cut left, you'll see a sign saying public footpath. Follow that, and it'll take you to the clubhouse. On the other side of that, you'll see Wildeve Avenue. Turn right, walk for five minutes and there're a couple of cottages, a newsagent and a chippie.'

'I'll have a saveloy and chips,' Jodie said, handing him a twenty.

'Cod and chips for me,' Rick said. 'Get yourself anything you want. Keep the change.'

Thoughtfully, Freddie rolled the £20 note between his fingers.

Jodie regarded him through the rear-view mirror. 'OK… how much?'

Freddie pursed his lips. 'Thirty at least.'

She swung around in her seat.

'Thirty's fine,' Rick cut in, putting a hand on Jodie's shoulder. 'Thirty's absolutely fine.' He adjusted his glasses and reached under his leather jacket, filching out a wallet, opening it and extricating a twenty. He passed it back. 'Because we're springing this on you, let's call it forty. In fact,' he dug out an extra tenner, 'let's not be stingy. It's no small thing we're asking at this time of night, Fredster ... so let's call it fifty.'

Freddie goggled as the additional note was placed in his open palm.

He pulled on his anorak, zipped it, and stepped out into the dank wind. It was twenty yards to the nearest streetlight, its glow repeatedly obscured as semi-naked branches danced around it. Not far after that, he found the path on the left and cut down it, the flickery light fading behind him. He emerged at the foot of a short but steep embankment. At the top, Black Brook golf course unrolled before him. Overhead, the clouds were grey smudges scudding across the moon, but there was sufficient light for him to see the flat prairie of neatly mown grass. Veering left, he came to a cruciform signpost stencilled with the words *PUBLIC FOOTPATH* and an arrowhead. Beyond that, the ground tilted gently upward. At the top, it flattened off and there was another sign: *BEWARE LOW-FLYING GOLF BALLS*.

Freddie pivoted around as if one such missile might be hurtling at him right now. His eyes were attuning, and here and there sat clutches of shrubbery. Ahead stood a third signpost. It directed him to the mouth of a narrow alley between two deep rows of thickets, into which the wind funnelled gusts of spinning leaves. Freddie ventured along this nervously, but after that it was open again and all downhill, and about a hundred yards to his left he saw a squat, single-storey building against a row of bright yellow streetlights. The clubhouse.

No lights shone out as he circled around it, while all the windows were shielded by steel lattices. The car park lay empty and on the far side stood a pair of barred double-gates. They were padlocked closed, but there was a single gate alongside them, hanging open.

Turning down Wildeve Avenue, the only sound was the wind. As promised, when Freddie rounded the first bend, he saw a row of buildings on the right. But something about them jumped out straight away.

No lights. At least, not from either of the two shops.

His dismay deepened as he approached. The newsagent and the fish-and-chip shop stood in total darkness. The notice hanging inside the chippie's glass door read: CLOSED.

He stamped back along Wildeve Avenue. At first he was fuming, but then he remembered the money in his pocket, and it dawned on him that he hadn't been too badly done to. Basically, they'd wanted him to take a half-hour walk, and had paid him well for it.

He re-crossed the clubhouse car park and re-entered the golf course. His eyes adjusted more quickly this time, and when he found the passage through the thickets, he entered boldly, determined to ignore any scary rustlings or creakings. However, when he was about ten yards in, there was a blood-curdling scream.

He stopped in his tracks.

It had been short but intense.

An idea occurred to him that it might have been a vixen; he'd heard such sounds in the woods near his home. A vixen then ... a harmless fox.

5

Or maybe not.

Freddie raced out of the thicket onto the open fairway, heading downhill. The signposts flickered by, the outer line of trees visible a couple of hundred yards ahead.

There was another intense scream. This one broke off abruptly.

Freddie jumped the small embankment and sped along the path to the road, but as the filtered glow from the streetlight grew brighter, he decelerated, mainly because he didn't want to look a soppy kid in front of Rick. Even so, he didn't slow to an actual walk until he was back on the pavement mopping sweat from his brow.

But when he was still fifty yards from Rick's Audi, he saw that another vehicle was parked alongside it, a van, with its rear double-doors hanging open. And that figures were in motion. Freddie squinted through the tumbling shadows. With thirty yards to go, he realised that a couple of the figures were wearing green boiler suits. He part-relaxed. Paramedics. The van was an ambulance.

Only for new fear to strike him.

Was someone hurt?

He hurried forward, belatedly puzzled that the ambulance, which was clearly marked as such, was dark inside. Its back doors were open, but there was no warmly lit interior.

Another scream ripped the darkness. The same as before: a wailing shriek from the bottom of someone's soul. And that someone, he now knew without doubt, was not a vixen calling for a mate, but his sister, crying out in sheer terror.

Freddie slid to a halt, watching from ten yards away as three figures in green manhandled someone to the rear of that so-called ambulance and threw them inside it.

'Jodie!' he croaked.

Two of the figures glanced round.

There was another scream as a second struggling shape was bundled into the back of the vehicle. This one had to be Rick because he was putting up more of a fight, and it was several seconds before one of the men in green was able to tear himself away and lurch towards Freddie, one hand upraised.

'OK, son!' he shouted in an accent Freddie couldn't place. 'There is accident.'

Freddie didn't know which he found the more chilling. That the guy approaching, who had lost one of his gloves in the struggle, was now showing a palm bearing the tattoo of what looked like a huge black spider. Or that his face was blacker still, blotted out by a ski-mask.

Freddie bolted, but not along the lane. The nearest houses that way were miles off. Instead, he went left, crashing into the bushes, trying to dodge his way through. He'd covered twenty yards when he heard angry shouts, and an explosive CRACK.

A slug zipped past him, ripping through the foliage.

It goaded him to maniacal efforts, ignoring the branches that whipped and snagged him. As he reached the other side, he heard a heavy crashing of leafage as larger bodies entered the trees.

'Mara!' a gruff voice yelled. 'This way!'

This voice was different from the first. With another CRACK, a second shot was fired.

It clipped Freddie's left earlobe.

Though it stung, he didn't so much as yelp as he staggered up the short embankment. He knew that he'd need all the breath he could muster. But common sense was vital too. If he headed left towards the clubhouse and the road beyond, they'd see him, his dark shape a moving target on the moonlit grass. So, he went right, hugging the treeline as he sprinted.

In no time he was two hundred yards away. He risked a backward glance.

They were in close pursuit. One masked figure only fifty yards behind, another twenty yards further back than that. Freddie swerved left.

A third shot sounded.

A divot of grass was kicked up close by. But Freddie was already into the rough, the terrain dropping downhill towards an ornamental pond and then sweeping up to the first fairway. He sobbed for breath as he galloped around the edge of the water, risking yet another backward glance. The pursuers were still close. Even as he looked, light flickered, there was another *CRACK*, and a leaden wasp whipped past his head. Freddie stumbled on, cresting a low rise onto flatter ground. He dug for his phone, wondering if it would be possible to place a call at the same time as going pell-mell through this half-darkness. But his vision was too filmed with sweat, his fingers too slimy with blood from his ear.

Metal clicked behind him. *Directly* behind him.

Just as the landscape tilted downward.

A vista Freddie hadn't previously seen unfolded below him, at its heart the linear glow of a major road. He could even see the headlights moving back and forth. The slope steepened, making it easier; he found new strength.

'Shit!' someone shouted.

Freddie glanced back. Their two black shapes were on the higher ground, framed against the night. They'd stopped chasing, though one was pointing down at him. Freddie thought to zigzag, but was travelling at such speed that he feared he'd trip.

A *CRACK* split the night.

The smashing blow of the bullet was the worst pain he'd ever known...

I

THE WORST PERSON
ON EARTH

I

Today

'Course, it's not a problem these days,' Connie said. 'Being a shirt-lifter.'

'We're not exposing Sleaman because he's a closet gay,' David replied. 'We're exposing him because he's been doing the dirty on his wife and kids.'

'Yeah, sure.' Connie's raspy cackle sounded especially unpleasant through his in-car speakers. 'Who'd have thought it? Barry Sleaman ... How long's this been going on?'

'I doubt it's just started,' David replied. 'But that doesn't matter, does it? The fact remains I've caught him on film. And it's clear as a bell. He has no deniability whatsoever.'

'And let me get this straight ... you staked out his house in Beaconsfield and followed him every evening he went out until you caught him?'

'It was only five times.'

'Even so, darling. Tailing someone from Beaconsfield to Soho. No one can say you don't earn your money.'

'You're happy, then?'

'How could I not be? You're getting the front cover *and* a centre-spread. Love your intro, by the way.'

He'd known that she would. The road divided; he went — left towards Tesco.

'"TV tough guy busts a different kind of nut,"' Connie

read aloud. '"Brit-grit film and TV star, Barry Sleaman, famous for his roles as hardcase cops hunting lowlifes through the backstreets of Broken Britain, has this week revealed that he's got more than a professional interest in those backstreets, not to mention those self-same lowlifes. The burly, bearded actor may be known worldwide as a fearless confronter of hardmen everywhere, but today *Scandalous* can exclusively report that confronting 'hard men' means much more to him than a mere profession. The Yorkshire-born Sleaman (48), who is married and has three children, has long been renowned for his portrayal of macho but tortured heroes, characters with shady pasts but a firm grasp on their personal principles. However, according to *Scandalous* reporter, David Kelman, it now seems that Sleaman doesn't just have a shady past but a shady present too, though when it comes to personal principles, he is distinctly lacking. What he has a firm grasp on at present we can only surmise, but last Saturday night it was a young man called Sid, who cheerfully admitted to our intrepid news-hunter: 'Getting some action from a good-looking celeb like Sleaman was fantastic. I know he's on the scene a lot. He'd never admit that, but he is. But what a coup for someone like me. I only usually get the scrag-ends...'"' Connie broke off reading. 'This guy Sid proved talkative, didn't he?'

'Spoke to him in the bar after Sleaman had gone home,' David said. 'You'd be amazed how much lads like him'll tell you once you've bunged them a few quid.'

'Whatever, darling... This is very impressive work.'

Again, he didn't need her to tell him. The zip-filed photos and videos he'd sent with the story had only been compiled after a considerable expenditure of time; after waiting for hours, night after night, at different points along the suburban avenue where Sleaman's family resided in their seven-bedroom villa, hoping against hope that each night would be the night. That said, when it finally *was* the night and the big guy came outside unusually late, it had been comparatively easy tailing his classic MG soft-top the forty miles to Stanmore, where the actor had left it at a row of clapped-out garages, and continued his journey to London in a rickety old Renault Clio.

'Where's Sleaman now?' Connie asked.

'Lanzarote. The rest of the family went over for the summer hols. Sleaman couldn't go with them then because he had to do some pick-ups for his latest picture.'

She chuckled again. 'Pick-ups of one sort or another, that's for sure. Well, I imagine he'll be back home pretty quick once this story breaks. You'll want your usual rate, I take it?'

'You can take it and shove it.' David pulled into the supermarket car park. 'We're talking double, or I'm going straight to *Tittle-Tattle*.'

'Double?' Even the unshockable Constance Curzon sounded shocked.

'Connie, I didn't just shoot Sleaman smooching this kid on The Men's Room dancefloor; I got him banging the little bastard over a dustbin out back.'

'David, daaahling…' She only usually stretched her vowels when she was angry but trying to keep a lid on it because she respected (or needed) the other party. 'I love you dearly, but I was *not* expecting to have to pay double.'

'How do you think I got this scoop? I have big enough overheads as it is. This time there were lots of extras. I had to pay the doorman at The Men's Room, had to hire different cars. And like I say, Oli Hubert at *Tittle-Tattle* will always talk to me …'

'I get you!' she said curtly. 'Just don't make a habit of this. It's a nasty trick.'

'Isn't that the name of this game?'

She cut the call and David drove into the first space he came to. Locking his red Fiesta, he set off on foot.

It *was* nasty. The whole thing. There were times when he didn't like to think just *how* nasty. At one time, he'd used his skills to hunt real stories, to track down people who hadn't just morally lapsed or had a distant past they'd rather forget, but who were an active menace to society. It was quite a comedown for a once-infamous investigative reporter, even if the work itself was easy.

Sleaman had looked like a frightened rabbit as he'd emerged from that broken-down garage in Stanmore, wearing a disguise that would have fooled no one: jeans, a hoodie and shades. Shades! When it was already mid-evening and the sun almost down. How easy he'd been to follow and photograph. DI Crankworth, the hard-drinking, ass-kicking Murder Squad detective he'd played in *Blood City* would have sussed that he had a tail in two minutes. Barry Sleaman, predictably, hadn't. Not even when David had shadowed him on foot from the multi-storey at the bottom end of the Edgware Road. The big oaf had even gone into The Men's Room through its front door. Any of that would have been good enough for David to make a bob or two, but for the idiot to then have taken his latest squeeze out round the back …

Of course, just because the bloke lacked any of the animal instincts that made his TV persona so appealing was no reason to dislike him. Not when there were four other reasons: his wife and three young children.

Not that *that* excuse would cut it. A story like this was

hardly in the public interest. So, it would sound pretty lame if they tried to sell that line as justification. Irritated by the ever-insoluble nature of the issue, David did what he usually did: wrote all these characters off as dirty, deceiving bastards and put them from his mind.

Inside Tesco, he grabbed a basketful of groceries before meandering to the magazines section. This week's edition of *Scandalous* was on the topmost shelf, its plastic-sheathed front page unmistakable as it depicted Sally Ripley, a popular TV weather girl, seated in a crowded pub, grinning bleary-eyed while pulling up her sweater and bra. Her breasts would have been clearly exposed had the magazine not pixelated them out.

RIPLEY RAT-LEGGED

ran the 60-point headline. Below that, the strap added:

*Barflies goggle as tipsy totty celebrates
big 3-0 by flashing her big 3-8s*

And in smaller print:

Uncensored images inside

Down in the bottom corner, a smaller sub-header:

Soap queen's mob links?

sat above the screen-grab of an older but well-regarded television actress, captured snarling during an intense moment from one of her recent dramas.

*Did popular TV postmistress strut her
sexy stuff with gangland killers?*

the caption asked.

David Kelman gets on the case.

David wheeled his basket to the counter, where, after paying, he stripped off the mag's plastic cover and flicked his way in until he'd reached his story.

In truth, there hadn't been much to it. It was common knowledge that faded glamour-puss, Edna Fairchild, once the buxom fall-girl to innuendo-specialists of the 1970s like Benny Hill and Frankie Howerd, had enjoyed a racy past. She'd been married several times and back during her heyday was for three years the wife of Adam Vaughn, a one-time associate of the Krays, though stories had been rife for decades that during the course of this wild youth, Fairchild had attended functions where numerous underworld figures were present.

David had simply regurgitated much of what was already known, but had spiced it up by visiting a few East End bars, where several inebriated old lags, now able to gossip because no one else from that era was left, had elaborated on some of the crazy booze-ups their one-time associates had hosted, which had often involved drug-taking, strip poker, group sex and such, and how it was possible that Vaughn and his then missus had been present.

There'd been so little fact to go on that the double-page splash mostly comprised blown-up photos from Fairchild's past, needless to say when she was being saucy and provocative, though here and there a few gangsters' headshots had been inserted for emphasis.

The aged actress, these days a soap opera stalwart and national treasure, would not be happy. But David was no newbie. He'd been careful how he'd worded the story, at no stage suggesting that Fairchild had actually attended any of these lurid events, just stating that people around at the time thought she might have. And if that didn't prove to be adequate protection, well... that was editor Connie Curzon's problem.

'Admiring your latest masterpiece?' someone asked.

An Indian woman in her early thirties stood alongside him. She was intensely pretty, with dark eyes, firm lips and lush black hair cut square at the shoulder. Such was the trimness of her figure that she even made her boring floor-manager uniform of dark skirt-suit and white, sensibly buttoned blouse look good.

'How you doing, Nushka?' he asked.

'Happy enough.'

'Yeah?' David wasn't sure he could ever trust an employer who insisted you wore a large name-badge on your lapel.

'It's life after journalism, David. We take what we can get.'

'That's my excuse too.' He scrolled the mag.

Anushka shook her head. 'They pay you for that stuff?'

'Not much for this one. But I've got other irons in the fire. How's Norm keeping? Any closer to finishing his opus?'

'Think he's about halfway through the first draft.'

'He was that far on with it six years ago.'

'He's semi-retired, you know.'

David pondered that. It was difficult to conceive of their energetic ex-colleague as being even *semi*-retired.

'Should give him a call,' she said. 'He'd love to hear from you.'

David eyed her. 'You genuinely believe that?'

'Well, can't hurt, can it?'

'I don't think it's the best idea.'

There was an awkward moment. Anushka had told David what she'd *hoped* would be the case where Norm and he were concerned. David, for his part, didn't need to be an arch-cynic to sincerely doubt that any contact with his old mate would be well received.

She looked worried. 'I take it you've heard about…?'

He nodded. 'Yep. Believe it or not, I sometimes check out the real news too.'

'So … are you all right?'

'You mean am I upset because I think it was my fault?'

'Are you?'

'I don't get upset, Anushka. I can't afford to.'

'Come on, David…'

'By all accounts the kid had been leading a pretty risky lifestyle. I'm sure there were lots of other factors involved.'

'That's probably true,' she conceded. 'You're looking fit, anyway.'

'Thanks. Lots of gym, lots of running.' He almost added, *Gotta find some way to fill the endless empty hours*, but resisted. He was glad that she thought he looked good physically. He'd rolled back the years with his recent PE: he was lean and fresh-faced for a forty-year-old, and at six foot three, with a shock of jet-black hair and grey-blue eyes, he might even cut a dash. But Anushka Chawla had been a newshound herself before all this, and wouldn't be fooled. One look at his shabby jeans and sweatshirt and his scruffy denim jacket, and she'd know that he wasn't doing well otherwise.

'How you keeping *really*?' she asked.

'Well … I'm working. Don't feel sorry for me, Anushka. I've got lots going on.' He headed for the door.

'See you around, David.'

He waved as he left.

2

Six years ago

The press room at Colchester Police Station sat in silence as Detective Superintendent Mackeson of the Major Investigations Team spoke from the low platform.

'We can confirm,' he said, 'that the two persons abducted near the Black Brook golf course on Monday night were Jodie Martindale from Dedham, who's twenty-three years old and the daughter of Ralph Martindale – you'll all know him, I'm sure. And her fiancé, Richard Tamworth, twenty-five, from Stoke-by-Nayland...'

There was a rush of questions. Mackeson held two palms aloft, shaking his head.

Three other people sat at the table. To his left a handsome mixed-race woman, Assistant Chief Constable Gina Dearborn, unrufflable as ever in her pristine Essex Police uniform; to his right, a studious-looking man in a suit and glasses, with a salt-and-pepper beard and moustache. His name was James Whelks and he was the Martindale family's solicitor. Last of all, on Whelks' right, sat a tubby, sandy-haired man, also in a suit, who'd been introduced simply as DCI Thackeray.

'How's the little boy?' was the first question the panel actually heard.

Mackeson nodded to Whelks, who adopted a sombre tone.

'Freddie's doing well under the circumstances. As you know, he suffered two bullet-wounds, one of which was relatively minor – it nicked his left ear, and one of which caused a compound fracture of the humerus in his left arm. He underwent surgery yesterday and is expected to return home tomorrow.'

'Is he talking, sir?'

Mackeson responded to this one. 'Freddie will be a key witness in this investigation, but it hasn't been possible to fully interview him yet.'

'How did he come to be separated from the other two when the abduction occurred?'

'At present, we're not really clear on that.'

'Was he able to tell you anything at all about the assailants?'

'Only that there were at least two of them, maybe three. And that they were in reasonably good physical condition as they were able to pursue him all the way across Black Brook golf course. We have Scenes of Crime specialists up there as we speak…'

'So Freddie Martindale wasn't able to give you any physical detail?'

'Not so far,' Mackeson replied. 'The boy's done very well to remember what he has, given the amount of blood he lost and the fact that he was in a severe state of shock when he received assistance from passing motorists.'

'Was he able to describe the vehicle the assailants arrived in?'

'Only that it was a van of some sort. One of our first lines of enquiry of course has been to check all sources of CCTV footage shot in that area between the hours of nine o'clock in the evening and midnight on Monday 26 October.'

'May I ask, sir, what DCI Thackeray is doing here?'

Mackeson and ACC Dearborn glanced at the questioner. He was a tallish guy in his early thirties, wearing a shirt and tie under a leather jacket. He had a shock of very dark hair and intense features, and held up a Dictaphone.

'We have a considerable number of assets at our disposal,' Mackeson said, 'and DCI Thackeray has recognised expertise in the field of...'

'He's from the Kidnap Squad, isn't he?' the questioner interrupted. 'National Crime Group... New Scotland Yard?'

There were mumbles of surprise.

'That's correct,' Mackeson replied. 'Sorry, you are ...?'

The questioner held up his press badge. 'David Kelman, *Essex Examiner*... Crime Beat.'

The body language of both Mackeson and Dearborn tautened. It was ACC Dearborn who spoke next. 'Mr Kelman, for a respected crime reporter, a man famous for having informants *everywhere*, you're surely not surprised that we've called in the Kidnap Squad...'

'It seems very quick, that's all I'm saying,' Kelman replied. 'I mean you've already got the Essex Major Investigations Team on the case. They usually handle all serious crime in the county. Unless this isn't a one-off, of course?'

'I'm not sure what you mean,' she said.

'Well,' Kelman gestured, 'it can't have gone unnoticed by anyone that one month ago, just outside King's Lynn, there was a very similar case. Darren Doyle and Cheryl Bryant, another courting couple, snatched from their vehicle while parked up in a lover's lane area?'

'There are similarities,' Mackeson admitted, 'but no obvious links between the two incidents that we've been able to establish...'

'There's no comparison in terms of ballistics? Presumably there've been tests made?'

'We're having discussions with Norfolk Constabulary as we speak,' ACC Dearborn replied, 'but that case ended very tragically, as I'm sure you're all aware.'

The press pack *were* aware of it.

Darren Doyle and Cheryl Bryant had disappeared from Doyle's car one Friday night the previous September. Both youngsters were later found on a landfill near Dereham, hands zip-tied behind their backs, gunshot wounds to the backs of their heads. The case remained unsolved, but the official line was that Norfolk Constabulary were investigating possible drug connections between Doyle and local dealers.

'Which means it's always advisable to tread lightly in these situations,' Mackeson added.

'Any further questions, anyone?' ACC Dearborn asked.

'There's a story doing the rounds,' Kelman persisted, 'that the hoodlums responsible for kidnapping Darren Doyle and Cheryl Bryant demanded an exorbitant ransom. The figure I was given was £500,000.'

Mackeson shrugged. 'That enquiry has nothing to do with Essex Police...'

'Because if that's true, such a figure would have been far more than Darren Doyle or Cheryl Bryant's families could have afforded. Doyle's father was a bus driver, I believe, and Bryant's mother was single and lived on benefits.'

'I'm sorry, Mr Kelman,' ACC Dearborn countered, 'but the murders of Darren Doyle and Cheryl Bryant are the subject of an ongoing investigation by Norfolk Constabulary...'

'There's another story too,' Kelman interrupted. 'That because neither the Doyle nor the Bryant families could afford to raise this ransom, it suggests—'

'We're here to discuss a different case entirely,' Mackeson butted in.

Kelman ignored that. 'Ralph Martindale, Jodie Martindale's father, isn't just a local businessman, is he? He's a business mogul: founder and owner of MD Solutions, or MDS, one of the biggest asset management firms in the City of London, and now CEO of the MDS Group overall. I dare say that *he* could afford to pay a big ransom. Have you any comment to make on that?'

'No,' Mackeson said firmly. Alongside him, solicitor Whelks looked shaken.

'What I'm getting round to,' the journalist said, 'is that if the Norfolk abductions were a dry run, this suggests there's a professional kidnap gang operating in East Anglia?'

Dearborn whispered something into Mackeson's ear. Further conversation filled the room. Other similar questions boomed from the floor.

The ACC rose to her feet. 'I think that's enough for today, ladies and gentlemen. We've now ranged far into the realm of guesswork and speculation...'

'If there *is* a kidnap gang operating locally,' Kelman shouted, 'might it be some consolation to those officers involved in the Doyle and Bryant case who failed to rescue the victims... I mean, knowing that those two youngsters were a practice run and would have been killed anyway?'

She stared daggers at him. 'No, Mr Kelman – were that the case, I assure you it'd be no consolation at all.'

3

Today

David returned home late-afternoon. His address was 22, Danson Court, a small dormer bungalow tucked away at the end of a cul-de-sac on a drab Colchester housing estate.

Alongside it, a rusted kissing gate opened onto a narrow path winding through a belt of trees to a playground that was mainly notable for its bottles, beer cans and spent tubes of nitrous oxide. On a day like today, of course, with the school holidays into their second week and the sun shining, it was teeming with youngsters. They were making their usual God-awful racket, but it didn't bother David much. He'd been here three years since separating from Karen, and anything unsavoury about the place had now blended into an all-in-one background that he barely paid attention to anymore.

As he walked round to his back door, which was actually at the side of the bungalow, located at the end of a narrow alley running between the garage and the house proper, his mobile rang, and when he checked, it was Karen calling.

'Hi.' He barged into the kitchen, his bag of groceries clutched under one arm.

'Hi.' As always, his ex sounded tired and frustrated as if already fed up with him. 'You got plans for this weekend?'

'The usual,' he replied. 'Work.'

'Any chance you can take some time off to see your kids?'

'What's this about, Karen?' He dumped his shopping on a kitchen worktop.

'I'll tell you what it's about, David. You haven't seen Tommy or Tabby since Christmas. The other day, your daughter asked me if you were still alive.'

He peeled his jacket off. 'I sent her some cash for her birthday.'

'That was in February.'

'And I sent them Easter eggs at Easter.'

'Yeah, that was in April. It's now July. What's the problem?'

He went through into the small living room, which was in its usual state of disarray. 'Do they really want to see me, Karen? Or do you just want a break from them?'

'There are two answers to that. Firstly, I won't be taking a break from them. I thought we might all go out somewhere together. Like a drive to the seaside or even a walk in the park. Secondly, why would they not want to see you? You're their dad and they love you. That's why you've got full access any time you want. Even though you never take advantage of it.'

He moved to the window. Beyond it lay a garden area, which even though it was small, had the potential to be pleasant had it not been for the heaps of rotting leaves left over from last autumn and the clutter of old garden furniture he'd inherited when he bought the property.

'If you guys want to hook up on Saturday, that's fine,' he said.

'Why so reluctant? Have you got someone else?'

He crossed the living room. 'Chance'd be a fine thing.'

'I know what it is, David. You don't consider yourself fit to be around them. Do you?'

'Christ's sake, Karen. Stop trying to psychoanalyse me…'

He called it a living room, but it was that in name only. He'd now pushed the sofa up close to the television, with a coffee table to one side of it, from where he ate his meals. This was to make room for the swivel chair and desk, from the top of which paperwork spilled in abundance. His laptop was on there too, along with several unwashed mugs, a pile of notebooks, a scattering of pens and Post-it notes and various other bits of stationery.

'Don't be evasive, David. It *is* that. And I know why. It's because of this latest death, isn't it? You think it's all your fault. You think it makes you a bad man.'

He sat at his desk. 'Let's not go there, eh? I've just had Anushka hit me with all that.'

'Anushka Chawla?' Karen sounded puzzled. 'You still in contact with her?'

'Sure, why not? It's Norm who can't stand the sight of me.'

'Where'd you run into Anushka?'

'Tesco. She works there now.'

'Well, sounds like Anushka's on the ball. It'd make a change, but even a stopped clock's right twice a day…'

'She isn't on the ball. And neither are you. So enough with the bad-mouthing people.'

'All right, OK…' Karen took a breath, and when she spoke again, it was a more conciliatory tone. 'No one is trying to psychoanalyse you, David. And no one here considers you a bad man. It's just that Tommy and Tabby are seven and ten, and they want to see their dad. Surely that's not too much to ask?'

He hung his head. 'No, course it's not. Let's do Saturday then. If the weather's good, we'll have a picnic or something.'

'That sounds nice, I suppose.'

Karen was the one who'd asked him to come up with an idea and even though he had, she still didn't sound as if she trusted him. It was always the case that she'd only believe things if they happened. But then that was understandable to a degree. David had never been the most reliable husband and father.

'And I am *not* feeling bad about that business down in Chatham,' he said. 'OK? It was sad but it was also predictable given what's been going on.'

'If you say so.'

'I'll call you back on Friday.'

'Speak to you then.' She cut the call.

He sat back, eyeing the wall above his desk. It was plastered with newspaper clippings, most of them old and faded and bearing his byline. In pride of place sat a huge double-page spread:

COPS CLOSING NET ON KIDNAP KILLERS

Further down, but much newer – as in added this very morning – was a story written by someone else. This headline was somewhat less sensational:

TROUBLED HEIR'S SUICIDE LEAP

4

Six years ago

'So, what's this grass of yours actually saying?' Stan Grimshaw asked.

With his squat, foursquare physique, bull-head, thick pebble-glasses and scowling features, he resembled either a rugby prop forward or an escapee from Devil's Island. David was never quite sure which, though Grimshaw had been News Editor at the *Essex Examiner* for the last five years now, and they'd developed a working relationship based on mutual respect if not exactly trust.

'He's saying that Norfolk bollocksed it,' David replied. 'Less than a week after Doyle and Bryant got grabbed out of Doyle's car, his family received an anonymous demand for five-hundred grand. Everyone was flummoxed. These were ordinary people. How could either of the families cough up a fee like that? Norfolk Police said they shouldn't try to raise it anyway. They arranged with the family to make a dummy drop-off – a sports bag with cash on top, but all the rest of it bundles of newspaper. Course, there was a tracker in there too so that an armed police team could follow it covertly.'

Grimshaw listened, oblivious to the noise and fury of the newsroom. They were standing at the entrance to the Crime Beat office; Norm Harrington leaning on the jamb, Anushka Chawla to one side, pad in hand.

'The hoodlums were clever,' David explained. 'The guy dropping off the bag was an undercover copper, but they ran him all over Norfolk. He picks up a typed message here, answers a ringing telephone there. In the end, he was instructed to leave the bag on a traffic island near Fakenham. The firearms response team had managed to keep tabs on him, so they lay low not too far away. Couple of hours later, it's picked up by a biker. They follow the biker. He takes it to a house on a brand-new housing estate. Knocks on the door, waits. That's when the firearms team pounce. Course, there's nobody in the house. Hasn't even been completed yet, never mind occupied. The biker's just a courier doing a job. He didn't know what was in the bag…'

'So they knew there'd be a tracker?' Grimshaw said.

David shrugged. 'They suspected.'

'And this is why the two captives were killed?'

David mused. 'In my opinion, that's the impression they were trying to give.'

'Because the real target was these rich kids they were going to snatch one month later?'

'Doesn't it seem obvious? By capping Darren Doyle and Cheryl Bryant, they were sending out two clear messages. A – we know what you'll try, so don't even think about it. And B – this is what happens if you do.'

Grimshaw pondered. 'But Norfolk haven't backed any of this up?'

'They've neither admitted nor denied,' David said. 'Officially, it's a double-murder committed by persons unknown, possibly connected to the drugs trade.'

'Who's handling it?'

'Norfolk have put a Murder Taskforce together, but I'd be

amazed if they're not liaising with Essex Major Investigations right at this moment.'

'Have Norfolk put out any info at all?'

'A single poor-quality video-grab.' David pulled out a printed but blurry image. 'This guy – described as white, late thirties, strong build, balding on top with a scruffy beard and what might be several old facial scars, wearing a zip-up hoodie, dirty dungarees and underneath those, what looks like a green overalls top. He called into a petrol station on the A47, which is six miles from the spot where Doyle and Bryant were abducted, at around two in the morning on 19 September, which Norfolk estimate was about one and a half hours after the abduction. He bought bottles of water, crisps and chocolate, and paid with a credit card that later turned out to be stolen. There was a camera in the station shop, but the hood took care of that. Also suspicious was the fact he apparently walked to the petrol station and then walked away again afterwards.'

Grimshaw arched an eyebrow. 'On foot, on a dual carriageway?'

'Didn't want any cameras clocking his vehicle.'

Grimshaw frowned, unsure.

'He may not be connected,' David conceded. 'Norfolk haven't confirmed whether he is or isn't, but they've marked him as a person of interest.'

'What do *you* think?' Grimshaw asked Norm, who was taller than either of them, but older and silver-haired and flamboyant as ever in his latest colourful Paisley shirt.

'David's theory's plausible,' Norm said. 'But we've got no evidence for it. Not if David's grass won't go on the record.'

'He's not going to do that, is he,' David retorted. 'He's a serving police officer.'

'This same Deepthroat guy who turned over the Lampwick Lane crew?' Grimshaw sounded as if he already knew the answer to this.

'Who else? And what a result we got that day.'

'But we can't get anything from anyone else? Not even off the record?'

'No.'

'That's probably down to Lampwick Lane too,' Norm said.

David made no response to that.

Two years earlier, he and Norm had made the *Essex Examiner*'s name as a regional newspaper by exposing a cadre of corrupt local police officers. By use of his own insider, the aforementioned Deepthroat,, David had learned that two senior detectives from the Essex Robbery Squad based at Lampwick Lane Police Station near Braintree had planned and organised their own series of heists, using a trusted informant to recruit fall guys to carry out the jobs, and then arresting the robbers themselves, in each case the informant claiming the official reward and sharing it with his corrupt police buddies while the fall guys drew long jail terms. After several weeks of painstaking work, the story, broken exclusively in the *Examiner*, was an absolute sensation, as a result of which the Essex Robbery Squad was disbanded and several bent coppers sent to prison: the two detectives and a firearms officer who'd acted as their enforcer.

'How did they react at the conference when you pressed them on whether a ransom had been demanded for Martindale and Tamworth?' Grimshaw asked.

'Wouldn't play ball,' David replied.

'No surprise,' Norm said. 'Kidnappings are hard enough to tackle without having to do it in the glare of publicity.'

Grimshaw wasn't happy. 'Are there any other possibilities – anything we could be overlooking?'

Norm shrugged. 'This lad, Darren Doyle, was known to the police. He didn't have much form, but he wasn't squeaky clean. It's not inconceivable that if he'd annoyed the wrong people in some way, they could have staged the kidnapping in the same way David describes, but used it as cover for a gangland hit.'

'But that seems less likely given the Martindale and Tamworth abductions,' David replied.

'Which we still don't *know* is a kidnapping,' Grimshaw said.

'*We* don't, no. But others may.'

Grimshaw frowned again. 'If this turbocharged informer of yours is part of Essex CID, how come he's got no info on whether the Martindales have received a ransom demand?'

'It's only been two days,' David said. 'It's also possible that they've already received one but, given the disaster up in Norfolk, are keeping it close to their chest. Could be that the majority of Essex don't know about it either. Especially if it's a massive demand. I mean, you're not going to kidnap one of the three heirs to Ralph Martindale's fortune and only ask five-hundred big ones, are you?'

'How many Martindale kids are there?'

David glanced at his notes. 'Jodie, her older sister, Hannah, and young Freddie. But Jodie already works for her dad as a kind of trainee Number Two. They've got big plans for her at MDS. Or they had. So that's two reasons why some firm might expect a big payday if they nabbed her.'

'How's the little lad holding up?'

'We're assured he's OK,' Norm said. 'He's back home today, but no one's allowed near him.'

'I'm not surprised,' Anushka put in. 'He must still be in a bad way.'

'Maybe,' David grunted. 'But it's no good to us.'

'Come on, David, have a heart.'

He glanced at her. 'Newsflash, Nushka – we've got column inches to fill, and this is the biggest story in town.' He swung back to Grimshaw. 'It's not like there aren't questions to be answered where the lad's concerned.'

'What do you mean?' Grimshaw said.

'Why wasn't he in the car with the other two?'

'Presumably they wanted some nookie and sent him for a walk,' Anushka said.

David shook his head. 'A couple in their mid-twenties? I get it with Doyle and Bryant. They were eighteen and nineteen respectively. But Tamworth owns his own place.'

'That's true,' Norm said.

'We need to talk to the kid,' David asserted.

'They've said no interviews for the next week at least,' Anushka said, irked by David's curt dismissal of her viewpoint. 'Plus, like I say, he's probably in shock. The whole of the Martindale family's probably a mess. Shouldn't we give them some space?'

'If we do, someone else won't,' David responded.

'We don't *know* that. It'll look terrible if—'

'Don't you owe me some copy from court this morning?' Grimshaw asked her.

Anushka glared at him. 'Suppose so.'

'Off you go, then. I'll see your first draft in twenty minutes.'

Grudgingly, she slunk away.

'Look, Stan,' David said, 'even if we can't find anything

to link these two abductions, we can dig for more on the current case. There are lots of unanswered questions here.'

'What was their body language at the conference?' Grimshaw asked. 'The Essex brass, I mean?'

'They weren't happy.'

'That could just have been because it was *you* firing questions at them,' Norm said.

'Jesus!' David snorted. 'Anyone'd think we did the world a disservice outing those bastards at Lampwick Lane.'

'It didn't reflect well on their bosses either,' Norm replied.

David waved that aside. 'Stan, come on. It was the line of questioning that was bugging them. I'm sure it's because we were getting close to something that's likely to be the biggest story we've had in ages.'

'Yeah, well...' Grimshaw handed David his screen-grab back. 'I'm not risking this paper's reputation on the basis that you *think* you're getting close. We need something that'll stand up – we need provable facts.' He moved away. 'Come back with something solid. Until then we're sticking with the official line.'

'You didn't think he'd buy it, did you?' Norm said as they went back into the Crime Beat office. 'I mean, without any proof?'

David sat at his desk. 'I'll get him all the proof he needs.'

'Don't do anything risky, David.'

'Do I ever?'

Norm snorted. 'You don't seriously want me to answer that question, do you?'

5

Today

As David drove to the Church of St Peter in the Fields, he wondered why he'd bothered to dress in black. It wasn't that the outfit didn't suit him; thanks to his recent spate of exercising, he could now get into his old black suit easily, his black shirt and tie finishing it off. But he had no intention of attending the funeral. For one thing, he wouldn't be welcome.

When he arrived, the church was typical of those you routinely found in bucolic villages scattered throughout Dedham Vale. Solid stone, clad with ivy, standing in a gentle green valley, cows at peace in the flower-filled meadows beyond. The only thing to sadden the pastoral scene was the presence of the burial party in the lichen-encrusted churchyard.

There were plenty of them, reflecting the huge number of cars lined up along the country lane adjacent. David remained in his vehicle, watching through the bars of the fence.

Family and friends stood in reverential silence as the pallbearers lowered Freddie Martindale's casket into the earth. David recognised one bearer as Jason Bulstrode, Ralph Martindale's son-in-law, who was also Senior Accountant for MDS, the family firm. Close by stood Jason's wife, Hannah, once the oldest of the Martindale children, now the only one left. Next to her, the grey, ghostlike form of Ralph Martindale sat stiff and silent in his wheelchair. David felt a particular kind of horror as he assessed the one-time hotshot financier. He too was in black, an overcoat as well as a suit, which seemed bizarre on a glorious day in August, though even from a distance, he was a frail wisp of a man, his face blank, cadaverous, tinted yellow. He looked ninety, yet was only in his mid-sixties.

David switched his attention back to the younger members of the family. With the casket lowered, Jason Bulstrode had backed from the grave and stood alongside his wife, one arm locked tight around her. He was youngish-looking and fresh-faced, with thick-rimmed glasses, a slim build and mouse-brown hair shorn at the back and sides. Altogether nondescript. In contrast, Hannah Bulstrode was more noticeable, only slightly shorter than her husband, but her shapely figure enhanced by a tight black dress, her fair hair held in coils beneath a black net full-head veil.

The whole event was as stiff upper lip as these affairs got.

David had his window open thanks to the summer heat, and all he could hear, aside from the low intonation of the vicar, was the humming of insects. No sizeable group of people he'd ever seen – and there must have been seventy mourners gathered – had conducted themselves with such immaculate dignity. Gazing through his windscreen, he wondered what it would be like to be *that* person. To be the object of so much respectful sorrow once you were gone.

I am not a bad man, he told himself.

OK, sometimes it was easier to say that than to prove it, sometimes even easier than it was to believe it. Especially after what he'd done to this particular family.

A few minutes passed and then a raft of people in black were swarming around his vehicle.

Up close, David spotted several celebrity faces. A Premier League footballer and his wife, both semi-concealed behind opaque sunglasses. A prominent broadcaster and notoriously outspoken TV personality. A cheeky Scouse comedian, who to the bewilderment of many, had now become famous in America. And Nick Thorogood, a big noise in the entertainment business, but a professional Jack the Lad too, legendary for his showy wealth and, thanks to some dodgy dealings during his days as a City trader, his roguish status, but a lifelong pal of Ralph Martindale.

Mumbling quietly, all these guests clambered into their own vehicles; there was every make and model there, from the Mercs, Rollers and Bentley Continentals of Ralph Martindale's close associates to the Skodas and Nissan Micras of his employees. Some distance up the lane, David saw Hannah Bulstrode, her husband and a security guy helping her bereaved father out of his chair and into the back of one of the funeral cars. When they'd pulled from the kerb, several other cars fell into stately procession behind them. Putting his Fiesta in gear, David followed.

But he had no real idea why he was doing this.

Something kept churning inside him. About trying to put things to bed with a simple, well-intentioned word or two. Except that he knew it wouldn't be so easy.

He flicked sweat from his brow as he drove, still following the bulk of the funeral traffic. In truth, his nerves were in shreds at the prospect of facing these people. And the closer he drew to Rosehill House, their country residence, the more unlikely it seemed that he'd be able to go through with it.

In Dedham Village, he stopped off and bought himself a bottle of Talisker.

Who knew, Dutch courage was sometimes a real thing.

But when he reached Rosehill, a Grade I-listed manor house, its electronic gates open for once, its long drive already filled with vehicles and milling with people, he halted in a tree-lined layby on the other side of Manningtree Road, and sat watching. And though he unscrewed the bottle and drank its contents in hefty gulps, he already knew that he wasn't going any closer than this.

When David's eyes flitted open, his vision was bleary. He sat up stiff and disoriented, wondering why he was in his car. When he noticed the bottle of Talisker lying on the front passenger seat, only a couple of fingers remaining, he had an answer of sorts. Not that this mattered. Of more concern was his pounding headache and an intense need to urinate.

Climbing out, he staggered to the bushes at the back of the layby, where he relieved himself copiously. It might still be early, but the sun was overhead and the heat muggy. He zipped up and leaned against his car for a minute, before ducking back inside, rooting in the glovebox and bringing out an unopened bottle of sparkling water. It wasn't cold, but at least it was fizzy, and it hit the spot when he gulped it down. He threw the empty back into the car and wandered to the layby entrance, to gaze up at Rosehill House.

It was quite something. Even in a part of the country where lavish rural residences were not the exception. It had the genuine look of a building from the past, one wing constructed from heavy stone, as though Tudor or medieval in origin, the other timber-framed and whitewashed in the Jacobean style. It occupied raised ground, overlooking

Manningtree Road, but sat on a broad terrace amid extensive gardens. When dealing with the Martindale family last time, David had researched the house's value. It had cost £3.5 million when Ralph bought it in the mid-1990s, so heaven only knew its worth now.

As he watched, he saw a lone figure coming down the drive. It was a woman, partly concealed behind a tower of cardboard boxes. When she reached the roadside, she laid the boxes down next to a row of different-coloured wheelie bins, and commenced emptying their contents into each relevant receptacle. Mostly it was cans, bottles, paper plates and general food waste. The woman herself wore slippers, scruffy pyjama bottoms and a T-shirt, but from the fair hair hanging halfway down her body, was recognisable as Hannah Bulstrode.

She hadn't seen him yet, but he already felt a crawling sensation in the pit of his stomach.

Before he knew what he was doing, he was crossing the road towards her, tucking in the flap of his sweat-damp shirt.

Astonishing even himself, he called out to her. 'Mrs Bulstrode.'

She turned in surprise, and then dropped the box she was holding.

She was a handsome woman, even scrubbed free of make-up. In fact, she looked better that way. Younger, more wholesome. But now her expression darkened, became a snarl. It brought David to a halt before he'd reached the pavement.

'What in the name of sweet Jesus Christ...' she hissed. 'Why are *you* here?'

David became flustered. 'I... I wanted to express my condolences. And I thought it would be cowardly if I didn't do it face-to-face.'

'Well, well…' She gave him a long stare. 'As it happens you've come at the right time. Perhaps I can reintroduce you to my baby brother, Freddie?'

David's brow furrowed. 'I don't understand.'

'Well, you wouldn't, would you. You don't understand anything that isn't of use to you. *Here* he is. *Here's* Freddie.'

She picked up the box, which had been bound with tape, and for a nightmarish moment David wondered if they'd had him cremated and were now disposing of his ashes in the trash.

'This is all that's left of him,' she said. 'A shoebox-sized pile of dog-eared paperwork, an armful of junk. The sum total of his final, frantic efforts to locate Jodie. So, Mr Kelman…' She gave him another level stare. 'Are you happy with the outcome of this thing you started? Or are you just sorry there isn't another front page you can milk from it?'

David regarded the box in horror and fascination, though more of the latter.

Freddie had been trying to find his sister. And *this* was the result of, well, of whatever he'd actually been doing…

'Famous people are so quickly discarded by journalists like you, aren't they?' the woman said. 'When their names don't sell papers anymore. Anyway…' She hefted the box, and dumped it onto the rubbish cramming the blue wheelie bin. It was already so full that the box sat on top, and even though she tried hard, she couldn't close the lid on it. She backed away. 'There you are, Mr Kelman. Pity you don't have a camera ready. That way you could have gone back to whichever publisher you've sold your soul to this time with undeniable proof that Freddie Martindale has finally been discarded in the most complete and irreversible way.'

'Please believe me… I just wanted to say I'm sorry.'

'Forgive me if I don't swoon with gratitude.'

She headed back up the drive.

'Mrs Bulstrode? Hannah!'

She spun back, fierce again. 'Don't you dare "Hannah" me! You've destroyed our family in more ways than one, Mr Kelman. You didn't just cost us Jodie and my mother and now Freddie. You cost us my father too. You realise he had a stroke the day he learned that Freddie was dead?'

David's thoughts raced back to the grey, shrunken figure in the churchyard.

'You saw him, didn't you?' Her expression changed again, this time to one of amused contempt. 'In his wheelchair yesterday. Were you skulking around the edges of the funeral to see if you could get something interesting out of it? Don't tell me that's why you're all in black? For God's sake, don't tell me you've camped out here all night?' She shook her head. 'You really are the worst person on earth.'

'I wanted to go to the funeral, yes. But in the end, I … I stayed away.'

'That must be the first decent thing you've ever done.'

She set off up the drive.

'I'm sorry,' he called after her again.

She said nothing. Further up, David saw that her husband, Jason, was coming down, wearing slacks, a sweater and white training shoes. Hannah stopped when she met him, speaking animatedly, gesticulating. The guy continued down, red-faced.

'Piss off, Kelman!' he yelled. 'Don't you think this business is difficult enough? Go on, sling your fucking hook!'

The older David might have waited defiantly, confident in the knowledge that he wasn't on their property. But that wasn't the way he responded now, backing across the road instead, palms raised in surrender.

Jason Bulstrode continued to hurl insults until David lost sight of him beyond the row of trees screening the layby.

As he climbed into his Fiesta, he was shaking.

Freddie Martindale had thrown himself off the top of a block of flats.

What on earth did it take to drive you to something like that?

And yet, though riddled with guilt, David was damn sure that it couldn't all be down to him. That was a momentous thing to do to yourself. There had to be more to it. And yet the sum total of Freddie Martindale's final few years now resided in a dustbin on the other side of the road, a shoebox-sized pile of – what was it Hannah had said: dog-eared paperwork.

Now destined for a furnace somewhere, or a landfill.

He drove to the layby entrance, where he halted, peering across the road. There was no sign now of either Bulstrode. But the cluster of wheelie-bins still stood by the left-hand gatepost at the bottom of their drive, the blue one still open because its lid couldn't be closed.

The sum total of his final, frantic efforts to locate Jodie.

David pondered that.

Freddie Martindale had spent his final years in self-imposed exile, in a squat, drugged up. But he'd also been looking for his sister? Who knew what evidence he'd managed to gather?

David glanced left and right. The road was still quiet. He pulled out, heading left. No one would ever know, of course, if it was dispatched to a landfill.

He drove a few dozen yards, at which point he braked,

knocked his motor into reverse and hammered the pedal, accelerating back to the foot of the drive. Without trying to think it through, he kicked his door open and walked to the bins, where he snatched up the box. Yes, it was shoebox-sized, but it was heavy, which meant that it must be jammed full. One glance up the drive showed that no one was watching. He flung the box into his back seat, and leapt behind the wheel again. Tyres squealing, he headed home.

He'd made it as far as the Colchester ring road before it occurred to him what he'd done and how it would be seen by the Martindale family.

Cold sweat trickled down his back.

OK, he'd stolen it, he'd removed something personal to them. But they'd binned it, for Christ's sake! Plus, he owed it to Freddie Martindale, didn't he?

Not that any of that counted for much now. He could hardly take it back.

6

Six years ago

When Marvin Kerwin came down to the gates at the foot of the drive, he was every bit the bruiser David had expected. Heavy brows, a dented nose, sloping, apelike shoulders. He wore an expensive suit and tie, but his veneer of civilisation was paper-thin.

David flipped open the wallet containing his press card. 'Kelman. Essex Crime Beat.'

Kerwin was too busy exuding hostility to do more than throw a quick glance at the ID, which in no way was adequate to distinguish it from an Essex Police warrant card.

'The liaison officer's been called away,' Kerwin said. 'Supposedly it's an emergency.'

'It's OK. Just need to go through a few things with Freddie.'

Kerwin hit a control, and the gates swung open. They walked up the drive.

'How's Freddie doing?' David asked.

'He'll live,' Kerwin grunted.

'Tough kid to go through what he did.'

'It's the family who're fucked up. Worried shitless about Jodie.'

'I presume they've heard nothing else from the kidnappers?'

47

David asked, aware that he had to be careful what kind of questions he posed.

On no account did he wish to reveal that he wasn't who the big lunk had assumed he was, but by the same token he didn't want it to appear that he was deliberately being deceitful. It was risky enough that he'd pretended to be a cop when texting the family's liaison officer from a burner phone and summoning her to a non-existent meeting at Colchester Police Station. If that issue ever arose, he'd deny any involvement and they wouldn't be able to prove otherwise, but here in the family home there'd be witnesses.

'Not since last night,' Kerwin replied.

David made a mental note that the villains had now been in touch. Presumably to demand a ransom. If it had been last night, that would have put it *after* the police press conference, though there'd still been no updated or additional bulletins put out to that effect.

They turned right and took a flight of broad steps up to the main building. From close proximity, Rosehill House was even more like a baronial hall: sprawlingly huge, this part of its façade comprising the restored beams and plaster of the seventeenth century. At its front, the drive swung up onto a gravelled area where there was parking space for several vehicles. In front of that lay an expansive lawn, neatly mown. It was an afternoon in late October, but cool rather than cold, the red and orange leaves all the brighter under a pebble-blue sky. About twenty yards away, a young boy wearing a dressing gown and with his arm in a cast sat at a wrought-iron table.

This was more than David could have hoped for. Freddie Martindale alone. Well, not completely alone. The grand front door was open and an adult woman with short grey hair and a stout physique stood shaking out a doormat. By her jeans and ragged sweater, she was a member of staff, possibly a housekeeper.

'Another copper,' Kerwin said, lumbering towards her.

David made a second mental note: to pretend that he'd never heard that.

'Needs to speak to Freddie.'

The woman glanced at David, but her eyes seemed glazed. She nodded and turned indoors.

David meanwhile, hands in pockets, ambled towards the child. He glanced casually at Kerwin, who seemed uninspired by his role here. Most likely there wasn't enough action. These people were rich and paid well. But maybe he was the sort who also needed to be slamming heads into walls to get full job satisfaction. The minder halted ten yards away and reached under his jacket, pulling out a crumpled tabloid newspaper. Within seconds, he'd become engrossed in it.

David glanced back towards the house. The front door was open; doubtless the housekeeper had gone to find the family. He'd been intending to talk to them, and still would if they came out, but having the youngster alone, even briefly, was an opportunity he couldn't pass up.

The boy was wearing pyjamas and slippers as well as his dressing gown, and sat propped on pillows. His left arm wasn't just in a cast, it was set into a steel frame, while an overlarge wad of Elastoplast bound his left earlobe. His hair was damp, his complexion pale.

'Sorry about what happened, Freddie. I'm David, by the way. David Kelman.' David spoke quietly, understandingly. He held up his ID card. 'Essex Crime Beat.'

The boy looked blankly up at him. For a horrible moment, David thought he was going to be asked directly if he was another policeman. That would be ironic, if the family's security man wasn't conscientious enough to do that, but the shellshocked child-victim was. Acting to head off any such inconvenience, he produced his Dictaphone and placed it on the table, using his body to block it from the view of either the house or the minder.

'You don't mind if I record this?' David asked. 'Want to make sure I get everything right.'

Slowly, the youngster shook his head.

'OK, cool.' Again, David glanced at Kerwin, but the guy was still ten yards off and deep in his newspaper. 'So ... let's take it from the beginning, shall we?'

Falteringly, the youngster spent the next couple of minutes going back through the events of *that* night. For the most part, David let him ramble, continuously glancing towards the house, inserting the odd question here and there.

'Why do you think Jodie asked you to get out of the car?' was one of them.

Freddie looked discomforted. He was still too immature to realise that minor sexual indiscretions between consenting adults was scarcely an issue in the light of a crime like this.

'I think ... they wanted some time alone.'

'That was all it was?' David probed gently. 'Seems to me they were a bit old for that?'

Freddie's expression changed, tightened. 'I did wonder.'

'About what?'

'Something didn't feel right. In the car.'

'How do you mean?'

'It was nothing much. But Jodie and Rick were being funny with each other. And with me. You know, not talking. Until they decided they wanted chips ...'

The boy paused again.

'OK,' David said. 'So you set off to get the chips. I assume there was no one else hanging around? There were no other vehicles parked up?'

'No, but I told the other police all this stuff.'

David nodded. 'Just out of interest, which other police are we talking about?'

Freddie shook his head. 'It was a police lady. Think her name was Hagen.'

David made another mental note – Lynda Hagen was a detective with Essex CID.

'So what happened when you got back to the car?'

Eyes glistening with tears, the boy spoke on, explaining about the ambulance, the violent movements he saw in the half-darkness, along with those terrible screams, and then the black spider tattooed on the palm of a hand, and those murderous shouts as he was chased from the scene. All of this was new to David of course, none of it having featured in the press material the police had put out, most notably the info about the kidnappers wearing green boiler-suit type clothing. That tied in with the description of the credit card conman at the petrol station up in Norfolk the previous September.

'I'll tell you one thing I'm keen to know a bit more about,' David said. 'When the men were shouting to each other, you said one of them used the name "Mara"?'

Freddie nodded. 'Think that's what it was.'

Newspaper rustled. David glanced round. Kerwin's tabloid still hung open in his grasp, but the minder was looking back towards the house as though wondering where the rest of the family were. David knew he was cutting it close, but again, the absence of responsible adults was a bonus he couldn't ignore.

'Do you want my dad?' Freddie asked. 'Because he's at Fen Court Garden with Jason.'

David said nothing. Fen Court Garden was the location of the MDS Group's head offices.

'They're trying to get some money out,' the boy added. 'I mean, people think we're super-rich. But even for my dad, it's not that easy to get £10 million.'

David tingled. Ten million was quite an upgrade on five-hundred thousand. So his theory was correct. That whoever these bastards were, they'd grabbed the first pair of kids, intending to kill them, making the correct assumption that this would give them all the leverage they needed when they struck their real target.

After Lampwick Lane, this could be the next 'story of his career'.

Freddie continued with his tale, tears breaking as he described the pursuit across the golf course, the horrendous realisation sinking through him as the bullets flew that these men were trying to kill him.

But David wasn't really listening. From this point on, the details were well documented, other civilians, road-users on the A12, having got involved. He nodded as the boy spoke, but in the back of his head he was trying to piece it all together into a coherent whole.

The kidnappers had used a fake ambulance as transportation. It was the perfect cover, of course. An ambulance could drive fast anywhere with its blues and twos activated. The green paramedic-type outfits were part of the same deception and clearly linked the kidnapping of Jodie Martindale and Rick Tamworth to the abductions and murders of Darren Doyle and Cheryl Bryant. Clearly, this *was* an organised kidnap gang. There couldn't be further denial.

They even had one of their names: Mara.

It must have happened during a moment of panic, probably created by the unexpected arrival of the youngster. But the kidnapper's error was the journalist's gain.

Mara sounded female, which in itself was a shocker.

David doubted he'd ever had so much sensation at his fingertips.

They'd hate him, of course. The cops, for treading on their toes. The Martindales, for deceiving the little lad into talking.

But what did people hating you matter if you sold a million newspapers?

7
Today

David stared long and hard at the box before he made any effort to open it.

He still tried to console himself with the knowledge that this was rubbish, that he'd removed it from a dustbin. So it hadn't been real theft. Yet he was in no doubt what the Martindale family would think about it. The whole thing was so sensitive to them that they'd sealed the damn box up with tape, presumably to ensure that no one in the waste disposal process would catch an accidental glimpse of the contents.

But no one had followed him from Rosehill, so now perhaps it was best to fall back on that oldest, most traditional David Kelman get-out: that he hadn't been caught, so why sweat? It was hardly in keeping with the way he'd felt this last couple of days, but again he tried to tell himself that if anyone could do something with this item, *he* was the guy.

The sum total of his final, frantic efforts to locate Jodie.

If there was anyone who could turn a pile of bumph into gold, it was him. He didn't just have the skills, he had the motivation.

And yet still he didn't touch it.

Instead, he glanced again at that story Blu-tacked to his living-room wall.

TROUBLED HEIR'S SUICIDE LEAP

Two grainy headshots accompanied the story. Freddie Martindale as he'd been at the age when his sister was abducted; he'd looked relaxed and happy, his hair combed, a school tie-knot showing through his V-neck sweater. And below that, the Freddie Martindale of one year ago, emerging from court after he'd been fined for possession: a wild-haired eighteen-year-old, thin-faced with spots, an emptiness in his bugged-out eyes.

'Do I really owe you, Freddie?' David asked. 'Simply because I was doing my job?'

Yet how noble, or otherwise, was his 'job'? Wasn't he doing it right now by trying to extract the last conceivable ounce of profit from the unfortunate youngster?

Of course, no action at all led to no answers.

He leaned forward with scissors and snipped the tape holding the box's upper flaps. When he opened them, he found what he'd expected: a packed jumble of dog-eared paperwork, most of the sheets scribbled back and front with blotchy biro. He pulled on a pair of thick leather gloves before rummaging through. Freddie Martindale had died an addict, and it wasn't impossible that his bumph might contain something nasty like a used syringe, but the paperwork itself, which was smudged and well thumbed, didn't just look dirty, it *felt* dirty. The same way this whole thing felt dirty. The same way David himself felt dirty.

He flipped through sheets of varying sizes. Some had been torn from A5-sized notepads, while others were more like script paper. There were photographs too – blurry printouts for the most part, as if they'd been taken on a phone and then run off a library computer. Nothing about them bore any degree of useful clarity, neither the places, which looked like subway passages or urban street corners, nor the figures featured in them, who mostly were unidentifiable shapes, sometimes alone, sometimes in groups. Their postures implied dealers and goodtime girls, though it was impossible to be sure.

David sat back, disheartened.

The sum total of his final, frantic efforts to locate Jodie.

In which, with his sister still among the missing, he'd clearly failed, though from this evidence he'd been in no fit state to make a serious investigation.

From what David knew, and after the big story broke in the *Examiner*, the family refused to entertain him, so he'd only been able to glean tidbits from other news sources – Freddie Martindale had responded badly to his sister's disappearance, suffering severe guilt issues, failing his exams, drinking, falling into drug abuse. As a consequence, he never made the university grade, which was a rarity for a kid whose education up to that point had cost twenty-five grand a year. All attempts by his family, his father in particular, to put him on the right path came to nothing, Freddie finally dropping out completely, leaving home and living in squats in resort towns on the Kent coast. Until ending it all by jumping from a rooftop so high that identification had to be made from dental records.

David extricated more sheets, checking them front and back for any bits of spidery text that might make sense, though most of it was incomprehensible. On some pages, times and dates had been scribbled in the top-right corners. Had Freddie logged his entries, or attempted to? That suggested a clearer head than one might expect, but it was still a fool's errand trying to make sense of this material. David sat back again, frustrated. Something had been going on in the doomed drug addict's mind. This was an exhaustive effort in terms of written work alone. Freddie must have felt that he was getting somewhere. And then David turned another page, and saw something that he *could* read.

Though it left him none the wiser.

The sheet bore only three sentences, each one written beneath the one before, and in descending order each one larger, though they all said the same thing:

Who is Saint Bridget

At the bottom, there was a single, very large question mark. David held it to the light, just to make sure that he wasn't misreading, because again it was scrawl rather than actual writing. But in this case, it was so large that it was legible.

So, who *was* Saint Bridget? Was this a genuine question?

David had been raised a Catholic, but hadn't darkened a church door since his teens and remembered nothing of his catechism.

He continued to root in the box, which now was half empty. As he did, something heavier than paper thudded in the bottom of it. Again, David was careful, working his way down cautiously until he uncovered the offending article. He picked it up, turning it around in his gloved hands. It was an old mobile phone, but a model that hadn't been used for years. Dead as a doornail, but also chipped and scuffed, ingrained with dust. When he scraped the fluff off what remained of an image transferred onto the back of it, it was only vaguely discernible, but it looked like the Marvel character, Ironman.

A young lad's phone, then. Freddie Martindale's, no doubt. Probably the last one he'd owned before the shocking event that had demolished his life.

David swallowed bitter spittle. The sight of this broken, dirty toy made him realise just how young Freddie had been at the time. It hit home to him how, a month before that incident, he'd been a typical happy-go-lucky youngster, born into a wealthier-than-average family but much like all the other lads of his age …

It was suddenly necessary to go for a run. And not a light, less-than-energetic jog, which would be David's normal routine early in the day, but, a punishing, long-distance sprint. It wasn't just *this* – his hand spasmed open and he dropped the phone back into the box – he had more than a few cobwebs to blow away after last night.

In the bedroom, he pulled on a vest, shorts and trainers, and grabbed a bottle of water. Heading back through the bungalow, he stopped again near his desk, peering at the phone in the box. He didn't want to touch it again. It was too ugly in everything it signified.

But then he glanced up at the news shot on the wall.

Freddie's haunted, lifeless stare hit him full on.

'I owe you this much at least,' David sighed.

He opened a drawer and lifted out a bunch of spare charger cables. In all likelihood this wouldn't work. The phone was ancient; it had probably died long before Freddie. It might not even contain a Sim card.

The first couple of cables wouldn't fit, but the third one did, and when he plugged it into the power socket atop the desk, he was surprised to feel the device buzz in his hand. This still didn't mean anything. It might contain nothing but gibberish, if it contained anything. Plus, if it had been returned to the family along with all the rest of Freddie's clutter, most likely they'd have passed it to the police, who would have checked it as well.

Except that there was no sign that this phone had been powered up recently. On top of that, if it was buried in all this junk, would the family even have known it was there?

David headed out. He'd leave it plugged in and have a look in another couple of hours. The way things had been going, he'd find a single message on it:

FUCK YOU, KELMAN

Which was all he'd deserve.

8

Six years ago

'You understand you're still under caution?' Detective Constable Hagen said.

David, seated alongside his solicitor, Jayne Pearson, nodded. 'I do.'

Hagen eyed him. 'You're aware that you've been arrested on suspicion of impersonating a police officer?'

Her looks struck him straight away: dark eyes, dark brown hair, a soft demeanour, though that was deceptive. He knew Lynda Hagen by reputation if not in person, and she was renowned as a tough, single-minded officer who wouldn't suffer fools. She was only in her early thirties but exuded no-nonsense authority; when she spoke it was terse, clipped.

'It's a load of cobblers,' David replied. 'But yeah, I understand.'

'That's very interesting. If it's a load of cobblers, how come I'm looking at this?' She presented a newspaper in a plastic evidence bag.

'For the tape, DC Hagen is showing the suspect Exhibit LH2,' the other copper present commented. He was DC Tony Jorgenson, a solid, craggy bloke with a mop of dark hair and a thick, dark moustache. 'That's the newspaper story Kelman admits writing for the edition of the *Essex Examiner* published on 2 November.'

David glanced at the edition in question. Its front-page headline ran:

LIVING NIGHTMARE
*Abduction survivor describes terrifying
ordeal but is grateful to be alive*

'As I've already explained,' David replied. 'At no stage did I tell any member of the Martindale household that I was a police officer.'

'You're sure about that?' Hagen asked.

'My interview with Freddie Martindale was above board. What's more, it was all recorded on an Olympus digital Dictaphone, the same Dictaphone that I voluntarily surrendered to you on my arrest this lunchtime. I'm sure you've now had the opportunity to listen to it a dozen times. Did you at any point hear me say that I was a police officer?'

Hagen appraised him. 'You certainly didn't deny it.'

'If someone had asked me the question, I would have. But they didn't.'

'When you say if someone had asked...The problem was, there was *no one* there to put such a question to you, was there? Apart from a thirteen-year-old boy. A child, a minor.'

'That's not true,' David said. 'Freddie had a chaperone with him all the time we chatted, a bodyguard called Kerwin.'

'You didn't think it would be better to wait around until members of Freddie's actual family appeared?' Hagen asked.

'I was doing that while I was chatting to the boy. But then the housekeeper came out and told me his father and brother-in-law were in London, that his mother was in bed, sedated, and that his sister was engaged in an important phone call with the child psychiatrist.'

'So you just legged it with your ill-gotten gains?' Jorgenson said.

'Nothing ill-gotten about them,' David replied. 'I interviewed the kid in the presence of a family employee and a responsible adult, who'd consented to it.'

'Because he thought you were a police officer,' Hagen said.

'If he thought that, it was his mistake. I didn't tell him I was.'

'So, you didn't inveigle your way onto the premises by pretending you were part of the investigation team?'

David shook his head. 'I presented my press credentials, which you've also seized as evidence, and identified myself as David Kelman from the Essex Crime Beat.'

Jorgenson snorted. 'Which some might think sounds rather... *policey*.'

'It's also well known as the crime desk at the *Essex Examiner*.'

'Essex Crime Beat.' Jorgenson looked amused. 'Did you invent that yourself? Did it make you feel big, like you're a crime fighter in your own right?'

David kept his cool. 'We adopted that name after we exposed the corrupt officers at Lampwick Lane. I'm sure you're not going to deny that on that occasion, we *were* the crime fighters – while you lot were the opposition.'

Jorgenson reddened. 'Don't try to be clever, Kelman. It doesn't go with your face.'

'OK, gentlemen,' Jayne Pearson intervened. She was a prim young black woman, very smartly dressed and wearing round-lensed glasses. She too spoke with authority. 'Let's try and keep things civil, shall we?'

'If Marvin Kerwin says I told you I was a police officer,

he's lying,' David told Hagen. 'Are you going to hinge everything on his word against mine? An ex-prize-fighter who still can't count to ten because he never heard the ref get that far? And me the hero of Lampwick Lane?'

'You're really proud of that bit of subterfuge you pulled, aren't you?' Jorgenson sneered.

'Wouldn't you be?' David retorted. 'If you'd even got close to a result like that. Not that I'd have expected it. You were quite friendly with Jack Pettigrew, weren't you? You'd be staggered how often *your* name came up during our investigation...'

Jorgenson curled his lip, showing unsightly yellow teeth.

As Norm had pointed out after the police press conference, Lampwick Lane was an open sore with several serving officers. While no one could deny that Detective Inspector Jack Pettigrew, Detective Sergeant Keith Elgin and Firearms Inspector Jerry Corrigan had all committed imprisonable offences, they'd been popular among the rank and file, and unspoken beliefs persisted that they ought to have been shown at least a bit of leniency for their otherwise impressive track records.

'You're obfuscating, Mr Kelman,' Hagen said. 'And it isn't going to wash. Especially with me. You see, I'm much more interested in knowing how it was that the family liaison officer at Rosehill House came to be diverted away from the Martindales to a meeting that never was, only twenty minutes before you rang the bell?'

'Another stroke of fortune,' David said. 'I'm sure that if she'd been there, she wouldn't have let me in.'

'You're damn right she wouldn't,' Jorgenson retorted, 'and with bloody good reason.' He slapped the newspaper. 'This lot for example. All this crucial detail, none of which was supposed to be in the public domain.'

Hagen's gaze bored into David. From such an alluring pair of eyes it was disconcerting, particularly as they'd now reached the part of the interview where David would need to be economical with the truth.

'I'm guessing *you* were the one who texted her?' she said.

'I didn't text anyone,' David replied.

'You're a snivelling, lying toad,' Jorgenson growled.

'That's quite enough of that, thank you,' Miss Pearson said.

'You can abuse me all you want.' David remained calm. 'I didn't text anyone.'

'That text was sent from an untraceable phone, of course,' Hagen said. 'Which presumably no longer exists. And whoever it was, they left no personal details.'

'Sounds like a crude diversionary tactic to me. Perhaps the family liaison officer needs a good talking to.'

'Don't worry,' Hagen said. 'That's exactly what happened. A bit more than that, actually. Though it wasn't completely her fault. The mysterious caller knew her first name and the name of the officer assigned to replace her in the event of her absence. There aren't many I know outside the police who'd have that kind of information to hand. But *you* are one of them, Mr Kelman.'

'You see,' David leaned forward, 'this is what gets the modern police a bad name. The Martindales' lives have been ruined by a gang of professional kidnappers. I'd be much more impressed if *that* was where you were concentrating your energies.'

'You sent that text, didn't you,' Hagen persisted. It wasn't a question.

'I can see that you're a focused interrogator, DC Hagen,'

David replied. 'Your reputation is well earned. But you should surely know not to ask questions during interrogations that you don't already know the answers to. The problem is, you see, you've then got to be able to prove these answers you think you already know. On which basis, how are you doing so far?'

She said nothing. Didn't even flinch.

'Or is it more the case that you think you're talking to some tealeaf scrote,' David added, 'who you can browbeat into coughing with endless, baseless assertions?'

There was another protracted silence, though Jorgenson's cheeks had tinged purple.

'I must admit, DC Hagen,' Jayne Pearson interjected, 'as the arresting officer here, it doesn't look as if you've got very much to put to my client. He's already explained that he was looking to get an interview with the family – what journalist wouldn't? This is one of the biggest news stories in the county for quite some time. He clearly identified himself, and even then, he only spoke to young Freddie in the presence of an adult. What exactly has he done wrong?'

'I'll tell you what you've done wrong, Mr Kelman...' Hagen never took her eyes off David, but tapped the newspaper with a fingertip. 'All these details were withheld for a reason.'

'Let me guess,' David said, '...to prevent the Incident Room getting crowded with cranks making false confessions?'

'You've been watching too much fucking telly, Kelman,' Jorgenson rumbled.

Jayne Pearson broke in again: 'Detective Jorgenson, I'm compiling a list of indiscretions on your part, and it's getting longer by the minute. Swearing at my client only makes things worse.'

'How would you feel, Mr Kelman,' Hagen said, 'if I told you that last night, the Kidnap Squad were about to make their move against the offenders and that, thanks to your revelations, when they went into action, there was no one there?'

'*My* revelations?' He laughed. 'You already know these guys are clever. They sussed Norfolk out easily enough. You telling me they couldn't pre-empt you and Scotland Yard too?'

'The Kidnap Squad have means and methods that divisional CID officers like DC Jorgenson and I aren't even aware of. And they were just about to swoop – to find that the birds had flown. And yes, it was thanks to *your* revelations.'

'Nothing to do with some operational screw-up on *your* part, then?'

'Believe that if you wish, but deep down I'm sure you realise that once the law has as much data to hand as this – the mocked-up ambulance, the black spider tattoo, the presence among the kidnappers of a female who goes by the name of "Mara", and perhaps more important than any of that, the evidential link to the Norfolk double-murder – the only thing to realistically do, if you're the offender, is abort.'

'Vanish into the darkness,' Jorgenson added. 'Taking your captives with you.'

'You don't know that's what they've done,' David retorted, feeling his first prickle of unease. 'They want their ten mill. They could easily contact you again.'

'You believe that?' Jorgenson snorted. 'How fucking naïve can you be?'

'DC Jorgenson,' Jayne Pearson said, 'if you don't mind—'

'I don't think it's anything to do with him being naïve,' Hagen said, watching David closely. 'What this was really about, like Miss Pearson said, was getting the big story first, securing the interview no one else could...'

'It's called doing your job,' David asserted.

'And now that we've established it didn't involve impersonating police officers, I'm not sure there's any need for us to extend this conversation,' Jayne Pearson said again.

Before Hagen could reply, the door opened and a uniformed PC stuck his head in. 'Sorry, Lynda – call for you. It's urgent.'

Hagen stood up, checking the clock on the wall as she left. 'Interview suspended 3.38 p.m.'

Jorgenson switched off the tape machine. 'You're a real case, Kelman.'

'Look who's talking,' David replied, 'oh friend of Lampwick Lane.'

'You come out with all this snappy stuff, but did it honestly never occur to you that in writing this story, you might be endangering a perfectly viable plan to foil these bastards?'

'Has it honestly never occurred to you that if you lot had done your jobs properly up in Norfolk, there wouldn't even have been a kidnapping here in Essex?' David said.

Even Tony Jorgenson seemed taken aback by such whataboutery. As if even he, who'd probably lied under oath many times, would have hesitated to offer something so patently tenuous in his own defence.

The door opened and Hagen came back in, scanning through a printed-out document.

'I've got some interesting news for you, Mr Kelman,' she said. 'Seeing as you're such an advocate of people doing their jobs, you ought to be very happy. Because Essex Uniform are certainly doing theirs. Half an hour ago, one of our mobile patrols found a body on a fly-tipping site near Little Bromley. Male, mid-twenties. Hands zip-tied behind his back. Single fatal bullet wound to the back of the head.'

David's stomach turned to water. 'If this is some kind of stunt...'

'I'm guessing Rick Tamworth wouldn't call it that,' she said. 'Not that we can confirm it's him. The body hasn't been identified yet.' She sat again, re-reading. 'From the state of things, that isn't going to be much fun for whoever draws the straw.' She glanced up. 'I know what you're thinking now. What about Jodie? Well, seeing as you're also fond of honesty, let's all be honest.' She eyed him frankly. 'What do *you* think her chances are?'

9
Today

David was on his eighth mile when he turned for home, the sweat coming off him in rivers. He still wasn't slowing down unless he had no choice, when he had to cross busy intersections perhaps. Most of the time, to avoid that, he kept to woodland paths and back-country trails, where he could stretch out. And if he tripped and fell, cutting or winding himself, well, that was all part of the price he was paying.

Pain was his new normal. And though he hated it, he took it on the chin.

Of course, that wasn't the only reason why he worked out so much these days. He also had a lot of empty hours to fill. He was self-employed, which meant that he no longer had to clock on or off, and didn't have some beady-eyed micro-talent of a boss scrutinising his every coming and going. That was the upside of it. The downside, apart from the irregular earnings, was that he had more spare time than he'd ever been used to before. When working full-time on a daily newspaper, he'd used to dream that when retirement came he'd write a book, savouring every leisurely minute of it because there'd be no rush, writing speculatively and yet calling on every inch of his talent and experience to produce something that would last, something he could consider his legacy to the world. Now, he had no stomach for that, because he wrote speculatively all the time. Through no choice of his own, he was under contract to no one, relegated to making a living, or trying to, as a freelancer. The thought of penning an opus that anyone would be interested in now seemed like a pipedream of epic proportions.

And again, any accolades he drew from that, even were he able to, would be unmerited.

Jodie Martindale had been twenty-three that night she'd disappeared. She'd be twenty-nine now. If Rick Tamworth wasn't lying in his family plot over at Hadleigh, he'd be thirty-one.

As David hammered his way home, he tried not to picture his own children in such circumstances, but couldn't help wondering which would be the worst of the two evils. For a family to know without doubt that their offspring had died so young and so violently, or for a family to never know anything about their youngsters' fate, the trail the police were following eventually turning cold, but the questions remaining.

Always those questions.

Why? How? Where? When?

David accelerated, his heart slamming his chest with car-wrecking force.

The vehicle mocked up to look like an ambulance had likely been torched. Anyone with a black spider on the palm of his hand would ensure that he'd had it removed. If he was already known to law enforcement for such a distinguishing mark, he'd have got his alibi sorted well in advance. Anyone who called themselves Mara, male or female, wouldn't do so any longer.

'You'd better hope that girl doesn't turn up in the same state as her boyfriend,' Stan Grimshaw had said to David outside the front of Colchester Police Station, after he'd been released without charge.

'Come on, Stan, *you* OK'd the story!'

'You assured me you'd got it legitimately.'

'I *did*. I haven't been charged with breaking any laws.'

'You mean they couldn't prove you'd broken any laws?'

'Stan…'

'You know what this is going to do to us?'

'We knew it would be controversial.'

'We didn't know the hostages were going to get killed because of it.'

David had been bemused. 'Isn't that the fault of the people who did the killing?'

'Don't you feel even a hint of responsibility?'

'Course I do, but look, it's early yet. They'll find the girl alive.'

'How can they, you dickhead… with the suspects in the fucking wind?' Grimshaw had then made an effort to get control of himself. 'You ought to know that the *Essex Examiner* is henceforth prohibited from attending Essex Police press conferences. But that's only the start of it. The Essex Police Press Office is going on a massive counter-offensive tomorrow. They're laying the blame for that boy's death on the *Examiner*, and on you in particular. They're going to say the entire police operation was undermined because *you* revealed crucial info.'

David got back home earlier than he'd planned, having pushed himself over the last couple of miles even harder than usual. He circled the bungalow's interior on rickety legs, while rubbing himself with the towel. After checking his mobile for messages, and finding none, he drifted across the lounge to his desk, to see if attempting to recharge Freddie Martindale's ancient mobile would have had any effect.

And was surprised to see a small green light.

He flipped it open. Remarkably, despite its beaten-up condition, the phone appeared to be working. On one hand, David now felt even guiltier about having pillaged the box from the dustbin (if they'd known this thing was still alive, would the Martindale family really have wanted to throw it away?). But on the other hand – he switched the device on – it wasn't inconceivable that it might contain something of use to his enquiry.

He paused to wonder.

His enquiry?

Was that it, then? Was that his solution? That he was going to look into the case himself?

The phone buzzed in his hand. He glanced down. If an entry-code was required, that was the end of it. But a code wasn't required, it seemed; Freddie had been a kid after all – it had probably been set up so that, if necessary, his parents and older sisters could also access it.

Instead, there was a message across the bottom of the screen:

You have voicemail

David's heartbeat had decelerated since he'd returned, his sweat cooling. But now everything was thrown into reverse. Because when he activated the voicemail, though there was only one item, it was dated Wednesday 21 July, just over two weeks ago.

'Two weeks …?' He put the device to his ear.

'*Freddie … Freddie …*' came a breathless female voice.

David stiffened.

'*Freddie, for God's sake, answer. Freddie, it's me, Jodie. You've got to help me, you've got to get me ...*'

Her voice became a muffled squeal as the call was forcibly cut.

II

THE INTRUDERS

10

David wouldn't have been surprised if the two civilian support staff manning the front desk in Colchester Police Station had recognised him. That would explain why one of them, having dealt politely and proficiently with the irate customer in front of him, now disappeared into the rear of their office somewhere, while the other one, a foursquare heavy woman with a short, neat cap of dyed dark hair and thick, black-rimmed glasses, engaged herself in paperwork, plodding her way through one form after another, in each case adding a squiggle of a signature at the bottom.

He cleared his throat.

'With you in a minute,' she said, not looking up.

A hundred of those smart-Alec comments rushed into his head.

No rush. There's only one kid trapped on the roof of the burning orphanage.

But none of that would have worked. Over the last few years, David felt that he'd learned a number of important lessons. One was that politeness costs you nothing whereas impoliteness could cost you a lot. That said, the seconds were rolling by.

'I was wondering if I could speak to Detective Constable Hagen?' he said.

There were two main reasons why he'd asked for DC Hagen.

Firstly, six years ago she'd let him off without even a caution. OK, she hadn't done that out of the goodness of her soul. Some tailor's dummy from the CPS would have instructed her that they didn't have enough evidence. But while she hadn't been his friend, at least she'd been civil with him. The second thing was that, back during his days as a full-time crime reporter, he'd heard her name mentioned in glowing terms several times. She was a proper copper who did her job conscientiously.

'Lynda Hagen's not with us anymore,' the woman said, still signing documents. 'It's DS Hagen now. And she's moved to the Roads Policing division. Accident investigation.'

'Oh. I don't suppose ...?'

'I can't send a message, no. If you want her, you'll have to go through the central directory.'

'It's about Jodie Martindale,' he said.

The woman didn't look up straight away. But when she did, it was sudden and quick.

'I've come into possession of some evidence,' he said, 'which might be of interest to whoever's still investigating the case. I'll go through the central directory, like you said. But who do I need to call?'

'That won't be necessary.' She turned to a desktop computer. 'Our Cold Case Unit is handling the Martindale enquiry.'

'So it's still open?'

'Oh yes.' She was distracted, flipping files onscreen. 'Who are you please?'

David hesitated. This was always going to be the risky bit.

'My name's David Kelman.'

She picked up an internal phone. 'If you'd like to take a seat, Mr Kelman.'

Relieved, he retreated across the foyer and sat on an empty bench.

Now that the wheels were in motion, he wondered if maybe it wasn't the greatest idea. Whoever came down from the Cold Case office, he'd have to admit to them that he'd stolen the Martindales' rubbish. Somewhere in the back of his head, he seemed to remember hearing that once disposed of in local authority receptacles – i.e. wheelie bins – household rubbish became the property of said authority. He doubted that anyone from the Essex Cold Case Unit would be too worried about enforcing an obscure bylaw like that, but given David's background, it would be yet another embarrassment.

With an electric buzz, an interior door opened. A hefty man in a shirt and tie came through it, pulling on a suit jacket.

David said nothing as the man headed for the main door.

Tony Jorgenson hadn't changed for the better. He'd been a big, heavily built brute of a bloke six years ago. Now, a lot of that had run to fat, but he was a no less physically imposing specimen. He still wore a tufty moustache while his hair was a greying mop.

'Inspector Jorgenson,' the woman behind the counter said. '*This* is the man you're looking for.'

Jorgenson pivoted around. 'Sorry, Nan ... what's that?'

She pointed at David, who sat rigid.

Jorgenson was now an inspector?

'Not looking for anyone, love,' Jorgenson said, half glancing at the civvie on the bench. 'Things I need to ...'

The penny dropped.

He strolled across the foyer. 'This is the guy you called up about? The one who's got something new for us?'

The woman called Nan nodded.

'I'll be damned.' Jorgenson almost seemed amused. 'David bloody Kelman. You've got some nerve, showing your face here.'

'You're a DI now?' David asked, rising to his feet.

'Why, that your worst nightmare?'

'With Cold Cases?'

Jorgenson sneered. 'And what are *you*, a washed-up local reporter who can't get a proper gig anywhere and so writes dirty stories purely for the fun of shaming people.'

'Suppose I should be flattered you're keeping tabs on me. Or do *you* read those magazines too?'

'I see the gobshittery's still the same.'

David held his ground. 'I'm here to help you. I know you'll find that hard to believe ...'

'What the fuck made you think that?'

'I've got something for you.'

'I've got something for *you*.' Jorgenson pointed at the door. 'The exit. Use it!'

'Look, Jorgenson – don't be a bloody idiot all your life!'

The copper's face darkened. 'What did you say?'

'OK, uncalled for.' David raised a hand. 'I'm sorry. But—'

The DI stalked forward, back hunched. 'You walk into my police station ...'

'*Your* police station?'

'Afternoon, Nan,' someone else said, breezing through the internal door. Another detective, younger and slighter-built than Jorgenson. 'I believe there's—'

'Over here, Timmo,' Jorgenson called.

The newcomer came over.

'Detective Constable Bly,' Jorgenson said, 'may I introduce

you to a gentleman of the press, and also the scum of the earth – the one and only David Kelman.'

Up close, Bly seemed young for a detective, with neat fair hair and schoolboyish features, but he evidently took his lead from Jorgenson. He didn't know who David Kelman was but already regarded him with hostility.

'The little shit who blew the Jodie Martindale case,' Jorgenson explained.

'Jodie's the reason I'm here now,' David said.

'Conned his way into the family's front garden,' Jorgenson added. 'Pretended he was a copper no less, interviewed the little lad who was half-dead with shock, thus fucking him up for the rest of his short, tragic life, and then ran the whole story in his paper. Made public knowledge of every single thing we had going for us. In consequence, the kidnappers were off on their toes and Jodie Martindale was never heard from again.'

'Until now!' David blurted.

Jorgenson's eyes narrowed. 'What are you talking about?'

'I've got some info for you if I can get a word in edge-ways.'

The detectives glanced at each other, faces inscrutable. Then Jorgenson pointed again at the door. 'I've already told you, Kelman – get your arse outside.'

David walked out, aware that the twosome were close behind.

'You're not so dumb as to still be working this case, are you?' Jorgenson said, grabbing his collar and steering him away from the station entrance and down a side passage.

David tore loose and backed away. 'Why would that be dumb? It's only what you're doing!'

The two coppers halted, regarding him balefully.

'Or are you not?' David asked. 'Is it now just a piece of paper in a file drawer?'

'What's this info?' Bly demanded. His voice was reedy, weaselly.

David felt uneasy. This passage presumably led through to a car park or somewhere similar, but at present it hid him from public view.

'You fucking us around, Kelman?' Jorgenson wondered. 'Again? Doing that twice is a bad idea. Doing it three times is really asking for it.'

'So exposing Lampwick Lane was a bad thing?' David replied. 'You give more away every time you open your mouth, Jorgenson.'

The DI lunged, grabbing him by a fistful of sweatshirt, slamming his back against the wall.

'We went fucking easy on you last time because you were a journalist working for a local rag. You had back-up. But you don't anymore, so take my advice and do not fucking wind me up. If you'd seen the state that lad, Rick Tamworth, was in ...'

Again, David yanked himself loose. 'I'm trying to make up for that ...'

'Spit it out,' Jorgenson said. 'And don't give us some boring load of investigator journalist bollocks in which you've cracked the case all on your own. Just tell us what you've got.'

David did so, explaining everything that had happened since he'd approached Hannah Bulstrode the morning after the funeral, and producing Freddie Martindale's mobile phone from his pocket, which he'd already inserted into an evidence bag (it was actually a peel-off sterile sack used for transporting fresh vegetables, but it would serve).

The two cops regarded the item with both bewilderment and unease.

'You dug around in someone's rubbish,' Jorgenson said, 'and found *this*?'

'I know it was wrong,' David replied. 'But if the outcome's good, where's the harm?'

The DI locked gazes with him. He seemed less angry now. Instead, there was a wariness about him. 'And you're telling us there's a recording on here of Jodie Martindale's voice asking for her brother to come and get her?'

'Dated two weeks ago,' David said.

Another silence.

'Anyone else touched this?' Bly asked.

'Not since I took charge of it, no.'

Jorgenson held out his hand. 'Give it here.'

David backed away. Their manner troubled him. 'What happens if I do?'

Jorgenson glared at him again. 'I'll tell you what happens if you don't. You'll be compounding the offence of theft with the additional offence of perverting the course of justice. Give it here!'

With no other option, David handed it over. Jorgenson regarded it long and hard before heading back along the passage, Bly following.

'Hey!' David called after them. 'You don't want a statement?'

Jorgenson half looked back. 'We can find you when we need you. Meantime, fuck off.'

They vanished around the corner. David hurried after them. When he skidded out onto the pavement, they were re-entering the station through its main door.

'Jorgenson!' he shouted. 'You're going to listen to that?'

Jorgenson turned back. 'When I have the fucking cheek to tell you how to write about some TV mum who advertises supermarkets on telly, and how she once used to drop her knickers for any producer that wanted a taste just so she could get enough work to eat that day, you can tell me how to investigate crime.'

He disappeared inside. Again, Bly followed, but not before giving David a threatening stare.

David was bemused. On this occasion it had gone against his every instinct to hand over such a crucial piece of evidence, even to the cops. He tapped his other pocket, checking that his Dictaphone was still inside it. But if nothing else, at least he'd made a recording.

11

'The situation's simple,' David said, laying his Dictaphone on the pub table. 'Freddie Martindale clearly missed this recent message.'

Anushka Chawla sipped her spritzer as she regarded the device. It was just after teatime on a weekday, so the Camulodunum in central Colchester was quiet by its normal standards. Anushka was still in her Tesco outfit. 'How do you know?'

'Firstly, because if he hadn't, wouldn't he have told someone? The police, for example. I'm telling you, Nushka, Jorgenson and that other fella – they looked surprised by what I had for them. That was definitely the first they'd heard about it.' David took a swig of lager. 'Secondly, from what I've been able to discover about Freddie's final months, he was a wreck. Homeless, addicted. His phone probably ran out of juice years ago, and he didn't have the means to power it up again.'

Anushka gave it some thought. 'Play it again.'

David hit 'play', and that tinny but plaintive voice emerged.

'Freddie ... Freddie. Freddie, for God's sake, answer. Freddie, it's me, Jodie. You've got to help me, you've got to get me ...'

She pursed her lips. 'You know that could be anyone?'

'She says she's Jodie.'

'Could still be anyone. Wind–ups happen.'

'Why bother winding up a homeless drug addict?'

'People are strange, David. And cruel. We don't know what enemies Freddie Martindale might have made. He could've been pestering all sorts of people. You said he'd been trying to find out where his sister was. And anyway, if that *was* Jodie, why would she call her younger brother? Why not call home?'

'That's a mystery, I'll admit.'

'That's the end of it, as far as I can see.'

'You're saying we just ignore it?'

Anushka arched an eyebrow. '*We?*'

'Nushka, this is the first evidence in six years that Jodie may still be alive.'

'And what's it got to do with us?'

'How about everything!'

'You mean it'll make *you* feel better?'

David reddened. 'That's part of it, yeah.'

'David...' She leaned forward. 'Freddie Martindale took his own life because he'd burned himself out on junk, not because of you.'

'Come on, Nushka. He did that to himself because he'd always felt guilty about the trick he'd allowed me to play on him, and the consequences that followed.'

'He was a kid. He should've been counselled that he wasn't to blame.'

'Obviously he wasn't. Not properly.'

'Well, that's not *your* fault at least. Look, leave it to the cops. You've done what you needed to. All you do now is sit back and wait for the result.'

'I don't know.' David couldn't hide his unease. 'That Jorgenson... I've never liked him. When me and Norm were working the Lampwick Lane story, he was, I don't know, he was pretty close to Jack Pettigrew.'

'Define close.'

'A friend, a confidante.'

She sat back. 'Doesn't mean he was involved in the scam you exposed.'

'Doesn't mean he wasn't, either. Could just be that in his case, we couldn't prove anything.'

'OK, for the sake of argument, let's say that he was as corrupt as the rest. Why would that stop him doing a proper job now?'

From her considered manner, Anushka had matured since her days as a wide-eyed cub reporter on the *Examiner*. She'd gone through a rough time at home since then, of course.

'What a feather in his cap it would be,' she said. 'The copper who rescued Jodie Martindale.'

'I just don't trust him,' David replied.

'He can't bin it, can he? The phone, I mean. Wasn't there another copper who saw him take charge of it?'

'Yeah. Detective Constable Tim Bly. I've done some digging on him. Sounds like he's Jorgenson's sidekick in every way. They call them the "Pantomime Horse" because wherever Jorgenson goes, Tim Bly is right behind him.'

'David, I know this whole thing has been bugging you all these years, but you're making an awful lot of suppositions here.'

'When I say I don't trust them, Nushka, I'm saying that I don't trust them to do as good a job as I could.'

'You can't be serious.' She shrugged. '*I* wouldn't know where to start.'

'No disrespect, love, but you're not me.'

She gave him a long stare before finishing her drink. 'On which basis, I've got to get home.'

'Hey, I'm sorry – I didn't mean that the way it sounded.'

She stood and grabbed her anorak. 'It was against my better judgement coming here.'

'Nushka! I didn't mean it like that. What I meant is, I've … I mean … Look, I've got more at stake here than you have. So maybe I'm more motivated.'

She pulled her coat on.

'I'm sorry,' he said again.

'It's all right,' she replied tersely.

'Nushka, come on …'

'It's all right, it's OK, I'm not offended.' She looked down at him. 'But those kinds of comments come out of your mouth too often for your own good, David.'

'I know, I know. It's something I'm working on.'

That much was true. He'd never be a suitable father or role model for Tommy and Tabby, in his own eyes at least. Far too often, his old charmless persona still peeked out.

She collected her bag. 'You know what Vijay's like. If he hears I've come out for a drink with another bloke, all hell's going to let loose.'

'It's a quick snifter after work with an old mate.'

'There's no such thing in Vijay's book.'

'I thought you two were separated.'

'Vijay doesn't believe it's permanent. And this wouldn't be the way for him to learn the truth, trust me.' She edged towards the door. 'Look on the bright side.' She indicated the Dictaphone. 'That may be kosher. It could even be the clue the Cold Case squad need to go and rescue Jodie Martindale. You'll have done your bit and it'll have paid off.'

'Nushka, don't go yet. Please.' He pushed her chair back out for her. 'If I'm going to look into this, I can't do it on my own.'

Her eyes widened. 'You've got to be kidding!'

'Why? You were a good journalist.'

'And now I'm a good shift manager at Tesco. And I earn a decent wage.'

'But wasn't investigative journalism what you really wanted to do?'

'Like you've just said, I'm single now. I have to look after myself.'

'Can't you help out in your spare time?'

She sat down again. 'David, it's over.' She tried a softer tone. 'Look … the *Examiner* closed down four years after you got your marching orders. And it was nothing to do with the Martindale scandal. It's local journalism. It's dying on its backside. Everyone's a journalist now. Look at them, they're all over the internet. And they do it for free.'

'They do a piss-ant job too.'

'Which makes it all the more painful, but there's nothing we can do about that.'

'*I'm* doing something about it.' He finished his drink and signalled to the barman for another. 'It's called the *Essex Enquirer*. It's going to be a local news website, and I'm going to use it to break major stories, all of which will be properly sourced and written.'

She eyed him. 'And you're going to do this as well as selling the dirty secrets?'

'Unfortunately, I have to look after myself too. But if this thing works, that sleazy stuff ends. Believe me, that'd be another welcome outcome.'

She nodded. 'And the staff of this exciting new venture – they won't be paid?'

'Not until we can sell enough advertising.'

'Wow. Be fun watching you make that happen, seeing as you haven't got an advertising department. And this staff – the plan is that they'll comprise you and me? Me part-time?'

'And Norm. If he's interested.'

'Norm?'

'Obviously. Look at some of the stories we broke together when me and him were running Crime Beat.'

'Wait a minute.' Anushka looked suspicious. 'That isn't why you asked me to meet you here?'

'What do you mean?'

She jumped to her feet. 'You cheeky bastard!'

David held out his hands. 'What?'

'So I could get Norm on board for you.' She shook her head. 'I thought it seemed odd that the first person you called was Nushka the ingenue.'

'It's not that at all.'

She grabbed her bag again. 'You're a bloody little swine, David Kelman!'

'Nushka, I need you too!'

She hovered there, glaring at him. Possibly, it was her hurt pride that made her linger, a vague hope against hope that there might at least be some truth in his words.

'I was only a couple of years past my probation when the *Examiner* closed. Why would you need *me*?'

'Because you've got an aptitude for this work. You always have had.'

'Yeah, right.'

'You came to Crime Beat voluntarily, Nushka. We didn't ask for you. You were a trainee, but you wanted in at the sharp end. And you more than held your own.'

She stared at him doubtfully. 'And that's the truth?'

'Sure.'

'Because after you got sacked, Crime Beat was closed

down and I was back on general duties until they kicked us all out. So I don't see how you can say I had an aptitude for investigation.'

'You were a like-mind. On our wavelength. Straight away.' Anushka placed her bag back on the table.

'I need the whole team, though,' David added. 'Which means I need Norm too.'

'Good luck with that.'

'Nushka ... Norm was like you. He made the switch from Features to Crime Beat *voluntarily*. He loved those investigative stories we worked on.'

'It's not about the job, David – it's about *you*. You let him down. Badly.'

'Come on, that was years ago.'

'What does that matter? He'd had a long and distinguished career, writing about everything that ever happened in this county. Everyone knew him and liked him. And then he gets blindsided by this Martindale business.'

'Jesus! You don't think there's a possibility he might have overreacted? *I* got the lead credit on the story, not him. *I'm* the one who got whizzed.'

'It may shock you to learn, David, but guilt by association's an actual thing. Anyway, Norm's retired. And I think he's happy with that. He was one of the first to leave when the cuts started. He volunteered for that too.'

David considered. 'Retired at sixty-one, Jesus.'

'Writing his book, isn't he.'

'Rehashing old stories.' He eyed her. 'You sure he won't find this more interesting?'

'Doesn't matter what I think, does it?'

'We won't know if we don't at least ask him.'

'Rather you than me.' She grabbed her bag again and headed for the pub door.

'Nushka, I *need* this!' he called. She turned. He tried not to look too sheepish. 'I know it sounds self-absorbed saying that. But this is literally all I've got.'

'So, it's not about rescuing Jodie Martindale, it's about rescuing you?'

'You prefer me to be honest, don't you? But if we rescue that girl in the process, how can it be wrong?'

I2

It was a row of semi-detached, three-storey townhouses near Lexden Park.

When David opened the front gate to the second one along, its small garden was ablaze with red and pink roses, their soil beds neatly and freshly turned. On the front door hung a handwritten notice.

Round the back

He couldn't conceal a wry smile as he walked back to the pavement, turned left and then left again along the entry between this house and the house next door.

At the back, Norm Harrington, his tall, rangy frame attired in flipflops, baggy shorts and a too-large Hawaiian shirt, reclined in a comfortable chair on the patio, a parasol erected overhead. There was a table in front of him with a laptop on it, alongside an open scrapbook filled with grubby newspaper clippings, though at present he seemed more interested in sipping through a straw at what looked like a large piña colada.

Norm was the usual picture of good health, with his tall, trim frame, bronze complexion, short, neat, chalk-white hair and almost impossibly handsome face.

David approached across the patio, Norm so relaxed that he still hadn't seen him.

About five yards away, he halted. 'Erm, hi. It's me.'

The householder didn't look around. 'I know it's you.'

'Erm, OK. Well, this is going to seem a bit ridiculous…'

'It doesn't *seem* ridiculous. It *is* ridiculous.'

'Come again?'

Norm sipped his cocktail. 'Anushka phoned me. Told me you'd be coming. She also told me why.'

'OK, so … what do you think?'

'About what?' Norm finally looked around. 'About the best way for you to rehabilitate yourself resting with an unidentifiable female voice on a second-hand recording?' He mused. 'Not much.'

David shrugged. 'I'm not sure we can call it "unidentifiable".'

'Well, the opposite of that is "identifiable", which Anushka says it isn't.'

'It's not that clear-cut. There're a couple of websites dedicated to finding Jodie Martindale. I mean, they're not official. But one of them is carrying video footage of her talking. It's poor quality. But, the two voices … well, they're not dissimilar.'

'Not dissimilar.' Norm looked frontward again. 'That's persuasive. Not that it matters. From what Anushka said, the police are in possession of the phone now. And unlike her, I don't believe that your personal quest to save face is so important that we should try to circumnavigate them.'

'Nushka *does*?' David was surprised.

'Something like that. She feels sorry for you. Also, I don't think she's enjoying life supervising shopping tills.'

David considered that. 'Having Nushka onside would be better than nothing…?'

'You seriously asked her?' Norm glanced round again,

affecting disbelief. 'To pack her job in? To come and work with you on this fantasy newspaper you're setting up?'

'I suggested she comes in part-time.'

'You're like bloody Napoleon, you, David. You'd sacrifice any number of others for personal glory.'

'Not exactly glory...'

'So, what was that bloody Martindale story about in the first place?'

David struggled to answer.

'We got a big score with Lampwick Lane,' Norm said. 'Or rather *you* did. And you couldn't rest after that until you got another one, could you?'

'You didn't think the Martindale kidnap was a story worth telling?' David replied.

'I'm not having this argument again. It was beyond irresponsible.' Norm pointed at him. 'I warned you beforehand that if you kept on playing things close to the knuckle, something was going to blow up in our faces. And it did – and note the "our". Because *I* got tarred with the same brush afterwards.' Norm shrugged. 'Not that it matters now. It's all in the past.'

'I was hoping you'd take that attitude...'

'And it *stays* in the past. What I mean is I'm not coming back.'

Despite everything, David was a little surprised by the determined set of his old mate's jaw. The hurt had lasted, that was for certain.

'Look, David,' Norm said, suddenly more conciliatory, 'I don't want to be your enemy. We were friends for too long. And I'm sorry what happened between you and Karen. I don't wish a lonely life on anyone. Good lord, I know all about that...'

A bachelor all his life, there'd long been questions among those only peripherally acquainted with Norm about his sexuality. David knew that he was gay, but also that he'd never played the field. On the odd, rare occasion Norm had mentioned someone he referred to as a 'companion', but none of those relationships had lasted. In the great man's own words, his standards were 'too exacting for anyone else'.

'But I'm not working with you again,' Norm added. 'Not after what happened last time.'

David hovered there. 'Anushka tells me you took early retirement?'

'So?'

'So, just answer me this: was that because you genuinely wanted to finish early or because you were depressed about what happened?'

'Who cares?' Norm looked away, but a pink tinge had crept into his cheeks. 'It's history.'

'We'd built something amazing, me and you. We turned Crime Beat into a major item.'

'Something you hoped to take to the nationals at some point. I know what the real plan was.'

'And if I had done, and I'd taken you with me, would that have bothered you?'

Norm said nothing.

'Look, Norm ... it wasn't just about personal ambition. It was great work. We didn't just expose the Lampwick Lane mob, remember. A year later we uncovered an Albanian gang who were selling smack out of a derelict shipping container for five quid a bag. We were the ones who found out that it was cheap because they'd cut it with quicklime.'

'We went to the police with that one first.'

'Because we thought we might need protection if we

broke it. We still got first dibs on the story. That one went viral too. We had the dailies on the phone every day, we had ITV Anglia knocking on our door. And then … then I blew it.' David shuffled his feet. 'I'm not pretending otherwise. I'm just wondering how big a loss to you that was?'

'Why?' Norm said. 'Because now we're going to put it right?'

'Norm, if you're not doing anything else …'

'I am.' Norm sipped his piña colada. 'I'm writing a book, as you can see.'

'Recollections of all the VIPs you interviewed when you were Features Editor, yeah?'

'Problem with that?'

'You couldn't wait to get off Features. You wanted to chase gangsters with me.'

Norm looked away.

'Suppose I come back with a couple more leads? Decent ones?'

Norm shook his head. 'Leave it, David. Don't make things worse for yourself.'

'Would you be interested then?'

Norm pointedly gave no answer.

David turned and walked towards the gate.

'I suppose it depends how you'd got them,' Norm said.

David looked back. Norm placed his cocktail on the table, positioning it just-so.

'You know, David, after the Martindale scandal, I spent the next three years knocking side-panel copy out of press releases.' Norm looked at David hard, his bright blue eyes written with accusation. 'I covered everything, from fêtes to garden parties to Nativity plays at Christmas. Not because Stan didn't trust me, but because he couldn't afford to have me associated with serious news anymore. I missed out on one story in particular that I was the only person on that paper qualified to cover—'

'I know about that,' David said. 'And I'm sorry...'

'So, does that answer your question about why I finished early?'

'Yeah, but what I meant—'

'So, if you fuck up again, David, and my name is once again linked to it – and remember, in this new plan we won't be paid journalists, just self-appointed busybodies – what happens to me *then*? At the very least, I can kiss this new book goodbye.'

'And what kind of book can you write if you save Jodie Martindale?' David asked.

'The police will save Jodie Martindale.' Norm toyed with his glass. 'If she's still saveable. God knows what there is left of her now, if she's even alive. You just stick to salacious gossip, David. You'll find that a lot less painful.'

13

An old sweat of a Major Investigations detective had once given David a wide-ranging interview about the hundreds of murders, rapes and robberies that he'd looked into. One key question David had put to him had been: 'It must be difficult when, every day at work, you have to deal with people who have been so grotesquely abused. You must be thinking about it all the time. How can you stand it?' The detective's response had been simple: 'You *don't* think about it. You can't afford to, otherwise you can't function in your role.'

As David drove home from Norm's, he wondered if he'd taken that lesson too much on board. In his own job, he too had found himself confronted by the victims of violence, and though it had undoubtedly been one of his tasks to tell their story, he'd also felt that it was at least as important to try to expose the worse-than-animals who'd harmed them. But he'd found that it wasn't possible to do that if you weren't objective, if you got emotional.

And yet somewhere down the line it had all gone wrong. That determination to be a hardass had somehow come to mean that there wasn't room for any kind of sentiment. That the people involved weren't quite so important. At least, not as important as getting the job done – and reaping the rewards, of course.

He pulled into his drive.

There'd long been a theory that Jodie Martindale was still alive, mainly thanks to her body never having been found. But as with other high profile and unresolved abductions, he'd often feared that this owed more to hope than realism. The common-sense opinion held that she was dead and buried. But even if she wasn't, as Norm himself had intimated, what would her condition be now? That was another of those 'best not to think about it' situations. But David *had* been thinking about it. An awful lot.

Once, while surfing the internet, he'd come across the story of an American college girl who'd vanished from a cruise ship in the Caribbean, and many years later, had been spotted – or so her family thought – on an obscure website advertising the services of South American prostitutes. There were unconfirmed horror stories like that all over the Net. But on that particular occasion, David had sat stock-still for a good five minutes. Time heals all hurts, he'd once believed. But what if that hurt was ongoing, continuing relentlessly in some faraway unknown place where no one could intervene?

He didn't go into the house, but used a side door to enter 'the Shed', as he called it.

It wasn't an actual shed. It was his garage, though he'd never used it as that. Its main door had once been electrical, but no longer worked and so was jammed closed. Its roof, which comprised rotted planks, had huge gaps in it, and the single cobweb-covered window, which was positioned at head-height, was letterbox-shaped and looked out on nothing but the wall of meshed vegetation bordering the playground. The interior itself was dust-shrouded and crammed with broken furniture. However, he'd now cleared the north end, where the side door stood, and where the garage's sole working plug socket was located. He'd moved his desk out from the house and placed it there. His laptop now sat on top of it, alongside the box of documents he'd brought from the bin at Rosehill House. He'd even screwed a noticeboard to the wall, though at present there was little on there, just the scraps of newspaper that had once decked the wall in his lounge. It was still a mess, but when he threw out all the rest of the junk, it would be more than adequate for the team of three that he'd hoped would be working here.

Well, that had been the plan.

It wasn't just that Norm was uninterested and Anushka, at best, indifferent. The voice on the phone had been his solitary lead. It had been poor quality anyway, but now he only had a second-hand copy of it. More to the point, there was no proof that he'd taken it from Freddie Martindale's mobile. He hadn't filmed himself recording it. He hadn't photographed the notification of the call, or the date and time it was received... all of which, on reflection, were big oversights. He'd written the number down, but a search online had found no trace of it. The enquiry was stymied already before it had even begun.

David had one other possible lead, but if the voice on the phone had been a long shot, he had no clue how *this* would be classified.

He lifted the topmost sheet from the box. It was the page bearing the question, *Who is Saint Bridget?* This was something he hadn't mentioned to the police. He would have done if Jorgenson had been more receptive to him. Even then, David hadn't withheld it deliberately. But the discussion had gone so badly that his thoughts had scattered.

He could still take it in to them. Perhaps he should. Perhaps he should dump the whole box at the Cold Cases

Unit office. They'd have more resources than he with which to comb through the indecipherable scrawl that covered every page in there. But thanks to Jorgenson, he wasn't inclined to. Not yet anyway.

He sat, opened his laptop and, on a pessimistic whim – mainly because it was better than staring at the wall – googled 'Saint Bridget'.

The amount of material he was rewarded with was astonishing. Website after website contained articles about her, not all of them religious in character, some very scholarly. He skimmed through, at the same time pulling a fresh notepad and pen from his drawer and scribbling down the salient details.

Saint Bridget had been an Irish abbess of the sixth century who was said to have worked many miracles, though the activities of early Christian missionaries had muddied the water. It seemed that Saint Bridget had regularly been syncretised with key mother-goddess figures in non-Christian belief systems to aid with conversion. In fact, some of the deities who later became conflated with Saint Bridget were unusual personalities by any standards.

Brigid of pre-Christian Ireland, famed for her ravishing beauty and command of sorcery.

Brigantia of the North Britons, a warrior spirit whose sigil was the Gorgon's head and whose main demand of her followers was the blood of their enemies.

'Great,' David muttered. 'And this is the person I'm looking to for help?'

14

'David Kelman.'

'David, it's me.'

'Morning, Nushka,' he said, focused on the dual carriage-way as it spooled out before him.

'So?' she asked.

'So … what?'

'So, how did it go with Norm?'

He smiled as he drove. 'Well, if you know I went to see him, you must know how it went.'

'Look, I dropped him a line the other day to let him know what was happening. That was all. And he sent me a text last night to say that you'd been.'

'That was all he said?'

'No, he said he'd sent you off with a flea in your ear.'

'So …' David broke off to navigate heavier traffic, 'why are you bothering asking?'

'Because I know Norm and I can't see him sitting around in his garden all summer while *you're* investigating a kidnapping. Assuming that's what you *are* doing. I mean, it's for real, this, isn't it? You *are* setting up this *Essex Enquirer* thing? It wasn't some flight of fancy?'

'Why so interested, Nushka? *You* sent me off with a flea in my ear, too.'

'If you must know, I've got some holiday time owing. Couple of weeks' worth.'

'You want in?' he asked.

'First, I want to know that this is real. You won't like me saying this, David, but you're not the world's most reliable guy.'

'I'm as serious about this as I can be, Nushka. But what I can't give you is a contract, a pay-packet, an expenses allowance – any of that stuff.'

She sighed. 'We can't have everything, I suppose.'

'What I *can* offer you is a desk in a proper newsroom.'

'A newsroom?'

'Of sorts.'

'Of sorts? I see.'

'And I've already spoken to a couple of web designers, so we'll have a professional forum in which to publish this material when we've compiled it.'

'It still sounds like you're playing at it.'

'What else can I do?' He swung left onto the M25. 'No one'll publish me outside the gutter rags. I'll tell you what isn't amateurish, though: mine and your expertise as investigative reporters.'

'Come on, David. That *sounds* good, but where would we even start?'

'I've already started. I'm on my way to Chatham.'

There was a pause. 'Chatham, Kent?'

'Well, not Chatham, Ontario.'

'What're you going there for?'

'That's where Freddie Martindale killed himself.'

'He jumped off the top of a derelict building in Keppel Hall, didn't he?' Anushka sounded uneasy.

'That's my understanding. Place called Somersby House.'

'So, you're going to the Keppel Hall Estate? Talking to street people?'

'Kent Police won't tell me anything.'

'David, that could be dangerous.'

'You asked me how serious I was being.'

'You'll end up getting knifed.'

'Some people would call that justice.'

Another pause. A long one this time. 'Just be careful, yeah?'

'Caution's my middle name. Gotta go now, Nushka. If you decide you want in, you know where to find me.'

He cut the call, hitting the gas as he sped south along the motorway, conscious that yet again he'd just lied to a colleague. Twice in this case. First of all, it was pure bravado that their investigative reporting skills would see them through this thing. To start with, Anushka didn't have any. She'd been an enthusiastic junior when all this happened before, and had spent the last two years out of the game. He, meanwhile, had not pursued anyone who was likely to, how had she put it – knife him – for a similar period of time.

The other lie was that caution was his middle name. He couldn't afford it to be on the Keppel Hall Estate, not if he wanted to get some answers. But it wouldn't be fun. Keppel Hall was a grotty area, and he was going in there with nothing.

Not even a press card.

The district wasn't appalling. Occasionally, David spied shadowy figures in darkened doorways or halfway down side alleys, motionless as they awaited customers, but there were normal folk around as well, going about their business.

However, when he came in sight of the now-derelict Somersby House, he couldn't miss it.

It wasn't high-rise, but was still a hulking, monolithic structure made from dingy concrete, its windows covered with green-painted steel. It only seemed to be accessible along a narrow side passage. At the end of this, he had to kick his way through a corrugated metal fence. After that, lines of police tape hung limp over heaps of broken bricks and shattered masonry. Beyond this, a doorway, previously crammed with bulging plastic bin liners had been cleared, said bin liners lugged out and thrown to one side.

David listened, hearing nothing, before edging his way inside.

It might be summer, but the pitch darkness was dank and chill. A stench of urine engulfed him; his feet kicked bottles and loose planks. He clicked on his phone-light, but the subterranean gloom only retreated a short distance. Every two yards, he paused to listen, but it was deathly quiet. When he came to a T-junction, the passage on the left ran about ten yards to the foot of a flight of concrete steps with a hint of daylight shimmering down. He ascended warily, reaching a switchback landing, where a single burned spoon lay in one of the corners.

'Great place to spend your final days, Freddie.'

On the next floor, there were windows, but again they'd been covered by steel hoardings, which allowed in minimal daylight. From here, passageways led off in two different directions. The one in front led to more stairs, but the one on the left travelled a significant distance, passing various battered-open doorways. David waited again, listening.

He hadn't planned what he was going to do once he got in here. Probably go from one flat to the next, looking for clues. Most likely, they'd show signs that vagrants had been living in them. Even here, on the landing of the first floor, there were tell-tale signs: crack phials, the occasional used syringe, but if there was anywhere it was obvious the police had been, that would be the starting point.

After that, though, it was anyone's guess what he might glean from this.

He went along the main corridor, steel-clad windows on his left, broken doorways on his right. There was nothing telling behind any of the latter. Fire-damaged walls, piles of masonry where ceilings had collapsed. His eyes were now attuning, however, and he came to an abrupt standstill when he saw what he thought was a figure waiting at the far end. He advanced again. Slower than before. The figure didn't move, but the closer David drew, the more distinct it became.

Whoever it was, they were wearing black. But had they also painted their face white?

About thirty yards away, he realised the truth. It was a piece of graffiti art; on a patch of wall, someone had painted a life-size figure dressed in black clothing. The face was alarmingly basic, the eyes two crosses, the nose a simple tick, the mouth a big, curved, clownish grin. David regarded it for several seconds, wondering if this whole thing was a lost cause.

On the second floor, it was the same. A litter-strewn corridor, more open flats filled with junk and dust. Obscene slogans slashed onto the walls. He mopped sweat from his brow.

A door slammed overhead.

David froze, ears pinging. He glanced up at the water-marked ceiling.

A heavy thud followed, and then another.

All along he'd been in two minds about what to do if he found that there was someone squatting here. He'd told Anushka that he would demand answers of the street people.

On arriving, he'd found that prospect less appealing. Now though, confronted by the surely hopeless task of working out Freddie Martindale's final movements simply by sniffing through an abandoned tenement block, it would be plain ridiculous not to at least speak to someone.

When he reached the third floor, he halted again, this time feeling a breeze on his face.

He crept to the first junction. Another corridor, similar to the ones he'd seen below, ran away to his left. However, on his immediate right, a shorter passage led to an uncovered window. He approached it, relieved to be breathing cleaner air. Shards of glass remained in the desiccated frame, but it stood at waist-height and he was able to look down. He must have entered through the back of the building, because this appeared to be the front. He saw a parking area covered with wastepaper; beyond that, a disused road led to another fence of corrugated metal.

He leaned further out. Forty feet below lay piles of bricks and other rubble. It was dizzying, yet poor Freddie Martindale had come down from a much greater height. The mind could only boggle at what degree of suffering could have driven him to such a deed.

Another loud thud. This time from somewhere behind him.

David moved back to the junction. To his surprise, he heard what might be music.

He followed it left, heading along the main corridor.

As he progressed, he realised that one flat, perhaps thirty yards ahead, was shedding a little more light than the others. This also appeared to be the origin of the sound, which was quite definitely music. And not just music; David heard the inane jabber of a radio DJ.

With the door just in front of him, he paused.

Taking a breath, he stuck his head around the jamb.

It looked like an empty room. He ventured in. It was a shell: peeling walls, bare floorboards. But no rubbish strewed it, so some effort had been made to clean. Meanwhile, the music, not to mention a little more daylight, were emanating from a doorway on the right. David approached, halting in the entrance to a second room, though this one was smaller. If it hadn't been a bedroom before, it was being used for that now. There were two camp beds. One had an empty sleeping bag laid on top, the other a backpack alongside bits of clothing and toiletries.

A battered radio sat in the corner, blaring away. But there was no one in there listening to it. David moved further in, scanning left and right. A recess closet occupied one corner, its door jammed open an inch or so. On the other wall, the single window was covered by a torn bin liner. It rustled and fluttered in the breeze, admitting plenty of daylight.

David tried to make sense of what he was seeing.

Dossers obviously. As Freddie Martindale had been. But, given that one of the beds was being used as a kind of sideboard, maybe there was only one of them here now. Did that mean this had once been Freddie's room as well?

David's eye was caught by something hanging from the door frame, glimmering blue and white. He stepped towards it and saw the tail-end of a strip of police tape. He felt a surge of excitement. This was it – this was where Freddie had been living. The police would have closed it off while investigating his death.

A floorboard creaked.

David tried to spin around, but it was too late. In the background, the closet stood wide open. In the foreground, a hooded figure filled his vision. He raised his arm, but was only partially able to block the wooden bat that came hurtling down. It bounced off his elbow, which itself was agony, before striking a glancing blow to his left temple.

The next thing, the floor was spinning up towards him.

Side-on, a vague, blurry figure grabbed the backpack, before vanishing from the room, footfalls hammering away into the distance.

David groaned, but remained conscious. Groggily, he got back to his feet.

His elbow stung, but he had full rotation in the joint. When he touched his temple, the blood smeared his fingertips. It was a moment or two before everything swam into focus. Meantime, he heard a banging of woodwork from somewhere below.

He stumbled to the window, ripping the plastic aside. It was the same view he'd had from the corridor, but directly below, the person who'd hit him came into view, jogging fast across the empty car park, the backpack on their shoulder. Even before the fugitive pulled their hood back, letting loose an untidy mop of dyed-blue hair, David realised that it was a girl. She might be in streetwear – a ragged anorak over a hoodie top, patched jeans and dirty trainers – but he could tell from the way she moved.

He glanced back at the camp beds, wondering if any telling personal items had been left behind, but a gruff shout, male this time, drew his attention back to the car park.

The blue-haired girl had stopped in her tracks.

David saw why.

The corrugated metal fence blocking the derelict road had been erected in two sections, but the left one had now been kicked aside, and a figure had stepped through. It was a heavily built man with a thick beard and moustache and long tangles of dark-blond hair. He wore boots with steel caps glinting through their toes, oily jeans and a tasselled leather jacket, which was unzipped, the hefty, hairy paunch of his belly protruding out. He shouted again at the blue-haired girl.

'Squeaky!' it sounded as though he'd said. 'Just the bitch I'm looking for!'

David watched, fascinated.

'Don't you run, you fucking bitch!' the biker type shouted. 'You owe me.'

A chain uncoiled from his right hand and swung by his side. It was thick and dirty with a heavy padlock on the end. That was enough for Squeaky. She flung the bat at him, missed, then turned and dashed back into the building.

'*You fucking bitch!*' the biker roared, pursuing her with heavy, clomping strides.

David lurched out into the corridor, where he halted and listened. Already he could hear the muffled thudding of running feet down below. He stayed where he was. There were stairwells both to left and right. It wouldn't help to pick the wrong one. But the footfalls were growing louder. He could hear a panting and whimpering as well. It came from the right.

He hurried that way. When he reached the top of the steps, he waited again. It sounded as though the girl was on her way up. By the angry bellows from further down, the biker had also entered the building.

David descended at speed, knowing that his timing was going to need to be bang-on, or else he'd get clobbered along with the girl. Maybe worse.

They confronted each other on the second-floor

switchback. The girl, who was rodent-thin, her face pale and spotty, looked appalled, staggering to a halt before shrinking back into the nearest wall. More gruff shouts rose from below. Iron-shod boots clumped on concrete stair-treads.

David put a finger to his lips, before moving along the second floor's main corridor, beckoning the girl to follow. She regarded him with bewilderment, hanging back.

There was another bass shout. 'Gonna kill you, Squeaky, you bitch! You owe me!'

The bastard sounded as if he was only a single flight down. David beckoned again, urgently. The girl ran towards him and they hurried along the passage together. On reaching the fifth flat, David clambered over the broken-down door and indicated the girl should do the same. Reluctantly, she complied.

In the first room, there was a neat stack of furniture, as if its former owner had intended to one day come back and retrieve it, though it was thick with dust and cobwebs. David grabbed a chair, pulled it out and placed it underneath the trapdoor in the ceiling. He'd noticed this during the recce he'd made earlier, but had barely thought anything of it at the time.

The girl gazed up, astonished. David jumped onto the chair so that he could reach the trapdoor. He pushed it and it lifted, black dust pluming down.

'Don't know what's up there,' he whispered, stepping back to the floor. 'But it's got to be better than down here.'

The girl held back again, baffled, unable to understand why he was helping her. But when a splintering crash sounded at the far end of the passage, she darted forward, climbed onto the chair, threw her bag up through the square hole and leapt after it, catching the edges with both hands.

David got underneath her, grabbing her legs and pushing. A second later she was out of sight. He climbed onto the chair as well, and thanks to his recent fitness regime, had no trouble swinging himself up there. Before he did, he kicked as hard as he could at the chair's backrest, sending it skittering across the room, where it fell over. And then he was up in the blackness and the dust and dirt, fitting the square piece of board back into place.

15

Seconds passed, during which the couple sat inches apart, blind in the blackness, but breathing hard and seeping sweat. David had no idea what kind of loft or crawlspace they'd infiltrated, but there were joists underneath them rather than a solid floor.

They listened to what sounded like a whirlwind of violence approaching along the corridor. The biker continued to rant and swear. There were crashing, smashing impacts. David pictured him twirling the chain, the huge padlock gouging chunks out of the plaster walls, shattering rotted woodwork.

'I'll find you, you druggie slag! I'll fucking slaughter you for this!'

It now sounded as if he was in the room directly below. Neither of them breathed, and David felt a small, claw-like hand clamp his shoulder in terror.

'Fucking bitch!' The voice was lower this time, a dull rumble.

Then it fell silent. David pictured the pot-bellied brute pivoting as he checked the room. Maybe wondering why most of the furniture was stacked but one chair lay in a corner.

What had brought him in here? Had they left a clue behind?

The silence persisted. Had the bastard's piggy eyes fallen on the trapdoor?

But the next thing they heard were his boots clumping away along the passage. There were further crashes and bangs as he kicked doors and slashed at the walls.

'I'll find you, Squeaky!' he shouted, his voice diminishing. 'You thieving little bitch!'

The hullaballoo continued upstairs onto the floor above. But then, at length, that too dwindled to nothing. They remained where they were, rigid in the darkness. Only after what seemed an age, did the girl unclasp David's shoulder.

'Think he's still out there?' she whispered.

'I think if he knew we were up here, he'd try to get up,' David replied. 'Could still be in the building, though. We should wait.'

He sensed her nod. More minutes passed until the silence filling the great, gaunt structure that was Somersby House seemed profound. The girl made no objection when David fingered the trapdoor open and peeked down.

'He's checked the squat,' the girl said. 'I'm not there, so he's probably gone.' Her accent sounded Northern. 'He'll think I've legged it through the back door. He'll be searching the streets now. There're other hangouts.'

'Even so, *I'd* better go first,' David replied.

'Hell with that.' She reached past him, lifted the trapdoor and lithely slid her lean body downward, dragging her backpack after her.

Even hanging full-length by the arms, she had to drop several feet. David cringed as she alighted on the bare floorboards, but it wasn't a loud impact. She got up, not waiting for him but rushing to the apartment's front door, checking the passage and hurrying out.

David jumped down and had to dash to keep up with her. They didn't speak as they moved warily but speedily along the corridor. At any moment, it seemed possible the long-haired ogre could step out of a doorway in front of them. But they made it to the stairwell unmolested and stood listening again, before commencing a slow, cautious ascent.

'You've got stuff up here that's actually worth this risk?' David said quietly.

'Shhhh,' she replied.

They peered along the third-floor corridor before proceeding down it. If this squat was the hub of Squeaky's operations, it stood to reason that her enemy would more likely be lying in wait here than anywhere else. But it also made sense that he wouldn't expect her to be hanging around, and so possibly had called off the search. David's heart still slammed his ribs as they approached the doorway in question. Squeaky seemed hesitant too. She was white-faced, strands of blue hair streaked across her sweat-damp features. They waited and listened. And listened.

And at last took the bull by the horns and ventured inside.

As expected, the squat had been trashed. There wasn't a lot the biker could have damaged, but he'd still managed it, throwing the two camp beds around and stamping on their rusty metal frames until they were broken and useless, tearing the sleeping bag apart, wrenching out its stuffing, and kicking the few personals the girl had left behind from wall to wall, including the radio, which lay in pieces.

She dropped to her knees, unperturbed, searching to see what she could salvage.

'Who was that nutcase?' David asked from the window, seeing no one below.

She glanced up at him, as if only now remembering that he was here. 'Never mind him. Who are *you*?'

'If I said a friend, would you believe me?'

She carried on sorting her stuff. 'I haven't got any friends.'

'I wonder why. I got spiders in my hair saving you from the ass-kicking of all time, and now I get the feeling I'm being given the brush-off.'

'It's not that I'm not grateful.' She didn't sound grateful. 'And I'm sorry for hitting you.' She didn't sound sorry either. 'But I've got to get out of here. Dane won't be far off.'

David glanced back through the window. The forecourt remained empty. 'That was Dane, was it?'

'Didn't you hear me say so?'

'And what is Dane?'

She glanced up again, this time suspiciously. 'You a copper?'

'Do I look like one?'

'Who are you then? Why you here?'

'Answer *my* question first, eh? Let's establish some trust.'

'Trust...Jesus.' She snorted again. 'You're no copper, that's for sure. I don't remember the last copper who wanted me anywhere near him, never mind tried to win my trust. For what it's worth, just so's you know what you've messed yourself up in, Dane's my dealer.'

'And you owe him, right?'

'Don't miss much, do you?'

'How much?'

She zipped her backpack closed. 'Five hundred...ish.'

'Five hundred! How you going to get that?'

'I'm not, am I!' She swung the pack to her shoulder. 'That's why I'm getting out.'

'I can't help, I'm afraid.' David flicked through the wad

of notes in his pocket. 'I've got a few quid on me, but not five hundred.'

She was halfway across the room, but stopped to stare at him. 'Who are you, mate? Seriously? You've just met me and suddenly you're looking to pay my debts!'

He offered his hand. 'My name's David Kelman.'

She backed away. 'I'm not shaking your fucking hand.'

The revulsion in her face was a shock. Normally, it was street people like Squeaky whom everyday citizens like him sought to avoid contact with. He'd no idea it cut the other way too.

'Don't need to tell me, anyway,' she said. 'Can't be any reason why you're round here unless you're up to no good. Even if you're not, you should get your arse out. If Dane catches you, he'll know you've helped me. Or he'll think you have. It doesn't matter either way. He'll beat the living shit out of you.'

She made for the door.

'I was a friend of Freddie Martindale's,' David said.

She glanced back.

'I'm here to find out what happened,' he added. 'Why he killed himself.'

'You knew Freddie?'

'Not as well as I'd have liked to.' That comment was honest at least.

She shook her head. 'You can't have known him that well. Otherwise you'd never have come here.'

She left the room. David went too, but in almost no time she was halfway down the corridor.

'Squeaky!' He hurried in pursuit. 'Help me ... please.'

She stopped again. 'You want to know why Freddie killed himself?'

He shrugged, awkward under her intense scrutiny.

'You fucking idiot. You're just like all the rest.' But the next look she gave him was one of pity. 'You really don't get it? Freddie didn't kill himself. He was murdered.'

16

'This is where they say he jumped off,' Squeaky said.

They were on the roof of Somersby House, though there wasn't much room up there. A kind of superstructure occupied the central area, brick-built and flat-topped, and when you looked inside, filled with the rusted remnants of long-disused cisterns and water pipes. There was only a narrow walkway, perhaps a metre wide, around its edges, a low brick barrier, no more than two feet high, separating that from the precipitous drop to the world below.

David wasn't afraid of heights, but it was a descent of ninety feet or more into the narrow passage running between this building and the next one. Again, fragments of police tape were visible down there.

'Was he killed instantly?' David asked.

'What do you think?'

'What I mean is, he wasn't able to talk to anyone before he died?'

She shrugged. 'Not as far as I'm aware.'

'So how do you know he was pushed?'

'Because I knew Freddie. He wouldn't have done that.'

An answer like that meant nothing. Many suicides' loved ones tried to deny that the deceased had been in crisis. It was a form of self-defence and certainly wouldn't have convinced police investigators. Not on its own.

'There's no chance he could have fallen off here?' David

said. 'I mean if he was zonked out of it and didn't know where he was?'

'Never knew him come up here voluntarily. Plus, he was trying to get clean.'

David considered that. It tallied with the toxicology report, which had recorded that Freddie Martindale's body had been clear of narcotics at the time of his death. The Coroner's officer had suggested that this might have depressed him even more. In other words, reality came rushing in and it was too much for him to handle.

'Plus he thought he was getting somewhere,' the girl added.

David glanced at her. 'What do you mean?'

'Trying to find his sister. He thought he was making ground.'

David considered again. 'I'm assuming that was Freddie's empty bed down in the squat?'

She nodded.

'So a lot of the time it was just you and him?'

'We weren't together, if that's what you're asking.'

'But you were close?'

'I suppose.'

'Close enough for him to confide in you that he was looking for Jodie?'

'Shit, everyone knew he was doing that. It's all he ever did. Anyone new in the area, he'd go straight to see them, ask if they knew anything.'

'And he thought that would work?'

'Why not?' She shouldered her backpack and set off along the parapet, David trailing behind. 'People do all sorts to feed their habits. Thieving's only part of it. But if someone had been on the rob, Freddie reckoned they might know someone else who knew someone else.' They descended the internal stairs side-by-side. 'Word gets around.'

'So he wasn't discreet about it? This search for his sister.'

'Wouldn't have made any ground if he had been.'

'But he *was* making ground?'

'He was excited. Said a couple of times that he was getting close.'

'I don't suppose he mentioned any names? Anyone I might be able to speak to?'

'People don't really have names out here.'

'Well, you've got a name. They call you "Squeaky".'

She glanced sidelong at him. 'So?'

'I'd like to know your real name.'

'Why?'

'Because I have to start somewhere.'

She pondered. 'You trying to find Jodie too?'

'I think it's the least I can do for Freddie.'

She mused on this. 'Laura. Laura Reynoldson.'

'You're not from this part of the world, are you, Laura? Let me guess... Manchester?'

She smiled without humour. 'If you're thinking you're going to send me back there, tough shit. You and your mates'll have to catch me first.'

'I've not got the power to send you anywhere.'

'The coppers have.' They'd now reached the ground floor, where they headed towards the main doors. 'Go and tell them, if you want. But you'll be wasting your time.'

'You wanted for a crime or something?' he asked. 'Up north?'

'Like I say, we do what we can to get by.'

They emerged into daylight. After the indoor gloom,

it was unexpectedly bright. David shaded his eyes as they walked into the abandoned car park.

'I don't talk to coppers,' Laura said. 'Not even when they came about Freddie. Didn't even tell them about the couple who were here.'

David glanced at her again. 'What couple was that?'

'The bloke and the woman. They wanted Freddie too.'

'When was this?'

'Couple of days before he died.'

'Did you know them?'

'Saw them before, sniffing around, like they were looking for someone. They didn't come inside that time. Second time, they did – Freddie was out. I told them I'd never heard of him.'

'They asked for him by name?'

'Yeah, but I told them to leave me alone.'

'They couldn't have been members of his family?'

'Wouldn't have believed them if they'd said that.'

'Why?'

'Something about them, you know. Something I didn't like.'

They strode along the derelict road.

'Could they have been police officers?' David asked.

'Didn't seem right for that either. Bloke had a tat on his hand.'

'Not on the palm, by any chance?'

She glanced at him. 'How'd you know?'

'Lucky guess. What was it?'

'Tangle of briars. With a rose in the middle.'

'OK...'

'Didn't sound local, either. She had a Northern Irish accent. His was like ... foreign, Eastern Europe somewhere.'

David's thoughts were racing. A distinct non-English accent had reportedly confused the young Freddie Martindale when he'd fled the scene of his sister's kidnapping.

'There were two of these people, you say? A man and a woman?'

'There was a third, I think. But I never saw him. The driver of the van they came in. He sat out there on the other side of the fence, keeping the engine running.'

'What kind of van was it?'

She screwed her face. 'Funny-looking thing. Could've been an ambulance, but the wrong colour... dark grey.'

'And these people were specifically looking for Freddie?'

'I've said that, haven't I!'

'Laura, Freddie never said anything to you about... well, someone being after him?'

'No, like I say.'

They approached the corrugated metal fence. From this close, the narrow gap between the two sections was clearly visible.

'What you actually said was that he was murdered.'

Laura sighed. 'The coppers thought he did it himself because he had to walk up three floors to jump off the roof. And you don't do that by accident. They didn't seem to take into account that someone else could've dragged him up those three floors.'

'Did you see that happen?' David put a hand on her arm, turning her to face him. 'You seem very sure this is how it went down.'

'No!' She tore free and hurried on towards the fence.

David followed. 'Laura, this is dead serious!'

'No!' she snapped back. 'Fuck's sake, I wasn't there when Freddie died.'

'Where were you?'

'I've already told you, I have to earn money. Or I have to try.' Fleetingly, she looked disgusted with herself. 'It's not as easy as it used to be. That's why Dane came wanting his pound of flesh.' She passed out of sight through the gap.

David scrambled through after her. On the other side, the road ran on, though from here there were markings along the gutters, while some of the shops were open for business.

'That was something else the coppers said.' Laura spoke with deep annoyance. 'That Freddie didn't want me on the game, so he got upset – they were trying to blame *me*, the bastards.'

'*Did* he get upset?' David asked.

'He didn't like it,' she admitted, 'but not so's he'd top himself. Anyway, he was too busy. When he wasn't out and about, he was writing up piles of notes on scrap paper. What he'd learned, what to do next.'

David's thoughts tumbled. Freddie Martindale, though his efforts to locate Jodie had been cack-handed, might actually have been closing in on some vital information. So much so that some very nasty people came out of the shadows to shut him up.

'How long were you with him, Laura?'

'Don't know. Couple of years.'

'In all that time, did you ever know Freddie use a mobile phone?'

'He had a phone, but it never worked as long as I knew him.'

The end of the street came in sight. About fifty yards ahead, it joined with what looked like a main road. Cars were passing, pedestrians crossing.

'Listen,' David said, 'I have a bad feeling that when we come to the end here, you and me are going our separate ways and will never see each other again.'

'Suits me,' she muttered. 'I'm grateful for your help, but I'm out of here.'

'Trouble is I've nothing to work with.'

'I've told you everything I know.'

'And Freddie definitely didn't mention any other names?'

'No, I've told you.' She was turning irritable again, walking faster.

'How about Saint Bridget?'

She glanced round at him curiously. 'Saint Bridget?'

'You've heard that name?'

'Now you say it...' She tried to recall. 'He *did* mention something like that. One night, couple of weeks before it happened. He was talking to himself while he was scribbling. I thought he was rambling. Said something like "Jodie met her"...'

David grabbed her hand. 'Jodie met Saint Bridget?'

She snatched her arm back. 'Not long before she got nabbed. Or something similar...'

'Any idea how long "not long" is?'

'I dunno. He said something else too – can't remember what. Didn't give it no mind at the time. But—'

'*You bitch!*' a harsh voice cut across them.

A brutish bearded figure had just stepped from an alley some ten yards ahead. He lumbered towards them at speed, chain-and-lock in hand. Laura seemed transfixed, before twirling and running. Not back along the road, but aiming for another alley entrance.

David went with her. At first, it looked good. The alley ran behind a row of shops that were in use; it was straight and clear, lined with dustbins. And of course, both of them were lighter and faster than the cumbersome figure of the biker. He followed anyway, shouting and swearing. They threw backward glances. They were well ahead of him, the gap growing.

Until Laura trod on a loose bottle.

It rolled sideways and her ankle rolled with it.

She went down, squawking in pain.

David stopped and turned. Dane was twenty yards away, barrelling towards them, his face beetroot red, swirling the chain around his head like a medieval flail. Laura whimpered as she scrabbled on the floor, trying to regather oddments shed from her pack.

David grabbed her by a handful of anorak, hauling her to her feet. She gasped as he dragged her along the alley. But Dane was less than five yards behind them now. They could feel the rage pouring off him. David shoved the girl ahead, then, with barely enough time to think things through, dropped and rolled into a tight ball. Dane had no time to stop, striking David with his knees and falling clean over the top of him.

His face struck the alley floor with a resounding *SMACK*.

David, agonised by the impact on his ribs, but adrenaline-fuelled, sprang back to his feet and tried to run past. Only for a ham shank of a forearm to jerk out and trip him. David also hit the ground with force, tumbling through a full somersault. As he did, he caught a sideways glimpse of Laura a dozen yards ahead, almost at the end of the alley. Though now she'd stopped and turned back.

A bear-like growl alerted him to the biker getting up again, bleeding from a split eyebrow but still clutching his chain-and-lock. Teeth bared through sweat-soaked bristles, he stomped forward. David tried to slither away on his back, but the biker was on him already, spinning his chain faster and faster, set to swing it down with brutal, bone-splintering force.

17

A wild blaring sound filled the alley. David glanced sideways, and, behind the biker's giant frame, saw a black car advancing fast along the narrow passage, its lights on high-beam, its driver hitting the horn. The biker also glanced back, and was just able to throw himself to the far wall to avoid being hit, where he collided with a wheelie bin, which fell over, its filthy contents exploding out. He rolled in it as he tried to scramble to his feet.

'*You bastards!*' he screamed.

David got up and also threw himself aside, but in his case the car screeched to a halt. It was a Fiat 500, and when he bent down to look, he was incredulous to see Anushka Chawla behind the wheel.

'Get in!' she yelled.

He wrenched the back door open. As he did, Laura came limping towards him. He threw her into the backseat, before flinging himself in after her. Anushka hit the gas as the immense, filth-covered figure of Dane ran at the Fiat's rear. Tyres spun, rubber stinking, as the car lurched out of his reach, accelerating all the way to the end of the alley, at which point Anushka spun them right into the mainstream traffic.

'Looks like you haven't lost your knack for pissing people off,' she said.

David was bright-faced with sweat, breathing hard. 'What're ... what're *you* doing here?'

'Couldn't leave you to do a dangerous job like this on your own, could I?'

'Aren't you supposed to be at work?'

Anushka got her foot down to beat the next lights. 'Told you I had some time owing.'

She was wearing a sweater and jeans rather than her supermarket uniform, he noticed. He glanced behind, but saw only cars and normal pedestrians.

'What happened to holidays in the sun?' he said.

'What?' she replied. 'For an adventurous sort like me? I won't pretend I didn't nearly give up, though. Been driving all over this neighbourhood for fifty minutes. Found your car but there was no sign of you.'

'And there was me thinking that you, being our techie expert, had used some electronic wizardry to track me down.'

'Don't start that,' she said. This was something he and Norm had used to irritate her with back on the *Examiner*, referring to her as their 'resident techie'. 'And it wouldn't be wizardry, just WhatsApp. Remind me to show you how to share your location on it. Anyway, who was that nightmare-on-legs?'

David wiped his brow. 'That was Dane.' He saw her expression in the rear-view mirror. 'I know ... even sounds like a Viking, doesn't he? Basically, he doesn't like being outsmarted.'

'Tell me later. Where we going?'

David looked at Laura. 'Where d'*you* want to go?'

She sat pale-faced, arms wrapped around her backpack. 'Anywhere away from here.'

'Railway station?'

'So I can sit at the door, begging? He'll soon find me there.'

David dug into his pocket, bringing out the same notes as earlier. 'If I give you the money for a ticket, will you use it for that?'

She eyed the cash uncertainly. 'Suppose. I know some people in Deal.'

He separated five tenners from the rest, folded them and offered them to her. But when she reached for it, he held it back. 'Answers first.'

She scowled. 'I've told you everything I know.'

'No, you haven't. You told me about Jodie meeting Saint Bridget. But you said you thought there was more. You just couldn't quite remember.'

She shrugged. 'It didn't make sense.'

'Let me worry about that.'

'Freddie was just talking. To himself, mainly. Kept saying "Jodie saw Saint Bridget at..." think he said "at Royal Wallasey". And that's it, I swear. I've no clue what he meant.'

David pondered. 'How about you, Nushka?'

She shrugged as she drove. 'Easy enough to look up.'

David filched his iPhone from his pocket, and made a quick search. 'There are references to Wallasey on Merseyside. Suppose it could be that. We've got Wallasey Royal Mail Group, Wallasey Royal British Legion ... neither use "Royal" as the prefix, though.'

'What do we mean anyway?' Anushka asked. 'Jodie met Saint Bridget?'

David explained the little he knew.

She mused. 'We couldn't be talking a vision or something, could we? You know, a religious experience? A hallucination? This Royal Wallasey might not even be a real place.'

David glanced at Laura. 'What do you think?'

'Dunno, do I? *Sounded* like he was talking about a real person.'

David turned back to Anushka. 'Was Jodie Martindale the sort to have hallucinations? She was deputy chair of a massive finance house.'

'Takes all sorts,' Anushka replied. 'We're here, anyway.'

They were now on the access road in front of the station. Anushka pulled into a small unloading area. Laura checked that her backpack was fastened, then produced a baseball cap and crammed it down on her mop of blue hair.

David offered the money again, and she snatched it.

'Whoa!' He gripped her wrist.

'Come on, mate!' she pleaded.

'Before you get out – you were lucky today.'

'You call that luck?'

'Yeah, I do. If I hadn't been there, Dane would've had his pound of flesh, as you called it.'

'Oh, I see. You saved me, so that gives you the right to give me a lecture?'

She met his gaze truculently. Realising how impossible this was, he released her. 'Just be careful, OK?'

She jumped out of the car, leaning back in for half a second, the pack already hoisted to her shoulder. 'When I said thanks, I meant it.'

'No problem,' David replied, getting out himself.

By the time he'd climbed into the front passenger seat, she was already out of sight.

Anushka pulled out. 'You know she's not getting on any train, don't you?'

'Yep. Just like I know her name's not Laura.'

'How'd you figure that out?'

'She's got a homemade tattoo on the inside of her left wrist. A back-of-the-bike-sheds job. Says "Yvonne". Think she'd go to all that trouble to write someone else's name there?'

'Who was she, anyway?'

Again, David went through what they thought they knew.

Anushka looked thoughtful. 'So you're thinking these three people who came to the flats were the same ones who kidnapped Jodie Martindale?'

'I don't know. The vehicle they used looked like an ambulance...'

'Laura said it was a different colour.'

'A spray job's easy enough to come by. So's a replacement tattoo.'

'You seriously think these three characters are still at it six years later?'

'If Jodie's still alive six years later, which we think she is, whatever *it* was is clearly still going on.'

Anushka mused. 'The woman had a Northern Irish accent, the bloke sounded Eastern European. Fits with Freddie Martindale's original story that at least one of them wasn't English. So, are we going to the cops with this stuff?'

'What's the point? It'd be hearsay. From a witness who's already disappeared.'

They headed back towards Keppel Hall so that David could get his car. En route, they watched the pavements, scanning doorways and side streets, but there was no sign of Dane.

'If there's CCTV round here, the cops could use it to trace the van,' Anushka suggested.

'How many grey vans do you think travel through

Chatham, Nushka? And it'd likely be travelling under false plates anyway.'

'There've been no others, have there?'

'Other what?'

'Well ... Darren Doyle and Cheryl Bryant were abducted first. Up in Norfolk. Then they were found dead. A short time later, Jodie Martindale and Rick Tamworth were grabbed. Rick was found dead and Jodie vanished. So ...?'

'So there haven't been any others because Jodie was the main target,' David interrupted. 'I've been saying this all along.'

'Or because the perps have been lying low,' she replied. 'Or because they've changed their MO. The police got close, and they didn't want a similar pattern to emerge somewhere else afterwards.'

'You mean like they're just serial killers? Three of them working together?'

'It's happened before.' She pulled up next to his parked Fiesta.

'That'd be bad enough, but I'll tell you, Nushka, I've got a gut feeling this is a whole lot bigger even than that.'

'Wow!' Anushka said, when David turned the main lights on.

In truth, she hadn't been familiar with the interior of his garage before, and so had no idea just how much cleaner it now was. After a busy weekend on his part, all the rubbishy furniture and spare bits of garden gear had been removed, the roof had been repaired, all cobwebs and other grot vacuumed away, the floor swept and laid with brand new carpet tiles and a couple of desks and swivel chairs brought in. He'd even had power-points installed at every work-station, the electricity supply having been restored.

'Welcome to Crime Beat Mark II,' he said, stripping off his anorak.

'You've constructed yourself a newsroom,' she replied.

'I still think of it as "the Shed", but it's doing its job. The landline's being installed tomorrow.'

'Landline?'

'Tip-line then. Call it what you want.' David sat at the desk he'd chosen as his own. 'But this is where I'm going to run the *Essex Enquirer* from.'

Anushka eyed the two framed pictures sitting alongside his laptop. The first depicted Tabby, blonde and pretty in a jumpsuit and trainers, the second Tommy in his football kit.

'I have to make it work for *them*,' David said.

'I thought you were ...'

'Estranged? Not quite. But I've had nothing to offer them. Nothing they could be proud of. Until now.' He lifted his laptop onto the next desk along. 'Maybe.'

'You're serious about this, aren't you?'

'After today, can you doubt that?' He picked up the box of Freddie's bumph and commenced leafing through it. 'Career-wise, I'm not going to pretend it's anything other than the longest shot of all time. But I only started this thing a few days ago, and already I feel better. Take a pew.' He indicated the laptop. 'It's already signed in. Have a look for Royal Wallasey, eh?'

Shaking her head, Anushka sat and opened the laptop. She glanced at Freddie's paperwork. 'What's that?'

He told her as he scanned the pages.

She looked discomforted. 'Shouldn't you at least give *that* to the cops?'

'It's not as simple as that.'

'Why not?'

'It's this guy, Jorgenson. I've already explained that I don't trust him.'

'David, come on ...'

'No!' he said adamantly. 'When I went to speak to him, his whole attitude seemed wrong. Gangsterish.'

'Gangsterish?'

'He was menacing, threatening ...'

'Some coppers are like that.'

'Not very often. Not anymore. But *he* was right at home with it. The other thing is ...' David paused as though struggling to articulate. 'He looked ... pissed off, you know?'

'No, I don't know.'

'When I mentioned the mobile phone and how I thought it was Jodie's voice.'

'If you'd just admitted to stealing it ...'

'It wasn't that. It was more like: "Shit! What do I do now?"'

'Maybe he's just lazy?'

He shrugged. 'If so, what good's he to us? I don't think it's even that, though. I'm sure there's something else going on.'

Anushka regarded him carefully. 'You sure it's not just a case of you wanting to get even? You missed him at Lampwick Lane, so you're not handing him another win now?'

David grabbed up a handful of Freddie's scribbled sheets. 'Look at this stuff, Nushka. It'd take an Egyptologist to decipher it. I *could* give it to him, but what difference would it make?'

'That's self-justification.'

'Hey, if you want to give it to him, go ahead.' He offered her the box. 'You're part of this operation too.'

She pointedly didn't take it. 'I'm not sure I am yet. Not one hundred per cent.'

'In that case, we do it my way and see if *we* get anything out of it first.'

They continued with their individual tasks, Anushka scanning various websites, David checking page after page for additional bits of scribble that might resemble the name Saint Bridget, and perhaps unexpectedly, finding one almost straight away, semi-concealed amid a mass of other scrawl. He leaned closer, squinting.

The line of writing underneath those two words also contained something which, on close inspection, might just be intelligible.

Anushka sat back. 'Nothing under Royal Wallasey.'

'Try spelling it differently.' He showed her the sheet, and the passage in question. 'I might be wrong, but does this not read as W-A-L-L-A-S-E-A?'

She examined it. 'Yes, it could. Hey, it might mean Wallasea Island. That's not far away.'

David took the laptop and began another search. It didn't take long. 'Here we go.'

Anushka looked down over his shoulder. It was the home page of a website depicting a green shoreline under a blue sky, and in the foreground sailboats and other swish-looking craft moored along a sun-bleached jetty.

'The Royal Wallasea,' she read aloud. 'Yachting Club and Marina.' They scrolled to the smaller print. 'Off the River Crouch. Looks expensive, exclusive even. Just the sort of place Jodie Martindale might have hung out...'

David gave her an impish grin. 'Do you reckon they'll let the likes of us in?'

18

'Wouldn't it just be easier asking your police insider, Deepthroat or whatever he's called, if he knows any St Bridgets?' Anushka said as she drove.

'Already done that,' David replied from the back seat. 'We drew a negative.'

'Because I feel ridiculous in this get-up.'

'You look *great*.'

He wasn't just soft-soaping her. The shirt and tie and the pin-striped three-piece suit fitted her female shape snugly. The high-heeled shoes set it off nicely too.

'Do chauffeurs really wear kit like this?' she asked.

'It's about looking smart and efficient.'

'At least you've not got me in boots, jodhpurs and a peaked cap.'

'That would've been fun too.'

They rode in silence for a while, the road from South Fambridge quiet on a late-morning midweek. The sleek, smoke-grey Mercedez Benz S-Class that David had hired for one day ate up the mileage smoothly.

'I don't think I'm going to fool anyone,' Anushka said, sounding nervous.

'I have two thoughts on that. First of all, there'll be no one for you to fool. You won't even need to get out of the car. Just park and wait...'

'And what if they ask me to bring it into the marina car park or whatever?'

'Same thing. You're a functionary doing a job. They'll probably just give you hand-signals. Won't even speak to you.'

That didn't appear to cheer her up. 'What's the other thing?'

'Oh, that's one of the tricks to investigative journalism. It's not letting it enter your head that you're doing something wrong.'

'We'll be infiltrating a private club under false pretences...'

'It's only private because the people who run it say it's private. We won't be breaking any laws.'

'They can still turf us out.'

'That's the worst they can do,' David said. 'But my point stands. We're trying to find out what happened to Jodie Martindale. On the scale of evil, how high does that register?'

She still looked worried. 'If you get into this place, it'll be because you told lies and used a fake identity.'

'Telling lies is wrong, but so is kidnapping and murder. Stand them against each other, Nushka, and what've you got?'

She said nothing. There was no way to argue with that point.

'Me and Norm did the same thing at Lampwick Lane,' David said. 'We told lies, used phoney IDs. Do you think we did wrong then too?'

Again she said nothing. The Lampwick Lane operation had skated along the edge of acceptable journalism but the outcome had been undeniable.

'What I mean, Nushka, is that the more you feel con-spicuous, the more you look it. In the end this job's all about bullshitting. I'm not the kind of actor who'd win Oscars every year. But I can put on a front when I need to. Because I know I'm doing the right thing.'

'Does that apply when you're chasing dirty stories?' she wondered.

'Let's just say it's a relief not to be doing that this time.'

She eyed him through the rear-view mirror, wondering how honest he was being. The David Kelman of old would have stopped at nothing to get a good story, *any* kind of story, while most of his recent scoops had been lurid beyond belief, career-ruining for those involved.

If nothing else, she had to admit that he looked the part. Aside from his fake facial hair, and a pair of Yves Saint Laurent sunglasses, he'd donned a Laksen Woodhay sports jacket, a pair of chinos and Gucci loafers. If that outfit didn't help him blend into the yachting set, she wasn't sure what would. And he'd come up with it on his own, along with today's strategy. She had to give David credit. He did his homework.

When his contact inside Essex Police had told him that a small cadre within the Essex Robbery Squad had been organising their own armed robberies, and that thanks to their devious informant, Malcolm Riker, lesser criminals were taking the fall for them, the operation David had put together to expose them had involved him living a lie not just for ten minutes or half an hour, but for several weeks. It had seen him sitting down and getting drunk with some very dangerous people. It had required him to create a covert identity, which, even if Riker hadn't been able to penetrate it, there was at least a reasonable chance the corrupt coppers would.

Some had later argued that David had been lucky, that the bent cops must have been ridiculously overconfident to have fallen for it. But others had responded that this wasn't the case at all, that DI Pettigrew and DS Elgin in particular were top thief-takers at Essex Robbery, but that even they hadn't seen through David's detailed preplanning and carefully constructed wall of lies, which admittedly he'd had help with from the criminal underworld, but which nonetheless he'd stress-tested himself while out there all alone, with only Norm's voice in his ear as back-up.

Compared to that, he ought to have this one covered relatively easily.

They were now on the approach road, the River Crouch lying to their left, a scenic sweep of glimmering blue water in the August sun. On the far shore, the emerald Essex flatlands rolled off to an indefinite horizon. A signpost appeared on the left.

Royal Wallasea
Yachting Club and Marina

A hundred yards past that, a barred electronic gate closed off the entrance to an expansive driveway. Anushka pulled in. The gate didn't open, but there was space for her to halt the car.

On the other side of the gate, a figure emerged from a small whitewashed building on the right. He was a solidly built chap with a square jaw and blond crewcut. He wore white flannels and a white polo shirt with a crest underneath a sky-blue blazer.

David climbed out and approached.

The gateman regarded him through the bars. 'Can I help you, sir?'

'I hope so,' David replied in his best well-bred English.

'I'm not a member, but I phoned earlier to make a lunchtime appointment with the club secretary. My name's Fosdike. Jon Fosdike. I'm thinking of joining. Looking for a year-round berth for my Intermarine Flybridge. She's a ninety-footer, but Mr Anderton said you could accommodate her. He was going to show me around.'

'Mr Fosdike.' The gateman threw a brief glance at the Merc before checking a clipboard. 'I'm sorry, Mr Fosdike, I don't have any record of that appointment.'

'You don't?' David feigned puzzlement. 'I see. Well, I understand that you can't just let me in, but I don't suppose you can phone the clubhouse? Speak to Mr Anderton maybe? I've come all the way from London ...'

The gateman glanced again at the Merc, which no doubt cost around eighty grand to drive from the showroom. 'Yes, I can do that, of course.' He backed towards his office. 'I'll not be a minute. You understand it's all procedure?'

'Absolutely. And I'm glad to see it. Oh, before you go ...'

The gateman came back.

David leaned towards the bars. 'Just to show I'm who I say I am ...' He slipped a fat wallet from the back pocket of his slacks, and made a show of flicking through. It was packed with twenties and a wide range of plastic. The latter was all fake of course, but the gateman wasn't to know that. He leafed out a Coutts Silk credit card and held it up. The name read 'Jonathan Fosdike'. Alongside it there was a driving licence, also belonging to Jonathan Fosdike but carrying David's headshot, again complete with fake beard and moustache. 'I hear this is one of the best places on the coast. You were recommended by Anton Tipping.'

'Oh, Mr Tipping, yeah.' The gateman smiled with recognition. 'Of course.'

'I know him from Brasenose,' David added. 'We were in the Dragons together.' Whether the gateman had ever heard about the semi-mythical Dragon's Head student society at Oxford and its 'Who's Who' list of mover-and-shaker alumni was immaterial. Cedric Anderton, the well-connected club secretary, almost certainly would have. Plus, it was effective added colour.

The gateman went indoors while David drifted back to the car, hands in pockets. Anushka sat po-faced in the driving seat.

'This was always the bit where the wheel might come off,' he said quietly.

'You mean if they do anything as outrageously unexpected as check up on you?'

'Depends how much of a check they make. Jonathan Fosdike's a real person. He runs the Kreditos Group, one of the largest multinational chemical companies in the world. And he has genuine college connections with Anton Tipping, a currency trader from Australia. Fosdike doesn't look like *this* of course.' He flashed her the fake driving licence. 'But I picked him because he's apparently quite reclusive. There aren't many pictures of him online unless you *really* look.'

'And if they *really* look?'

'The worse they can do is tell us to fuck off.'

'David,' she stared dead ahead, 'you put fake plates on the car. That's called deception.'

'No way. I'm not trying to obtain money from anyone.'

'In seeking to join this elite club, it could be construed as attempting to gain pecuniary advantage.'

'Except that I'm not trying to join. I just want to get inside so that I can talk to a few people.'

'They still might call the police.'

'Won't be the first time for me.' He slid his wallet away. 'Anyway, I can't converse with you too much. You're the help, remember?'

The gateman re-emerged from the building, smiling broadly. There was a *buzz* and a *clunk*, and the gate swung inward.

'Mr Fosdike, terribly sorry. There's obviously been a mix-up. If you'd like to come through, you can take the car up to the club and park in the members' area. Mr Anderton will meet you there.'

'Excellent,' David said, climbing back into the Merc.

Anushka drove them through the gate and along a lengthy drive with manicured parkland lying to either side. 'So much for thinking I could make a quick getaway,' she muttered.

David knew what she meant, but said nothing.

The car's air-conditioned interior was all leather and varnished woodwork. It was a dream just riding in it. The engine purred as they glided towards their destination. He'd driven here from Colchester with a low sense of anticipation but an air of fearless superiority, almost as though the plush surroundings of the vehicle had lulled him into a confidence he ought not to feel. But now it was exactly the opposite. As the driveway dipped downhill and the expanse of sun-splashed water came into view again, it felt as if he were digging himself deeper and deeper into something that was more than a little bit nefarious. He'd experienced the same in the past when pulling other similar stunts. But this one was post-Freddiegate. How would he be regarded this time if it all blew up? The roofs of the clubhouse came in sight, serried rows of masts in front of them.

David had told Anushka that he wasn't committing a criminal offence. But strictly speaking, that wasn't true.

Swapping the plates on the Mercedes could certainly get him into trouble. It might even be construed criminal damage by the hire company. There were lots of things here that could see him arrested.

'We brazen it out,' he reminded himself.

'What was that?' Anushka watched him through the rear-view mirror.

'Nothing.'

'Brazen what out?'

'All we need do is play it cool. Just like it's any other day.'

'Sure. Should be a doddle.'

19

'Mr Fosdike, so sorry about this. What a ridiculous mix-up.'

Despite being somewhere in his mid-seventies, Cedric Anderton came hurrying out of the main building in the regulation white flannels, white crested polo shirt and blue blazer, and before David had even climbed from the car, was pumping his hand apologetically. He was of average height, but lean and tanned, with a head of snow-white curls. He seemed sincere in the welcome he was extending.

'I honestly had no idea you were coming today. Do you know who it was took the booking?'

'I'm afraid I don't,' David replied, signalling to Anushka to park in one of the visitor bays. 'My secretary rang it through. A young man, she thought.'

Anderton shook his head, disappointed. 'That'll explain it. During the summer we have a lot of students working here. They're not always tip-top quality. Heads in the clouds, every spare minute playing on their phones. I mean, give them an actual job to do and they're fine. But when they're just required to be around the place and be efficient … well, that can be a problem.' He indicated that they should go indoors.

David checked out the building as he entered. It was the usual thing: a clutch of low whitewashed structures with red pantile roofs. Here at the back, where the members' car park was, it could be any country club: well-tended grass verges, islands of shrubbery and flowers, a range of international flags hanging over the glass doors of the entrance. On the other side, facing the marina and the river, it would be pure summer: verandas, terraces, masts and rigging as far as the eye could see.

'Even so, for an august person like yourself, there should have been something in the club diary.' Anderton approached the Reception counter. 'We ought to have laid something on actually.'

'There's no need for that,' David replied in a magnanimous tone. 'I have another appointment at three anyway, so I'll have to be on the move shortly.'

Anderton nodded at the young woman behind the counter, presumably implying that there was no need for this particular guest to do anything as vulgar as sign in or be issued with a visitor tag.

'Well…' he headed left, 'the very least we can do is treat you to lunch.'

'If you don't mind, I'll pass on that too,' David said. 'I'm having a bit of a hectic day and I've already eaten.'

'Fair enough. Can I ask chef to dish something up for your driver?'

'She'll be fine, trust me.'

'As you wish.'

They were now in the clubhouse proper. It mainly comprised open-aspect bar and lounge areas, wood-panelled and carpeted, everything shipshape and nautical, even down to the seafaring implements of former days mounted on the walls and pillars. On the right, a succession of French windows had been opened wide, not just to admit the warm breeze, but to allow outdoor dining and grand views of the many luxury craft moored here. One or two couples were dotted about, most dressed casually but fashionably.

'So, you're visiting us on the advice of Mr Tipping?' Anderton asked.

'I am indeed.'

'He's been a member for the last decade.'

David already knew that from his researches, which was why he'd chosen him.

'You can see his Flybridge over to the right.' Anderton moved out onto the clubhouse's main balcony, gesturing towards a section of the marina where larger craft rode at anchor. 'It's down at the east pier. Perhaps you'd be interested in having the berth next to his? It's not vacant at present, but we can always juggle things around.'

'Well, as I say, I wouldn't want you to go to any trouble.'

'It's no trouble.' Anderton led him back inside. 'Just out of interest, was Mr Tipping expecting you today?'

'Oh, no. We were chatting in The Ned the other night, and he just happened to mention the Royal Wallasea.'

'That's so good of him. I think it's so much more effective when the recommendation travels by word of mouth rather than through advertising. I firmly believe that one shouldn't feel the need to advertise if one provides a service of genuine quality.'

'I couldn't agree more,' David said.

A waiter appeared with a cloth folded over his arm. 'Anything from the bar, Mr Fosdike?'

'I'm good, thanks,' David said. 'While the sun isn't yet over the yardarm.'

Anderton gave him a mischievous sideways look. 'Isn't the sun always over the yardarm?'

'Not in my line of work, I'm afraid. As I say, I have a big afternoon.'

'Of course.' The secretary became serious again and

despatched the waiter with a curt nod. 'I should think this will be quite a surprise for Mr Tipping?'

'Well, yes. I'll let him know beforehand, of course.'

'You won't need to. He'll be here in the next quarter-hour.'

'He will?' For the next couple of seconds, David waged an epic struggle with himself not to look shaken. 'He's coming here, you mean?'

'Oh yes,' Anderton said. 'Tuesday lunchtime, he's regular as clockwork. One o'clock on the dot. When he's in the country, of course. Whether he'll sail or not, I've no idea. The weather's very good today, but sometimes he's just happy to sit and chat with the members. I presume you'll be here long enough to at least say hello?'

'Yes, I ... I hope so.' It seemed politic in that numbing moment not to give commitments either way.

Anderton led him down a flight of steps and out to the marina, though already David was throwing furtive glances at his watch. It was just after quarter to one. Anderton chatted amicably as he led his guest along a kind of esplanade and showed him the marina office, which was separate from the main club, and located between the boat park and the slipway, introducing him to the staff there, and then strolling out onto the network of timber piers spread before them. All the way, David battled to concentrate, let alone ask intelligent questions.

'You say you have a ninety-footer, Mr Fosdike?' Anderton asked.

'Erm, that's correct, yes,' David replied.

They were now on the aforementioned east pier, the motor yachts ranged alongside them huge and of the most extravagant variety, though David's thoughts were spinning too crazily for him to be impressed by rich men's toys.

He glanced at his watch again. It was ten to one. When he looked up, the clubhouse seemed a considerable distance away.

'May I enquire about the depth of your vessel's draught?' Anderton asked.

'I'm sorry, oh, erm, the draught, yes. Well, I'm afraid I don't have the *Andromeda*'s specs with me at present.'

He'd prepared the name beforehand, having noted online that the names of female figures in mythology, particularly those associated with the ocean, were popular among the yachting clique. But he'd no clue what the draught might be for a ninety-foot motor launch.

'Not to worry,' Anderton said. 'If you opt to join us, you can have the details phoned through, but I doubt there'll be a problem. As I say, these are our deep-water berths. You'll notice there are larger craft here than yours.'

David nodded, glancing at his watch again. It was eight minutes to.

They headed back and re-entered the main building, though Anderton now insisted on showing him around the club's various indoor attractions, its gym, its spa, its swimming pool.

'May I enquire where the *Andromeda* is berthed at present?' Anderton asked as they trekked back through the main bar.

'Ah, well…' David's mouth dried.

This was another thing he hadn't thought about. What other marina could he currently be using, a man like Jonathan Fosdike (net worth $4 billion), which he'd now found inadequate for his needs? Before he could bumble his way to another unconvincing response, an attractive dark-haired woman, again in the Royal Wallasea uniform, came hurrying up.

'Cedric …?' she interrupted.

'Charlotte, my dear?' he replied.

'So sorry to butt in.' She smiled at David. 'Afternoon, Mr Fosdike.'

'Charlotte Derbyshire,' Anderton said. 'Our Marina Manager.'

'Lovely to meet you, Charlotte.' David fought the urge to look at his watch again.

'It's O'Neil & Sons,' she told Anderton with a pained look. 'They need to speak to someone urgently about the work on the breakwater.'

Anderton sighed. 'So sorry, Mr Fosdike – I must take this.'

'Absolutely fine.' David was more relieved than he could say. 'I'll wait at the bar.'

While Anderton and his underling bustled away, David found himself a stool at the end of the bar nearest to one of the windows looking out at the clubhouse's rear. From here, not only was the members' car park visible, but the drive as well. He sat down, tense and torn about what to do next. He'd barely spoken to anyone, and already it was five to one. A scrunch of gravel alerted him to the window again.

A car had pulled up outside. A red BMW.

David watched, rigid.

Only for another member of staff, a second young woman in Royal Wallasea livery, to jump out and enter the building.

'Can I get you something, sir?' a Scottish voice asked.

David realised that one of the bartenders had come down to his end. He was a well-presented chap in his late thirties, with short red hair and a trim red moustache.

'I'm fine, thank you,' David replied.

The barman nodded, before picking up a cloth and

mopping down the bar-top. David noticed the name tag on his polo shirt.

'Graham, is it?'

'That's right, sir. Graham Montgomery.'

David pursed his lips as though thinking something through. Again he kept one eye on the drive. Surely he was out of time? He had no choice but to leave, even if that meant exiting the place without speaking to Anderton again. But still he hung on.

'Changed your mind about a drink, sir?' the barman asked.

'Oh, sorry, no thank you.'

The barman went back to his cleaning.

'By the sounds of it you're an Edinburgh chap?'

'That's right, sir. Though I've been down here the last fifteen years now.'

'You must be at the top of your game to secure work in an establishment like this?'

The barman smiled as he mopped. 'I like to think so, sir. I was previously at the Caledonian Club, and for a short time at the Churchill Room in the Houses of Parliament.'

'Wow, good on you. That's quite a CV.'

'Thank you very much, sir.'

'I bet you've seen some characters in your time …'

'That'd be true, sir. Here as often as anywhere else. I assume you're thinking of becoming a member, is that correct?'

'That's correct,' David replied. 'So it gets raucous, does it?'

'Och, no. I don't mean that, sir.' The barman became thoughtful. 'Different kind of celebrity here. We get the jet-set crowd, of course. But when they're here they're trying to relax, you know … get away from it. They're not at the end of a chaotic day in London.'

David nodded his understanding, glancing along the drive. The coast was still clear.

'Anyone I might know?' he wondered.

The barman reeled off the names of several members, stars either of stage or screen.

'And they all have boats here?' David glanced along the drive again and now saw a car approaching at a stately pace. Tension crackled through him.

'Not all,' the barman replied. 'Some just enjoy the peace, the quiet, the ambience. We're a way out here. A kind of country club on sea.'

'Anyone from the business world?' David watched the approaching vehicle. Even from this distance he could see that it was a Rolls Royce, metallic-blue in colour.

'Well, Mr Tipping, who you already know about. In fact ...' The barman also glanced through the window. 'In fact, I think that's his Silver Shadow on its way in now, sir.'

David worked his dried lips together.

'One or two others, of course.' Graham related several names from big business while David worked frantically on his exit strategy. Outside, the Silver Shadow had come to a halt, but at present no one was getting out of it. 'And of course it would be remiss of me not to mention Mr Martindale, though he's hardly a regular these days ...'

'I'm sorry,' David blurted. 'You said ...?'

'Mr Martindale. Ralph Martindale. Obviously, we don't see too much of him at present.'

David glanced through the window again. A tall man with a shock of sandy hair, wearing shades, stonewashed jeans and a pink silk shirt, had climbed from the Silver Shadow's back-seat. However, he was deep in conversation on his phone, and remained beside the car.

'Terrible what happened,' the barman said.

'Yes, I remember hearing,' David said quickly. 'Ralph Martindale was a boating enthusiast, was he?'

'Don't know as you could call him an enthusiast, sir. But he kept his boat here. That's all I know. I used to see the young lady quite often.'

'You mean Jodie Martindale?'

'That's right, sir. I mean ... before she disappeared, obviously.'

'Of course.' David watched Tipping, who was still talking on his mobile.

'*She* wasn't much for sailing, sir,' the barman added. 'But she came here regularly to meet friends. She was very close to Ms Carter – you know her, sir? Miranda Carter?'

Tipping had finished his call; he slipped the phone into his pocket.

'The name sounds familiar.' David was barely listening.

'Quite famous in her day.'

Outside, Tipping reached into the backseat and brought out a haversack.

'Not anymore?' David asked.

'She starred in that Essex reality show.'

David's memory was tripped. '*Essex Unwound?*'

'That's right, sir. Few years ago now. Don't think she's in anything at present.'

Tipping headed for the clubhouse door. David lurched off his stool, but hovered there, thoughts spinning.

'That was their table over there, sir.' The barman nodded across the room. 'Ms Carter and Ms Martindale's favourite. Now Ms Carter tends to sit there alone. Sad thing really.'

David looked, but was distracted by the sound of a deep,

resonant voice in the Reception area. A voice with a light but distinctive Australian accent.

'Sounds like Mr Tipping now, sir,' the barman said. 'Be quite a surprise for him, finding *you* here.'

'It certainly will. I'll tell you what, Graham ...' David leaned across the counter conspiratorially. 'I'm going to make it even more of a surprise. First of all, if you can direct me to the little boys' room?'

The barman pointed left. 'Straight down the corridor, sir.'

'When Mr Tipping comes in, don't mention that I'm here, OK? I'm going to creep up on him.'

'As you wish, sir.'

The barman didn't seem surprised by such juvenile silliness, presumably a legacy of all the 'characters' he'd had to deal with. David hurried towards the corridor in question, acutely aware that the voice he'd heard was now booming from just beyond the door at the far end of the bar. Once in the corridor, he sped up, but managed to avoid breaking into a run. He passed the door to the Gents on the right, but kept going. The back of the building was somewhere on his left, so it stood to reason that the next left turn was the route he wanted. One came up, and he rounded it. A short passage led to an open door with daylight shining through. Now, David did run, but once he got there, it was an office. There was no one inside it, but from the paper strewn on the desk and the fan humming in the corner, it was in use. Most frustrating of all, its windows looked out onto the car park – he could even see the Merc waiting in the members' zone – but only the windows' narrow upper panels were open.

He doubled back along the passage. He'd hoped that the ruse with the barman would buy him a little more time, but as he came back to the turn, he again heard the booming voice of Anton Tipping, now in the bar itself and, by the sounds of it, in conversation with Cedric Anderton. David listened with bated breath.

'Old Fozzy? Wants to become a member here?' The Australian sounded stunned.

'And it's all down to you, Mr Tipping,' Anderton replied in his obsequious tone.

'Fozzy can't even swim. He doesn't go anywhere near the water.'

'He said that you and he were discussing us a couple of nights ago. In London.'

'That's ridiculous. I've been in the States for the last five days.'

David took the corridor at a run, his back to the bar, but going left again and then right. It brought him, rather abruptly, into one of the balcony dining areas, where a couple eating lunch at a nearby table gave him a curious look. He smiled and straightened his lapels.

From here, a flight of steps led down to the marina. He descended, yanking his phone from his pocket.

'Yes?' Anushka answered.

'Get out of there now.'

'Why?' She immediately sounded panicky. 'What's going on?'

'We're about to be rumbled. Move it.'

'But what do I say?'

'You don't have to say anything to anyone.'

'I mean at the gate?'

At the bottom of the steps, he turned left along the esplanade, the boats and piers to his right. He walked past the entrance to the boat park and then the marina office, all the while attempting to look calm as he chatted on the phone.

'They can't stop you leaving, Nushka,' he said. 'Just drive straight out.'

'And where do I go then?'

'I don't know. A few miles along the road. Find yourself a layby and park.'

'For God's sake, David! I knew this would happen.'

'Put yourself in my shoes. I'm still stuck in here.'

He cut the call and put the phone back into his pocket. It now felt as if he was approaching the marina's western edge. The esplanade had narrowed to a footway, its smart paving replaced by timber. A brick wall stood on his left; he thought it might be the exterior wall to a boat shed or some kind of repairs area. On his right, water sloshed against the pilings rather than lapped, picking up a heavier current from the river. Further to his right, the interconnected web of footways and moored craft angled away from him.

From somewhere to the rear, he heard a shout.

It was distant and he wasn't sure what it signified, but he broke into a trot. Ahead, he could see a barred gate. When he reached it, there was a notice.

Staff only beyond this point

Dreading that it might be locked, he lugged on its lever, but it moved and the gate swung open. Sweating with relief, David slid through and closed it behind him, then took a left-hand path, which brought him to a door in the wall of an old hangar-type building. He listened, but there was no sound. He pushed at the door and it opened. As he'd suspected, he'd entered one of several large, shed-type structures. It was spacious, but there was lumber everywhere, along with work tools and piles of wood shavings. Thankfully, there was no one else here.

He scurried to the next door, which stood ajar. Beyond that lay an area of beaten earth and gravel. Another boat shed stood facing him; its double-doors had been flung open, and he could see a boat inside, resting on a wheeled trailer. He also heard voices.

David held his ground, heart hammering. He appeared to be in a cul-de-sac. Left, the mud and gravel wound back towards the main buildings. Right, further egress was blocked by a brick wall, though several lidded dumpsters were arrayed in front of it. The wall was only ten feet or so high. If he climbed onto one of the dumpsters, he could easily scale it.

He heard another shout, this one closer.

He dashed to the right, dreading that someone would come out of the building opposite. No one did, though one of the voices inside raised itself to be heard. He thought it said: 'Excuse me?' Again thanking his new-found fitness, he vaulted up onto the first dumpster and from there levered himself up and over the top of the wall, dropping nimbly down the other side, where he found himself in overgrown woodland.

Over in the repairs area, he heard a rumble and skidding of tyres, the *clunk* of a handbrake being applied. There was a quick exchange of voices.

David darted forward, winding through the trees. The wood sloped, and it was plainly obvious that to get back to the road he'd need to head uphill. He tried this, only to encounter a towering fence of barbed wire. He hurried along it, searching for a gap while struggling through thickets of thorns, ripping his flesh as well as his expensive clothes. The fence veered downhill, but he followed it anyway, finally stumbling out at the foot of the slope, the river sliding by in front of him. The fence didn't even stop there; it extended several yards out into the water before terminating at an iron post.

Again, David heard shouts; they were somewhere in the wood.

He waded out, his expensive loafers plunging into the slime of the riverbed. He was almost thigh-deep when he sidled around the post and headed back towards shore.

Once on dry ground, he ran freely uphill. The woods here were thinner, and he was able to find a new burst of energy. But as the slope levelled out and he approached the road, he only pushed through the last line of bushes with extreme care.

There, he squatted in deep summer grass, panting. Satisfied that no vehicles were coming, he pulled out his phone, but before he could make a call, a car horn tooted no more than thirty yards away. He twirled around, and on the other side of the tarmac saw the flashing lights of the Mercedes, where it had just emerged from the well-concealed entrance to a layby. He scampered over there, Anushka pulling out in front of him, powering her window down.

'I said a few miles,' he shouted.

'And how would you have found me?' she retorted. 'Anyway, you said find a layby. Did I do good, or what?'

'You did good.' He yanked open the front passenger door, at which point she saw the state of him.

'Hey, don't mess the car up!'

He climbed in and slammed the door behind him. 'The car can be cleaned. Drive.'

'Where to?'

'Home. Quick as you can.'

Anushka hit the gas, the Merc accelerating away.

For several hundred yards, David peered backward over his shoulder. But the road remained empty. 'Ease down a bit,' he said. 'We're back in the real world now. Don't want to look too conspicuous.'

She shook her head, having now spotted the cuts on his hands and the tears in his trousers and jacket. 'This is unbelievable.'

'No, Anushka. This is the job.'

20

'So let me get this straight,' Norm said. 'You used a panto-mime disguise to impersonate a real individual, who's probably got more power in his little finger than you would have in a hundred lifetimes, to con your way into this elite establishment, for which under normal circumstances you wouldn't even come close to qualifying, having driven there all the way from Colchester in a hire car, the identity of which you'd illegally altered. You then left said establishment by nipping out through the back door, no doubt trespassing in half a dozen staff-only areas, and then having altered the vehicle back, drove home again – and you don't expect the police to come knocking on your door in the next half-hour?'

David sat back in his swivel chair. 'The police investigate crime, Norm. What crime did I commit? I didn't steal anything, I didn't attack anyone, I didn't damage anything... well, nothing I didn't restore to perfect condition afterwards.'

Norm, who, ten minutes ago, had entered the Shed for the first time ever, shook his head in exaggerated disbelief. 'You cloned a car.'

'Yeah. For half an hour.'

'Using an illegal registration number.'

'Of which, mysteriously, there is now no trace.'

'Jesus, David, haven't you heard of roadside cameras – of number-plate recognition?'

David smiled. 'Which is why, once we were several miles away, I got my trusty screwdriver out and swapped the plates back.'

Norm shook his head. 'They'll still trace you. They'll go through all the necessary footage until they find another Mercedes Benz S-Class in roughly that area, and they'll just follow it back to the place where you hired it.'

'A process which, in that sparsely filmed district, would take days and days of man hours, as well you know. And like I say, for what? A minor infringement?'

'They might be interested in knowing who provided you with the fake number plate.'

'And why would they hear that from me? I've already told you, there's no such number plate in my possession. How could I tell them anything?'

Norm stood speechless. He'd come over here reluctantly in response to David's insistent phone call that there was something going on that he'd genuinely be interested in.

'Did you touch anything while you were inside this clubhouse?' he asked. 'I mean, they'll have your prints on file from when you were arrested six years ago.'

'Your concern is noted and appreciated, but fortunately, no.'

Norm blew out a long breath. It was difficult to tell whether it was one of relief or annoyance.

'So what next?' David asked. 'Will they send forensics teams to sweep the whole premises, in case there's a tiny speck of my earwax or a droplet of sweat?'

'It wasn't a pantomime disguise either,' Anushka cut in; she was seated across the room at one of the other desks. 'It was pretty effective.'

Norm glanced at her. 'And what possessed *you* to partake in this hare-brained caper?'

'I had reservations, I'll admit,' she said. 'But it seemed like the only way to go.'

'The only way to go?'

'To get the answers we need.'

'That *we* need?' For the first time Norm seemed to register that she was wearing a T-shirt and jeans on what would normally be a work day. 'So you're now part of this *Essex Enquirer*?'

'You can keep pretending you're turning your nose up, Norm,' David said. 'But I saw your face when you first walked into the Shed.'

'Well ... Shed is a good name for it.' Norm swung around, determinedly unimpressed. 'Because it certainly isn't a newsroom.'

'Not yet,' David replied. 'But it will be.'

'I just can't believe you took such a risk on the word of some poor girl who doesn't know what day it is ...'

'I won't pretend it was a promising lead,' David said, 'but sometimes you can't afford to leave any stone unturned.'

'It's the methods, David. That's the concern I have.'

'Is it really a concern, Norm? Or are you just fishing around for reasons not to get involved?'

Norm's face tinged pink. 'I don't need to go fishing.'

'I think you may. You were already long in the tooth when I was a cub reporter. You had plenty of tricks up your own sleeve back then.'

'Nothing like this.'

David sat forward. 'Harold Willoughby?'

Norm's cheeks flamed red; he struggled to respond.

'It was you and others like you who taught *me* everything I know,' David said.

Still Norm couldn't say anything.

In his days before Crime Beat, Norm Harrington might have courted a reputation for being the family face of the *Essex Examiner*, for being the Features chief, the guy who wrote about celebrities and produced frothy editorials on the county's prettiest villages. But before then, when he was covering news, he'd written a big story about the outspoken Essex MP and government minister, Harold Willoughby, an ex-British Army colonel and public school headmaster who, when he entered politics, was famous for his uncompromising position on the permissive society. After Willoughby's 'wild child' daughter, Samantha, was arrested for dancing naked in the fountains at Trafalgar Square, and then released with a police caution, Norm interviewed her and she told him that her father's prudishness was a masquerade. Not only that, she passed Norm a photograph of Willoughby from the 1980s, in which the bastion of public decency was shown riding in the backseat of a car with Cynthia Payne, the celebrity brothel-keeper.

The subsequent front-page lead Norm wrote for the *Examiner* was light on accusation, but the picture was its centrepiece and the public were invited to draw their own conclusions. Willoughby retaliated by claiming that his daughter was a troubled fantasist and that the picture was a product of Photoshop, which was in its infancy at the time but fast gaining notice as an effective means by which to edit photography. When it was discovered that Sam Willoughby's boyfriend was a digital artist, Willoughby announced that he was preparing a lawsuit against the *Examiner*. Norm was nervous until an anonymous phone call advised him that

Willoughby, who was still married to his wife of forty years, was a regular at the weekend parties hosted by a certain Madame B.

The aforesaid Madame B, an outwardly respectable and wealthy widow, occupied a large private house at the end of a swish cul-de-sac on the outskirts of Chigwell. Norm was told that if he arrived there incognito at a certain time on a certain date, all his problems would go away. Norm did so, disguised as Zorro, and was admitted through the back door by an unsmiling young man who never spoke but who was clearly an insider connected to whichever political opponent had tipped off the journalist. Inside the house, Norm found himself in the midst of a drugs and sex orgy, not just being attended by Willoughby, but several other recognisable faces. Even more damning, the Minister of Clean Living was wearing an SS uniform, which apparently he always wore, and requiring to be addressed by the various naked women present as 'Herr Doktor'.

Norm was able to take several covert photographs, none of which could this time be written off as Photoshop hack-jobs, and the following day, he and Stan Grimshaw went back to Willoughby's legal team and laid it on the line that if the minister didn't withdraw the lawsuit and give the *Examiner* an exclusive interview about his long-standing use of prostitutes, they'd print all the gruesome details. Willoughby had had no option but to comply, resigning his position and adopting a remorseful tone as he told the world, via Norm's sensational centre-spread, how he'd gradually drifted into a dissipated life after suffering with his nerves due to his military experiences in Malaya. It was no more than a pile of self-excusing horseshit, but it still amounted to a news story so massive that it gained international attention.

In effect, Norm had blackmailed a government minister into giving him the scoop of a lifetime. It made his name in journalism over a decade before Lampwick Lane made David's.

'I just hope you consider it worthwhile.' Norm edged towards the door. 'I'm not even sure it was worthwhile coming over here today.'

'That's because you've not done your bit yet,' David said.

'Excuse me?'

'You've not even asked if we got a result.'

'I thought you'd run for your lives.'

'That's because we had to leave it till the last second. But seeing as you finally *are* asking – yeah, it was worth it.'

Norm shrugged and opened the door.

'Miranda Carter,' David said.

'I'm sorry?'

'You interviewed her once, didn't you?'

Norm pondered. 'Miranda Carter?'

'*Essex Unwound*,' Anushka put in.

'Oh yes...' Norm nodded. 'Blonde. Big lashes, big nails, big boobs... now mainly known for being a glamorous drunk.'

'That sounds like her,' David replied.

'I did interview her, yes. Way back. So?'

'Apparently she's a regular at the Royal Wallasea. Has been for ages. And she knew Jodie Martindale well. Two "it girls" together, you could say.'

Norm pushed the door closed again. 'And let me guess – you think she may know something?'

'Specifically, she may know about this mysterious Saint Bridget I mentioned, who supposedly met Jodie at the Royal Wallasea not long before she disappeared.'

Norm snorted. 'Good luck. Miranda was difficult enough to pin down even in her heyday.'

'We've discovered that for ourselves,' David replied. 'When she was in *Essex Unwound*, she was represented by Healey & Dawkins Management. But she isn't anymore, and they don't know who represents her these days, if anyone. So, the obvious place to find her – the only place, in fact – is the Royal Wallasea, where she still goes all the time.'

Norm glanced from one to the other. 'And you want *me* to do it because you two can't risk being seen there again?'

'And also because you're known to her,' David said. 'Anyone asks around, they'll learn that Norm Harrington is writing a book about his halcyon days on the celebrity trail and in fact is looking to re-interview a few people he interviewed in the past.'

Norm made no reply, but at least he didn't turn red in the face again.

'No one'll suspect anything, Norman,' Anushka said.

'How am I supposed to get in touch with her?' he replied. 'I'll have to contact her beforehand.'

'Do it through the Royal Wallasea,' David said. 'They can ask her on your behalf. And if she consents, Bob's your uncle.'

'And what kind of questions am I supposed to ask?'

'You never had a problem with that in the past ...'

'I mean about your bloody case!' Norm was finally getting het up, but it encouraged David that he hadn't dismissed the idea out of hand. 'I've hardly been following developments.'

'That's where this comes in.' David opened a drawer and brought out a roll of insulated wire with a power-pack and covert microphone attachment. He also produced a wireless earpiece. 'Remember? Last time we used this was at

Lampwick Lane, only on that occasion *I* was the one sitting out front.'

Norm gazed long and hard at the kit. 'You're going to be prompting me? Are you serious?'

'We did it before.'

'And it was nerve-shredding. If we'd got caught...'

'Norm! She's a sozzled docu-soap star, not a gangster. You think she'll even notice?'

'Come on, Norm,' Anushka said. 'You'll be killing two birds with one stone. Getting another interview for your book as well as helping us.'

Again, Norm looked from one to the other. 'I can't believe I'm even considering this.'

'It's a win-win,' David said.

'Don't be so bloody ridiculous! We'll be going out on a limb. With no safety net.'

'But it's an exciting prospect, eh? Come on, don't make like it's something you don't want to do.'

'There's one thing you *haven't* thought about,' Norm said.

'Go on?'

'If the police are also reinvestigating the case, they'll likely get there first.'

David made a carefree gesture. 'Just as good.'

There was a prolonged silence.

'You mean that?' Norm asked.

David didn't even glance at the box of scruffy documents sitting under his desk. 'The priority is returning Jodie Martindale to her family, not writing a blockbuster news story. If we get the news story too, who's complaining?'

Norm pursed his lips. 'On that basis ... I'll think about it.'

And he left, the door closing loudly behind him.

Anushka looked at David. 'Being economical with the truth again?'

David glared at her. 'I *do* want Jodie back safely. That's my entire motivation.'

'And yet still you won't surrender Freddie Martindale's paperwork to the cops?'

'If I told Norm my reasons for not giving this stuff to Jorgenson, he wouldn't buy them.'

'Because he'd know the simple reason is you and Jorgenson can't stand each other.'

'I don't trust the bastard.'

Anushka stood up. 'Well, the day you *do* tell him, and it's going to come, make sure you let me know beforehand.' She too headed for the door. 'So I can be somewhere else.'

21

'Well, the police eventually dropped the charges against Alan for so-called lack of evidence.'

The voice emerging from David's computer was not quite what they'd expected. It didn't sound cultured, but gone was the comedy Essex girl twang that had made blonde and bubbly Miranda Carter an instant TV hit all those years ago. It was deeper now, inevitably given that a decade had passed, but also harder and croakier, doubtless the legacy of her thirty-a-day habit. If there was a vague slushy edge to it, that was probably because she'd already been at the yachting club an hour before Norm had arrived.

'I don't know what they thought the bruises on my body were if not evidence,' the voice added. 'I lost the house at Brentwood because of the break-up, and it wasn't long after that that I lost my book deal because of the cocaine arrest. The reason I'm telling you this, Mr Harrington, is because there's so much fake news out there ...'

'And very little of it's about you,' David chuckled. 'I bet there's been no news about you for the last five or six years.'

Anushka glanced around from the Fiesta's passenger seat. 'Don't be cruel.'

She was tense and uneasy, unused to eavesdropping on conversations in this blatant way. Even though she and David were a distance up the road from the Royal Wallasea, where

Norm was holding the actual interview, she almost seemed self-conscious about what they were doing.

'So many lies are told that just seem designed to ruin reputations, don't you think?' Miranda Carter said. 'It doesn't matter about all the hard work a girl does to try and make something of her life, they just want to drag her down...'

'What did she do before they picked her for *Essex Unwound*?' David asked.

'Worked in a nail bar,' Anushka said.

'And is that classifiable as hard work?'

She gave him a look. 'It's a job. You have to be good at it, you have to practise...'

'Fair enough.'

They were parked in the same layby where Anushka had picked David up a few days earlier. It was just within range of the Royal Wallasea but secluded enough, hopefully, to prevent any of the comers and goers at the club from noticing their presence.

'On this subject,' Norm's voice said, 'we perhaps should mention the, erm, video?'

'Ah, yeah,' Miranda replied. 'The one that has now streamed a million times on Pornhub.'

David chuckled again. Anushka gave him another look.

'That wasn't fake news?' Norm asked with mock-innocence.

'More like a typical aspect of life in the twenty-first century, wouldn't you say?'

'You've never tried to deny that it was you in that film?'

'Would it serve any purpose? It was obviously me.'

'I wouldn't know,' Norm replied. 'I haven't looked at it.'

'I'll bet he hasn't,' David sniggered.

'Why would *Norm* be interested in that?' Anushka replied.

'Hey, he has to do his research ...'

'What no one ever says is that it was a private video,' Miranda added, 'which I made for a bit of fun with my partner, Niles McCleash. But the moment we got hacked, the whole thing went viral. And of course ... I didn't earn a penny from it.'

'Excuse me?' Throughout, Norm had been his old urbane self, relaxed and non-judgemental. But this comment seemed to throw him. 'You didn't earn a penny?'

'I was offered five hundred grand to pose for *Mayfair* before the first season of *Essex Unwound* had even ended. I turned them down on the advice of my agent. He reckoned that in time, I'd be able to get a lot more. Course, the moment that film came out, all my leverage was gone. They weren't even interested in bikini shots for *Esquire*. So I lost money all round – as well as my dignity.'

David glanced at Anushka. 'The money sounds like it's the main thing, though.'

'Only someone who's never been short of cash could come out with a comment like that,' she replied.

'You're joking, aren't you? After the last six years *I've* spent? But you're right, I'm being a twat.'

He resolved to try to be less scornful. It was that side of his personality, the sneering predator, that he'd supposedly been trying to get away from.

He listened as Miranda spoke on. It was easy to think of her as a dim blonde, an English blue-collar version of Marilyn Monroe minus the actual talent. But the fact that she'd made an effort to change that voice – had had elocution lessons of some sort – seemed to signify a desire to improve herself. Despite the court cases, the bankruptcies, the cancelled book deals and advertising contracts, she had money – was probably rolling in it, otherwise she wouldn't be a member at the Royal Wallasea – but who was *he* to get uppity about the way she'd earned it? *Essex Unwound* had been shallow TV, but it was hardly Miranda Carter's fault that the networks these days found it more profitable to produce lightweight 'reality' crap than original drama. You played with the hand fate dealt you. His hand, however, he'd dealt to himself.

'Would you say that that video was the beginning of the downturn in your career?' Norm asked.

'It didn't help,' she replied. 'But, no, the other bits of bad publicity didn't help either. Look, I won't pretend that I haven't mucked things up. I wasn't used to that kind of lifestyle, and no one taught me what I needed to know. God, people can be cruel … and just because they were getting bored with me. The "Spray-Tan Queen" one of the tabloids called me. It was a total shock, and so bloody untrue. I'd never used a spray-tan in my life unless I couldn't find a decent sunbed. The scandal sheets loved it, of course …'

'This giving you ideas in case Crime Beat Mark II doesn't work out?' Anushka wondered.

David shook his head. 'She's soiled goods already. None of my readers'd be interested.'

She tutted in disbelief.

'Exactly,' he said, 'now you know why I'm sitting here with you.'

'Can we talk a bit more about your family?' Norm asked. 'And the way you say fame and fortune estranged you from them.'

'Christ's sake,' David muttered. 'How about getting to the point?'

Miranda appeared more comfortable moving onto that

subject, though it wasn't uplifting stuff. She spoke about her father, who was a drunk, and how he used to beat her. About how her mother worked two jobs just to feed them all. On a happier note, she reminisced about her late grandfather, who couldn't do enough for them, even though he'd been retired from the rubbish collection business for thirty-odd years and was by then in his eighties. Miranda bemoaned the fact that he didn't live long enough to see her success, but expressed relief that he didn't see her downfall either.

David glanced at his watch. 'This is all great for Norm's book. Not so good for us.'

'We had to offer him a carrot to get him involved,' Anushka reminded him.

'And he's not half chowing down on it.' David grabbed the mic.

'Wait...'

'Jodie was the only person I felt I could talk to,' Miranda said.

They leaned forward, ears pricked.

'In what respect?' Norm asked.

'We got to know each other here just by chatting now and then. And, well, seems we had stuff in common.'

'That's interesting,' he replied. 'Jodie Martindale was being groomed to inherit her father's business empire...'

'And I was an entertainer.'

'Well, yes, so what makes you think you had something in common?'

'I think maybe we both worried we were a bit out of our depth.'

'You both earned good money.'

'True, but that doesn't help either. It builds a wall be-tween you and everyone else. To find someone in a similar position ... well, that's different. Jodie was engaged to be married of course, to the same bloke she'd been going out with when she was school age, while I'd already had a load of different boyfriends and none of them had worked out very well. But somehow we hit it off. We could talk to each other.'

'Hmm ...' Norm was clearly thinking. 'This is slightly off topic, but I'm sure it's a question an awful lot of people would like an answer to. I don't suppose you've any idea what happened to Jodie?'

'Oh my God – if only I did.' Miranda's voice thickened. 'I've never known anything as terrible as that week when news of the kidnapping broke. And then I heard that they'd found Rick's body. Oh Christ, I must have cried for hours. I was sure Jodie would turn up next. As the days rolled by and she didn't, I almost became hopeful. But then more days went by, and then weeks and months, and eventually you realised there was no hope at all. But you were asking me about my family?'

'Of course,' Norm said.

'*No!*' David put the mic to his lips, shouting even though he knew he'd be coming through loud and clear in Norm's earpiece. 'Get her back onto Jodie.'

'So, your family?' Norm said pointedly.

'Norm!' David cut in. 'We need to know more. Did Jodie say anything odd or unusual in the days leading up to her abduction? Was there anything different about her behaviour?'

'Your family,' Norm said again. 'You must have some fond memories.'

'Norm, get this bloody sorted!'

'For Christ's sake!' Norm snapped.

'I'm sorry?' Miranda sounded bemused.

'I beg your pardon.' He became ingratiating. 'You were saying?'

'Erm, you asked if I had fond memories of my family. Beyond my grandad, not many.'

She then went on to list a number of people, none of whom the rest of the world had ever heard about, whose troubles had ranged from the mundane (Cousin Agatha, who was 'driven loopy' by the voices she kept hearing in her bedroom, never having realised that it was her neighbour's portable TV), to the serious (ex-brother-in-law Vernon, who got into a violent fistfight with a police officer and in two minutes turned a £70 speeding fine into a seven-year prison sentence), to the bizarre (Great Uncle Billy, who lost his left arm in the machinery at work while trying to demonstrate to his employers how he'd lost the right one). All of which was great copy for Norm, of course.

'Then there was Aunt Belinda,' Miranda added sadly. 'She committed suicide.'

'How terrible,' Norm replied.

'To the outside world, she was happy. Had everything going for her. But, well, all I can say, and this is reading between the lines – she had secrets.'

'Do you have secrets, Miranda?' Norm asked.

'Nice,' Anushka whispered.

'How do you mean?' Miranda replied.

'This is your way back in,' David told the mic.

'I don't need *you* to tell me that,' Norm retorted.

'Pardon me, but you asked,' Miranda said.

'No, I mean, I'm sorry,' Norm laughed awkwardly. 'Only if you want to.'

'Do I have any secrets?' Miranda said distantly. 'I don't think so. With me you always get the truth.'

'But you have a sense for when someone else is in that position?'

'I think so.' Again, she sounded distant.

'Jodie, for example!' David hissed into the mic. 'Come on, Norm... Jodie Martindale.'

'Jodie, for example,' Norm said.

'Jodie. Yeah, I think there was something going on. The last time she was in here with me... but I told the police all this.'

'Of course. But my readers will be interested too.'

'I don't think the cops believed me anyway. I mean, when I told them I thought there was some kind of problem.'

'How so?'

'I don't think they thought I was the sort of person who'd know anything about that.'

'Keep probing, Norm,' David urged him. 'Come on.'

'Would you have said that Jodie was your best friend?' Norm asked.

'Probably... at the time, yeah.'

'So – and I only ask this because I think it's relevant to your situation today – when you say Jodie was your best friend, and you lost her in those strange circumstances, and it no doubt had a huge impact on *your* life as well, have you never looked back to those final moments with her? It was *here* at the club, you say?'

'This very table, Mr Harrington.'

'Do you ever wonder if there was something you missed? I mean during those final moments?'

'As I say, I told the police everything.' She was finally

sounding puzzled about the line of questioning. 'Even the black lady.'

David and Anushka looked at each other.

'I'm sorry?' Norm said. 'The black lady?'

'I had no idea who she was. I'd never seen her at the club before. But she was a real glamour-puss. Dressed to the nines, but a genuine looker. Fabulous figure.'

'I'm sorry, Miranda, I don't understand.'

'Jodie and I were seated right here when this total eye-catcher came sashaying up to the table. Dripping with gold, diamonds. Wore these three adorable pendants, obviously a set. Think they were platinum. A lightning bolt, a sword and what looked like a little tornado—'

'But you didn't know her?' Norm interrupted.

'Had no clue who she was. And Jodie? Well, Jodie didn't seem to know her either.'

She relapsed into contemplative silence.

'And?' Norm pressed.

'She asked if she could have a minute of Jodie's time. Strange accent, she had. Not British. I thought French, maybe. Or African. But Jodie went off with her. Came back, I don't know, ten or fifteen minutes later. Said it had been an old schoolfriend. Nothing for me to worry about.'

'She didn't name her by any chance?' Norm asked.

'No. Definitely not ... I'd have remembered that. The weird thing was that comment – that there was nothing for me to worry about. Because, you know, I *hadn't* been worrying. Which is what made it seem like a strange thing to say.'

'So ...' Norm sought clarity, 'the fact she said there was nothing to worry about made you think that maybe there *was*.'

'That and Jodie's behaviour, yeah.'

'Jodie's behaviour?'

'After that, she was ... well, different. Something about her, I don't know what. But she wasn't happy or relaxed anymore.'

'And she didn't say what the cause of this was?'

'No, but I felt sure it was something to do with this black lady.'

'I don't suppose you remember what date this happened on?'

'You'll need to look it up, but it was the day that truck bomb went off outside the Louvre in Paris. It was all over the news. It was on the news while we were in here.'

David made a hurried note.

'The weird thing is ...' Miranda sounded vague again, 'this black lady. The police searched, I understand. But they couldn't find anyone like that in Jodie's background.' Suddenly, Miranda sounded suspicious. 'Is that what this is really about? What happened to Jodie?'

'Oh, no ... absolutely not. This is about my book and your place in it.' Norm resumed soft-soap mode. 'You may not believe this, Miranda, but *you've* been one of the glowing personalities in this part of the world for the last decade. I know things haven't been great for you recently but I think it's about time we accorded you the status you deserve.'

David dialled the volume down to look at Anushka.

'You don't ask,' he said, 'you don't get.'

'You think we've learned something?' she replied.

'You don't?'

'You mean this mysterious black woman?'

'Or as we might alternatively call her ... Saint Bridget.'

22

'You a Catholic, David?' Anushka asked.

David was distracted by the Fiesta's rear-view mirror. 'I was born one. But I don't think I've led a very Catholic life.'

Anushka stared ahead as they drove. 'I'm just wondering if that's why you're fixating on this Saint Bridget business?'

'I wouldn't say I was fixating on it.' Again he checked his rear-view mirror. 'But it's a lead.'

'It's a bit of scribble on wastepaper, while the only witnesses to it are a homeless smackhead who's now done a runner and a fading reality star who drinks too much.'

'Bit harsh on Miranda Carter.' He braked as they approached a red light, again scanning his rear-view mirror. 'She seemed to have good recollection of that meeting Jodie had.'

'Yeah, so good she can't remember whether this mysterious beauty spoke with a French accent or African.'

'She was also certain there was no one else at the Royal Wallasea who she'd ever heard referred to as Saint Bridget.'

That had been Norm's final question. Had Miranda ever heard of any member there going by such a curious nickname. And it had drawn a puzzled but firm negative.

'Which narrows it down, you must admit,' David added, again eyeing the mirror.

'What's the matter?' Anushka asked. 'Someone following us?'

David set off driving. 'I'm not sure.'

She looked back. There were other vehicles behind them, but only by some distance.

'First saw it in Colchester.' David got his foot down as the A12 opened up. 'Brown Toyota Prius. I didn't pay much attention at first. Then, five minutes ago, I thought I saw it again.'

Anushka glanced again over her shoulder, but saw no car matching the description. 'Think it's connected to the yacht club?'

'Nah.' David turned into an unmarked side road. 'The police would just knock on my door.' He checked his mirror a final time. 'No one's behind us now. Getting paranoid in my old age.'

'Well, if there *is* someone,' she replied, 'they'd better be on the right side of the law seeing as today's main assignment is the cop shop.'

That morning, they'd checked into the Shed to assess the previous day. Despite her reservations, Anushka was in broad agreement that the unknown black woman at the Royal Wallasea *could* have been the Saint Bridget referred to by Freddie Martindale. But her main concern was that this new info had not yet been shared with the police. David had dismissed this, pointing out that the police had already investigated the unknown woman and discounted her. Anushka had replied that the cops hadn't at that stage known about Freddie's cryptic reference to someone called Saint Bridget. In addition, and this was the thing that really worried her, they didn't know that a witness was now claiming Freddie Martindale had been murdered.

After some protracted thought, David had agreed that maybe it could be construed as withholding evidence if they didn't reveal this latter detail. Though his response hadn't been as straightforward as Anushka had hoped. Instead of driving to Colchester Police Station and asking to speak to the Cold Case Unit, they were now en route to Chelmsford.

'Assuming we don't have to spend too long chatting with this expert you've dug up,' Anushka said, wondering why they were suddenly on single-track lanes.

'"Dug up?"' David smiled. 'Apt phrase in this case.'

'Why? Who is it?'

'Just a scholar. He's written a number of books on the lives of the saints. Particularly the Irish saints.' He checked his rear-view mirror again, but the road behind was deserted. 'Heard of Dr Dermot O'Malley?'

'O'Malley, Dermot…' She frowned as she glanced outside again, noting the sun-drenched fields stretching to every horizon. 'I know that name… *God!* Wasn't he the headmaster at St Balthasar's? The one who got sent to prison?'

David nodded. 'Correct.'

'On multiple counts of sexual misconduct with the pupils?'

'Also correct.'

'You're saying he's out?'

'As of last year. But he's still an expert on the Irish saints. Probably the best in his field.'

Anushka looked a little shaken, most likely because she remembered the ghoulish details of the case that David had highlighted in the story he'd written for the *Examiner* at the time of the priest's conviction. 'He's back at St Balthasar's? For real?'

'St Balthasar's didn't survive the scandal. It's been closed for ages.'

'But he *lives* there?'

'In an old groundskeeper's cottage somewhere on the premises. Probably the best place for him. There are no children anywhere near.'

'Does he know we're coming?'

'He's not on the phone.'

'So we're calling cold?'

'Seems rude, I must admit.' David pulled off to the right, onto an area of raised ground that was tarmacked but cracked and weedy. 'But given that he didn't just do lengthy jail time, he was also laicised from the Catholic clergy, forced to resign as an honorary fellow at Oxford University, kicked out of the Royal Historical Society and lost his publishing deal, I don't think an unexpected visit from us is going to be the worst thing that's ever happened to him.'

He applied the handbrake.

'And all this just to see if the Saint Bridget thing actually means something?'

'Where's the harm? It's en route.'

They locked the car and walked across the road. On the other side, a wide entrance was partially concealed by dense bushes. Its two concrete posts were massive and mottled with lichen, the wrought-iron gates between them padlocked and hung with a plywood notice.

Property For Sale
View by Appointment Only

Beyond the gate, a narrow track wound off between thick rhododendrons. David went left of the entrance, to a tumble-down section of boundary wall. He clambered through, signalling Anushka to follow.

She hesitated, remembering the details of the priest's

offences. The police enquiry had taken evidence from over thirty students, past and present, painting a picture of decades-long sexual grooming and assault by a man the trial judge described as a 'total beast'.

'How old is O'Malley now?' she asked, climbing through.

'Early to mid-fifties.'

They followed the drive, which again was broken and tufted with weeds. Around the first bend, St Balthasar's Catholic College came into view. It was a huge, rambling place of mid-Victorian design, with abundant ivy, crenellated gables and paved paths between the buildings. It looked wholesome, but the silence was eerie.

'Whereabouts on the grounds is he supposed to live?' Anushka asked.

'Dunno.'

'This is going to take ages, isn't it?'

'At least there're two of us to share the load.'

'I just hope this leads to something, David. Because ...'

'Because *what*?' He looked at her. 'You're getting to the point where you've had enough?'

A snappy response came into her head. About wild goose chases, about wastes of time. But he was watching her with interest, and she wondered if she was being tested. It occurred to her that this was investigative journalism, and much of that often started with nothing more than a vague suspicion.

'Lead the way,' she said curtly.

They walked on, circling the buildings via paved footways. Despite the blue sky, the silence and solitude of the ornate but semi-derelict structures quickly became oppressive. There were so many windows, it was impossible not to imagine they were being watched.

'Where's the intel for this come from?' Anushka asked.

'My usual source,' David replied, referring to his pet police insider.

'Suppose this time he's wrong and O'Malley's not here?'

'There's a first time for everything.'

'But—'

David held up a hand for quiet. Anushka realised that an exit door at the rear of one of the buildings was wide open. They approached it, spotting splintery damage along the jamb.

'It's been forced,' David said.

Before Anushka could reply, he'd gone inside. Glancing warily around, she followed.

They walked along spacious passages. Fleetingly it seemed that the school was not disused, just between terms: the floor was tiled and smooth, coat-pegs jutted in rows.

They stopped at a junction of corridors, on the other side of which another door stood open. A notice on it read:

Boys

Someone had underscored it twice with thick lines of black spray-paint.

'Won't be a sec.' David crossed over.

'You need to pee now?'

'Just checking something…'

He entered the lavatories, finding them damp and cold. Faint fragments of age-old graffiti were visible on the white-tiled walls, though one huge illustration dominated all. It was done in crude black spray-paint, and portrayed an archetypical devil, all horns, folded bat-wings and evil slits for eyes. It also, quite clearly, was wearing a clerical collar.

Underneath it, again spray-painted, was the caption:

In flaming fire take vengeance on them that know not God…

He took several photographs of the image with his phone, then backed from the room.

Outside, he found the corridor deserted. There was no sign of Anushka.

She approached the object with fascination.

Up close, it was no less disturbing than when she'd glimpsed it through one of the classroom windows while waiting for David.

She'd had to go outside to get a proper look, but that had been easy. Some thirty yards down the left-hand corridor from the boys' toilets, there'd been another exit door. From there, she'd rounded a corner and found herself in a quadrangle, its central green deeply overgrown, the centrepiece a white marble statue of the Virgin Mary standing on a plinth.

Sometime in the recent past, the image had been spray-painted by vandals. Variously coloured veins circled the Virgin's body, but a particularly intense blast had been directed into her face, leaving it completely crimson except for the eyes, which remained white, as if they'd been closed at the time but were now open and staring reproachfully down.

Anushka felt so unnerved by the unblinking gaze that she retreated a few steps before turning to walk away. Only to discover that a man had come into the quadrangle from behind, and now stood watching her.

A man carrying an axe.

23

David strode along several corridors, calling Anushka's name. He wasn't concerned for her safety. The graffiti artists had been and gone, and the only other person here, theoretically, was Dermot O'Malley, who though he'd been considered a serious criminal in his day, had only offended against children. But her sudden absence was more than an inconvenience.

She'd been right to query the usefulness of this sidetrack they'd taken. It was gobbling up the time they had available.

'Anushka, where the heck are you?' He kicked open every classroom door as he passed. All were empty, denuded of furnishing, but through the seventh or eighth one, via its far window, he caught a fleeting glimpse of the higher ground beyond the school's front gates.

He saw his own red Fiesta parked there.

And a second car wallowing into place alongside it.

A brown car.

David stopped. He entered the classroom, hurrying to the window. As he did, the perspective altered, leafy branches rising into view, obscuring the car park. When he backed to the door again, the brown vehicle was no longer there.

'Shit,' he said under his breath.

He ran the rest of the way back to the exterior door, the echoes of his footfalls clattering behind and ahead of him. Outside, only the tweets of birds disturbed the sun-soaked noon.

Irritably, he rounded a few annexes. Playing fields appeared on the left, rugby posts standing amid knee-deep grass.

'Shit!' he said, louder.

He'd been trying to get back to the front, but clearly didn't know which way he was going. He stood with hands on hips.

'Looking for your missing white hat, Mr Kelman?' a voice called. 'Because you won't find it here.'

David spun. Two figures approached along an arbor on his right. Anushka was one of them, but though she walked level with the other person, she was keeping her distance.

Dermot O'Malley had changed dramatically since the final day of his trial, his last public appearance. Gone was the tall, well-built priest with the charismatic air, square jaw and swept-back fair hair. In his place, there was a tall but cadaverously thin man with straggling white locks and white bristles on his chin. Instead of clerical garb, he wore baggy jeans tucked into a pair of scuffed boots, a plaid shirt open on a stained vest, and work gloves. A hand-axe and various other tools were slotted into a low-slung belt.

David regarded that latter item warily.

'Don't be alarmed,' the ex-priest said. 'I'm chopping wood. That's all.'

'In summer?' David reached out as Anushka came over to stand with him.

'Autumn will be here soon enough. And when you're living off the grid, it comes with teeth.' The ex-priest assessed them carefully. Up close, his eyes didn't look as old as the rest of him. They were still the piercing pale blue David remembered. 'I've already apologised to Mrs Chawla for coming on her by surprise,' O'Malley said. 'Not everyone who trespasses here is well intentioned towards me.'

His voice was cultured, minus accent. He wasn't menacing, but he wasn't welcoming either. If anything, he seemed indifferent to them, and now that he'd established who they were, he strode away along the paved path.

'I'm surprised you're still here,' David said, walking quickly to catch up. 'Having a disgraced priest in residence can hardly be a selling point.'

'There are worse stumbling blocks than me,' O'Malley replied. 'The dispute about what to do with this place rumbles on eternally. Local people would have it razed and the ground sown with salt. Others would leave it standing but rotting in the fields. More pragmatically but still unrealistically in my view, the Diocesan Board of Education feels it can eventually be reopened and used as a school again, while the local authority, who are doubtless in bed with various builders, wish it to be sold for redevelopment. In time I'll be required to move. And then I'll be lucky to find anywhere so far removed from our unforgiving twenty-first century society.'

They ascended a flight of steps, alighting on what might once have been an old running track, though it was now mostly grass. A few yards along on the right, stood a small house.

'Unforgiving?' David said. 'Quite a judgement considering the things you did to that society's underage sons.'

O'Malley half smiled. 'Well, Mr Kelman, none of them *died* because of my indiscretions.'

'Whoa…' David retorted slowly. It would have been louder had Anushka not caught up and grabbed his arm. 'Don't try to categorise *me* with *you*.'

'And why not?' the ex-priest wondered. 'Has society welcomed *you* back with open arms?'

'I ...' David struggled to find a response.

'I didn't think so.' O'Malley made his way around the residence.

It was extremely basic: a two-up/two-down cottage, made from rugged stone with odd-angled window frames and distorted, grubby panes. At the side of it sat a chopping block and a heap of freshly hewn firewood. O'Malley threw a sheet of canvas over the wood and left the axe on top.

He stripped off his gloves and tucked them into his belt. 'It's explainable in your case, of course. You've not repaid your debts as yet.'

'You served seven years out of twelve,' David countered. 'That wasn't much of a repayment either.'

'You should try it.' O'Malley smiled. 'Who knows, maybe you will.'

He went inside, leaving the cottage door ajar.

David shook his head. 'You were right. This was a crap idea.'

'Now we're here, we might as well talk to him,' Anushka said.

The cottage's front door had evidently been left open for them, so David knocked.

'Can we come in?' he asked of the dimness within.

'I assume that's what you're here for,' the voice inside replied.

They entered a small cluttered room which smelled of tobacco. Embers glowed orange in a small fireplace, while a worn but well-swept carpet covered the floor. An armchair faced the grate and there were several bookcases, their shelves crammed with leather-backed volumes. Candles stood on some of the shelves and the mantelpiece. None were lit, but lengthy tendrils of cold wax dangled beneath each one.

'I'd offer you tea,' O'Malley said, indicating a flame-blackened kettle suspended over the hearth, 'but I'd have to build up the fire and I think that would take a little longer than you were hoping to spend in my company.'

Anushka stared at the kettle, and then at the candles. 'You really *have* retreated from the world, haven't you?'

O'Malley settled into the armchair. 'I think that's best for everyone, wouldn't you say?'

'Thought the Church would be looking after you better,' David commented.

'Oh, they would if I'd let them. These days, there are Church-run hostels for men like me. Halfway houses for the clerically insane, if you like. I'd be out of sight and out of mind, but I'd have central heating, three meals a day ... But you know, something about the hermit lifestyle always appealed to me.'

'I see they're letting you write another book.'

David had ambled to one of the small windows, beneath which a rickety, ink-blotted desk creaked under the weight of pens, notebooks, an ash-tray filled with twisty dog-ends, a heavy, old-fashioned typewriter, and a neat pile of typed documents, which when David leafed into it, was filled with Irish-sounding names.

'You consider it outrageous, Mr Kelman?' O'Malley wondered. 'Should I be denied that privilege too?'

'No, I'm just surprised.'

Their host touched a roll-up cigarette to the embers. 'Every scoundrel needs a last refuge, and writing books does it for me. Even a book like this one, which will never be published.' He stood up, blowing pungent smoke. 'I don't need the Church's permission to do this. Just as I don't need a publisher's permission, as none of them will even come near me.' He wandered over, clamping the cig with his lips as he gently wrested the paperwork from his visitor's grasp and re-ordered it. 'It's purely therapeutic.'

'Actually,' David said, '*this* is what we've come to talk to you about.'

O'Malley chuckled. 'You've developed an interest in theological history?' He moved back to his chair. 'I'm afraid you won't find absolution that way.'

'I aim to find absolution by finding Jodie Martindale.'

O'Malley looked around, puzzled. 'Hasn't that horse already bolted?'

'Not necessarily.'

'And how is that relevant…' O'Malley nodded at the desk, 'to *this*?'

'I don't think it is, personally,' Anushka said. 'But David's more attached to his Catholic upbringing than any of us knew.'

O'Malley arched an eyebrow at David.

'We believe that a woman who may be connected to Jodie Martindale's kidnapping goes under the street name "Saint Bridget",' David explained.

'Can't be many of those.' O'Malley blew more smoke. 'Surely the police are all over it?'

'It's not really a street name,' Anushka put in. 'Truth is, we don't know what the Saint Bridget reference actually means.'

'I see.' O'Malley sat in the armchair again. 'So you thought you'd find an expert to interpret it for you?'

'The woman who may be our Saint Bridget,' David began, 'is black, beautiful – or so we're told – and speaks with a non-British accent.'

O'Malley eyed him. 'I must admit, I'm speechless.'

'I appreciate none of that seems to fit with the Saint Bridget of Christian belief,' David said, 'but it gets weirder. The woman we're interested in was well dressed, moneyed. Wore expensive jewellery. Three items stood out apparently. A trio of platinum pendants. A lightning bolt, a sword and what might have been a tornado. I know that last one sounds odd...'

O'Malley tapped ash into the palm of his hand. 'When I say I'm speechless, what I mean is I'm speechless at your audacity.' He tossed the ashes into the fire. 'That you should come to me for help when you wrote the most terrible things about me in your newspaper.'

'Well, only after you'd been convicted of abusing children.'

'Details about my family background, my relationships with my parents...'

'I was a crime reporter and it was a big story. If I'd just regurgitated the official account, I wouldn't have been doing my job properly.'

'Doing your job is one thing. Crude muck-raking is another.'

'Look, I owed it to my readers to present a full picture. I had to speak to your victims and their families, look into your past...'

'And you gleefully believed everything you were told. That my entire life was darkness and woe.'

'Wasn't it?' Anushka asked.

O'Malley gave her a long look. 'I think you need to leave now. Both of you.'

There was clearly no point arguing. But when they exited, he followed them to the door.

'I'm trying to put things right, O'Malley,' David told him. 'I'm surprised you don't want to do the same.'

'Spare me your pseudo piety, Mr Kelman. I know what you are. And I'd respect you more if you just said you were stuck and needed a helping hand.'

'Don't beat yourself up,' Anushka said a couple of minutes later as they threaded back through the school grounds. 'It wasn't a bad idea. But he's a surly old bastard. Acknowledges his faults, but thinks he should be a special case because he's an intellectual.'

When they got back to the car, it sat alone. They climbed in. The interior was hot and stuffy.

'Sorry, Nushka,' David said.

She powered her window down. 'For what?'

'For involving you in this. It's already taken us to some pretty shitty places.'

'Or alternatively, nowhere at all.'

He frowned.

'We're not getting anywhere,' she said. 'That's the main problem as I see it.'

'You have to chase every lead. It's inevitable some will lead to dead-ends.'

'Well...' She glanced across to the padlocked entrance gates and the thicket of leaves enmeshing them. 'I wouldn't disagree that this place ticks that box.'

A nicotine-yellow fist thudded on the window next to David's head.

They jumped before spinning around.

It was O'Malley.

Warily, David rolled down his window.

'One question,' the ex-priest said sternly. 'This sword

pendant the beautiful black woman wore – could it have been a machete?'

'Erm, I don't know,' David replied.

'But the other two items were a lightning bolt and a tornado?'

'That's correct.'

O'Malley blew another cloud of smoke. 'The connection you could be looking for is Oya.'

'Oya?'

'An ancient goddess. A guardian of the dead. An invincible warrior. She has various sacred symbols, among them a lightning bolt, a machete and a whirlwind.'

David was still puzzled. 'I'm not following. How is …?'

O'Malley flirted away his fragment of roll-up. 'On the plantations in the Caribbean, the slaves were only able to worship their old deities by conflating them with spiritual powers acceptable to Christianity. The Yoruba goddess, Oya, was conflated with the Haitian goddess, Maman Brigitte, who had already been syncretised with the Catholic Saint Bridget. They thus became one and the same.'

'Yoruba?' David asked.

'An ethnic group indigenous to West Africa. Much enslaved during our glorious white past.'

'Africa …' David's thoughts were suddenly racing. 'Father O'Malley …?'

O'Malley was already walking away. He stopped and turned. 'I'm not a father anymore, Mr Kelman. I was defrocked, remember?'

'*Mr* O'Malley. Thank you.'

Briefly the raggedy beanpole figure looked awkward. 'Like you said. Maybe I haven't repaid enough yet.'

'Before you go, can I ask – do you ever get any other visitors here?'

'Is that a serious question?'

'Someone who might have a brown car. It could've been a Toyota Prius.'

'Mr Kelman, you are the first people I've seen on these premises since January, and that was someone from the estate agent's making an up-to-date recce.'

'No one else then?'

'What on earth would motivate them?'

David put the car in gear. 'What indeed?'

24

'So what did he say?' Anushka asked.

David lowered his phone. 'Nothing much. Apart from calling me a cocky little prat.'

'Hmm.' She glanced through the wire-mesh fence in front of the car. 'He didn't care much for you prompting him during the interview yesterday. I suspected that when he didn't come to the Shed this morning.'

'I think he doesn't like it that he's getting interested in what we're doing.'

'If he was interested, wouldn't he be with us now?'

'Says he's got more of his book to write. The Miranda Carter chapter, I'd imagine.'

'Just out of interest, what did he say about this new Oya thing?'

'Said he supposes it's a possible link but also that it's so unlikely as to be "barely worth two seconds of a genuine newsman's consideration".'

'Well…' She still didn't sound sure about it herself.

'Come on, Nushka. Let's not be dismissive for the sake of it. Look at what we've actually got. We know that Jodie Martindale had a meeting with someone called Saint Bridget shortly before she was abducted. We also know that Jodie met a mysterious, unnamed black woman at the Royal Wallasea shortly before she was abducted. On top of that, we now know that one of several Saint Bridgets existing in mythology was a goddess worshipped in pre-Christian West Africa. And that this black woman at the Royal Wallasea might have had an African accent *and* was wearing symbols of that same goddess.'

Anushka shrugged. 'I wouldn't say it adds up to very little, but...'

'It's slim, I suppose.'

'So slim that I'd suggest you don't mention it to the police.'

They glanced again through the mesh fence into the car park attached to the austere, official-looking building that towered over them. They were at Chelmsford, parked in the visitor car park of the Essex Police HQ, where Essex Traffic, specifically the Serious Collision Investigation team, had their offices.

'How long do we think this is going to take, anyway?' Anushka asked. 'We've been here an hour already.'

'According to my info, Lynda Hagen finishes at five-thirty.' David glanced at his watch. 'That's five minutes from now.'

'Suppose she's on overtime?'

'Could be a problem.'

'She's also a DS. You said she'd been promoted since you and she last spoke?'

'That's true.'

'So she may have to stay behind routinely...'

'Anushka, I'm doing what I can, OK?' He tried not to raise his voice. 'I'd like to think that this impatience you're displaying was because you had four or five other promising leads that you yourself had developed and were keen to be following, but somehow I don't think that's the case, is it?'

'Whoa, isn't that her?'

A woman was crossing the staff car park wearing a smart

skirt and jacket, and carrying a shoulder bag. She had long, dark brown hair and even from a distance was distinctly good-looking. Several years had passed, but David recognised her immediately as Detective Sergeant Lynda Hagen. She hit a key fob as she approached a parked Qashqai, which chirruped and flashed its lights.

'Excuse me!' David shouted, climbing from the Fiesta.

DS Hagen glanced around, registering the figure on the other side of the fence.

He waved an arm. 'Yeah! Over here!'

She walked forward cautiously, halting about ten yards short.

'Mr Kelman...' She spoke distastefully, as if his name itself was unpleasant to her.

'You don't seem surprised to see me,' he said.

'Nothing you do would surprise me, I'm afraid.'

'You don't seem happy either.'

'Is this important?' she asked. 'I'm quite busy.'

'It's to your benefit,' Anushka said.

Hagen glanced at her. 'Who are you?'

'My name's Anushka Chawla. I, erm...'

'Anushka works with me.' David placed a business card against the wire mesh. 'We're part of the *Essex Enquirer*.'

'It's a new online newspaper,' Anushka explained.

Hagen looked at David. 'So it only took you six years to find someone who'd let you back in. That's pretty amazing work. I'd say well done but I wouldn't really mean it.'

She turned to walk away.

'Can we just talk to you?' Anushka asked.

Hagen glanced back. 'We have an official press office. They handle all enquiries from journalists and reporters.'

'We want to return a favour.'

Hagen looked bemused. 'I'm sorry?'

'We've come to you because, well…' Anushka shrugged, 'David said that when you arrested him six years ago, you were very polite, very proper. And of course you let him go.'

'I didn't let him go. The CPS decided we didn't have enough to beat the defence that he'd already prepared for himself beforehand.' The cop shook her head. 'You could learn from this man, Anushka. But if it had been down to me, I'd have thrown the book at him and taken my chance in court.'

'I know you won't believe it,' David said, 'but I'm actually sorry for what I did.'

'Try telling that to Freddie Martindale – except you can't, can you.'

'It's Freddie Martindale we're here to talk to you about,' Anushka put in.

Hagen remained where she was, listening.

'There's a girl,' David said. 'An addict called Laura Reynoldson. Or that's what she calls herself. Her real name might be Yvonne. I can't tell you exactly where you'd find her. She's homeless, but she seems to live in and around Keppel Hall in Chatham.'

'So take it to Kent Police…'

'She says that Freddie Martindale was murdered,' Anushka said.

Hagen eyed them both. 'What're you talking about?'

'She says he didn't throw himself off that roof, but that someone else did it to him.'

Hagen regarded David doubtfully.

'That's what she says,' he confirmed. 'She seems adamant.'

'She actually *saw* this?'

'Well, no. But she's pretty certain about it.'

Hagen smiled. 'I see. So she's adamant that this *might* have happened.' She edged away. 'Like I say, get in touch with Kent.'

'You don't want to do anything yourself?' Anushka asked. 'Weren't you involved in the Jodie Martindale enquiry?'

'I was peripherally involved because I was a divisional CID officer,' Hagen explained. 'You may have noticed, but I'm now Essex Roads Policing division. I look into traffic accidents. And that's *all* I do.'

'Snagged yourself a bunch of blaggers a few months ago, didn't you?' David said.

'You follow the news, very good. But that was my case. This isn't.'

'Look ...' David gripped the mesh. 'You may as well know. I brought this to you because I thought I could trust you.'

'No, Mr Kelman. You brought this to me, I suspect, because you've become conscience-stricken about what you did all those years ago. The problem is that making things all right with me doesn't make them all right generally. Now, as I've said, Freddie Martindale is Kent's investigation, not mine.'

'I don't suppose you know anyone in the local underworld with a street name Saint Bridget?'

Hagen smiled again. 'I see ... So, in truth, you didn't even come here to make yourself feel better. You came here for information.'

'It's just a question. A name that's cropped up.'

'You take my breath away.' She turned to walk back to her car.

'So, for clarity, you've never heard of a Saint Bridget?'

Hagen answered over her shoulder. 'Ask at a church.'

'How about Oya?'

This time the cop glanced back.

'There can't be too many you've come across called Oya, can there?' David said.

'And you call yourself a crime reporter?' Hagen looked at Anushka. 'I said you'd learn from this fella. Seems I was wrong.'

'So who's Oya?' David asked again.

'Like you say, it's an unusual name. You should be able to find it.'

'In relation to what?'

Hagen set off back to her car. 'Only the biggest investigation Essex Police have ever been involved with.'

They stood in silence while she drove away.

'What a cow,' Anushka said.

'Everything she said was true,' David replied. 'Everything about me, anyway. But it was still worth coming here. I knew we were going to get something.'

He jumped eagerly behind the Fiesta's wheel, Anushka rushing to get into the passenger seat.

'How'd you mean you knew?' she said.

He accessed his laptop. 'You think I came all the way here to help the cops?'

'We came here to tell them about Freddie Martindale being murdered.'

'Yeah, but only to cover my arse. Someone tells you about a murder … you don't *not* mention it or you're next to get nicked. If they want to kick it down the line and let it get lost in the paperwork, that's up to them. But we've done our duty. And on top of that, we learned something.'

Anushka still didn't know what he meant, but now he showed her his laptop, on which he'd called up an old newspaper website.

The central image depicted a figure humped under

a blanket, hands cuffed behind as he or she was escorted by uniformed police to a waiting transport, while in the background an angry crowd raged behind temporary crash barriers. Down the right-hand side, a column of headshots depicted the faces of six women. The overarching headline read:

MONSTER CAGED

A strapline added:

Restless mob restrained as 'Medway Slasher'
James Lynch convicted on all counts

They didn't have to read very far into the intro to find the quote from Major Investigations boss, Detective Superintendent Mackeson, that this was 'without doubt the biggest investigation Essex Police have ever been involved with'.

'Check out the victims,' David said, indicating the column of faces.

Anushka did, and saw that under each one there was a caption bearing a name.

'Sadie Johnson,' she read, 'Tia Wells, Lola Mackenzie, Briony Williams, Jean Baker...' She hesitated with the one at the bottom. 'Oya Oyinola.'

The snapshot over the top of this one portrayed a black woman.

A black woman, at whose throat hung three pendants, one of which was clearly a lightning bolt, another a sword... or machete.

25

Over a fourteen-month period, James Lynch, 44, a delivery driver from Harlow, whose routes regularly took him back and forth between London and the south-east coast, murdered six female sex workers in the back of his vehicle, having first been able to lure them in there because he'd installed a camp bed. Once they were in his grasp, he strangled them unconscious, raped them and sliced them down the middle, opening them throat to crotch. Their bodies, he would afterwards dispose of on open countryside.

Lynch killed four women in Kent, mainly around the Medway area (hence his moniker) and two in Essex, so the two police forces concerned combined their resources to put together a dedicated taskforce, Operation Redwood, which, augmented by expert investigators from the Serial Crimes Unit at Scotland Yard, led a fast, efficient enquiry, resulting in Lynch's arrest.

In due course, having confessed to most of his offences, Lynch was sentenced to a full-life term at HM Prison Brancaster, the UK's own version of a supermax, which occupied a bleak stretch of the Norfolk coast and was known locally as 'Gull Rock'.

During the course of his depredations, a frenzy was stirred up in the districts where the killer was believed to be hunting. Scathing criticism was directed at everyone from the police to the government. There'd been marches in solidarity with the victims, some of which had turned into public order situations, curfews imposed, roadblocks set up. Vigilante groups had served threatening notices on individuals they had suspicions about (in all cases men who had nothing to do with the crimes). News crews had poured in from everywhere, even far-flung locations like New York and Hong Kong.

Rural England, it was said, was 'in the grip of a monster'. The 'land of green fields, country churches and thatched-roof villages was under siege by a faceless death-dealer'. The fact that most of the victims had been procured in run-down resort towns was ignored. The *Essex Examiner* itself, recently denuded of its Crime Beat office, had been guilty of the same offence. With Norm Harrington 'the only man in the newsroom qualified to cover the case', to use his own words (and desperate to get involved because he'd hoped it might restore his damaged reputation) refused permission to go near it, others who were less well versed in local crime had been assigned. And perhaps inevitably, with no contacts, no leads, no expertise of any sort, they'd restricted themselves to parroting the official line trotted out by police press officers, doing zero digging of their own and asking no searching questions of anyone involved, and, to fill the empty spaces that resulted, reprinting the many scurrilous rumours and scare-stories doing the rounds in pubs and workplaces:

The sole of each victim's left foot had been carved with a black magic symbol.

People were drawn to several of the crime scenes by hysterical laughter.

The Victims' families had received gloating postcards written in a blood-red, spidery hand and describing with fiendish glee their loved ones' final moments.

None of which transpired to be true.

More important than any of this, however, at least from David and Anushka's perspective, was a quick Google search once they returned to the Shed confirming that one of the killer's victims from Kent, the fifth in order, had been a sex worker of African origin called Oya Oyinola. Further searches uncovered a few extra details about her, including her status, which was high-class call girl rather than street-walker, and that, of the six victims, she was the only one whose death James Lynch had denied responsibility for.

David pondered the printout depicting Oya Oyinola's face.

It was a grainy reproduction of the official police pic, but unlike so many other photographs of prostitutes, which were often tearful custody shots, this one was tagged in its lower left-hand corner *OnlyTheBest.co.uk*, and was softly focused. Its subject was proud and beautiful, the three pendants at her throat only adding to an array of glamorous jewellery.

The Shed door swung open and Norm stood there, a jacket draped over his shoulder.

'Yeah,' David said, 'I thought the words "Medway Slasher" would bring you running.'

'This had better not be a joke, David.'

'Course it is. I thought it'd be really funny dragging you away from your Piña Colada for nothing.'

Norm approached the huge whiteboard that Anushka was plastering with printed-out images and using marker pens with which to scribble notes and draw arrows between them.

'Good lord…' One by one, he took in the tragic faces, then the maps, e-fits and crime-scene images, the latter not just from Black Brook golf course but relating to the deposition sites where the Medway Slasher had dumped his victims. 'So we're not just a newsroom – now we're a police incident room too?'

'If you like,' David said. 'But only where *one* of Lynch's victims is concerned.'

Norm said nothing, awaiting further explanation.

'So … you on board?' David asked.

'You'll need to give me a bit more than that.'

'You had even less when you agreed to help us at the Royal Wallasea.'

'I was interested in that because it gave me a potential new chapter for the book.'

'OK, but don't deny you're interested in this too. Come on, Norm, you came here so fast the only question in my mind is whether the cops do you for speeding or low-flying.'

'Don't push your luck, David.'

'You need to be reasonable, mate. We've got good leads here. We're not going to share them with just anyone, are we?'

'What leads?'

'You on board or not?'

Norm glanced at Anushka, who'd broken off from what she was doing to nod encouragingly.

'For God's sake!' He gestured irritably. 'Yes, I'm on board. For the time being.'

'OK …' David eyed them both. 'But from this point on, all work we do on this story will be under the banner of the *Essex Enquirer*. Agreed?'

Norm blew through gritted teeth, but didn't say no.

'Excellent,' David said. 'Because I've now registered the company. I've also installed the landline and ordered some *Enquirer* ID cards for you two, plus spare keys to the Shed …'

'David!' Norm blurted. 'You don't even have a story. Not a real one.'

'You think so? Well, let's take a look.' Anushka stepped aside as David moved to the whiteboard, running through the events that had led to this point. Freddie Martindale's oblique reference to someone called Saint Bridget and the meeting she allegedly had with Jodie Martindale. The info about the goddess Oya, also a Saint Bridget, and the symbolism around her, and then the beautiful woman who spoke to Jodie at the Royal Wallasea.

'And now we learn,' David tapped the whiteboard again, 'that the only Oya the police around here seem to have a record of was an African-born escort, Oya Oyinola, who was brutally murdered less than two years after Jodie was kidnapped.'

'It took nearly two years?' Norm said sceptically.

'If she went into hiding, maybe that's how long it took for them to find her. Or maybe they were waiting for a window of opportunity, and the Medway murders presented one?'

'Why didn't this Oya speak to anyone else?'

'Too frightened?' David suggested. 'She saw what had happened to Jodie.'

Norm still looked unimpressed. 'Look, anyone can wear exotic bling. There's no absolute proof the woman at the Royal Wallasea and this Oya Oyinola are even the same person.'

'No *absolute* proof,' Anushka agreed, 'but it's coming together.'

'Bear in mind,' David said, 'that the man convicted of Oya's murder, though he freely admitted to killing five other women, denied any involvement in that one. You honestly don't think there's something here we need to look into?'

Still, Norm seemed unsure. 'I won't pretend there aren't a couple of coincidences.'

'Excellent, we're making progress. But what this essentially means is that we have a job to do. It's not just Jodie Martindale's kidnapping we're investigating. There are murders to be solved too.'

'Suppose I go along with you,' Norm said. 'I still think this whole *Essex Enquirer* thing is a non-starter, but just say for the sake of argument that we're all in. How's it going to look that we first got onto this story by scavenging in the Martindale family's rubbish?'

'Depends where we end up,' David said. 'We might never need to mention that.'

Norm snorted. 'I know you gave Freddie Martindale's mobile phone to the police, but it's still going to cast us in a terrible light.'

'Especially as there was something else we *didn't* give to the police,' Anushka muttered.

Norm glanced around at her. 'What?'

David sighed.

'Come on, David,' she said. 'Let's get this over with.'

Reluctantly, David reached under his desk and pulled out Freddie Martindale's box. He also opened a drawer and took out the Saint Bridget document, which he'd now sheathed in plastic. He kicked the box across to Norm, at the same time explaining its relevance and how he'd got hold of it.

'It was this that first got me interested in the name, Saint Bridget,' he said. 'But that homeless girl in Chatham mentioned the name too.'

Norm flicked through the box's contents. He glanced up. 'That girl who we'll probably never see again?'

David shrugged.

Norm frowned. 'In which case we'll yet again be producing evidence that you obtained by stealing. Only this time
it's a theft you haven't owned up to.'

'Norm, we're not putting a court case together.'

'But the police are, David! And they might be able to use
this stuff.'

'Did I mention that the cop in charge is one Tony
Jorgenson? Does that change anything?'

Norm looked troubled by that, but didn't immediately
respond.

'Think about Lampwick Lane,' David said. 'We couldn't
find the smoking gun where Jorgenson was concerned, but
he was part of Essex Robbery back then, and he was the
fourth man that night – I've always said that.'

'You've also said that you weren't so sure that you'd put
your life on it.'

'When we were first looking into it, Jorgenson's name
came up again and again.'

'Even if he was corrupt back then, why would he not
investigate *this* crime?'

'To answer that, we need to know whose payroll he's
currently on.'

Norm walked around the office, visibly discomforted.

'There was a time when you trusted my instincts,' David
said. 'You're going to have to trust them again now.'

In truth, David didn't think this was too much to ask.
Their police insider had long ago advised them there were
dirty coppers dotted throughout the police forces of England
and Wales. In many cases it amounted to no more than lazi-
ness. In others, though, it was about taking bribes, losing or
falsifying evidence, telling lies in court. In a few more, not
many but some, there were police officers actively conspiring

to commit serious criminal offences. With his long experience, Norm would have known this anyway, especially where Tony Jorgenson was concerned.

'Even if we took it to other coppers, it'd end up in Jorgenson's hands,' Anushka said. 'He's the Cold Cases boss.'

Norm sat down. 'If your instincts tell you this guy is bad news, David, then so be it.' He leafed through the box. 'I can't see what all this crap would be worth anyway. But the fact remains that we're going out on a limb. Again.'

David indicated the whiteboard. 'The alternative is we pretend none of this matters and that we shouldn't do anything about it because I gathered the intel by underhand means. We can also pretend that because what we're doing here is looking to start an online newspaper, it's simply too immoral to intrude on the Martindales' grief any further by reopening this case. But I can't unhear the voice I heard on that phone. And even if Jodie Martindale has died since she made that call and there is no ticking clock, the people who did it should not get a free pass just because we don't feel good about our methods.'

Norm looked far from convinced.

'Look,' David said, 'if this works out, we save someone's life, get justice on a bunch of villains, and relaunch our careers. Everybody wins.'

'*If* is a big word, David,' Norm replied. '*If* is a very big word.'

III

SHOTS IN THE DARK

26

Eight years ago

The worst part was always the waiting. Your imagination played its nastiest tricks on you then. Not that David had been waiting long; the Frontera's dashboard clock indicated that Riker had only left him alone five minutes ago, even if it seemed more like fifty.

Though it wasn't as if David didn't have real things to worry about.

He hadn't invented Oakwood Farm, a country cottage sitting isolated several miles south of Wix. It was a real place, but it was empty following the death of its owner, an octogenarian called Barraclough, and was now awaiting probate to be finalised, and there was nothing of value inside it. The coppers from Lampwick Lane would have been able to find that out if they'd made the necessary enquiries, but if they'd made those enquiries, it would be on record, and given what they thought was about to happen there, that would be something they definitely wouldn't want. They'd never trust *his* word of course. They didn't know him. But they'd trust their regular informant, Mal Riker. And that was the point where David worried that he might be on thin ice. He'd made it his business to get to know Riker over the last month, but whether he'd genuinely managed to convince the guy that he was an active criminal himself was another matter.

'Stop chunnering,' Norm's voice mumbled through the earpiece.

'Sorry,' David replied quietly.

'Makes you look like an amateur.'

'There's no one else here, you know.'

Norm said nothing for a moment. 'How long's he been gone now?'

'Eight minutes.'

'Remind me the reason he gave?'

'He didn't.' David glanced through the Frontera's windows, eyes roving the scrapyard.

It was night-time, and they were somewhere near Braintree. He knew that much, but he wasn't sure where exactly. But there was no ambient light seeping from nearby housing into the black alleys between the teetering stacks of rusty, mangled cars. No sounds of vehicles coming and going on nearby industrial estates. Even the yard office sat in winter darkness.

'This has got the hallmarks of every thriller I've ever read,' David muttered. 'Where the undercover journo thinks he's about to get his scoop, and instead gets topped.'

'If they've sussed you, let them know you're not working alone,' Norm replied. 'Show them the wire and camera, and ensure they know that everything's already been transmitted back and that if you don't come home again, it'll be on the internet in the next half-hour.'

'That'd be an awful lot of work down the shitter.'

'Better the work than you.'

'If my cover story doesn't hold...'

'I thought you trusted Clayton.'

'What I trusted was his determination to get even with Riker and his crew.'

'So, he won't have sold you a pup.'

'It's whether he knows what he's doing. He was the fall guy, remember. He was the one who went to jail while Riker walked free.'

After first learning from a police insider that career criminal, Malcolm Riker, was setting up the blags, which his friends in the Essex Robbery Squad could then 'solve' before splitting the rewards with him afterwards, David and Norm had traipsed from prison to prison, interviewing many of those men serving time for the crimes, until they'd found one Terry Clayton, who was better connected than the others and so stunned to learn how he'd been hoodwinked that he was determined to have payback. It was Clayton who'd agreed to use his own connections to set David up as a supposed blagger from the Midlands, Ryan Raeburn, and arrange for him to meet Malcolm Riker...

'Hang on,' David said. Four indistinct figures had emerged around the side of the yard office. 'Jesus! I think they're here!'

'OK – be sure to hide the earpiece.'

David yanked the hi-tech plug from his left ear and pushed it into the crack between the cushion of his seat and the backrest. As the gangling shape of Riker came round to his side of the car, David opened the passenger door.

'Out you get,' the informant said, an odd 'Cheshire Cat' grin splitting his lean features.

David did so, and was confronted by two men he recognised as Detective Inspector Jack Pettigrew and Detective Sergeant Keith Elgin. The former was aged about fifty, with short grey hair and steely good looks, the latter in his late thirties and of solid, stocky build, his reddish hair also cut very short, his face brutish. Both wore overcoats, gloves and scarves. The third man hung around in the background. He was bigger than either of the other two, both in height and breadth, and somewhere in his mid-forties, his hair hidden under a black baseball cap. His clothing was also black, his gloved right hand resting inside his zipped-down jacket, probably because he had a concealed weapon there. David only knew Inspector Jerry Corrigan as a specialist firearms officer; from the way he kept a watch on everyone, he was providing security. Way back near the office, possibly so that he could keep an eye on the scrapyard's front gate, there was yet another man, though he was nothing more than a burly outline.

The two detectives regarded David curiously, before Elgin came forward, pulling off his gloves, and without preamble, gave him a thorough search, checking his pockets, around his belt, under his clothes and collar, even down his trousers and into his socks, taking his wallet away for further examination but at no stage detecting the button-cam. Elgin instructed David to roll back the sleeve on his left arm, which he did, exposing the 'rising sun' symbol that he'd recently had tattooed on the back of his wrist. Elgin tilted the arm so that Pettigrew could also see it, and then licked his thumb, attempting to smudge the image. It was real, so no smudge resulted.

Elgin re-joined his gaffer, who was now on his phone, evidently comparing the figure in front of them to some kind of photograph. Terry Clayton had warned David about this, but had added that it was less to worry about than he might think as villains on the lam often affected physical change. The blond rinse David had sported ever since he became Ryan Raeburn looked like an obvious fake, and that was just what the cops would have expected. The same could be said of his tattoo. The original one that Pettigrew and Elgin would have been looking for was a plain old rising sun, but on David's arm it was partly obstructed by jungle leafage; again that was the kind of quick and easy change they'd have anticipated.

For all this, David felt increasingly twitchy. Their eyes probed him like laser beams.

'So, Mr Raeburn,' Pettigrew said in a voice that was almost BBC English, 'how is it you don't look anything like the last photograph taken when you were in custody?'

David adopted his best Brummie accent. 'Don't want to get caught again.'

'Well, the beard and shaggy black hair were easy enough to dispose of, I imagine, but three and a half stone in weight? And that's a conservative estimate.'

'I run, I work out.'

'How come you're here instead of overseas?' Elgin asked. He was a Cockney.

'Can't watch the Villa overseas.'

Neither of them smiled. 'Where you living?' Pettigrew asked.

'All over the place.'

'You don't look like you've been on the run?' Elgin said.

'Haven't been. I'm not the same bloke who busted out of Durham. Got a different life now.'

They glanced at his wallet, flicking through the various documents in there, the driving licence, the credit cards, all belonging to another non-existent person with a made-up name.

'If you want to know how I got out ...'

'We know how you did it,' Pettigrew said. 'It was all over

the news. I'm more interested in who you knew when you were in there.' He eyed David with interest. 'We've sent plenty up to Frankland ourselves.'

David shrugged. 'Lots over the years. People come and go. Faces change.'

'You must remember some of them?'

David pondered. 'Lennie Albright.'

Pettigrew arched an eyebrow. 'You knew Lennie Albright?'

'We were on the same landing. He was doing fourteen for aggravated burglary.'

'How about Dougie Lane?' Elgin asked.

This was a name David hadn't heard before, despite his prep. Which meant that it could be a trick. 'I didn't know him, no.'

'That's unusual,' Pettigrew said. 'Big character, Dougie. How about Roy Barnes? You must remember him. "The Big Key". They called him that because he was such a big fucking unit he didn't need any kit to get through a door.'

Again, David knew that he couldn't risk giving any of these names the nod in case there was the slightest chance they were bogus. He shook his head, but was getting worried, because if these had been real inmates at Durham while he was supposedly serving time there, why on earth didn't he know them?

'Tod Lacy?' Elgin asked.

'No.'

'Yorkshire Mike?' Pettigrew again, though this was one David *had* heard about.

'Yeah, I remember Mike Thompson.'

Pettigrew nodded. 'Always claimed he was innocent of that post office job they got him for in Dulwich.'

'Sorry to correct you,' David replied. 'But no, he didn't.

The Flying Squad caught him gun in hand as he left the premises. He had to cough, throw himself on the mercy of the court.'

The two cops pondered this.

'There's another thing,' David said.

'Yeah?'

'It wasn't Dulwich, it was Croydon.'

Pettigrew put his phone away, took the wallet from his sidekick and gave it back to David. 'Let's get in the car. It's nearly Christmas and we're all freezing our knackers off.'

David stood back while the two cops climbed into the front, Elgin taking the passenger seat. His nerves jangled as it occurred to him that Pettigrew's junior might now search that area, in which case he'd have to be a total buffoon to not find the earpiece slotted inside the seat. Despite this, as he opened the back door, David ensured that for a few seconds at least, he was facing Riker and Corrigan, who stood in conflab a few yards away, the hefty firearms cop a massive unit in contrast to the underworld beanpole. The button-camera was on night-vision, so with any luck he'd get clear unobstructed shots of both their faces.

'You know what really swung this for you, Ryan?' Pettigrew said, when David had climbed into the back seat and shut the door.

'Don't know what you mean.'

The DI's dark eyes fixed on him through the rear-view mirror. 'We went to visit your big sis up in Wolverhampton. Silka, is it?'

'Shawna.'

'That's it, Shawna. Reminded her we were still looking for you. She got shirty. Called us pig bastards, all the usual shit. Wasn't difficult flushing her out, though. We mentioned what a chicken-shit arsehole you must be, running off to some other country with your tail between your legs. You know what she said?'

'Hopefully nothing.'

Pettigrew chuckled. 'Said you'd fucking show us. Said you were still in the UK, doing jobs right under our fucking pig noses, but that we'd never catch you ...'

'Shawna was never the brightest,' David replied.

'You got that right. But she's helped you out today, even though she doesn't realise it. I've still got one question though. You've got yourself this nice new life, Ryan ...' The two cops turned around to face him. 'Why decide to go back to your old one?'

'Nice new lives cost money too,' David said. 'Besides, I do what I do. I'm no good for anything else.'

There was a protracted silence.

'Tell us about Oakwood Farm,' Pettigrew said.

'Hasn't Mal Riker told you everything?'

'He hasn't told us why you won't just hit it clean. If there's only a man and wife caretaker living on site, it wouldn't take much to overpower them even with a green crew. You could fence the antiques yourself. Probably get a tidy sum.'

'The problem is the stuff in the cellar vault is mainly sentimental value. Family heirlooms and that. Most of it's probably old and dirty. But it matters so much to the Barraclough family that the reward will be high.'

'What are we talking in total?'

'I reckon a million. Even split three ways that's not to be sniffed at, eh?'

Pettigrew looked amused. 'Three ways?'

'You, me and Mal.'

The DI snorted with laughter. 'No, it's two ways, Ryan. You and Mal get one half, we get the other.'

'That's hardly fair.'

'Fair's got fuck all to do with it,' Elgin said.

'There's more than just us two, as you've probably seen,' Pettigrew added. 'Plus, we take the bigger risk.'

'*You* take the bigger risk?' Even though this job was non-existent, David was stunned by the cheek of that.

'Listen, Ryan – you go back inside, you're on fucking holiday. It'll be you and your mates together again. If *we* go in, it's a different story.'

David glanced from face to face. They weren't scowling, but there was a deep ruthlessness imprinted there, which he could sense even if he couldn't see it.

'OK,' he said. 'Fifty-fifty. Does Mal know?'

'He knows,' Elgin said. 'That's always the way we do it.'

That unguarded comment delighted David no end, as it would prove that this wasn't the corrupt trio's debut at ripping off both armed robbers and insurance companies together.

'It'll be different this time,' Pettigrew said, 'because normally he doesn't have to share his whack with anyone, but I'm sure he won't mind for quarter of a million quid.' He frowned. 'So long as you're sure your intel's good.'

'Hasn't been wrong so far,' David replied.

Elgin looked curious. 'What other jobs have you done? Since you escaped from Durham.'

'That'd be telling.'

'What – you think we're going to lock you up? After what we've shared so far?'

'It doesn't work like that, and you know it.'

David didn't think he was taking a chance in refusing

to entertain this latest test. No self-respecting bank robber would show any more of his hand to the cops than he needed to.

'Mal tells us you've picked a three-man team,' Pettigrew said.

'Correct,' David replied.

'You sure you need that many when the opposition's so light?'

David affected puzzlement. 'You need someone to send down, don't you?'

'A crew that size might look suspicious.'

'These live-in caretakers are loyal to the family. We'll need to go in hard and heavy. There's going to be rough stuff if we want them to open that vault. A couple of the lads I've chosen are just right for that kind of work.'

The cops considered this, but neither seemed unhappy. Quite the opposite. The more violent the crime, the better the arrests on their CVs.

'OK, Ryan,' Pettigrew said, 'here's the deal so pin your fucking ears back. I've no doubt you already know who we are. If Mal Riker hasn't told you, it won't be hard to find out. But as far as we're concerned, this meeting never took place – OK? And as you've already seen, we've got at least two witnesses with us who'll confirm that. So ... as things stand, we know nothing at all about you or Oakwood Farm. From this moment on, we'll have nothing to do with it, until the job is done and dusted and our reliable CI blows the gaff on the evil twats who did it. But ... and this is the most important thing, from this point and forever fucking more, you will make no attempt to contact us, yourself.' Pettigrew's eyes gleamed like dark jewels. 'You understand that, Ryan?'

David shrugged again. 'Why would I?'

'Never fucking mind why would you. Do ... you ... understand?'

'Sure.'

'All contacts go through Mal Riker. And *only* through him. He's the broker. That means, he's the one who dobs your crew in, he's the one who collects the reward and splits it. If you're not happy with the final take, if you've any beef at all ... take it up with him, not us. Because we're just hardworking coppers who've got no clue who the fuck you are, and will be too busy getting slapped on the back for locking up another bunch of loser scumbags who actually couldn't knock over a bangtail in a brothel. You got all that?'

David nodded.

'You sure, Ryan?' Elgin asked again, flicking his torch on and shining it into David's eyes. 'You sure?' He switched the torch off, and then on again, spearing David's face, dazzling him, causing him to raise a hand.

Pettigrew did the same, flashing his torch on and off in perfect synch with his mate, slamming the double-glare into David's filmy, sleepy eyes ...

Today

And only then, did David realise that he wasn't in the backseat of Mal Riker's battered old Frontera, but in the front seat of his own Fiesta and that the lights emanated from a clumsy old motorhome pulling a multi-point turn in front of him.

In a vague daze, he sat upright.

He'd hit the M3 late the previous night, only to find

himself mired in slow-moving summer holiday traffic, and having made nothing like the distance he'd hoped for, pulling off at Fleet services to grab a catnap, though from the dashboard clock, which read 5:30am, that catnap had lasted over four hours.

He lumbered across the car park, looking to grab himself a coffee and a bagel.

As he did, the memories hit him again.

Had that really been all it had taken? That one meeting?

Once the bent cops had departed into the night, Riker had allowed him back into the Frontera's front passenger seat, and had driven him back the agreed drop off point, chatting amicably. He'd been so garrulous on the journey back that he hadn't even noticed David covertly retrieve his earpiece from between the cushions, so, once the journalist was back in his own car, he'd been able to converse with Norm again.

Norm, who'd listened to the whole thing via the buttoncam, was able to confirm that they'd got everything on film and tape, the entire exchange.

So yes, that really had been all there was to it.

Of course, no real burglary had ever been planned for Oakwood Farm. There'd been no bunch of naïve fall guys heading blithely towards the biggest disaster of their careers. There'd been no stockpile of dust-furred antiques of interest only to the Barraclough family, waiting to be lifted from a cellar vault. There hadn't even been a cellar vault.

What there was was a shocking news story just waiting to be written.

And a Mount Everest-sized pile of shit set to fall on the heads of certain officers in the Essex Robbery Squad.

David mulled it over as he pulled out of the services car park, heading south. His mind strayed again to that tension-filled winter eight years ago, and how Crime Beat was born off the back of what a significant number of police officers had complained was straightforward entrapment.

It *had* been entrapment. David had assumed a false identity and had lured those corrupt bastards into his confidence by fabricating a lucrative crime. OK, they'd got on board eagerly and had soon taken charge, revealing the depth of their guilt, their unwitting confessions alone kickstarting the internal enquiry that uncovered the other occasions when they and Mal Riker had pulled this stunt. Riker had responded by cutting a deal for himself, ensuring that his former mates' full villainy was exposed. Afterwards, everyone had proclaimed it an intense, efficient and very worthy piece of investigative reporting. But if that was the case, why did David feel as if the whole thing had been rather seedy?

Almost certainly, that was an effect of the Martindale affair. It had been one thing to deceive a bunch of dirty cops and their pet gangster, but it had been something else to do that to a tormented family.

If David was honest with himself, he felt bad about what he was doing now.

Though Norm and Anushka had both come on board, they'd made demands, the key one being that he had to bring the Bulstrodes in on what they were doing. And it couldn't be done by text or email. He had to sit down with the survivors of that decimated clan, and explain things face to face. It was a near certainty that, given their progress so far, Hannah Bulstrode would OK it, though not until she'd verbally ripped him a new one. But he'd had no option but to agree. He'd even admitted to himself that *he* would probably feel better if the Martindales/Bulstrodes gave him their blessing.

And then what had he done?

After returning to Rosehill House and being told by a gardener that Mr and Mrs Bulstrode had gone away on a short holiday, he'd called in at the nearest country pub, producing another of his fake IDs, this one claiming that he was from the BBC, and explaining that he was looking for Rosehill House because, by long-standing arrangement, they were planning to film some scenes there for a new drama. A bunch of locals had replied that the Bulstrodes were either at their villa in Italy or down at their house in Cornwall, somewhere near Port Izal.

David had thanked them and left. If the Bulstrodes were only away on a 'short' break, it seemed more probable it would be the latter. It was so easy, he thought, and yet it was all so devious, so fraudulent. And the worst thing was that he was good at it.

'You must have an honest face,' he told himself as he drove.

Or you're just 'the worst person on earth,' as Hannah Bulstrode had declared.

27

'Not in this universe!' had been Norm's view.

Anushka had looked to David for support.

'Forget it,' he'd responded. 'It's way too dangerous.'

'But surely it'll take a female to do a job like this,' she'd argued. 'You think those women will open up to two men?' They hadn't been able to dispute that, which had given her extra confidence. 'Doesn't matter how many fake identities you produce, David. These are women who've spent their entire adult lives, maybe longer, being exploited by blokes. Why would they tell you two anything?'

As far as Anushka was concerned, it was a damn good idea.

Drive back to Chatham, hang out around Keppel Hall and other red-light areas, get talking to some of the girls who stood on street corners. Maybe even lie to smooth the way for herself. Tell them she'd been a friend of Oya Oyinola's. Perhaps explain that she didn't think the woman had been a victim of the Medway Slasher, that something else had been going on ... It could even be that Oya's killer was still walking the streets. Surely that would generate some intel?

'Nushka ...' David had said. 'If Freddie Martindale, who lived in that area for the last couple of years, couldn't learn anything of value, what makes you think *you* can?'

'Like I say, he was a bloke.'

'Yeah, but he was part of that world. They'd *know* he wasn't a copper – or a journalist.'

'So it's a "no"?' she'd said grumpily.

'Absolutely it's a "no",' David had confirmed. 'I'm not saying we won't do it at some point. It's a plan. But it can't happen tomorrow because I'm going to see Hannah Bulstrode, and Norm's following his own line of enquiry.'

'So you two get the good jobs while I'm left out.'

'You're not being left out,' Norm had said. 'We need you in the Shed tomorrow.'

'Why?' she'd demanded. 'Because I'm the woman!'

'Because you're our top techie,' David had replied. 'The printer's being delivered, and someone needs to set up the drivers on all the laptops, so that it can scan and print wirelessly.'

She'd fumed again at their apparent technophobia, especially as in David's case she suspected it was assumed (he was the one who'd installed the mini-spy software that had snagged Lampwick Lane, after all). But it had made no difference. Their decision was made.

Deep down, of course, Anushka had known that they weren't just displaying old-fashioned chauvinism. The 'techie-girl' thing was an excuse, but not because they mistrusted her gender. Because they worried about her lack of experience. When she'd first arrived at the *Essex Examiner* as a teenager on work experience, she'd been blown away by the hive-like atmosphere of the newsroom. David had been on general duties back then rather than a crime specialist, but was already a go-getter. She'd shadowed him on several different stories, everything from the dark and scary (the Borley Rectory-type haunting of an abandoned farmhouse), to the hilariously funny (a package delivered to the doorstep of a local council official, which began *whirring*, but when the Bomb Squad opened it, turned out to be a vibrator). She'd enjoyed every minute of that first week, but even more so the following one, which she'd spent with Norm, who at the time had been Features Editor. In her own words, in the intro to the first story that carried her byline, an interview with a former glam rock star of the 1970s, she'd 'never met so many fun and famous people in such a short period of time'. On return to the paper several years later, as a trainee reporter, Crime Beat had been up and running, and Anushka was even more impressed to learn about the sting by which David and Norm had snared Jack Pettigrew and his cronies.

She'd known from that first day in full-time employment that she'd wanted to be part of Crime Beat. Even though she had no experience, she'd cajoled Norm and David to take her on as an assistant. Eventually, with Stan Grimshaw's reluctant permission, they'd agreed, and to be fair to the guys, they hadn't used her simply to make the tea. They'd taken her on the job, given her her own research assignments, and most important of all, shared their contacts with her so that in time she could develop her own stories and investigations.

Of course, that incredible new career path had ended with the Martindale kidnapping.

To an extent, all their careers had.

David was given the heave-ho, Stan Grimshaw severely reprimanded and Norm kicked back to Features, while she, the trainee, was back making the tea.

So, no, she didn't feel that Norm and David's refusal to allow her to drive over to Chatham and try to make allies out of the working girls was out-and-out sexism. It was more that she still lacked the essential journalistic nous. On top of that, they were genuinely worried that it might be dangerous.

'Well, sorry gentlemen,' she said, getting her foot down. 'That's tough.'

Somehow she had to break some ground on her own. Had to show the guys that they could trust her. Otherwise there'd be no point even considering this new path when she already had a perfectly adequate job at Tesco.

A road sign flickered by on the left. It read:

Chatham 3

28

David never found trips down to Cornwall anything less than tiresome, especially at the height of summer, the traffic log-jammed at every point. If nothing else, though, at least he didn't see any more suspicious brown Toyotas in his wake, and on top of that, the weather was glorious. When he entered Cornwall itself, the undulating grasslands of Bodmin Moor rippled in the gold-hued heat, a vista broken only by the odd sentinel outline of a tor. The iconic Cornish villages of Helford Passage and Gweek were postcard-perfect and thronged with cheerful visitors. The holiday vibe would have got to David too had he not been focused on the job.

He still didn't know the exact location of the Bulstrode house, but Port Izal, on the Lizard Peninsula, had been easy enough to find online. The Travel Cornwall site had described it as 'an idyllic former fishing village, occupying a scenic coastal cliff location, famous for its steep central street, which plunges down to a small but busy harbour, and for the many pretty shops and cottages that line it on either side'.

He arrived around mid-afternoon, parking in a public car park at the top of the main street. There, he changed his T-shirt for a button-up, short-sleeved shirt, and added a clip-on tie. In a tourist info kiosk, he flashed his fake delivery driver ID to the young girl behind the counter, and told her that he had a package for the Bulstrode house.

She responded: 'Take the coast road. It's a five-minute

drive to White Horse Point. You can't miss it – there's only the Bulstrode house there.'

Deception again, he thought.

Though this time at least it was in a worthy cause.

The house itself was called White Horse Point. It didn't need a street number because as the Port Izal girl had said, it was the only habitation there.

It was every inch the palatial summer residence David had expected. Sitting at the extreme end of a private road, which ran for several miles through open grassland, it occupied a clifftop position, only the vast, aqua-blue expanse of the Atlantic beyond it. It comprised several whitewashed build-ings with pink pan-tiled roofs and a number of good-sized palm trees, all nestling behind a high whitewashed wall and a pair of even taller electrically operated gates.

David made no effort to ring the bell. Doubtless, it would be a security man who'd answer, and that would be the end of the matter. Instead, he pulled a quick, three-point turn, hoping to make it look as if he was lost, and headed back to the main road. As he did, he mulled over his position.

He felt it was more likely he'd get a hearing if he spoke to Hannah Bulstrode herself. He wasn't quite sure why. Whatever security team worked here, they'd be well in-formed about the way he'd fooled the minder at Rosehill all those years ago. But it wasn't just those guys that David suspected he'd need to be wary of. He barely knew Jason, Hannah's husband, but though the bloke hadn't looked like a hardcase, appearances could be deceptive, especially in the world of big business. As Senior Accountant at MDS, Jason Bulstrode was virtually running the company since Ralph

Martindale had succumbed to ill health. He'd be no slouch when it came to defending his own.

Was he the sort who'd jump to conclusions? Would he be so convinced the caller was up to no good that he'd have his men kick the irritating bastard off his property without even asking what he wanted? That didn't seem too likely. He'd surely want to weigh up what it was David said he was offering. But by the same token, David couldn't see the bloke allowing anyone near if they were going to upset his wife. And like any normal man, he'd be furious that his family had been followed to their holiday haven.

Before doing anything else, David opted to make a recce.

About a mile from the house, he pulled up on the side of the road. His car would be conspicuous, but it didn't look as if there was much traffic along here. And in any case, he had a cover story pre-prepared. He swapped his shirt and tie for a T-shirt and windbreaker, and replaced his trainers and jeans with all-weather leggings and a pair of walking boots. Mussing his hair and donning a pair of false glasses, he reached into a holdall and took out his camera with its super-powered telephoto lens. He'd used this on the job on a number of occasions, but this time it was a prop.

Outside, the warm sea breeze caressed him. There was no one and nothing in sight. He couldn't even see the main coastal road. With the camera strap looped around his neck, he set off on foot, heading back towards the coastline, but now over open grassland rather than along the road. The ground was baked dry, the vegetation thick and spiky. Every twenty yards, he stopped and lifted his camera, clicking non-existent shots of whatever seabird came into his eyeline. When the house reappeared, it was on the right. He veered further left, but not too far, as he needed to stay close enough to the property to check it out from the side and the rear.

It wasn't long before he was level with it, but he still couldn't see much. The ten-foot wall that fortified the frontal approach also circled around to the side. However, things changed when he reached the clifftop. He ventured the last few yards and found himself teetering above a sheer drop. A hundred feet below lay mountainous jumbles of seaweed-covered boulders. The ocean, normally a raging beast in this part of the world, was at peace, a glimmering cerulean blue, barely a hint of froth as it lapped and spilled through the rocks.

David raised his camera again, still feigning interest in the local wildlife. This was hardly difficult. There were any number of gulls, gannets and razorbills lofting by. It was a grand view all round. White Horse Point sat at the tip of a minor headland. From here, to the left, though it was several miles away, he could make out the harbour and harbourside buildings of Port Izal. Directly in front, the Atlantic extended to the far horizon, but on a day like today was dotted with leisure craft. To his right, some sixty yards off, he could now see the rear of the Bulstrodes' holiday premises.

It was impressive by any standards.

Whatever buildings comprised the property at the top of the cliff, there were more on the way down. A flight of concrete steps, with a handrail attached, descended steeply from one cliff-face platform to the next, on each one of which whitewashed outhouses were located. One particularly large one, about halfway down, boasted a huge set of panoramic windows, with sliding glass doors in the middle, and a balcony in front, on which garden furniture was arranged. David imagined that it was a kind of sunroom;

there was probably plusher furniture inside, perhaps a bar and billiards table. Other smaller buildings looked equally cosy; guest rooms, maybe, complete with beds and en-suites.

At the bottom, the property had its own quay, a flat concrete platform extending out into the sea, where two speedboats were tethered.

All of that was interesting enough, but something else now caught David's attention. Down on the waterside, he spotted a sun-bronzed body, naked except for a pair of green bikini pants, lying on a lounger.

'Hannah?' he whispered.

He raised the camera, adjusting the telephoto lens. She lay face-down, glistening with sun oil, her hair hanging to one side in a tawny, sweat-damp mop.

'You there!' came a gruff Cornish voice.

David turned abruptly, still with the camera to his eye. His vision filled with a frowning, bearded face. He dropped the device to his chest.

The man approaching along the clifftop from the house wasn't quite as close as the telephoto lens had made it seem, about thirty yards off, but he was already menacing. Balding on top but with a thick red beard and moustache. Though somewhere in his forties, his hefty, over-muscled physique all but burst from his light grey polo shirt and white slacks.

'What are you doing here?' the man, who was obviously a security guard, demanded.

David put on a broad Lancashire accent. 'I'm on my holidays. What's it got to do with you?'

'I asked what you're doing, not why you're here.'

'What does it look like I'm doing, chief?'

The man came on fast, face reddening. 'Don't get funny with me, mate. This is private land.'

David glanced around. '*This* is?'

'I presume that's your Fiesta back there?'

'And?'

'It's parked on a private road. Did you not see the sign when you turned in?'

'Just because you put a sign on that road … does that mean you own all this land as well?'

'I'm not debating it with you.' The security man was genuinely angry. 'Get your gormless arse back to your piece-of-shit motor, and get on your way!'

David didn't want to overplay his hand. He edged in the direction of his vehicle. But it often paid to stay in character. 'I bet you were one of those locals who were telling tourists to keep the fuck away during the Covid crisis, weren't you?' he sneered.

'Move it!'

'And then whinged for England when all your bars and restaurants had to close.'

'Move it now!'

'Fucking yokel.'

The security man lurched towards him, so he turned and walked quickly away. When he'd covered thirty yards, he glanced back. The man had stopped and was watching him with hands on hips. Clearly it had been the correct decision not even attempting to reach Hannah Bulstrode through her security detail. Not that it mattered. David now had a better plan.

29

When Anushka found a quiet side street, she parked her Fiat and sat nervously.

Now that she was here, the reality of what she'd done was kicking in. From the outset, she'd opted to 'dress down', donning jeans, trainers and a well-worn T-shirt. She also had a scruffy anorak and one of her older handbags, inside of which she stowed a small amount of money and her *Essex Enquirer* business card. None of this made her feel armour-plated. However, she commenced strolling, and at first Keppel Hall didn't feel especially risky. The buildings around here were old and scabby, some disused, but mid-afternoon had felt as if it might be a relatively safe time.

'Them jeans touch where they fit, don't they, love?' shouted a fat, bald-headed man, his unbuttoned shirt showing multiple neck chains, as he sat on the wall opposite. He had two equally disreputable-looking characters alongside him. All three were eating bags of chips.

Anushka strolled on, undeterred. She had to come back from here with something. Norm and David would have words to say as it was, but particularly if this trip proved fruitless.

The first person she approached was a shapely blonde, whom she'd glimpsed swaying down an alley wearing a short denim skirt, thigh boots and a strappy top. Anushka hurried to catch up, only for the girl to swing around. Up close, she wasn't even glamour-girl sexy, with a thin, pinched face, too-heavy make-up and dry, bottle-bleached hair.

'Sorry to scare you,' Anushka said. 'Can I talk to you for a minute?'

The girl regarded her suspiciously.

Anushka dug into her bag, realising that she should have had her ID in hand already.

'I can jill you off,' the girl said, her accent Geordie. 'Cost you fifty.'

'Oh, no ...' Anushka found herself blushing. 'I'm not looking for sex ...'

'Don't waste my fucking time, then. Bitch.' The girl spun and strode away.

Anushka watched her go. The girl halted at the next street corner, where another similarly clad woman stepped out and spoke to her, the pair of them glancing back along the alley. Anushka headed the other way. When she looked back a half-minute later, one of them was on the phone.

The working girls would have learned that she was on the plot at some point, she supposed.

She wandered the maze of alleys, again spying women hanging around in ones or twos, but this time she avoided them, only finding what she was looking for when she spotted the neon glow of a gaudy shopfront.

As a junior on Crime Beat, she remembered hearing David comment how the sex-for-sale industry had changed beyond recognition since the advent of the internet. Porno cinemas, for example, no longer existed, while sex shops were often fronts for so-called 'interactive services'. These would be organised operations, she reasoned, so, even though they wouldn't necessarily be any more co-operative, they'd probably be safer for her to poke her nose into.

This first premises was every bit as seedy as she'd imagined, comprising a single garishly lit room, its floor made from grubby lino, its walls lined with shelves on which imported magazines were visible. Four or five men were browsing, but the moment Anushka joined them, they scurried out of the shop, heads down.

'Fantastic, yeah!' said the Fagin-type character with the long hair and sunken eyes, who sat behind a high counter. He spoke with a near-incomprehensible accent. 'You tarts not know to come through back door.'

Anushka was caught off balance. 'I'm sorry, I ...'

'You here about job?'

'No, I'm sorry ... I'm ...'

'So if you not selling, why you here ... buying?'

'Certainly not.'

'Then get out!' He pointed at the door. 'I know you feminist people. Stop honest man like me make honest living, and then go home and drop knickers for husband's camera ... show every wanker online what you got! You already cost me fortune! Get the fuck out!'

She scampered out, cheeks burning. No one around here who'd seen or heard the kerfuffle was likely to care. But that was the second time today she'd been aggressively insulted, which was twice more than it happened during her average working day. For this reason, Anushka wasn't focused on where she was headed, not that she knew the district anyway, and before she'd realised what she was doing, she was following a side passage with dirty flagstones underfoot and brick walls to either side. As this one had an arched roof, it was darker than any of the previous backstreets. In addition, there was an even darker recess about twenty yards ahead on the right. Anushka veered left to avoid passing it too closely, but when she was still ten yards away, a figure stepped out and looked at her.

A figure wearing jeans, a dark hoodie top with the hood pulled up, and a red leather gimp mask. The mouth was closed behind a zip-fastener, but the eye slots, which also had zips on them, were open. And the eyes behind these pierced her with their intensity.

Anushka came to an automatic dead-stop.

The figure didn't move, just remained where it was, watching her.

Slowly, heart banging, she backtracked.

Still it didn't move.

When twenty yards away, she turned and walked swiftly in the other direction, only risking a backward glance when she was clear by maybe forty or fifty yards.

The figure had either withdrawn or she'd lost it in the shadows. She didn't care, she kept walking. When she passed the shop she'd been thrown out of, she could hear Fagin's evil twin still ranting and raving inside. She glanced back again.

No one was following her, but still she kept walking.

30

The atmosphere at Port Izal harbour was again one of lively holiday, the bars and eateries fronting onto the quayside and the craft shops and water-sports kiosks thronging with visitors, the air ringing with a good-natured gabble of voices from all over. It might once have been a fishing village, but the many boats bobbing at anchor now were of the leisure variety, most of them for hire, and David, who, thanks to happier times during which he'd enjoyed several adventurous holidays with Karen and the kids, already held a basic navigation certification, had no trouble acquiring one for the afternoon.

It was a small motorboat with a 150-horsepower outboard engine and was ideal for exploring the coves and zawns of the Cornish coast. Of course, plenty time had elapsed since David had sailed solo on the open sea, so he couldn't pretend that he wasn't nervous. If nothing else though, the safety instructions were straightforward, mainly ensuring that he wore a lifejacket, while motoring across the harbour was a doddle; all he had to do was follow a straight route defined by red and green buoys. However, when he left the harbour, the swell increased; it wasn't a rough day but he was on the Atlantic.

At least his boat, the *Nep-Tune*♫, handled as easily as the hire office had said it would. Within a few minutes, he was easing his way at thirty-five knots in a southerly direction, following the cliff wall. White Horse Point was already visible, the house of the same name a small but impressive fixture on the jutting promontory's highest point. The problem now was how best to approach the miniature harbour at the foot of it. Because if the Bulstrodes' men were watching the sea as well as the land, wouldn't they spot him from some distance? And if it was the same guy who'd warned him off before, there was every likelihood David would be recognised. He'd changed his clothes since then, now wearing shorts and a loose-fitted vest, but if the guy had his own telephoto lens, he'd still identify the snooper from the clifftop.

All David could do, he decided, was hold a straight line as he boated past, swinging towards the White Horse Point landing area at the last possible minute. He veered a little closer to land beforehand, but could still see no obvious activity on the house's sunbathing platform, which sat at two o'clock from him and was soon no more than a hundred yards distant.

At three, he'd swing in.

Another minute passed, David watching the stairway leading up to the main building. When he glanced down again, the fair-haired woman wearing green bikini bottoms was visible, still lying face-down.

'Here goes nothing,' he muttered, rolling the wheel to starboard.

The swell reduced as he approached, the wind dropping, the intense heat of the afternoon striking him. He was about fifty yards from the landing area when he observed the two craft tilting at their moorings. While he was riding a motorised tub with an upper limit of fifty knots, these things were rather different, possessing the sleek outlines, twin engines and predatory air of high-powered speedboats.

For some reason, that unnerved him.

He was now only thirty yards out. The woman, who looked as if she'd been half asleep, levered herself up on her elbows, brushing hair out of her eyes and fitted on a pair of sunglasses. David cut his engine, trusting that his momentum would propel him forward, but hoping that it wouldn't take him too close as that might constitute a genuine intrusion.

He stood up, swaying, one hand gripping the wheel.

'Mrs Bulstrode!' he shouted. 'It's David Kelman. I need to speak to you.'

The woman pivoted around at the waist.

David shouted again. 'I don't mean to cause you any problems...'

She spotted him, and was visibly shocked, jerking her entire body around as she sat bolt-upright, baring her breasts in the process.

'Shit!' David said. 'It's me! David Kelman! I didn't want to...'

She screamed, and he realised that he'd made a terrible mistake. Because so swiftly did she move to cover up with a towel that her sunglasses flew off, and he saw that it wasn't Hannah Bulstrode at all. It was a much younger woman, no more than eighteen. She screamed again.

'Please!' David shouted. 'Please... I didn't mean...'

On the next level up, a young guy had emerged from one of the small outhouses. He had slicked fair hair, and wore white deck shoes, white trunks and a white hoodie zipped open on a bare, muscular chest and washboard stomach. He immediately took in what was happening, leaning forward over the barrier.

The girl wasn't screaming anymore, but calling for assistance, shouting: 'There's a pervert!'

On the level above the young man, an older figure came out onto the sunroom balcony.

David recognised him as Jason Bulstrode.

He wore an open Hawaiian shirt and slacks, and had a cocktail in his hand. He banged the drink onto a table and adjusted his glasses to glare at the intruder. David didn't wait to see any more. With luck, the myopic Jason hadn't recognised him, so he hit the ignition, the *Nep-Tune♫*'s motors churning to life, spinning the wheel as he tried to turn it around.

'Gideon, get hold of the peeping bastard!' Jason Bulstrode roared.

David glanced back as he motored away. The younger guy, Gideon, was already hurrying down the steps to the landing area. David had initially made him for the sunbathing beauty's other half, but now it seemed more likely that he worked here. Was he yet another of the Bulstrodes' endless cadre of security men?

'See if he's got a camera!' Jason Bulstrode shouted. 'Zak . . . *Zak!*'

David glanced back and saw that the angry homeowner had turned and was calling indoors.

'All I need,' David chunnered, now on a straight course for the distant outline of Port Izal. '*All I bloody need!*'

The engine was grinding. When he glanced at its gauge, the *Nep-Tune♫* was doing its top speed. And yet it felt as if it was covering no distance at all. Behind him, alarmingly close, came the deep belly-growl of two infinitely higher horsepower engines.

31

On the phone the previous evening, Maxine Mulgrave, Governor of HM Prison Brancaster, had sounded amused. 'You want to include James Lynch in a book about Essex VIPs?'

'That makes it sound a bit more frivolous than it is,' Norm had replied. 'When I was Features Editor on the *Essex Examiner*...'

'I'm well aware who you are and what you did, Mr Harrington.' Her delivery was slow, her tone so stern that it made him feel as if he'd been caught mucking about at the back of the class. 'What I don't understand is how someone who wrote articles about pop stars and celebrity chefs could possibly have interest in a serial murderer.'

'During my journalistic career, I've interviewed all kinds of people who made the headlines. It wasn't just the lighter end of the market. We had the actor Charles Bulford... you know, the one who almost drank his career away and then fought his way back to fame and fortune in his seventies? We had Danny Ricketson, the striker who started at Southend, transferred to Liverpool and then suffered a career-ending injury a month after he'd been selected for England. All these people had dark stories to tell...'

'With all respect, Mr Harrington, these people, while they might have seen hard times, were essentially on the right side of civilisation. None were even remotely in the same category as James Lynch.'

'It takes all sorts, Governor Mulgrave. Essex, like any other part of the country, boasts the good, the bad and the ugly. James Lynch has a place in our history, like it or not.'

'James Lynch was known as the Medway Slasher. That's because most of his murders occurred in Kent.'

'But two of them didn't. They were in Essex. And Lynch himself was born in Harlow ...'

The fact they'd responded to his email overnight, when he'd expected that it would take days, had encouraged him. If nothing else it meant that the authorities at Brancaster were at least intrigued by the prospect of his visit. And Norm knew why.

'It might also interest my readers,' he'd said, 'if I spoke to Lynch about his experience of life in custody. I mean, Brancaster has a fearsome reputation. And yet very few commentators will have the first clue what it's actually like inside.'

She'd said nothing, simply listened.

'Even by Category A standards, it houses the worst of the worst, and accordingly the regime you supervise, by repute at least, is tough. What I could maybe investigate is – how tough? For example, I don't believe that conditions inside Brancaster are even close to being as brutal as some rumour-mongers insist. I'd imagine that, considering the convicts in your charge are all lifers, it would be in the interest of you and your officers to be even-handed. You have to live with these people after all.'

He'd waited tensely, hoping that he wasn't dangling too obvious a carrot.

HMP Brancaster, or Gull Rock, had terrifying renown. Britain had no death penalty, but most of the inmates there had no hope of release. Not only were they all lifers, in many cases they'd had tariffs imposed, minimum sentences to be served: thirty years, forty years, even fifty, while in several notorious cases no parole date would ever be granted at all. Horror stories had thus spread far and wide about a regime of ultimate punishment, the damned souls trapped there suffering as they did in no other prison in the UK...

A sharp electronic buzz broke Norm from his reverie. He peered up the towering slab of riveted steel that was HM Brancaster's inner gate.

He huddled deeper into his anorak, not that it was offering great protection against the swirling gusts of rain, and glanced irritably at the heavy cloud cover as another zigzag of lightning split it end-to-end. To think that all the way north from Colchester he'd seen nothing but blue skies and summer sun. How quickly, as he'd neared his destination, all that had changed.

With a hefty *clunk*, a single-door section of the gate swung inward.

Norm stepped through into semi-darkness. Bare brick walls stood to either side; damp paving stones lay under his feet. He pulled back his hood and unzipped his anorak as two unsmiling officers emerged from a side office, checked him over with a portable metal detector and then subjected him to a vigorous body search. He'd already been advised not to bother bringing a notebook or pen, as both would be taken off him. Instead, he'd equipped himself with his Dictaphone, which, despite having told the authorities about it beforehand, the officers regarded with grave suspicion before handing it back without comment.

One of them withdrew into his office, while the other indicated that Norm should accompany him. They left the gatehouse, passing along a covered corridor, on top of which the rain thundered. Through its high letterbox windows, he saw the glare of moving spotlights.

'This the way prisoners are brought in?' Norm asked.

The officer, a tall, angular, lugubrious sort, seemed surprised to have been addressed.

'They come in round the back, by secure transport,' he said. 'They only see this side of the prison if they're being released. And that almost never happens.'

'So, all this stark functionalism ...' Norm tried to sound as if he was being light-hearted. 'That's purely for the visitors?'

'Visitors?' The officer cracked a smile.

They came to another steel door, which swung open when the officer tapped in a key code. 'Through there. Surrender your valuables, and you'll be escorted to the Special Supervision Unit.'

'Special Supervision Unit?' Norm queried.

But the officer was already gone, headed back the way he'd come.

Norm passed through the next door and found himself in a small waiting area with a low ceiling, a row of chairs on the left and a wall of bricks painted gunmetal grey on the right. There was a hatch and counter, behind which sat another prison officer.

'I'll take charge of your valuables, sir,' the officer said. 'It's a straightforward precaution, just to make sure you don't accidentally leave anything around that one of our inmates can make use of. We're talking watch, keys, loose change, that sort of thing.'

Norm slipped everything into an envelope. 'I was told I could keep my Dictaphone.'

'That's fine, sir.'

The officer issued him with a receipt and a visitor pass inserted into a plastic sleeve. As Norm clipped this to his shirt, the next door slid open, admitting a black man in a neat three-piece suit rather than a prison officer uniform. He was somewhere in his mid-thirties, bespectacled and handsome.

'Mr Harrington?' He offered his hand. 'Jackson Clarke, Security Governor.'

'Thanks very much for having me,' Norm replied.

'Our pleasure. What do you think of us so far?'

'Everything feels very secure.'

'We can't afford it not to be.' Clarke smiled briskly. 'Right – one or two basics. Much of this you can file under common sense, but it's best if we go over it. When you speak to Lynch, it will be in the SSU's interview room. There are no tables in there, just chairs. All are fixed to the floor, while the chairs facing each other are seven feet apart, so, as Lynch will be shackled in place, there's no danger of him being able to reach you. That precaution is nullified, of course, if you approach him yourself. Don't do that under any circumstances.'

Norm didn't think he'd needed to be told that.

'If there's something you wish to show to him, a photo-graph or whatever, give it to me first and if it's appropriate, I'll do the necessary. You've nothing on you like a pen or notebook?'

'Just my Dictaphone.'

'Fully powered? It's best not to take anything in there like a spare battery. If you drop it and he gets hold of it...'

'Fully powered. I've got no spares.'

'You're a seasoned journalist, Mr Harrington, so I'm not presuming to tell you your job, but when you're in ordinary conversation with someone, I'm sure it's normal to make constant and prolonged eye-to-eye contact?'

Norm was puzzled. 'Well... yes.'

'In a prison situation that's a no-no as it can be deemed a challenge and might provoke an aggressive response. By the same token, constantly looking away might be deemed rude. As I say, Lynch will be securely shackled, but if you want his co-operation, it's best to find a point midway between the two.'

'I understand.'

'You know the interview's being recorded, and I'll be in the interview area with you at all times. We'll also have support staff in close proximity.'

'Fine.'

'Any questions?'

Norm couldn't help wondering how safe he was actually going to be with no one but this slim, besuited young man in the same room as James Lynch.

'You're not armed?' he asked.

'If there's ever a need for firearms in this prison, the police are called in. We don't deploy them ourselves. I'm assuming it's firearms you're referring to?'

'Well...'

'The disadvantages of keeping firearms here would out-weigh the advantages twenty-to-one. The danger of any of our inmates getting hold of a gun ...' The Security Governor shook his head. 'I mean there are plenty of men here who would kill each other the very first chance they got. And us, of course. And anyone who happened to be visiting at the time. Anyway,' he half smiled, 'time's getting on. Shall we go in?'

32

There had to be all kinds of freaks around here, Anushka reasoned. Fetishists who got their kicks from dressing up, play-acting. Hell, the figure in the red mask hadn't even needed to be a freak. It could be some bored everyman who'd bought it from the local bondage shop, something he could take home to liven things up in the bedroom for himself and his missus. Jumping out at a stranger like that had been a trial run, a bit of stupidity, a joke.

But even in the unlikely event that *had* been the case, Anushka was uneasy.

As she prowled one dingy street after another, she glanced continually over her shoulder. Thus far, however, the coast was clear, and she wasn't going to prove to David and Norm that she'd been wrong and they'd been right by scuttling home at the first sign of trouble. It wasn't as if the place itself was terrifying – this was an old part of town, there were lurid storefront displays and men around who eyed her in unsavoury fashion. But there were others here too who were clearly just passing through, carrying briefcases or chatting on their phones. When she heard what sounded like a rumble of thunder, she went into the next shop to avoid getting wet as much as to evade the attentions of an oddball in a mask.

Beyond the strips of ribbon covering the shop's entrance, she found herself in a dimly lit corridor leading towards a drab purple curtain. Muffled rock music pumped from deep within.

It wasn't promising, but outside she could hear that the rain had now started.

'Help you, love?'

She turned, shocked. A man leaned out of a nearby room, wearing pin-striped trousers, a waistcoat and an open-collared shirt. He was young, with short white-blond hair and bright blue eyes.

'Yes, I'm sorry, I'm a journalist.' She offered her card. 'Anushka Chawla. I'm with the *Essex Enquirer*.'

He waited for more.

'I ... I just wanted to ... I wondered if I could talk to some of the women who work here?'

Those blue eyes hardened. 'What makes you think there are women working here?'

Anushka was close enough to the purple curtain to be able to tell that the rock music coming from the other side had a raunchy vibe.

'Come on,' she said, humouring him. 'You're not telling me there's nothing going on back there? Why else would anyone come in here?'

He shrugged. 'OK, they're peepshow booths. There's nothing illegal about it.'

'I'm not saying there is. But we're putting a series of features together on all aspects of life on the Kent coast.'

'And why would that be of interest to the *Essex Enquirer*?'

'Erm, well, a lot of the girls you have here originally came from Essex.'

'Yeah? There was me thinking most of them were from Poland and Russia.'

'There are some from Essex. We know that...'

'And you're just popping round to see how they're getting on?'

'Look, cut me some slack, eh?' Anushka adopted a wearisome tone. 'I've been charged with finding Essex sex workers who've ended up on the Kent coast. We've got someone else tracking drug addicts, someone else talking to the homeless. We're doing a big story on the fallout.'

'Fallout of what?'

'Modern life. Essex has a rep for being one of the Home Counties. You know, prosperous, pretty. But we're on the trail of those who fell through the cracks.' She was making this up as she went along, she realised. 'Look, I didn't ask for this story.'

'I can see why.' He smiled like a cheeky schoolboy. 'Look, darling, I don't know whether we've got any Essex girls here or not. But we've got one or two blondes with nothing between the ears, so I suppose it's possible. Go through …' He indicated the curtain. 'Have a look round, chat to the girls in the rest room. We've nothing to hide.'

He slid back out of sight.

Heart thudding, Anushka progressed along the corridor. The music behind the curtain was quieter now, but sleazier. Then a bass bellow of laughter sounded, followed by a muffled female yelp.

She halted.

Another laugh followed, equally loud and harsh. Anushka's skin tightened.

A third laugh. Slower, a sinister version of the Sid James cackle.

She turned and strode towards the front door. As she passed the room, she heard the blond guy come out again.

'It's all right!' he said. 'What's the matter?'

She staggered outside into a downpour. It was still officially daylight, but the sky was slate-grey, fracturing repeatedly as lightning sizzled across it. The rain fell incessantly, those few out and about flitting past like hooded phantoms. Anushka pulled her own hood up as she scampered from one backstreet to the next. She wasn't sure where she was going, but she knew that she'd had enough of this neighbourhood. She turned another corner blindly, hurrying along the next narrow street at random, head bowed, only to realise that the car parked just ahead on the left was her own black Fiat.

Relief shuddered through her. She prepared to cross over – and halted at the sight of the darkened recess on the other side of her car. It was too dim to see into, but suddenly she was certain that she'd detected movement there.

Probably just some homeless guy ...

But her gaze narrowed as she tried to scrutinise the upright shape in that unlit cubby hole. Waiting, or so it seemed. More lightning crackled. So short-lived that it barely illuminated anything. But not so short-lived that something shiny and red didn't briefly glint in that recess.

Anushka retreated.

Slowly at first, but when she'd backed away five or six yards, she spun around and walked stiffly in the opposite direction.

33

At first David appeared to be doing better than he'd expected. Possibly it was the coastal current or the turning tide, but though the twin-engine powerboat had made a great, ponderous show of reversing away from its mooring, eating up the time while he'd skipped away over the rolling blue hummocks, he'd still expected it to surge around in a tight circle and come revving after him at mind-boggling speed. And yet, he was now about halfway back, and while it was gaining, it was still a significant distance behind. Fifty knots was faster than David had realised. He was having to squint in the headwind and the blasts of sea spray.

But then another problem arose.

He glanced up towards the coastal clifftop, and a couple of times, at points where the road came close to the cliff's edge, thought he glimpsed an orange sports car bulleting along. It wasn't possible to work out who was at its wheel, but an inner voice told him it was likely to be the bearded guy with the bad attitude. At that speed, it was impossible to imagine that the bastard wouldn't get to Port Izal ahead of him. And with the powerboat at his rear, David would be caught in a pincer.

He throttled the outboard for all it was worth. The 150-horsepower engine ground and whined, the vessel jolting and leaping. However, the harbour drew steadily closer, the hulls of its leisure craft sparkling white and gold beyond the granite bulwark of its quayside. He might make it into that lower section of town where the pubs and bars and shops were, before Growler from the cliff edge appeared at the top. That meant that if he could duck indoors somewhere, or down a side passage, he could still evade capture.

And yet another voice in his head asked why he was running at all. He'd been trying to speak to Hannah Bulstrode, stumbling upon the half-naked girl by accident. It wasn't as if he'd even been trespassing. The problem was, of course, that he could try to explain his way out of it, but those security goons wouldn't understand what he was talking about, and wouldn't care. The whole thing had gone belly-up, so it was best to run, regroup and try to work out a different angle of approach.

He glanced behind again, and was stunned to see how closely the powerboat had stolen up. It was no more than two hundred yards to his rear. When he got into the harbour, there wouldn't be much time to tie the *Nep-Tune♫* up and return the key. He was going to have to dump the bloody thing and run.

He glanced backward again, and already his opponent had closed the gap to one hundred and fifty yards. At least now David could see who was on board – it was the young guy with slicked fair hair, white trunks and the white hoodie. Gideon, was it? He obviously thought he looked cool, standing tall in the cockpit, one hand on the wheel. He'd even donned a pair of mirror shades.

David decelerated as the harbour mouth came up at eleven o'clock, with one hand unstrapping his lifejacket. He dropped it onto the deck, and then swung the wheel 90 degrees.

Doubtless there were all kinds of rules about entry and

exit procedure at Port Izal, which lane to use and so on. The harbourmaster would likely be a stickler. Probably some old seadog who'd spent his life following strict regulations and now got his own back by imposing them. But David didn't have time to worry. He veered left towards the nearest empty mooring. As he'd expected, there was a gruff shout. He paid it no heed, cutting the engine and gliding in the last thirty yards, coming up hard against the jetty, the *Nep-Tune♫*'s nose caroming sideways off its wooden under-structure.

David dropped the ignition key on the seat and climbed the ladder. There was another shout, but David didn't look around as he hurried along the jetty, breaking into a trot when mounting the stone steps onto the quayside, jogging towards the buildings. He slowed again as the crowd thickened, and soon was threading among tourists, glancing repeatedly over his shoulder. On the third occasion, he saw the powerboat easing through the harbour entrance. The kid at the helm didn't look so cool now. He was hunched over the wheel, and had taken off his shades as he scanned the mass of people.

David slowed down to make himself less conspicuous. Rounding the north-east corner of The Sea Shanty pub, he entered the lower end of Port Izal's main street and relaxed. He was now out of view from the harbour, though he had to keep going. Ahead, the street rose up and up, becoming steeper and narrower. It was pedestrianised, so, from halfway up, it became stepped terracing rather than actual road. Many of the side passages winding away between the shops and cottages were also stepped. But again, the whole town was crowded with people.

David peered up. Growler had to be up there somewhere. In fact, he'd be on his way down by now, and on a thoroughfare as busy as this, they wouldn't necessarily see each other until the very last minute. David could make his way up incrementally, calling constantly into shops, only leaving each one when the coast was clear. But he didn't want to be hanging around here. Suppose Jason Bulstrode had got the law involved? David hadn't committed any crime, but the bastard had clout. Suppose he'd reported their intruder as a peeping tom, or even worse, a stalker? That would be the end of David's attempt to reinvent himself, of the *Essex Enquirer*, of everything.

His gaze roved left to right as he tried to devise a better plan, and fell on something he hadn't expected. An arrow-headed signpost hung on the wall of a cut-through on the right.

Lifts

At first he was confused, but then the meaning struck him.

He hurried along the alley, expecting something scenic, and when he got to the end, he wasn't disappointed. On the north side of Port Izal, a beach ran along the footing of the coastal cliff. It was pebbly rather than sandy, but there were lots of people using it. The cliff itself was impressive, a sheer granite face broken by tufts of scrub vegetation, rising a majestic hundred or so feet. Hugging the town close, however, two parallel railway tracks emerged from a small platform at the foot of the cliff, and ran upward at a steep incline to a similar installation at the top. David had heard about this sort of thing before: the two passenger vehicles currently in motion on the tracks – one heading up, one heading down, both in perfect synch – were connected together by steel cables and counterbalanced by water tanks built into their undercarriages. It was a Victorian-age design and so ingenious that it would function under its own gravity all day.

He hurried along a wooden footbridge, which brought him onto the platform from its south end. Here, a station guard type in a blue and yellow floral jacket sold him a ticket, and he climbed aboard the right-hand lift, which had just docked.

Like a small version of an old-fashioned London bus, its boarding area was at the rear and open to the elements, but inside it looked more like a cable car: rectangular in shape, about fifteen feet by ten, and occupied by a horseshoe of leather-covered seats. There was seating space for about ten, while the narrow aisle down the middle provided standing room for about six or seven more. At present, David was alone on board, but he remained standing, nervously watching the platform through the open boarding area. On one hand, a couple of extra people coming and joining him could be good; it would make things look normal. But on the other, he couldn't be one hundred per cent sure that it had been Growler driving that orange sports car, so someone else getting aboard might mean they were onto him and he wouldn't realise it.

With a lurch, the vehicle commenced its ascent, which meant that David had the entire uphill journey to himself. On reflection, that was for the best. Most likely it *had* been Growler in that car, and he'd now be making his way down Port Izal's main street, searching every doorway and recess, while David rode in the other direction.

It wasn't a quick journey, however. The two vehicles were powered by hydraulics, so it wasn't even as quick as one of those old-fashioned cage lifts. He walked along the aisle to the upward-facing window.

And stiffened with shock.

Growler was waiting at the top with arms folded.

David was briefly dumbfounded.

The bastard would snag him as soon as he got off. He supposed that he might be able to dodge around him and leg it. But where to? Into the town car park? Growler would give chase, and in the kerfuffle as David had to unlock his Fiesta, would catch up easily.

He was going to get nabbed.

There'd be no other outcome.

Unless...

The ascending lift was now almost halfway up the cliffside rails, which meant that in the next twenty seconds or so it would bypass the descending lift. David dashed to the back of the vehicle and onto its boarding area, leaning out on the left side of it to look uphill, and saw that the other lift was only metres away as it glided down towards its twin.

There was perhaps a yard of space between the two of them.

If he was actually going to jump from one to the other, he'd need to know the exact moment when the two vehicles perfectly aligned, and he wouldn't *really* know that until it happened, and even then it would be for less than a second.

Good God, if he got it wrong...

He backed to the other side of the boarding area to give himself a run. Glancing back through the interior windows, he saw the downward lift coming alongside. He charged forward just as the other lift's boarding area emerged into view, launching himself bodily. If he'd miscalculated, and landed on the rails, he'd fall clean through and crash fifty feet down the cliff-face. He was in the air for less than a moment, but it still seemed a lifetime before he landed squarely, like a cat, on the opposite boarding area.

He got to his feet, sweating. Then glanced inside the vehicle. An elderly couple were riding down, staring at him with slack-jawed disbelief.

'*Where Eagles Dare* eat your heart out, eh?' he said, swaying past them along the aisle to the front of the vehicle.

He peered up through its window. The top platform was receding upward again, but Growler was still visible. Whereas he'd previously been relaxed and comfortable, now he gazed downhill in something like stupefaction, before vanishing hurriedly from sight. He'd descend by the main street this time, no doubt jostling his way through the crowd, which meant that, when David got to the bottom, he'd have to move sharply.

He lumbered back onto the boarding area. The platform at the bottom was ascending with painful slowness. Thirty yards ... twenty-five ... twenty ...

'Come on, come on!' David muttered.

Surely Growler couldn't get down there ahead of him. But it was taking a long time.

Fifteen yards ... ten ...

David scanned the platform, wondering what he'd do if he saw Gideon from the powerboat waiting. But there was only a young family present.

He jumped. He was still short of the buffers, but landed upright, hitting the concrete running, heading leftward along the platform and taking the wooden footbridge across to the same alley as before. At the far end of it, he paused, glancing uphill. Huge numbers were in the process of surging up and down the main street. It would be difficult spotting even a brute like Growler in such a mob, but David reckoned that if he could get to the other side, there'd be a different route to the top. Port Izal wasn't just a harbour and shopping street. There were layers of residential terraces on the south side. With luck he could work his way up via backstreets, side-passages and the like.

Head down, he crossed. There was an entry opposite, leading away between shopfronts with mullioned windows. He reached it and kept on walking. The shop on his left sold antiques; the one on his right appeared to be an art gallery. David feigned interest in the latter before continuing, relaxing as the crowd fell behind him. The alley reached a point where entries led off in different directions. A woman in flipflops, shorts and a strappy top passed him, looking cross. A sniffling child scuttled after her.

David shook his head. Everything was so damn normal here. It seemed ridiculous that he'd got involved in the thing he had. Then a foot scraped behind him. Inordinately close.

He half turned. To see that Gideon had had the temerity to put his shades back on before he lunged. It wasn't a punch, more an attempted grab. David was able to duck underneath it, and by instinct rather than intent, slam a right hook into the side of the young fella's ribs.

He thought of Gideon as young, but up close he looked to be in his mid twenties. Even then, he lacked combat experience. He staggered away gasping, holding his side, looking as shocked as he was hurt, before coming back with a haymaker. David blocked it with his left, drove in with his knee, and as Gideon doubled, slammed an elbow into the nape of his neck, sending him sprawling to the cobbles.

David didn't consider himself a great fighter. But with

fitness had come greater awareness, speedier hand-eye co-ordination, and lean, taut muscles.

'You came at me first.' He backed away. 'If you know what's good for you, stay down.'

Gideon *was* staying down. He was conscious because he moved slightly, but he lay face to the floor, groggy. David wheeled around to walk away … and caught a slap to the side of the head that sent him staggering. He bounced from the nearest mullioned window before he was able to look around.

It was Growler, coming straight at him, again attempting to grapple rather than strike. David tried to dodge, but was grabbed by the vest. Another hefty slap swept down, but he got a head butt in first, crunching the big guy's nose. Growler looked stunned, allowing David to tear himself loose and swing back in with a right to the guy's belly then a left-handed uppercut.

Neither seemed to make any difference.

With casual ease, Growler punched David on the point of the chin. He tottered backward, hitting the shop window a second time, his world spinning. The big guy came again, but David only evaded him by falling over and scrabbling away on all fours. He struggled back to his feet, but his legs were so shaky that they carried him sideways across the passage towards the art gallery entrance, just in time to almost collide face-on with a female customer as she emerged from the premises. He halted at the last second.

And found himself gawking into the astonished face of Hannah Bulstrode.

34

In some ways, James Lynch was exactly what Norm had expected.

In others, not so much.

The original police mugshots had depicted lean, aquiline features, a sharp nose, narrow eyes, a crooked smile. Thick black hair, damp with sweat and mopped back so that it looked greased.

He'd almost been handsome. If you went for the predatory type.

Today, they brought him into the interview area via a passage directly facing the chair Norm had been allocated. All the way along it, a succession of barred gates slid open and closed as the inmate approached. When Lynch entered the room, he was escorted by two prison officers and wore a distinctive high-security green and yellow boiler suit. His hands were cuffed in front of him but also linked to a leather belt. His feet were not shackled, but the overall effect of his encumbrance saw him hunched between his two guards and shuffling rather than walking.

Everything about Lynch's advance down that passage had suggested murderer, madman, monster. And yet, when he seated himself in the bolted-down chair seven feet in front of Norm, and his tethers were locked to a steel ring set in a concrete square underneath, he seemed less than remarkable.

He wasn't a big man, but neither did he resemble the

sneering, feral vampire in his arrest photo. His hair was cut very short, which revealed that his front hairline had receded. He'd also put weight on. He was pudgier-featured than Norm remembered.

Once the prisoner was secure, the two officers withdrew, which left just Norm and Security Governor Clarke, who stood about ten yards away. Aside from the chairs, the room was bare: brick-built, again painted that soul-sapping gun-metal grey. There were no windows.

While Norm placed his Dictaphone upright on the floor, Clarke addressed his charge. 'You know the situation, James. Mr Harrington is compiling a book about famous people from Essex. And if you give an inoffensive account of yourself today, you might make the final edit.'

Norm was amused. Clarke was laying the ground rules for the prisoner's behaviour, but he was also, either by intention or habit, laying them down for the visitor too.

You will write 'inoffensive' material if you ever want to see it published.

Lynch stared at Norm with empty grey eyes. He was blank-faced, unreadable.

'How do you do?' Norm said.

'I'm very well, thank you,' the prisoner replied. He was soft-voiced and spoke with a faint rural accent.

'I'm Norman Harrington, and I'm interested to know all about you, Mr Lynch. Where you came from. What your upbringing was like … who you are.'

'Can I ask *you* a question first?' Lynch said.

'By all means.'

'How do you think it will be received, in this woke age, that when you publish your book about Essex celebrities and the light-hearted occasions during which you interviewed them, one chapter will be devoted to a man whose main interest in life was the sexual murder of women?'

'That will be down to me,' Norm replied. 'I'll need to balance the book responsibly.'

'With what? I imagine there'll be very few others in there whose main pastime was as distasteful as mine. Perhaps if you placed the scandalous homosexual affairs of Larry Nightingale at the front of the book, in advance of my own section, that will prepare your readers?'

Norm was intrigued. Lynch had done some research. Born in Southend, Larry Nightingale had been a popular comedian of the 1970s. His TV show had been notable for its sauciness and double entendres; those on the receiving end usually drawn from the stable of busty beauties that British television had produced by the bucket-load in that era. And yet Nightingale had long been gone from the public eye by the time Norm sought him for interview in the *Examiner* in the mid-1990s, blacklisted because of his previous brand of non-PC humour, and thus leading a sad, lonely life in a flat three streets from where he'd been born, the abode in which it was also revealed (despite his best efforts) that he'd had a number of assignations with male pick-ups.

'The late Larry Nightingale's secret gay life wouldn't be seen as scandalous these days,' Norm replied.

'Of course not,' Lynch said, in that strange soft voice of his. 'And yet conversely, your coverage of my murders will be looked upon with suspicion. Isn't the new public attitude to serial killers that they should be ignored? Denied the oxygen of publicity? And that to do otherwise would be an insult to their victims?'

'Unfortunately, the public, whatever they may say, are fascinated by murderers.'

'And which part fascinates them most? The horror and abuse endured by those murderers during their own childhoods, which duly turned them into devils capable of atrocious acts, or the atrocious acts themselves? Would your readers be more interested in knowing that I'd once been shaken to the core by the glimpse I had of my maiden aunt's stocking-tops when she was kneeling in church and was thus scarred for life in sexual terms, or in Sadie Johnson's desperate pleas for mercy as I dragged her by the hair into the woods at Gads, having already beaten her black and blue?'

'If you continue to be flippant, we won't get very far,' Norm said.

Lynch arched an eyebrow. 'You consider what I've just told you to be flippant?'

'You don't? Trying to claim that a glimpse of stocking ruined your life.'

'I said a glimpse of *my auntie's* stocking. You never saw her.'

Norm didn't laugh. 'I'll tell you what – forget your auntie, and forget Larry Nightingale. For real balance, how about I put you right at the back of the book, and Neil Lawson right at the front. Neil Lawson – do you remember him? A Romford boy. Became a hero during the *Herald of Free Enterprise* disaster. Made his body into a human bridge so that other passengers could cross over it to safety. Won the George Cross. There'll be no grey areas at all, then. Front of the book – the very best of us. Back of the book – the very worst.'

Lynch responded with a cool smile, though thanks to his crooked mouth, it was twisted. In tandem with his empty eyes, the effect was soullessly horrible.

'So, what do you think?' Norm asked.

The prisoner said nothing.

Norm shrugged. 'You don't need to speak to me if you don't want to. But I'm still going to write about you. The difference being that if you clam up now, you won't have any say in it.'

'So, you're pretending you're here to give *my* side of the story?' Lynch said. 'Warts and all? I'm sure that Jackson over there, and the Queen Bitch, who's no doubt watching through a live feed, will have expressly forbidden that.'

'The problem here, Mr Lynch, is not the Governor or her deputy,' Norm said. 'It's you. I've only been here a couple of minutes, and already you've tried to take control of the interview. Which simply isn't happening.'

Lynch glanced at the doorway, perhaps wondering if his best course of action would be to go back out. If he couldn't have things his own way in here, what was the alternative?

'Why don't we just talk?' Norm said. 'Man to man.'

Lynch smiled again. 'Pardon me, but you have the look of someone for whom phrases like "man to man" would have a special meaning.'

'And you'll never know one way or the other. Because we're not here to talk about me.'

'There's a lot of that goes on in here, you know ...'

Norm could sense Clarke shifting uncomfortably.

Lynch was aware of it too. 'It's no reflection on the regime. It's inevitable, in a world where men are cooped up together.' That twisted smile again. 'I could tell you some stories ...'

'No doubt,' Norm replied. 'But not today.'

There was a lengthy silence, before Lynch sighed and shrugged.

'In that case, I suppose you'd better ask me about the murders.'

'No.' Norm shook his head.

Lynch looked puzzled.

'I'm going to ask you about the victims.'

Lynch frowned. 'Sadly, my memory's sketchy on those details. You see, to me they were mere objects...'

'But they weren't to others,' Norm said. 'Lola Mackenzie – does that name mean anything?'

'Sounds Scottish.'

'She was, by family connection,' Norm said. 'But she never lived there and didn't have an accent. She was your fourth victim, but she'll be of interest to my readers because she came from Clacton. She was a shopworker and housewife originally, but her husband beat her and her two children, driving her to drink. Led to her getting arrested a few times. When her husband finally abandoned her, her children were taken into care. Lola, now a jobless alcoholic, slipped into prostitution. Finished up in Medway. Even so, she tried to see her two children whenever she could. Brought them presents on their birthdays and at Christmas. Couple of weeks before she met you, she'd enrolled with Alcoholics Anonymous.'

'Well, it wasn't working,' Lynch shrugged. 'The night I took her, she was rat-arsed.'

'So you *do* remember her?'

The killer gave a sheepish smile. *Hell ... you caught me.*

'Well, they say it's a long, hard road, beating addiction,' Norm said, 'but in Lola's case, her children will never know whether she'd have succeeded. You may recall that you murdered her on 6 July, but that her body wasn't discovered until after 5 November. Bonfire Night was another day Lola always tried to keep with her kids, usually bringing them a box of fireworks. This time she just didn't turn up.'

Lynch pondered. 'I imagine if those children led the life

you've described, terrible things would be fairly common-place for them. So, in truth, it might not have been as awful for them as it would have been for you or me.'

'That's an interesting way to rationalise it.'

'We must always look for silver linings if we can.'

'In the case of Briony Williams, there were few silver linings of any sort. Remember her?'

'As I've already intimated, I don't do names.'

'Briony was from Colchester, and was only twenty-four when she encountered you. She'd been in the sex trade since she was sixteen. She ran away from home at that age, when her father died and she didn't want to be left alone with her abusive, drug-addicted mother. First of all she got work as a so-called model, then in massage parlours, and eventually, when her own drug habits became overwhelming, as a street prostitute. It was a common enough story, but when she was young they said she was a promising artist. She used to take her paintbox and easel out to farms in the surrounding countryside and paint horses. At her funeral, one of her junior school teachers said that she was a bright and pretty girl, who always entered class with a smile, and that she'd possessed a remarkable talent ...'

Lynch yawned. 'Sorry, but as I say, I didn't know these creatures at the time and getting to know them now would serve no purpose.'

'It's that easy for you, is it?'

'It's easier if I don't waste time thinking about it. You look at me as if I repulse you, Mr Harrington, but why should I pretend I care? I'm never coming out of here, whatever I say.'

'So, basically you don't give a fig for any of the women you murdered?'

'That's a stronger way than I would put it, but—'

'What about Oya Oyinola?'

For half a heartbeat, the killer seemed discomforted. 'What about her?'

'I see you have no difficulty remembering that name?'

'It's ... unusual.'

'You flinched when I mentioned it.'

'I don't like being accused of things I haven't done.'

'You're maintaining that line?'

'Why would I not? As I say, I'm never coming out of here. Why should I lie about anything?'

'So the police framed you with that murder?'

'Again, that's a stronger term than I would use. The circumstances of that crime were very similar to mine.'

'Some would say identical.'

'You've heard of copycat killing?'

'Of course,' Norm said, 'but in the end, you pleaded guilty to it.'

Lynch nodded. 'On the advice of my defence team, who believed that if I admitted guilt across the board it might go easier for me at sentencing because I wouldn't have put Oya Oyinola's family, if any such persons could be found, through the agony of a trial. In the end, of course, it didn't, and I now carry the mark of Cain for a crime I didn't even commit.'

'Mark of Cain?' Norm was amazed by that choice of phrase. 'You seem particularly upset about *this* case, Mr Lynch?'

'How would you feel if someone committed a crime and you served their sentence for them?'

Norm was fascinated. While indifferent to any mention of Lola Mackenzie or Briony Williams, the killer had become agitated on hearing Oya Oyinola's name. He clearly did not want to be tarred with that poor woman's death.

'If it wasn't you,' Norm said, 'who was it?'

Lynch eyed him curiously. 'Are you investigating an un-solved murder now?'

Norm was caught on the hop. He sensed Jackson Clarke standing still by the wall, as if interested to hear his answer.

'Your … opinion,' Norm stuttered, 'on what sort of person might really be guilty would obviously be of interest to my readers.'

'I already told you. A copycat. Some pathetic inadequate too frightened of his own shadow to stand up and be counted.'

Norm didn't bother commenting that the act of stran-gling someone unconscious and then slitting them open from collar to crotch was not the sort of thing he'd readily associate with an everyday inadequate.

'But if you and your readers want a more specific answer,' Lynch said, 'I suggest you speak to Detective Jorgenson.'

'I'm sorry?' Norm couldn't pretend that he wasn't startled. 'Detective Jorgenson? You mean DI Tony Jorgenson?'

'Probably the same person. I can't recall what rank he held back then.'

'I, erm …'

'He was part of the police team who came to arrest me. And I told him at the time that I didn't murder Oya Oyinola. That I couldn't have.'

'What do you mean – *couldn't* have?'

Lynch smiled. 'And there was you, coming here all busi-nesslike, acting as if you knew so much and quite patently knowing very, very little.'

'You said *couldn't* have?'

'For your information, Oya Oyinola was murdered on the night of 15 December. That same night I spent in Romford, in the company of two workmates, Brian Fairclough and Chris Jaycox. We drank into the early hours, and all that time I never once left my friends' company.'

'And you told this to Tony Jorgenson?'

'I didn't just tell him – he made a point of writing it down.'

'And yet you were still charged with Oya Oyinola's murder?'

'You see?' Lynch lowered his voice, made a pantomime face. 'It's a conspiracy, I tell you.' He slumped back, looked tired. 'Some of it, at least.'

'But what did Fairclough and Jaycox have to say for themselves?'

'Oh, nothing.' Lynch smiled again. 'A couple of years after my conviction, I exchanged some letters with Brian Fairclough. And he confirmed that, despite what I'd said when I was arrested, no policeman ever came to interview either of them about the night of Oya Oyinola's murder. Not even Tony Jorgenson.'

35

'Mrs Bulstrode,' David said. 'I know you think I'm a lowlife, but do you honestly believe I'd come all the way to Cornwall just to play some silly game?'

'You said you had important information, Mr Kelman,' Hannah Bulstrode replied. 'For my ears only, you said. Otherwise I'd never have entertained inviting you into my car.'

He turned in the front passenger seat and glanced out through the silver-grey Land Rover Discovery's window. The Port Izal car park was crammed with people, mostly families heading back to their vehicles. Close by, two men stood unmoving. It was Growler and Gideon. Growler was still dabbing at his nose with a blood-blotted handkerchief. The pair of them fixed David with intense, hate-filled gazes.

'But I warn you, Mr Kelman,' the woman added, 'if this is another ruse ... if you're here purely to get some kind of interview ...'

'I don't need an interview from you, Mrs Bulstrode,' he said. 'I need a thumbs-up.'

Her brow creased. 'I beg your pardon?'

'Call it conscience,' he said. 'Call it guilt. But I'm determined to try and put right the wrong I facilitated. And I can't do that and be comfortable with it unless I have your permission.'

'My permission?' That seemed to bewilder her even more.

'It's going to involve me poking my nose into personal affairs, but this time I want you to know that it's for the right reason.'

'And when did you undergo this Road to Damascus transformation?'

'Eleven days ago, when I first heard *this*.' He held up his Dictaphone.

'And what, pray, is this?'

David took a breath before telling her about the box of paperwork he'd purloined from the bin at Rosehill, and the mobile phone inside it.

'You stole rubbish from our dustbin?' she interrupted.

'I'm not sure it could be classified as stealing, Mrs Bulstrode. You offered it to me, if you remember. But surely the main thing is the phone – and the fact that Jodie had left a message on it only two weeks earlier.'

She regarded him with slow disbelief. 'You ... you're saying you have evidence that my sister's still alive?'

'You tell me.' David hefted the Dictaphone again. 'This is the message. I recorded it hand-to-hand. For that reason, it's not great quality, I'm afraid.'

He played it, but her response wasn't what he'd hoped for.

'All these years,' she said, after he'd turned it off. 'All these years ... as hope diminished, gradually coming to accept that Jodie was dead, refusing to consider anything else ...'

'Was that not her voice?' he asked. 'Can't you tell?'

'I wish I could.' She glared at him. 'Don't you understand? This is my sister we're talking about. So I need to be certain. It can't be another vain hope.'

'Doesn't it at least sound like her?'

'Of course. It also sounds like a hundred other young women. You said so yourself, it's the recording of a recording.

278

The quality's terrible. And it isn't as if we haven't been the recipients of hoax calls before. Cruel buffoons claiming to have seen Jodie, even to have spoken to her.'

'But it was left on Freddie's phone. Surely that counts for something?'

'If so, why didn't Freddie himself do something with it?'

'He likely didn't even know it was there. He was living rough. The phone had probably been dead for ages.'

'And why would Jodie even have called Freddie? Why not someone like me?'

'I've tried to puzzle that out, but I've got no answer yet. That doesn't mean I *won't* get one, though.'

She glanced away, but the disdain for him had gone. Instead, she looked worried and hurt.

'Where's the phone now?' she asked.

'I gave it to the police. I had to. It would have made me an accessory to kidnapping.'

'When was this?'

'The first day I heard it. They obviously haven't been in touch with you yet?'

'Not yet.' Her expression became curious. 'Which is odd, wouldn't you say?'

He shrugged. 'The investigation's being handled by the Essex Cold Cases unit. It's headed up by DI Tony Jorgenson. He doesn't sit high in my estimation, to be honest. But even if he did, a crime from six years ago would be a low priority.'

She looked troubled again, as if she didn't know what to believe.

'I don't know if it'll help ...' David produced a notebook. 'But I've been investigating, and frankly, a whole series of unusual events have followed since that message was recorded, perhaps the most significant of which was the death of your brother.'

She closed her eyes at the mention of it.

'That's another tragedy I feel responsible for,' he added.

'Well, my God. If the cap fits ...'

'I know, but *I'm* not the one who actually killed him.'

'You realise Freddie was never the same again after the way you tricked him?'

'What I mean is – someone else killed him. It wasn't suicide.'

A protracted silence followed, during which Hannah Bulstrode went through a gamut of emotions: first contempt, then confusion, then grief.

'I'm sorry if this is upsetting,' David said, 'but I honestly don't believe that Freddie jumped off that roof. I have it on reasonable authority that he felt he was close to discovering something, and it's my conviction that, whatever that some-thing was, it led to his murder.'

She didn't respond, so he continued, explaining about the girl nicknamed Squeaky, what it was she'd said that Freddie did all day, the copious notes he scribbled, his odd comments about someone called Saint Bridget who might have encountered Jodie at the yacht club, and then about the three people who came looking for Freddie, maybe as a result of this.

'You understand what I'm telling you?' David said. 'This girl, Laura Reynoldson, or Yvonne, or whatever her real name is – she was certain that a trio of killers, two men and a woman, did this thing to your brother. And this might be a spurious point to make, but wasn't it supposedly two men and a woman who kidnapped Jodie?'

Hannah shook her head. 'None of that was proven.'

'We don't have much proof of anything. But these are all leads, you must admit?'

'Did Squeaky give descriptions of these men and this woman?'

'The woman spoke with a Northern Irish accent, one of the men sounded Eastern European. The same guy had a tattoo on the palm of his hand. Doesn't all this sound familiar?'

'The tattoo? Was it a spider?'

'No, a rose amid briars. But that would be one way to disguise a spider, don't you think?'

'You've told all this to the police?'

'I have, but my opinions aren't worth much in their view.'

'And you think Freddie had been looking for someone called Saint Bridget who'd had this meeting with Jodie at the Royal Wallasea not long before she was abducted? And when you went to the Royal Wallasea, you spoke to people who remembered Jodie having a meeting with a beautiful black woman whom none of them knew?'

'That's the strength of it.'

She blew out a long breath. 'And you think this Saint Bridget and this mysterious beauty are one and the same?'

'There's a good chance of that, surely? It sounds as if that meeting had quite an impact on Jodie. Seems she was non-communicative afterwards and wouldn't go into detail about who this woman was. Police later investigated and found no such person in Jodie's past.'

'Have *you* found her yet? I presume all this is leading somewhere?'

David shrugged. 'Unfortunately, Mrs Bulstrode, if Saint Bridget is the person I think she is, she too is now dead. Also murdered. Even more brutally than Freddie was.'

Hannah listened in disbelief as he explained his theory concerning the fate of Oya Oyinola.

'Suppose it's just coincidence,' she said. 'Suppose the woman at the yacht club *is* the same woman who was murdered – she could still have been a victim of the Medway Slasher.'

'That's the thing,' David said. 'James Lynch insists that he *didn't* murder Oya Oyinola. We're trying to speak to him ourselves to confirm that, but—'

'We?'

'I have a team of journalists working on this, Mrs Bulstrode. It's not just me.'

'How efficient. Especially as I haven't yet given you that *thumbs-up* you were seeking.'

David stumbled on red-faced. 'We're trying to find out what the story is there. If Lynch still insists that he didn't murder Oyinola, that's another mystery. Who did? Why make it look like something it wasn't?'

'There could be any number of reasons.'

'Yes, and one might be connected to the meeting she had with your sister. Look, Mrs Bulstrode – again, I know this is distressing – but have you ever wondered if Jodie's kidnapping had more to it than met the eye?'

'What do you mean exactly?'

'You've presumably had it explained to you that professional kidnappers often take an easy victim first, someone whose family can't pay the ransom, and then kill them – to prove to the police that they mean business. Then they move onto the real target. That's seemingly what happened with your sister. Unless the kidnapping of Jodie was designed to *look* that way – just like Freddie's death was made to look like suicide, just like the murder of Oya Oyinola was made to look like the work of a serial killer.'

'You're suggesting some kind of conspiracy?'

'Mrs Bulstrode ...' He shook his head. 'I was Chief Crime Reporter on the *Essex Examiner*. I had a lot of dealings with criminals. I picked plenty up as I went along. And, well, it's my view that real kidnappers would have killed Jodie as well once they were compromised, and dumped her body the same way they dumped Rick Tamworth's. Thanks to me, they knew the police were getting close – why bother making life difficult for themselves by keeping one of the hostages alive?'

'Jodie's kidnappers weren't real – is that what you're saying?' She'd become thoughtful. 'It was all play-acting, to conceal something else?'

'Isn't that plausible?'

She glanced at him hard. 'It's not the case that you *want* to believe this because it will exonerate you? I mean, if it wasn't a run-of-the-mill kidnapping, but something more complex, Rick would have died anyway and Jodie would never have been returned to her family whether you'd revealed secret information about the gang or not.'

David shrugged again. 'I can't pretend that it hasn't crossed my mind. I'd do anything to restore my reputation. Who wouldn't? But – that will only happen if I can save Jodie. And I can only save Jodie by following the evidence, such as it is.'

'And how much do you want paying for your pursuit of this evidence?'

'I'm sorry?'

'Do you think I'm a dullard, Mr Kelman? Do you think I've never read up on the world's most famous missing persons cases? Do you think I know nothing about the legions of enthusiastic investigators who put their services at the disposal of the aggrieved families – for a fee of course? And how almost none of them ever uncover a damn thing, even though they're invariably well paid for their trouble.'

'I've already told you why I'm here.'

'Ah yes, you feel guilty…'

'If you doubt that, I can't change your mind. But neither can I force any money out of you. The worst I can do is ask, and I've no intention of doing that at any stage.'

She remained sceptical. 'So, you don't want anything? Not even expenses?'

'There is one thing.' He'd been going to mention this later on, but now seemed opportune. 'I'm a journalist. I want to be able to write the story afterwards. Exclusively if possible. But only on the condition we find Jodie alive. And only if you're agreeable.'

She watched him carefully.

'I don't blame you for not trusting me, Mrs Bulstrode. But surely the fact I've come to you is a sign of good faith? I didn't need to. I could have kept looking without ever mentioning it.'

'You've clearly done a lot of digging already, and a lot of surmising I might say, but do you possess any actual facts? Any useable witness statements, any dates, times…'

'About the only thing solid I have is the date of Jodie's meeting with the unknown woman at the Royal Wallasea – it was 9 September 2015.' He flicked through his notebook. 'We know that for a fact because, according to one of the witnesses, there was a terrorist incident in France on the same day. It was all over the news channels…'

His words dried. She was looking at him with renewed but apparent intense shock.

'Does that mean something?' he ventured.

Hannah stared out through the windscreen.

'Mrs Bulstrode?'

When she turned to look at him again, it was with concentrated scrutiny. 'You categorically promise me, Mr Kelman, that this isn't some devious attempt to elicit information?'

'I promise, yeah.'

'I mean, you're not the sort of man who ever felt he needed *permission* before.'

'I know that.'

'Never in your past would you refrain from nasty tricks so long as they led to a story. I'm not just talking about Jodie's kidnapping, I'm talking about the career path you've followed ever since then. I've seen the dirty secrets you've happily publicised. I've heard about the attempts to sue your publishers, and how they've always failed because men like you are so skilled at covering your backs ...'

'Not so skilled that earlier today I didn't blunder onto private property and disturb a half-naked girl who had nothing to do with any of this ...'

Hannah snorted. 'I'm sure Loretta won't mind that too much. You wouldn't be the first to see her without any clothes on. Loretta is Jason's younger sister, by the way.'

'The point is, I'm not this stealth super-predator you seem to think.'

'Nevertheless, you seem to have got further than the police.'

David didn't respond to that as he would have liked to. The cops were unlikely to keep him updated on their progress since he'd handed over the phone, but they ought to have spoken to the Bulstrodes by now. All that did was reinforce his belief that they – or rather, Jorgenson – weren't doing very much at all. But to mention that again might make him sound overly paranoid.

'I can't explain that. But what I can do is give you my solemn guarantee that any info you share with us will go no further – until, as I say, you tell me otherwise.'

'You're quite certain that Jodie had her meeting at the Royal Wallasea with this beautiful black woman on 9 September?'

He nodded, waiting.

'After …' She hesitated. 'After Jodie was abducted, the police searched her room and her private things, and they found a diary. There was a sole entry on 9 September. It was a curious one, which none of us were able to explain. It said: "Must go and see Daddy".'

'That was all?' he asked.

'That was all.'

'And no explanations were ever offered?'

'Well, Jodie wasn't there to explain. And when the police spoke to my father, he swore that she'd never been to see him about anything that wasn't run-of-the-mill company business. Certainly nothing so weighty that she'd needed to make a note of it in her diary.'

David scanned back through his own notes. 'If that entry was made on 9 September, and Jodie was abducted on 26 October, two months later, it seems unlikely she wouldn't have had the opportunity to go and see him, if she'd wanted to.'

'She saw him all the time. She lived at home.'

David's thoughts raced. This diary intel was new, and

while it didn't put a different complexion on the case, it was definite food for thought.

'Was there anything unusual about Jodie's behaviour after 9 September?' he asked.

'To be frank – yes.' Hannah looked troubled again. 'Once we became aware of the diary entry, we threw our minds back and we all agreed that she'd seemed rather withdrawn. Wasn't her usual bouncy self. I mean, you only need to go through the diary to see what she was like before then. It was all light-hearted stuff, total frivolity. Not so after that date.'

'Maybe she wanted to speak to her father about something important, but couldn't work out the best way. Perhaps it was bothering her. Perhaps it was bothering her so much that she was going to ask Rick's advice the night she was kidnapped. Could that be why she sent Freddie to buy chips?'

'The police wondered that, but none of us could think what kind of trouble Jodie might have got into.' Hannah's eyes moistened. 'Daddy especially. He was distraught. Felt he should have been there for her and wasn't.'

'Your father was very close to Jodie, was he?'

'She was always his favourite, though I think that was kind of inevitable.' Hannah dabbed at her eyes with a tissue.

'Do you mind me enquiring why?' David asked.

'Mostly because she was so interested in the family business. I mean, Daddy built MDS up from nothing. Turned us into multi-millionaires overnight. It's no wonder it was so important to him. Everything in the Martindale world centred around MDS. Look at me – I didn't have a business-minded bone in my body. I was an airline stewardess. That was the height of my ambition, but I ended up marrying the firm's senior accountant, which even brought *me* into the company fold. But Jodie, well, she wanted the top job. Her entire education had been geared towards it. She was twenty-three and already Daddy's official deputy. She'd have taken the CEO chair at some point. He was grooming her for it.'

Before David could reply, she appeared to reach some kind of decision.

'Do you have a car near here, Mr Kelman?'

'The other side of the car park.'

'Go and get it.' She put her key into the Discovery's ignition. 'And follow me.'

'I'm not sure your husband will be pleased to see me.'

'We're not going to White Horse Point. We're going to Merrivale.'

'Merrivale?' David was puzzled. 'Isn't that in Devon?'

'It's a one and three-quarter hour drive from here.' She fastened her seat belt. 'But that's on the main roads. I know some that are lesser used.'

'I don't understand.'

'Merrivale is the location of the care home in which my father is now a permanent resident.'

'I see …'

'I believe it's time you and I had a chat with him.'

'Aren't you supposed to be on holiday?'

'It was only a weekend break. We were heading home this evening anyway.' She turned the engine on. 'Ralph Martindale was once a mogul among his kind, Mr Kelman. A financial whizz-kid with Morgan Stanley, an office junior who later made the City of London his own. But these days he's ailing fast. Trust me, the sooner we go and see him the better.'

36

The two women watched Anushka across the table.

'The point is that no one tells *your* story, do they?' Anushka said. 'The general assumption is that anyone involved in sex-for-pay is a victim; has been railroaded into it ...'

The door to the greasy spoon café rattled loudly, and she glanced nervously over. It was only the storm. Rain still gusted along the drab street outside, streaming down the exterior of the windows. But no one was attempting to enter.

She looked back at the two women. 'I mean, after the ... the enquiries I've made so far, I now realise that's not always the case. I mean, no disrespect, I'm sure this is not the life-style that you ladies set out intending to follow, but you're both in good nick. You're both attractive, you don't look beaten up or worn out ...'

That was partly true.

The older one was somewhere in her forties and had a punky look with tousled bleached-blonde hair and heavy black eyeliner. She wore lots of cheap jewellery and had long, lacquered fingernails. Her clothes comprised a short plastic raincoat, silky tights and strappy high-heeled shoes. The younger one was in her early twenties, with freckles and red hair tied in bunches. She too wore heels, but also hotpants and a sleeveless summer blouse. There were several indications that life had been tough, which Anushka had quietly taken note of. The older one sported a couple of missing teeth, while the younger one seemed to wear a permanent smile, which, while it had initially encouraged Anushka to introduce herself, was so fixed that it was increasingly disconcerting.

They'd both been sitting here when she'd come stumbling in. It probably hadn't seemed too weird. As far as the women were concerned, she'd been flustered because she'd got caught in a horrendous downpour. In its turn, their presence had meant that she'd then been able to continue her enquiry.

'As I say, I'm a journo.' She showed them her card again, as she had done on first inviting herself to sit at their table. 'And we're doing a story on life in the resort towns.'

The older one slurped what remained of her coffee.

The café door rattled. Anushka threw another wary glance at it.

'What you paying, babes?' the older woman asked.

'Oh, yes, erm …' Anushka realised that she ought to have known this would happen. She had about sixty in her purse, but she was damned if she was offering that much. She filched out three tens. 'I can give you thirty up front …'

The older woman snatched them away and held them up to the light.

'There'll be more to come later,' Anushka said, 'if we write the story.'

Another protracted silence, before the woman crumpled the notes in her hand.

'Make it forty.' Her accent was local, her voice harsh.

Anushka slid another tenner over. The woman handed that and one of the others to her younger compatriot.

'So, what do you want to know?' the older one asked.

Anushka shrugged. 'Well, your names would be helpful. I'm Anushka Chawla.'

'Marie,' the older woman said. 'This is Antoinette.'

'I see. Marie and Antoinette.'

'Antoinette doesn't talk much, but don't think that means she's simple.'

Anushka glanced at the younger woman's doll-like smile. 'Wouldn't dream of it. So, erm, one of the things I'm interested in ...' Her words petered out as it occurred to her that she'd been so unexpectant of getting this far that she'd prepared no real line of questioning.

'Is why we do it?' Marie suggested.

'I suppose so, yes.'

'Money, babes.'

'You need to live, I get that ...'

''Cause it pays. If you don't mind opening your legs for scallies all day.'

'Not everyone would consider that an ... ideal arrangement.'

'You get used to it.' Marie shrugged. 'Sometimes you get roughed up, but that could happen anywhere, couldn't it?'

Not in the average office job, Anushka thought, though she didn't say it out loud.

'Do you manage your own affairs?' she asked. 'I mean financially?'

Marie gave her a hard look. 'We don't talk about stuff like that. What do you think we are, grasses? For forty fucking quid?'

'No, no, whoa!' Anushka held up her hand. 'I don't want you to break any confidences. I'm just trying to get a picture of this life. You're obviously OK with the cash situation. But surely there are some inherent dangers?'

Marie sniffed. 'It's not so bad these days. Not like it used to be. Everyone wears condoms.'

'But aren't there risks just going off with men you don't know?'

Marie fidgeted with her coffee cup. 'The weird ones … there's not too many of them. Mostly they're just lonely guys. Plus, we can look after ourselves.'

Antoinette's hand whipped out from under the table. With a *snick*, seven inches of razor-edged steel flicked into view. Anushka froze. Fleetingly, it was surreal. As though a grinning, painted dummy had pulled a switchblade on her.

'Fuck's sake, Chelle!' Marie pushed the blade out of sight. She rounded on Anushka. 'Don't mention *that*, yeah? Rozzers pull us over enough.'

Anushka shook her head, still semi-mesmerised.

'We protect each other,' Marie tried to explain. 'That's all it is.'

'And …' Anushka struggled to articulate. 'What … what about when someone like the Medway Slasher comes along?'

The silence at the table was abrupt. Marie clamped her mouth shut. Antoinette smiled on.

'Didn't he find two of his victims in this area?' Anushka pressed.

'That's a once-in-a-lifetime thing,' Marie said.

'It still must've been frightening. I mean, were you here at the time?'

'*I* was,' Marie admitted. 'Won't pretend it wasn't scary. You had to make sure of whoever you got in a car with … make sure you liked the look of them first.'

'But, James Lynch … he wasn't a monster. Not physically.'

'There are things you can look for.'

'That didn't save Oya Oyinola,' Anushka said. 'Wasn't she picked up in Chatham?'

The silence this time was different. Tenser, tauter.

'If you can't help me with that, perhaps I could speak with someone who might've known her,' Anushka said.

'Who are you?' Marie whispered. 'I mean, *really*?'

'I've told you …'

'No! No more of this journalist bullshit! You come here chucking your money round, so-called wanting to talk to us about what skanky lives we've led. And in no time at all, you're onto Oya.' She pushed her chair back and jumped to her feet. 'What's your game, eh?'

'I …' Anushka could only offer empty hands.

Marie yanked her eerily-smiling compatriot to her feet and spun from the table.

'Don't walk away!' Anushka begged. 'Look, I've got some more cash …'

'Keep your fucking money! Probably Monopoly paper anyway!'

The café door slammed closed behind them.

'Hmm …' a voice said, 'that went well.'

Anushka glanced around. A woman she hadn't noticed come in was seated at a table on her own in one of the café corners. She was nursing a bowl of soup.

'Sorry about that,' Anushka said to her. 'Small disagreement.'

The woman, who was somewhere in her mid-twenties, chuckled. 'I'd hate to see a big one.' She was pretty and bright-eyed, with short spiky black hair. She wore a white T-shirt, jeans and heeled boots. 'You want to find out about Oya, that's not the way to do it.'

'Sorry …' Anushka faltered. She would never have

considered this new person a sex worker. 'Did you know her?'

The woman laid her spoon down. 'Maybe.'

'It's just that ... Sorry, are you a case worker or something? Probation officer?'

The woman tittered. 'Dearie me, love. Me have a normal job? I should be so lucky.'

Looking more closely, Anushka now spied what might be needle tracks on the insides of both the woman's arms, though they'd faded over time.

'So is it possible you can help?' Anushka asked.

'First I need to know who *you* are?' the woman said.

Despite the tracks, everything about this one was different from the others. Not just in terms of looks, but manner. She seemed relaxed, confident, affable.

Anushka reiterated that she was with the *Essex Enquirer*. She also explained that she was here to speak to some of the women who worked the red-light district, adding that she wanted to make a new evaluation of things in light of the Medway Slasher case, particularly as two of the women, including Oya Oyinola, went to their deaths from these very streets.

'This is the age of the Me Too movement,' she said. 'But despite that, there's still a pervasive feeling in wider society that ... well, "whores get what they're asking for". I want to challenge that by writing a feature on the effects that a tragedy like Oya's murder had on her fellow sex workers. If the new Me Too mood makes them feel any safer. If I can speak to some of Oya's friends ...?'

The woman dabbed her lips with a napkin.

The door to the café banged open. Anushka jumped,

spinning around. But only a couple of middle-aged men in builder's garb came in, guffawing as they chatted.

'I'm not going to discuss it in here.' The woman stood, pulled on a lightweight jacket and moved to the counter.

Anushka hurried to get there ahead of her. 'Can I get that for you?'

The woman stepped back. 'Never been one to look a gift horse in the mouth.' By the sounds of it, she was a Londoner. 'Name's Sable, by the way.'

Outside, the rain had eased off but the maze of sodden backstreets was still quiet. They walked around a corner and followed a side alley lined with dripping wheelie bins.

'Any particular reason why you homed in on our Bridget?' Sable asked.

'I'm sorry?' Anushka had to bite down on her excitement. 'Bridget?'

'Or Saint Bridget, as we used to call her.'

'*Saint* Bridget?'

Sable smirked. 'Kind of nickname. Something Oya was christened with before she even came here. You know she was from Ivory Coast originally?'

Anushka nodded. 'Think I read that.'

'She was a real babe.' Sable sounded wistful. 'Always too good for this place. Isn't that why you chose her instead of Tia?'

'Tia?'

Anushka's thoughts still spun as they crossed a narrow street. It was black and grimy, only a couple of rust-bucket cars parked at its far end. If she remembered, Tia Wells had been the other prostitute that Lynch had picked up in Chatham.

'Not especially,' she said. 'I think the name stuck in my mind – Oya Oyinola.'

'Kind of unusual, I suppose,' Sable said.

They passed under a heavy brick arch and turned along a narrow, dingy passage. Bulging rubbish bags were piled in several recessed doorways.

'Where are we going?' Anushka asked.

'Meeting some of Oya's friends.'

They entered a yard, which, when Anushka looked up, was overhung on all sides by the yawning cavities of broken, empty windows. There were three doorways, those to the left and right nailed over with planks, though the one directly in front stood open.

'Here we are.' Sable walked across, heels clipping on the wet, litter-strewn concrete.

'In there?' Anushka halted in front of the entrance. It was so dark inside that she couldn't see anything, but a rancid stench seeped out. 'You serious?'

'I thought you wanted to talk about Oya?'

'I do, but—'

'In that case,' Sable bunched her fist in the back of Anushka's anorak, shoving her forward, 'get the fuck in!'

37

There'd been thunderstorms and heavy rain all down the east coast, but here in the West Country, the sun still shone. It was early evening, but Dartmoor basked in heat, its rolling, rugged uplands turning red as the day drew down, the occasional granite outcrop glinting a fiery orange.

When David parked his Fiesta alongside Hannah's Discovery and climbed out, he couldn't help likening the Merrivale Residential Care Home to Baskerville Hall, the bleak, weather-beaten edifice towering over him, its doughty walls clustered with ivy, its roofs made from heavy slate, broken here and there by turrets or rows of misaligned chimney pots.

Neither of them were properly dressed for visiting. David had several changes of clothes in the car, but Hannah had driven so speedily along the narrow moorland lanes that it was all he could do to keep up with her without making a pit-stop to don some new gear. As such, he was still in his shorts, vest and trainers, while Hannah wore a T-shirt, a short denim skirt and white deck-shoes.

'How much do you know about my father, Mr Kelman?' she asked.

David shrugged. 'Only that he is, or was, the king of the asset management game.'

'*Was* is the term you're looking for. Back in the 1980s, he and his associate, Nick Thorogood, started out together as high-flying young bankers with Morgan Stanley.'

'Nick Thorogood, yeah,' David said. 'He and your dad were pretty tight, weren't they?'

'In their early days, yes.'

David pondered. All the public really knew about Nick Thorogood was his flamboyant image today. That he was an older man who behaved as if he were a lot younger, that he wore top-dollar suits and snazzy jewellery and set it all off with a straggling mane of platinum hair. That he was often to be seen in the redtops, on the arms of glamour models, necking champagne or posing next to his Aston Martin. It was a cavalier lifestyle in the responsibility-conscious twenty-first century, but the guy tended to offset any really negative publicity by donating big sums to charity, organising fun runs for hospitals and the like.

'Thorogood still entertaining the elite of the elite?' David asked.

'He is,' Hannah confirmed. 'His main company is London After Midnight.'

David already knew about London After Midnight. It sold itself as the only contact rich visitors to the capital ever needed. And when they said rich, they meant super-rich. Corporate giants, rock and movie megastars, oil sheiks. Whoever they were, LAM was their one-stop-shop for fun, fun, fun.

'He does it in regal fashion too,' Hannah said. 'Looks after their every recreational need while they're in town. That was his big new idea after he was dismissed from Morgan Stanley.'

David considered this. A couple of times he'd sniffed around Nick Thorogood. But Connie Curzon had always advised that it would be a waste of time.

'Where would the scandal be?' she'd asked. 'Everyone already thinks the guy's a sleazoid.'

'But Daddy branched out too,' Hannah added. 'And unlike Nick, he didn't have the shadow of insider trading hanging over him. As such, he went on to create a tour-de-force asset management business. But he's only human.' She glanced at David. 'You saw how poorly he was at the funeral?'

'Yeah, I was surprised by that – and not a little horrified.'

'Jodie's abduction had an horrendous impact on him. Over the years that followed, he became less and less involved in the real world, especially after the death of Mummy in 2018. Before you ask, that wasn't directly related to Jodie's disappearance, but it wasn't helped by it either.'

'I don't suppose it's any consolation,' David said, 'but the business seems to be doing fine. The last time I checked, the MDS Group had a £4 billion IPO, with assets under management totalling over £500 billion.'

She nodded. 'Father's always been smart enough to install able deputies.'

'Your husband, Jason, is one of them, I imagine?'

'Jason's running things in Father's absence. What will happen in the long term, though, we're still not sure.' She took a moment to think. 'Father was already a mental and physical wreck by the time Freddie died. But the day the news reached him, he suffered a stroke. What you'll see here is near enough a lifeless husk. He only has full movement in his right hand.'

'Dear God...'

She appraised him again. 'If you're doing what you say you are, Mr Kelman, which is seeking to return Jodie to us ... Even if it only leads to her grave, you'll have gone a considerable way towards repairing the harm you did our family. Until that time, though, you'll understand that I remain sceptical about your motives.'

David nodded.

'Daddy may appear a vegetable, but he has some awareness. When we speak to him, he hears us and will sometimes make efforts to reply. If he recognises you, you can expect a negative response.'

David was discomforted by that, even though he'd expected nothing less.

'Ignore it,' she said. 'Let me do the talking.'

Inside, the building was modern and well lit. A matronly black woman, the plastic tag on whose pale-yellow scrubs said that she was Nurse Powell, greeted them very pleasantly, but asked if they wouldn't mind switching their mobiles off, before leading them through one expansive room after another, wherein elderly people sat in armchairs and read, or focused on jigsaws and puzzle books. At length, they went outdoors again, onto an extensive patio overlooking manicured gardens. Here, other residents were to be found, though these looked more infirm. Most were in wheelchairs, several sleeping, some drifting along to the accompaniment of music filtered through earbuds. One or two were noticeably non-responsive, either to the relatives who spoke with them, or, in a couple of cases, to the nurses who sat close by and read aloud.

In the shade of a bay tree, they found Ralph Martindale. He sat motionless as they approached, but even from a distance, David was still shaken by the emaciated outline under his pyjamas and dressing gown, by the lankness of his prematurely whitened hair, by his rheumy eyes and thin, grey features.

'I'm not going to mention the possibility that Jodie might

still be alive,' Hannah said as they drew close. 'It sounds wonderful when you say it, but we don't know what it means, do we? And God knows what Daddy's muddled head would make of it.'

David hung back, not wishing to get any closer than he needed to.

Hannah pulled up a chair and sat herself down.

'Afternoon, Daddy,' she said. 'How are you feeling today?'

Martindale's eyes rolled towards her, and seemed to brighten a little. His right hand flexed on its armrest.

'Shall I get your father his usual pad and pencil, Mrs Bulstrode?' Nurse Powell asked.

Hannah nodded but didn't look away from her father. 'I'm sorry, I know you were only expecting me next weekend, but something's come up and I want a chat with you.'

Martindale watched his daughter steadily. Nurse Powell returned, sliding a small notepad under his right hand, and slotting a sharpened pencil into his feeble grasp.

'I know it's a strange subject to bring up all these years later, Daddy,' Hannah said, 'but I was wondering how much you remember about the weeks leading up to Jodie's abduction?'

Martindale's face seemed to lengthen, the pencil to slacken in his nerveless fingers.

'I'm sorry, but some new information has come to light and I'm wondering if you can help? Do you recall an incident not long after Jodie disappeared, when we looked in one of her diaries and saw an entry "Must go and see Daddy"? I know you won't remember the exact date, but that entry was made on 9 September that year, just short of two months before she was snatched.'

Martindale remained motionless, but was it conceivable, David wondered, that the guy had stiffened, tensed even?

'Again, I'm sorry to rake all this up again,' Hannah said. 'But it's really very important.'

The patient commenced writing, using short, stiff movements. David leaned down to read, which wasn't easy given that the words were scratched onto the paper in weird, jagged letters.

'"Too long",' he said aloud.

Martindale ignored him, remaining focused on his daughter.

Hannah nodded. 'We'd all agree that it's been a long time. But we have to try and remember, Daddy. Did Jodie come to see you about anything in particular around that time, to discuss something that might have been bothering her?'

Martindale scratched on the pad again.

As before, David read aloud. '"Jodie gone too long".'

'I'm asking you about that particular week of 9 September,' Hannah said. 'Jodie didn't come to you with any particular concerns? Something related to the company, maybe? Something serious?'

Martindale just stared at her.

'You see, Daddy,' Hannah added, 'someone's told us that on 9 September that year, Jodie had an unscheduled meeting. We know it was unscheduled because it wasn't in her personal diary or her office diary. This meeting was held at the Royal Wallasea Yacht Club, and the person she met there was a young black woman. Very good-looking.'

A gobbet of drool ran down the side of Martindale's chin.

'Oh dear.' Nurse Powell leaned down and tissued it away.

'Does that mean something to you, Ralph?' David couldn't resist asking. 'Did Jodie mention this meeting to you?'

Martindale gave him a fleeting glance but registered nothing, his eyes rolling back to his daughter.

'Any thoughts, Daddy?' Hannah asked. 'Was there anyone in Jodie's professional life around that time, or yours, who might match that description?'

Martindale's hand clenched. The notepad page tore off, scrunching into a ball.

'Ask him if the name Saint Bridget means anything,' David said.

The patient's eyes fixed on him, and narrowed. For the first time it seemed to register on Martindale who David was. His mouth became even wetter. Visible shudders passed through his withered frame.

'Now, Daddy, don't overexcite yourself,' Hannah warned him. 'I know you recognise this man. It's David Kelman. He was the newspaper reporter who covered the kidnapping when it first happened. But he's on our side now. He's trying to help.'

Martindale clutched his pencil all the harder as he scrawled forcefully onto his pad.

'I'm not sure this is a good idea, Mrs Bulstrode,' Nurse Powell said. 'He's rarely this animated and he is being treated for high blood pressure...'

Hannah ignored that. 'Daddy, something's troubling you. Try to write it down.'

Martindale's chair shook as he scrunched another page into a rag of paper and dropped it on the patio, and then another after that. His body juddered; more drool emerged.

'Mrs Bulstrode, I think that's enough for today,' Nurse Powell said.

Hannah sat back. 'I'm sorry, Daddy, but we had to try

and talk to you. I wish I could make you understand how important this is.'

She stood up and kissed her father's head before the nurse wheeled him away. As she did, David scooped up the crinkled scraps of paper and tried to read them.

'I thought for a minute we'd succeeded,' he said.

'There's nothing useful, then?' Hannah replied.

'Couple of oblique references to the yacht club. And his opinion of my disgrace, which is no more than I deserve.'

He didn't bother elaborating on that last message. It simply said:

ENJOY WHAT YOU FUCKING EARNED

38

On first being shoved through the door, Anushka tottered sideways, bouncing from a wall and falling onto her bottom. Behind her, the door crashed closed, plunging her into dank blackness.

At first she was shocked rather than frightened. She didn't remember the last time anyone had laid a violent hand on her. But now, as the silence and darkness lingered, and a stench of decay clogged her nostrils, that shock turned to numbing fear.

She scrambled frantically to her feet.

'Sable!' she called. '*Sable!* What're you doing?' Again, silence and darkness. 'Good God, this is not funny!'

A low, snickering laugh sounded on her left.

She lurched away, hitting a solid wall again, this time with her shoulder. Something scampered across her left foot. She yelped, hopping, trying to follow the wall by groping along it, and when she came to a sudden gap, stumbling through it.

She sensed that she was in a room.

She also sensed that she wasn't alone.

A dull, hoarse breathing emanated from the far corner.

It didn't even sound human, more like an animal.

Terrified, Anushka tried to backtrack, but broken, rotted woodwork crunched and splintered under her feet, and she half stumbled again. There was a hiss of exhaled breath. So close that she felt it on her right ear. She squealed, blundering backward and sideways. Was she out in the corridor again? She had no clue, but the next thing, she'd stepped over an edge and was falling, head over heels, clattering and banging down a steep, wooden staircase, coming to rest at the bottom amid what felt like bricks and chunks of shattered stone.

She sat up quickly, albeit stiffly. Every part of her had been pummelled, but she wasn't hanging around to see if anything was broken...

Another low snicker, somewhere on the right.

Anushka jumped to her feet, eyes attempting to penetrate the blackness. But it was beyond opaque. As though she no longer had vision. More heavy breathing. The direction was indeterminate, but it appeared to be drawing closer.

She dug desperately for her phone, to find her anorak pockets empty. Had she dropped it during the fall? She staggered backward, feeling behind her for the stair, but finding a wall. It was scabbed and broken, huge patches of putrid plaster having fallen out.

And then... silence.

The breathing stopped.

As if a switch had been thrown.

Anushka's eyes bulged in the blackness.

And then a switch was *really* thrown. And a light came on. It was searingly bright.

It dazzled Anushka, made her cover her eyes.

As they adjusted, she realised that it came from a portable lamp hanging from an overhead beam by a coaxial cable.

A single figure stood underneath it, facing her square-on.

A figure in jeans, a black hoodie top, and a red leather gimp mask.

She turned to run, only to find seven or eight other people in the room behind her. All women. All garishly dressed and made up. Even so, she might have run to them for protection – had each one of them not raised a weapon. Her disbelieving gaze darted from rusty pipe to buckled belt, from Antoinette's switchblade to an old-school military bayonet.

'Please ... I haven't done anything ...'

'Not yet maybe,' came a voice from behind.

Anushka spun back. Leather Mask advanced, offering a raised right fist encased not just in a black leather glove, but in a moulded brass knuckleduster.

'And you won't be able to,' the nightmare figure added. 'Not when we're done ...'

It was a woman, but she spoke in a harsh Northern accent. Her stance was hunched, hyena-like.

'She wanted to know about Oya,' one of the others said, as the rest of the women fanned out, encircling their captive, 'and who her friends were.'

The speaker was Marie. Anushka couldn't believe it. Before she could even complain that she'd bought the ungrateful cow a cup of coffee, someone came up behind, threw a looped ligature over her head and yanked it tight, twisting it at the back. Anushka gagged and choked. It was another of the women. She could tell that from the cheap perfume.

'You bitch,' Leather Mask said, coming very close. 'Asking about Oya's one thing. But asking about her mates?'

'Why'd you want to know about *them*?' one of the others demanded.

'So they can be killed too?' Leather Mask said.

Saliva burst from Anushka's mouth as she struggled to breathe.

Leather Mask nodded almost imperceptibly, and the ligature slackened.

Anushka drew a deep, sobbing breath. She tried to grab at the noose with her right hand, but Leather Mask slapped it away.

'I told you,' Anushka stuttered, 'my name's Anushka Chawla. I'm a journalist. Don't hurt me, please ...'

Leather Mask was nose to nose with her. The dehumanised horror of those gleaming scarlet features, the eyes in the zippered slots shining with hatred, was almost too much.

'I just ... I wanted to tell Oya's story because no one else would,' Anushka wept.

'Lying sow.' Leather Mask removed her brass knuckles before going roughly through the captive's bag. She pulled out the purse, and rifled through it until she found an ID card.

'"Anushka Chawla",' she read aloud. 'Says you work for fucking Tesco!'

'No, look ...'

'You a journalist or a till girl?' Leather Mask demanded. 'Who the fuck are you?'

'I'm a part-time journalist ...'

'Smack her!' one of the others shouted. 'Smack the cow! She'd have us all ripped open like Oya was!'

'I wouldn't do that,' Anushka wept. 'Look, there's another card. Look for it please. I tried to give it to Marie and Antoinette ...'

Leather Mask glanced at Marie, who shrugged. 'She *did* try to give us something.'

'If you're lying to me, girl,' Leather Mask growled.

'I'm not,' Anushka sobbed, 'I swear.'

Her captor fumbled through the bag again, and this time came out with a small rectangle of card. '"Anushka Chawla, reporter, *Essex Enquirer*"?'

Anushka nodded desperately. 'That's it. That's the one.'

'You passing this off as proof? It doesn't even look as professional as the other one. You made this in your fucking bedroom, didn't you?'

'No, I didn't, I promise, look – there's a number there. A landline. Ring that.'

Leather Mask stared at her. 'Ring it, eh?'

'Yes, ring it, and when it's answered, you'll know the truth.'

Anushka could only pray that it *would* be answered. She had no clue where either David or Norm were up to with their days' schedules.

Leather Mask thought about it for a second or two. 'Anyone got a burner?'

A mobile was tossed across to her. She stepped back from Anushka, who stood rigid and sweat-soaked, tears streaking her dirtied face. She watched helpless as her tormentor tapped in the number, activating the speaker at the same time.

The call rang out at the other end. And rang. And rang. Until it switched to the standard messaging service.

Leather Mask slipped the phone out of sight. 'Well, well.' She refitted the brass knuckles. 'Look who hasn't got the back-up she thought she had...'

39

'Well, he's a mess, of course,' Hannah Bulstrode said out on the car park. She was talking on her phone. 'Agitated as hell, but I had to speak to him.'

David waited by his Fiesta. Behind her, lights were appearing in windows as the evening drew down.

'All I can say is that his motives appear to be genuine,' Hannah said, glancing at David. 'No,' she sighed. 'Not a scrap of *actual* evidence. Well of course we will. No, he's not asked for any money. Yes, I will. Speak to you later.' She tucked the phone away. 'My husband wants me to pass on our thanks for your help.'

David smiled. 'Something tells me he didn't quite say it that way.'

She shrugged. 'The main gist of it was "*we'll* take it from here".'

'I see.'

'However,' Hannah looked thoughtful, 'those are *Jason's* thoughts.'

'Meaning *yours* are different?'

She unlocked the Discovery and threw her shoulder bag inside. 'I'll be honest, Mr Kelman, I still don't know whether you're being of genuine assistance to us, or whether you're raising all our hopes for no reason.'

'I've only told you what I heard, Mrs Bulstrode. I've given no guarantee there'll be a happy ending.'

'I accept that. But … on the basis that all this is well within your area of expertise, I personally would have no objection if you continued to look into the matter.'

David shrugged. 'OK, but … well, if the police make ground on their own, you'll let me know, won't you? Because they won't tell me anything, and if this mystery looks like it's going to be solved officially, there are other things my team and I can be doing.'

'I'll let you know. Here's my card.'

She handed him a small, neat business card. David responded by giving her one of his own.

'You need to understand something,' she said. 'While I've no doubt that you regret what you did to us all those years ago and are now trying to make up for it, only if Jodie returns to us can there be any possibility of forgiveness. I don't know if that matters to you or not.'

'I don't know if I ever expected that, Mrs Bulstrode. I'm sorry your father got upset.'

She pondered. 'I hoped he'd be more helpful than he was. Just out of interest, what did he write down on those pages you picked up?'

David retrieved them from his shorts pocket. 'Well, apart from making it crystal-clear what he thought about me, just vague references to the yachting club.'

She frowned, as if that didn't make sense.

David squinted at the crumpled second sheet. 'Which he referred to as the "shipping club", strangely.'

'Shipping club?' Hannah came over to look.

David indicated the jagged inscriptions. 'It's scribble, but it looks like "Sh Club". He's written it twice.'

'Sh Club,' she said aloud.

'Does it mean something?' David asked.

'It could be a reference to the Share Club.'

'Share Club?'

She stepped away. 'The Share Club was the origin of Daddy's success.'

'Sorry, I don't follow.'

'Daddy set it up with Nick Thorogood after Nick left Morgan Stanley.'

'Thorogood again?' David said.

'It worked for him too,' she said. 'Allowed him to set up London After Midnight, as well as a few other ventures. You remember *Night Prowler*?'

David did. *Night Prowler* had been a short-lived TV series of the 1990s, a dance music show that had run on ITV's night network. Thorogood, by then gaining a reputation as a celebrity club-owner, had presented it, touring the UK's nightclubs, ostensibly to comment on Britpop and the general club scene, but also to chat up beautiful girls, and whenever he stole a kiss, to announce it with a wolf's howl, a semi-comical but saucy reaction, which had become one of his trademarks over the years. The press had even taken the piss, referring to it as Night Howler.

'That was entirely his concept,' Hannah said. 'He also put up quite a bit of the development money, thanks to the Share Club.'

'What was the Share Club?' David asked.

'Think of it as a kind of game they used to play. To top up their regular earnings.'

'To top up their earnings?'

'Sometimes very substantially.'

'And it was a game?'

'Only inasmuch as nothing was really at stake.' She saw his confusion. 'You need to understand, Mr Kelman – when

Daddy and Nick Thorogood were twenty-something best friends, they had an experience of life that would be unknown to other people of their age. As young bankers, they turned over a hundred grand a month each. But that was never enough. Not in those days. Back then, in the City, amassing wealth was a virtual religion. The Share Club was just another way to make this happen.'

'How did it work?'

'It was an amazingly simple concept. A Share Club itself is an unofficial syndicate, but perfectly legal. The way this one operated was that, periodically, Daddy and Nick Thorogood and a few of their banker buddies who were also members would put a chunk of spare cash into a central pot, about fifty grand each, and from this pot they invested in various going concerns. Many of these ventures came to nothing, but the fact that it was a syndicate spread the risk, so these weren't major losses. Some of them paid off handsomely though. Back in those days, you only really needed one of your investments to strike gold, but if you had knowledge of the markets and a gambler's instinct, which all of those guys did back then, you could pick out a number of potential winners. And they did; several of the businesses the syndicate invested in subsequently grew rapidly, enabling them to sell their shares at huge profit. As a result, the syndicate became phenomenally wealthy, which enabled the members – most of whom were still youngsters, remember – to seed and build up their own companies.'

David was fascinated. 'So that was how Nick Thorogood was able to underwrite his new entertainments career?'

'Yes. Even though he'd just been sacked from his main job. It was also how Daddy set up MD Solutions.'

'But why would your father mention this in the same breath as getting angry?'

Hannah seemed unsure. 'Daddy's riddled with guilt. He considers that if he'd never created MDS, we'd never have become the prominent family we are, and Jodie would never have become a target.'

David understood that. As a crime reporter, he'd met lots of people who felt guilty for the violence done by others. *If only I hadn't let her go out on her own ... If only I'd agreed to pick him up instead of telling him to get a taxi ...*

'Don't waste time trying to fathom it out,' she said. 'I'll speak to Daddy again when he's in a more responsive frame of mind. Don't take this the wrong way, but your presence here today didn't help.'

'No, I saw that.'

'But as I say,' she moved to the driver's door, 'if you want to follow any other lines of enquiry, I'd be grateful.'

'Sure,' David said. 'Erm, with regard to Cornwall, are we good?'

'We're fine.' She hesitated to climb in, seeing that he was struggling with something. 'Mr Kelman, it won't pay to ruminate on the Share Club. It's long been discontinued. I know it's a fashionable thing these days to blame all the world's ills on bankers, hedge-fund managers and such. The slightest misstep by one of those gents and the whole of Twitterati comes down on them. So I understand that it's tempting to go there. But the truth is, no one involved in the Share Club – and it wasn't just Daddy and Nick Thorogood, there were quite a few others – did anything wrong. It was all legal and above board and all the companies that sprang from it were completely legit. You can check, but you'll be wasting your time.'

David watched as she drove away.

'Sorry to differ, Mrs B,' he said to himself, 'but I've only glimpsed the kind of wealth at play here, and in all my years I've never known that much money be generated by anything that was completely legit.'

40

When Norm got back to Colchester, the rain and thunder had moved west, leaving a wet and glittering landscape, and an indigo sky, in which, one by one, the stars winked open.

He saw none of this, his mind focused on one thing: the story they were working on, and what its wider significance might be.

From the commencement of this business, Norm had been an uneasy participant. He'd never stopped liking David. He'd been left bitter and depressed by the rift in their relationship, infuriated by the cavalier way David played fast and loose with the rules. But inside, Norm had also been aggravated with himself. It was too easy to say that it had all been someone else's fault. *He'd* gone along with it too. His occasional words of caution had meant nothing in reality because David got a buzz from courting danger, and Norm had known this full well. When David had needed a leash, Norm had only paid lip-service to that.

And the reason was simple.

Norm had the bug too. He'd always had it. Why else was he a journalist?

He also got off on writing shock-copy. He too loved it when his name was up there. And when Crime Beat was first floated by this cocky young reporter called David Kelman, Norm had known that he'd been waiting for it all his career. Though a long-serving hack by then, he'd realised that he'd got lost in Features, writing nothing but fluff. Yes, the readers had liked it, but Norm hadn't. Not when the alternative was a darker, edgier world.

It was no surprise that he'd come aboard the *Essex Enquirer*. A lot had changed in the last six years. Norm was older these days, more relaxed, but he'd still seized the opportunity. Primarily because he'd felt so short-changed to have been denied access to the immense story that was the Medway Slasher. In some ways, he'd done 'a David' today. Had acted on impulse, charging in there and interviewing James Lynch with no real idea what the potential outcome might be. He hadn't even expected that it would give them a good lead. But then that name had come up. Again.

DI Tony Jorgenson.

Norm walked up David's drive, only becoming aware that there was a large box with shipping tags on it in the alley alongside the garage when he almost tripped over it. The new printer, he realised. The one Anushka had supposedly been supervising the installation of. He used his new key to enter the small building, humping the box along with him, turning the lights on.

It was amazing how smart it now looked in there: the desks and tables, the filing cabinets, the noticeboards on the walls, the working tip-line. All he'd needed when he'd set out that morning was the firm conviction that he was chasing a real story.

And now he had it.

Tony Jorgenson.

Norm had assumed that David's mistrust of Jorgenson was nothing more than an excuse for his refusal to hand over the remainder of Freddie Martindale's evidence. But now, it seemed, David's hostility to the guy was founded on more than personal pique.

And he didn't just have a convicted serial killer's word for that.

'Oya Oyinola was murdered on the night of 15 December,' James Lynch had said. *'That same night I spent in Romford, in the company of two workmates, Brian Fairclough and Chris Jaycox.'*

The surname Fairclough was too common to follow up easily, especially when you were sitting behind the steering wheel. But the man called Jaycox had been traceable with little effort. Norm had simply called Directory Enquiries and asked for 'C Jaycox, Romford'.

'I remember that, yeah,' Jaycox, a real country bumpkin, had replied. *'I don't have any contact with Lynchy now, for obvious reasons. But we were workmates, and we were out drinking that night. And no, no coppers rang me up or came to see me about it afterwards. I found it amazing he ever got done for that murder. I'm not saying he didn't do them other women. But he never left us all night that night.'*

When Norm asked why he hadn't volunteered the information, he'd become defensive.

'Look, mate, I never knew Lynchy had those inclinations. If I did, I'd have had nothing to do with him. After he got nicked, I kept my head down. Yeah, if the coppers'd asked, I'd have told them what I knew. But if Lynchy was happy to cop for that black bird, why should I have stuck my neck out?'

'I'm not sure he was happy,' Norm had replied.

'Sounds like you know more than me, then. Maybe you should be talking to the cops.'

'Not bloody likely,' Norm muttered.

Jorgenson had been connected, by reputation if not name, with the Lampwick Lane case. And now he was being mentioned in the same breath as the Medway Slasher, but not as the cop who caught him, as the guy who'd deliberately not taken the action that might have cleared the suspect of one of the murders he was charged with. OK, perhaps that was the sort of thing any bullish, old-school copper might stoop to, taking underhand action to ensure that the sissy rules the rest of society had to live by wouldn't interfere with bringing a killer to justice. The problem was that on this occasion it could mean another killer was still out there.

A killer who, in some tenuous and uncertain way, might be connected to the murder of Freddie Martindale, if not to the kidnapping of his sister.

Norm plonked himself into his chair.

Tony Jorgenson was a dodgy character. There was no question. They'd felt it in their bones the first time they'd looked into Lampwick Lane. But that on its own didn't mean anything.

'There's no link,' Norm said aloud. 'There's no link between Tony Jorgenson and Jodie Martindale's kidnapping.'

But actually, there was. There had to be. Otherwise Jorgenson's role in the Oya Oyinola cover-up, if that's what it was, would be the coincidence of all time.

He thought about contacting David again with this new info. He'd already tried several times, but David's mobile had been switched off. Before he could make that call again, the tip-line began to ring.

Norm stared at it. It had only been installed last week and it was ringing already?

Nervously, he reached for the receiver. 'Newsroom, *Essex Enquirer*. Norman Harrington speaking.'

'Hello, erm, yeah.' It was a woman with a Northern accent. 'I wanna speak to Anushka Chawla.'

'I'm sorry,' Norm replied. 'Anushka's out of the office at the moment. Can I take a message?'

'She's one of your journalists, yeah?'

'Absolutely. Anushka's …'

With a *click*, the line went dead.

41

'Who'd have thought it,' Leather Mask said. 'Someone answered after all.'

Anushka stood stiff as a flagpole, throat constricted by the ligature. She wasn't sure how she'd persuaded her captors to call the number again. But for someone to have actually been there on the second occasion...'Who answered?'

Leather Mask turned probing eyes on her. 'Perhaps *you* should tell us that one?'

'Either David Kelman or Norman Harrington?'

Leather Mask remained unreadable.

'They're news reporters,' she added.

Her chief captor pondered. Evidently, she was weighing up the voice she'd heard.

A taut second passed, before she slid the phone into her jeans pocket and gave a terse nod. The ligature slackened and fell away, and Anushka stumbled forward, rubbing at the welt on her throat. Leather Mask reached to the back of her neck, unsnapped a catch, and peeled off the mask. Revealing the sweaty features of Sable.

'You're a silly cow, coming here,' she said, reverting to her native Cockney. 'You realise that, don't you?'

'Depends whether you can help me out with some answers,' Anushka wheezed.

'Why should we?' one of the other women asked. She was older than the rest, grey-haired, but so heavily built that her five-inch heels, zip-sided miniskirt and black lace bustier looked vaguely obscene. 'What's in it for us?'

Anushka stared around at them. 'You don't want your story told?'

'So we're not getting paid?' Bustier shook her head. 'There's a fucking surprise.'

'I took a chance coming here,' Anushka stammered. 'I realise that. But it's for a good reason.'

'Which we don't get to hear about?' Sable asked. 'You're still not telling us why you want to write about Oya. Unless you think we buy that BS about street women and their sad lives.'

The hostile atmosphere had diminished, but the faces encircling Anushka were still hard.

'Look,' she said, 'the truth is that we don't think Oya was murdered by the Medway Slasher. And we want to find out who really did it.'

She'd not been expecting an astounded reaction to this, but neither had she anticipated the complete lack of emotional response.

'You sure you're not a cop?' Sable asked.

'Wouldn't it be a good thing if I was?' Anushka said.

There were snorts of laughter.

'Fuck's sake!' Bustier scoffed. 'How do you think they got to Oya in the first place?'

Anushka pivoted from one to the next. 'Who's *they*?'

'They … *them*,' Marie said. 'How do you think they found her?'

'Oya wasn't a streetwalker,' Sable explained. 'So they didn't just drive around till they spotted her.'

'So, you're saying …' Anushka was incredulous. 'You're saying the police directed whoever it was to her?'

'Someone in authority did. Someone who knew where she'd be, which as you can imagine, makes the whole situation a lot shittier for the likes of us.'

'Can't you tell me more?' Anushka said. 'I'm sure I can help?'

'You really want to get involved?' Sable asked. 'Why do you think we lured you down here? Because we thought you were one of them. We were going to give you more than a kicking. Because that's the only thing we can do if we want to stay alive.'

'We're investigative reporters. We don't care about the danger.'

'What about the danger you might bring to *us*?' Bustier asked. 'Especially as you're not paying.'

'Look, I'm sorry I can't organise any payment at the moment,' Anushka said. 'But that doesn't mean it won't be possible at some later date.'

'Some later date ... yeah, right. We do deals like that with all our tricks.'

'She's right about the danger, though,' Sable put in. 'It won't just be you.'

Anushka shrugged. 'You seem to think you're already in danger.'

'At present it's theoretical. But if whoever it is finds out we're talking to the press, it becomes very real.'

'Don't you want to see these people in prison? Because by the sounds of it, this is the only way that's going to happen.'

A brief silence followed.

'Are you for real?' Sable asked. 'I mean, you just seem like a nice girl to me. A nice, naïve girl.'

'It's not just me,' Anushka said. 'My colleagues are tough. And clever.'

'So clever that they let you come here on your own?'

Anushka blushed. No riposte was possible to that.

'Walk with me.' Sable moved to a nearby door, swooping up Anushka's phone from where it had fallen, and handing it over along with her bag. 'No sense the rest of the girls getting involved.'

Back upstairs, Anushka saw that a door now stood open at the front of the grotty old building, evening light flooding in. She wondered how on earth she'd been blundering around lost and terrified in this place. It was no more than the ground floor to a derelict tenement. Outside, Sable led her back across the small courtyard and onto the network of backstreets, which, the rain having cleared, had returned to life. Soon, they were on shopping streets, cars moving, pedestrians on the pavements.

Sable gazed ahead as they walked. 'Sorry about the mask. Belonged to an ex-client of mine.'

'Good God.'

'It's not as bad as it sounds. He liked to role-play. But I appreciate it's a scary thing. So, yeah, sorry.'

'I don't know how you got onto me so soon.' Anushka shook her head. 'I'd barely spoken to anyone when you started following me.'

Sable shrugged. 'Like I say, we're not taking chances at present, and you stood out like a sore thumb. But that's one of the two reasons I'm prepared to talk to you. Because I don't believe that anyone capable of doing to any human being what was done to Oya would use a total bungler like you. Don't be offended. Most decent people would've been lost back there too.'

'OK, but what's the other reason?'

'Well, even though I don't think you're one of them, it's

not impossible that your stupidity could rebound on me and the rest of the girls. But that's a risk I'm prepared to take because, stupid or not, you said something that made an impression on me: who else is going to get justice for Oya?'

'I can't promise anything,' Anushka said. 'But we'll do whatever we can.'

'Even if you did the bare minimum, it'd be more than is being done at present. You see, if it was me who'd been slit open like a fish, I've got family back in London who wouldn't let it drop. But Oya was different.'

'She was an immigrant, yeah?'

'She was. *And* a friend of mine. *More* than a friend.'

'Can you elaborate?'

'Well, all the girls back there were friendly with her. Partly because she was hot stuff. You stood on a street corner with Oya, you were going to get a lot of business.'

'I thought you said she didn't work the streets?'

'She did at first. That was around the time I showed up. It was ten years ago, and I was eighteen. The reasons I left home ... well, never mind that. But I was still a kid, I didn't know the ropes. Things looked bleak, but then I met this glorious-looking African lady, and she took me under her wing. Lucky break, really. I was a tough little druggie and she was ... well, the polar opposite. Miracle, given what she'd been through. In fact, she was a miracle all round. When she was born, she wasn't breathing. The midwife couldn't resuscitate her, but her mother prayed to Saint Bridget and it paid off – her lungs started working on their own.'

'Amazing,' Anushka said.

Sable chuckled. 'Who knows what it really was, but Saint Bridget was a big deal in their family, or so she said. They were Catholics, but Saint Bridget had some kind of connection, I don't know what, with a goddess called Oya who'd once been worshipped in that part of Africa. So, if you prayed to either of them, you got the best of both worlds. Something like that. Anyway, that was where she got her name from. Course, it was just Oya when she arrived here, or plain old Bridget, but she once mentioned they'd used to call her "Saint Bridget" back home, and the name stuck, especially as she was such a good egg. Like I say, she got me clean, got me on the straight and narrow. As much as it was possible.'

'You seem like a very together person, Sable, that's all I can say.'

Sable smiled. 'Who are you kidding? I've got a vicious streak a mile long. I may have a family who'd come looking for me, but I've had a shit life too. It gives you an edge.' She paused to think. 'But there's two sides to every coin. And that was Oya's doing. She always said I'd move on at some point, so I had to be ready for the real world. By the time she left the streets herself, I was in reasonable shape, I suppose.'

'Why did she move off the streets?'

'Before I tell you that, you need to know about her background.'

'OK...'

'I don't know what her life was like back in Ivory Coast. I'm sure it was happy enough at first. She had a decent education for one thing. Spoke English perfectly with this beautiful half-African, half-French accent. But something went wrong, and it sounds like her family fell into poverty. And when they're talking poverty over there, they're talking poverty with a capital P.'

'My family came here from India,' Anushka said. 'So yeah, I know.'

'Oya was in her early twenties when she tried to emigrate. I don't know what the circs were, but she made it as far as mainland Europe, at which point she met the wrong crowd.'

Sable let that hang.

'Who?' Anushka asked.

'Russians of course. They're all over Europe. At least they made the last part of the trip quick for her. I talked to her about it a lot, and she didn't even remember how they trafficked her in, just that she was gagged and blindfolded in this steel container. Her and a few others.'

Anushka shuddered with horror.

'Once she got here she was held for a few months in some kind of secure building. Oya thought it was only a staging post, but it was the usual rathole. That said, she was a stand-out girl, so, whoever was running things, they'd realised they could get top-dollar for her. They kept her in reasonable conditions. She was able to get perks and privileges for some of the other girls too. But she knew where it'd end. So, when someone took their eye off her, she escaped – made her way overland. Finally came to a road, got a lift off a lorry driver. Turns out she was on the Isle of Sheppey. She didn't even know where that was, but she stuck with the lorry for the full ride. Ended up here, where she had no choice but to live on the streets. She wasn't even close to being legal, so she didn't dare go for help. Eventually, though, she fell in with some of the other girls. It was the only option she had. Couple of years later, when I turn up, she's already a seasoned hooker.'

'But with a heart of gold?' Anushka said.

Sable glanced at her. 'You think that's a cliché, eh?'

'Isn't it?'

'Just remember, we're not all victims out here. We may not

like it, but we can hack it if it leads to better things. And that was Oya all over. She firmly believed that a decent future was waiting. So she kept herself in good nick. Minded her looks. At some point, a better class of pimp spots her, tells her she's too good for the streets, that he can get her a decent pad, earn her good money catering to high society.'

'She became an escort?' Anushka pulled a face. 'Hardly a better future.'

'You'd be surprised. We kept in touch. She came back here every so often because she had plenty of money and she wanted to share it with her old mates.'

'And that's why you think the Medway Slasher didn't kill her?' Anushka asked.

'Top quality call girls are out of reach for shitheads like James Lynch.'

'So what *did* happen to her?'

'What happened, or so Oya said when she made her last visit down here, was that she was worried. She'd been at this swanky party in London, doing her thing, when she saw someone she recognised from the house on Sheppey.'

'A punter?'

'A punter at this party, yeah. But not on Sheppey. On Sheppey he'd been a boss.'

'A Russian?'

'That's the thing – no, he was British. She called him Lou Garoo. Foreign-sounding name, but he *was* British, and he'd been the one Brit she'd seen on Sheppey. Apparently, he'd been there now and then, helping himself to the girls and giving orders, and the Russians had been jumping to it…'

'Did she describe this Lou Garoo?'

'No.'

'So that's all we've got to go on? That he was British?'

'And posh.'

'She must have said something else. Did he recognise her in return?'

'She didn't think so.' Sable looked amused. 'You'd think it'd be hard for him not to, a babe like Oya. But maybe not. It's all just meat to these scumbags, isn't it? The main thing is, she wanted to turn him in. She knew that'd be a risk to her. But all she could think of was the pain of the women she'd left behind in that halfway house. Said she couldn't live with herself if she didn't tell someone.'

'Who did she settle on?'

'That's where the intel ends. I never saw her again.'

'But you're certain she spoke to someone?'

Sable gave her a pained look. 'Course she did. And whoever it was, they didn't just sign her death warrant, they ensured she got carved open like a hog roast.'

IV

DIFFERENT WAYS TO DIE

42

David reached Andover by nine o'clock and the M25 by ten. Here, he encountered wet surfaces, though whatever storm had caused them had burned itself out. Warm, damp air rushed through his open windows, but the sky was ablaze with stars.

He barely noticed any of this, because he was lost in thought.

Hannah Bulstrode had been persuaded that he was trying to help. But she clearly hadn't felt the desire to make a plan with him, and he couldn't blame her for that. He'd brought her family nothing but anguish, and his attempts to atone for it had amounted to very little so far. Ultimately, he supposed, he was a journalist – not a cop, not even a private investigator. Yes, if Jodie was still alive, he wanted to help find her – he felt he owed them that. But his primary interest was always going to be the column inches he could generate. And that would only ever be something the survivors of tragedies could do without.

On the other hand, if the *Essex Enquirer* wasn't reinvestigating this case, who else would be? Investigative reporting was not just about sensationalism. It could also be a positive force.

Again, he considered Tabby and Tommy. They weren't old enough yet to understand his disgrace. But they would be in time. Unless he headed it off first.

The London Orbital was quiet, though it was now late. He sailed unhindered past junctions 15 and 16, and only now did it seem odd that he hadn't heard from either Norm or Anushka. Picking up his phone, he realised that he hadn't switched it back on. He hit the button and saw that he'd had several missed calls from both. In addition, Norm had left three text messages. David thumbed open the first one.

Lynch has proved that he did NOT kill Oyinola. Call me.

Before David could call back, the phone thrummed in his hand. Anushka's name appeared.

'Nushka?' David answered. 'Where are you?'

'On my way back,' she said. 'Listen, you're not going to believe this—'

'On your way back from where?'

'Chatham. Listen—'

'Chatham! I thought you were holding the fort?'

'David, stop being an arsehole, OK? This is important.'

'I hope you've not been doing something silly and dangerous, Nushka.'

'If I hadn't, you'd still be groping in the dark, whereas I've found something that could crack the whole case.'

He sighed. 'Go on …'

She told him everything that had happened to her in shrill tones, so excited that she struggled to keep her thoughts in order.

'It's gratifying to know we were on the right track,' David finally said. 'But you've only got the word of a bunch of hookers that this is all kosher.'

'You only had the word of a drug addict that Freddie Martindale was murdered, but *you* went with it.'

'We still have to be wary.' He tried to think. 'Some might argue that girls like that are screwed up. That they could have fantasised this whole thing. That it might make them feel less like easy victims if their friend had been chopped as part of a high-level conspiracy rather than by some kerb-crawling deviant.'

He was playing devil's advocate, of course. Whatever Norm had uncovered also appeared to reinforce the theory that Oya Oyinola was not part of the Medway Slasher series. But Anushka sounded overly animated. He had to know that she hadn't gone in too eagerly and that the prostitutes hadn't responded by taking the piss.

'The main girl I spoke to, Sable – she seemed very genuine. She said that Oya had been a big sister to her. Said that after she got off the streets, she'd even come back and given them money.'

'Regular goodie two-shoes, wasn't she?'

'There are good people out there, you know. Even on the backstreets.'

'Will this Sable let you contact her again?'

'I know where to find her.'

'This Lou Garoo character she saw at the posh shindig – that's all we've got on him, a name?'

'I'm afraid so.'

'Ironic or what? The first key person of interest was a beautiful black woman – we had the description but no name. The second one, we've got a name and no description.'

'Isn't a name enough? Surely you can run it by Deepthroat?'

'I can try, but this isn't even second-hand information.'

'You sound like bloody Norm!' she snapped. 'You really don't trust me, do you?'

'We've got to stress-test everything, Nushka. We can't keep running on suppositions.'

'Well, at present this is the only hypothesis we've got. Let's at least try it out for size.'

'Go on...'

'Oya recognises this guy at a party who's clearly involved at the British end of a sex-trafficking ring. He might even be running it. He was the one giving orders, and the Russians were snapping to it. The obvious thing is to go to the authorities, but Oya doesn't want to do that because she doesn't want to get deported.'

'So why go to Jodie Martindale?'

'Maybe Jodie was there too.'

'At a party where there were escort girls?'

'Jesus, David – you know it happens.'

He supposed that he did. The average punter might assume these City rave-ups would be like the drugs and sex-fuelled orgies depicted in *The Wolf of Wall Street*, the girls immediately getting on the tables and stripping. But more likely, they'd each turn up on some rich guy's arm, looking beautiful and elegant, and would behave like duchesses all night. Sex with the rich guys would come later.

'Let's take a guess that Oya saw Jodie interacting with this Lou Garoo,' Anushka said. 'Perhaps he was someone she and her father were going to do business with. Perhaps it was someone they were already doing business with. Maybe Oya was just giving them a heads-up: "You don't want to get in bed with this character".'

'How would Oya know who Jodie was?'

'They were at a party where everyone was talking. How difficult could it be to find out?'

David frowned as he drove. 'So what are we saying? Jodie's

abduction was retaliation? That Jodie confronted this sex trafficker, and got kidnapped? Why not just kill her?'

'I don't know. But there is one other possibility. A pretty nasty one, if I'm honest.'

'Let's hear it.'

'It's not very PC of me, but let's deal in realities. If we *are* talking about sex traffickers, a pristine English rose like Jodie Martindale could fetch a lot more than some poor immigrant mother-of-three who's been starved and beaten and dragged all over the place.'

David didn't reply. That was indeed a nasty thought.

Ahead on the left, he now saw a signpost for South Weald Services. He realised that he hadn't eaten all day. 'Nushka, you've done a hell of a job.'

'Well, there's no smoking gun.'

'No, but we've got something to go with at least. Where you off to now?'

'Back to the Shed.'

'Bit late, isn't it?'

'I've got to get my laptop. I want to write this stuff up tonight.'

'OK...'

'Also, if that new printer has arrived, it could still be sitting on your drive.'

'Don't worry about that. I'll sort it when I get home. I'm only an hour away.'

'I'll do it,' she said. 'I'm almost there.'

'OK – we get our heads together tomorrow. See what we come up with.'

He cut the call as he swerved into the service station car park. Inside, he bought a burger and chips, and coffee. At this time of night, he was alone when he took his tray into the seating area. The few members of staff around were pushing brooms.

Before eating, he made a quick phone call.

'Deepthroat', as Anushka and Norm referred to him, was a veteran these days, and though retired from CID, still with Essex Police, working as an intelligence analyst. David was happy to let the others refer to the guy by that time-honoured nickname because he would never divulge his real name. They'd first got to know each other during Lampwick Lane. In fact, it was Deepthroat who'd originally brought David the crucial info. Of course, that had been on the condition that David would ignore his own peripheral involvement in Jack Pettigrew's racket. David had been as good as his word, and Deepthroat had assisted him ever since.

However, there was no answer. There never was. David left a recorded message: 'Lou Garoo. It's all word-of-mouth, so all we can do is spell it how it sounds.'

He commenced eating, at the same time trying to put together the bits of data they'd gathered. Many of them fitted, but there were still questions.

The main one still being that if this Lou Garoo was someone Jodie Martindale had known through her business connections, and she'd confronted him, and her disappearance was a result of that, would it not have been better for him if he'd had her killed rather than abducted? Why go to the trouble of making it look as if a professional kidnap gang were at work in Essex and then not complete the illusion?

Sure, it might have been lucrative to sell Jodie into slavery, but wouldn't that have been a risk? As Oya Oyinola herself had proved, escapes happened.

David opened his laptop.

Was it conceivable that this guy had been connected to

Jodie's father? That seemed more likely; Ralph Martindale had done business at high level for decades. Suppose Jodie had gone to see her father after all, her father had confronted the trafficker, and Jodie's abduction had been some kind of insurance taken out against Ralph saying anything?

That would explain things but was it conceivable? That a man – and not just any man, a man like Ralph Martindale – would sit there as the years rolled by, knowing that his daughter was being held against her will, and never once trying to rescue her or informing the police?

It was ridiculous. No parent would allow that to happen.

Frustrated, David made random searches on the Martindale family. Much of the information he turned up related to the kidnapping. He even found his own story and follow-up articles relating to his own downfall as a result of it. But he also located references to both Ralph and Jodie Martindale from before that fateful day.

On one occasion, father and daughter were interviewed for a financial services blogsite. On another, Jodie was photographed while speaking on behalf of her father and MD Solutions at a Young Entrepreneurs conference. But nothing referred to anyone called Lou Garoo.

He went and got himself a refill from the coffee machine. On returning, an electronic ping alerted him to a text. He checked the phone. It was from Deepthroat.

No intel

David deleted it. That wasn't completely unexpected, but it was annoying. Deepthroat had access to police databases all over the country, and that didn't just mean Criminal Records, but known associates, known aliases, the works.

David mulled it over. It stood to reason that whoever Lou Garoo was, he'd be a business contact of the Martindales, otherwise why would they have been with him at some function in London? He sipped coffee as he threw a wider net online, looking not for Ralph Martindale and his daughter, but for Ralph Martindale and business associates.

This time, something caught his eye straight away.

The second link down connected to an FT article from 1985, referring to Ralph Martindale and Nick Thorogood. They hadn't just been work colleagues of course, they'd been best friends, for which reason David hadn't even considered Thorogood in this context, but this particular item referred to a court case.

David opened it. The first thing he saw was the grainy image of a much younger Nick Thorogood than he was used to, wearing a smart polo shirt, his platinum locks cut short.

Alongside it, the story read:

City trader, Nicholas Thorogood, sensationally walked free from Southwark Crown Court today when the prosecution failed to offer evidence.

Thorogood, 29, a trader with the high-yield bond division of the British branch of US multinational investment bank, Morgan Stanley, had been accused of making unauthorised and fraudulent trades. Despite his acquittal, Thorogood has been dismissed from his post, and was severely criticised by former colleagues. June Mycroft, General Manager of the London Branch, said: 'Party lifestyles and cowboy practices are not what this business is about. For whatever reason, the CPS opted not to proceed. But this is not exoneration. Incidents like this cast us all in an undeserved bad light.'

However, not all his fellow employees were so scathing.

Ralph Martindale, 28, Thorogood's fellow trader at MS, said: 'Nick took chances, but that was how things were done in the City when we arrived here. I know what everyone will say. "Oh, another City slimeball got caught with his fingers in the till but managed to wriggle out of it." But let's be fair, Nick's now out of a job. He's also out of trust. Plus he's had a big scare. For a natural-born chancer, that'll be a sobering lesson.'

David was reminded why he hadn't pursued his interest in Thorogood previously. Scandal mag editors like Connie Curzon and Oli Hubert had expressed no enthusiasm, having argued that he was one of those personalities who thrived on controversy. But David had also been put off because Thorogood's main notoriety stemmed from financial double-dealing, which wasn't just boring but had also been standard for the wideboy culture of the City back in the 1980s.

Even so, he flipped through his files.

The groundwork he'd done on Thorogood was easily located, but the Southwark court case aside, it was petty stuff: a cannabis bust shortly after Thorogood had left the City, for which he'd received a police caution; accusations by an ex-girlfriend that he was 'mentally cruel'; a brief wave of negative publicity in the late 1990s when he'd been involved in a violent incident in a central London strip club. None of which, of course, had seemed too problematic in the light of his much-publicised good works.

His entertainment company, London After Midnight, was a more secretive operation, but then it would be if it catered purely to the mega-wealthy. With no magazine to back him, David hadn't even tried to penetrate it, though he had scanned one of their calling cards.

He summoned the relevant images onto the screen. The

top one was the front of the card. It depicted Big Ben silhouetted against the moon, the fingers resting at one minute
past twelve. Alongside it:

London
After
Midnight

The lower image, which was the back of the card, bore
all the essential contact information, and underneath that a
company motto:

Enjoy what you've earned

David regarded it tiredly. And then sat up.
Was it his imagination or ...?

Enjoy what you've earned

He dug the scrap of paper from his pocket, the one on
which the zombified version of Ralph Martindale at the
Merrivale care home had written:

ENJOY WHAT YOU FUCKING EARNED

A few minutes later he walked out into the car park and
climbed into his car, but didn't turn the engine on. It could
not be the case that Nick Thorogood was implicated in this.
The guy had flourished since he'd been railroaded out of
the finance industry. A regular on TV and in the tabloids.
He had so much to lose.

Unless, of course, he was one of these villains who hid out in the open.

Another thought occurred to David. All along, they'd wondered why Jodie Martindale, on the one occasion she'd managed to get a phone call out, had rung her younger brother rather than her home or maybe her father. But suppose she'd done that because she'd been wary of someone her father might be very close to? Someone he might unwittingly confide in?

It couldn't be real? Could it?

Who the sodding hell was Lou Garoo?

It struck David that Hannah Bulstrode might know someone of that name, but it was too late to try her now. Then again, if Hannah Bulstrode knew him, that meant it was a real name, probably belonging to some fellow high-flyer, so it was impossible to imagine that it wouldn't be traceable online somewhere. He'd already searched for it exhaustively, but now he reopened his laptop and tried again. Still with no result.

He sat back, thinking hard, trying to come at this thing laterally.

Like he'd told Deepthroat, the info had only been provided by word of mouth. So could it be a spelling issue?

He searched again, this time keying in 'Lew Garoo'.

It brought the same negative result.

He tried 'Lew Garou', but again to no avail.

Stiff with fatigue, David sat back. It felt hopeless. He was more than ready to chuck it in. But one last throw of the dice never hurt.

He tried 'Lou Garou'.

And something appeared. It wasn't quite the same phrase; it was *loup-garou*. Which apparently was French.

David sat upright.

French?

Oya Oyinola was an Ivory Coast national, whose first language was French.

He leaned forward. The website he'd opened was a French–English dictionary.

He gazed long and hard at the phrase *loup-garou*, and then hit the translate tool.

Its meaning came up: *Werewolf or wolf-man.*

'Jesus H,' David breathed slowly. It wasn't a name, it was a description...

Wolf-man. A guy who behaved like a wolf? That could be any number of vicious bastards. But Oya Oyinola had been quite specific. He wasn't a beast or a brute. He was a *wolf*.

David's thoughts strayed unavoidably back to that cheap 1990s TV show, *Night Prowler*, on which Nick Thorogood had established his signature wolf's howl.

At Junction 28, David swung east onto the A12, multiple images flickering in his mind's eye.

Nick Thorogood, the king of high-roller entertainment. Flamboyant, eccentric, famous for his platinum mane and chunky bling, but also for his genial personality and witty comments. For appearing in lifestyle mags to give insights into his luxurious private world, but also making presentations at charity galas, snipping ribbons...

It was the proverbial life in a fishbowl. It was being a celebrity for the sake of being a celebrity. But clearly Thorogood enjoyed that, and it paid him well. Would he endanger it all with reckless criminal activity?

The truth was that David couldn't assume he wouldn't,

because aside from the superficial glitz and glamour, he didn't know anything about the guy.

Though he knew someone who would.

He scrabbled with the knobs on his dashboard, intending to call Norm. And then remembered that Norm had left him two other texts, which he still hadn't checked. He snatched his phone, calling up the most recent message.

> Trying to get you all day. Don't call back now. Too late. Speak in morning.

David used his left thumb to key in a response.

> No probs

According to the dashboard clock it was after midnight, which again made him realise how fatigued he was. Perhaps that was one reason he never noticed the spinning blue light closing from behind. He didn't even spot it while he was texting, this time because he was hard-focused on the message, determined to give Norm something to think about the moment he woke up.

> But how's this?
> Nick Thorogood – long-term family friend of Martindales
> Nick Thorogood on Night Howler
> Lou Garoo . . . loup-garou
> Oya Oyinola spoke French

The phone slipped, landing in the passenger seat footwell.

'Shit!' He reached down, scraped about and picked it back up, continuing his message.

What do we really know about Thorogood?

At which point he realised that he still had an unopened text from Norm. He clicked it, and a police siren activated behind him. David almost jumped from his skin.

He dropped his phone into his lap, though it was already too late.

'Christ's sake,' he groaned. They'd seen him texting at this time of night? In near-darkness?

The car behind flashed its headlights aggressively. David indicated left and veered onto the shoulder, decelerating. As he did, his eyes flickered down to the phone and Norm's message.

You were right. Watch Jorgenson. Bent as they come.

David brought his Fiesta to a halt.

The police car drew in behind him, where it was more visible in his rear-view mirror. He was surprised to see that it wasn't a uniform car; wasn't even Division, let alone Traffic. As David wondered about this, an officer strode up the Fiesta's offside flank, leaned down at the window, and grinned behind his torch.

It was Detective Inspector Tony Jorgenson.

43

'You don't have to say anything,' Jorgenson intoned, cuffing David's hands behind his back and patting him down, finding his car keys and pocketing them. 'Though it may harm your defence if you fail to mention when questioned something you later rely on in court.'

'What am I being arrested for?' David asked as Jorgenson opened the rear door to his unmarked car, a gleaming black Ford Kuga.

Jorgenson pushed him down by the head and thrust him into the back seat. 'I've already told you – assaulting members of Jason Bulstrode's security staff down in Cornwall.'

David straightened himself up as the DI climbed in behind the wheel, closed the driver's door and switched the engine on. Aside from the two of them, there was nobody else in there.

'Let me guess,' David said. 'Devon and Cornwall couldn't handle it, so the big, bad boys of Essex had to step in?'

Jorgenson pulled out onto the empty carriageway, David's Fiesta receding behind them.

'Cross-force cooperation. One of their yobs comes round here and causes trouble on our patch, and then runs home, thinking he's safe ... they arrest him, send him back to us.' Jorgenson spoke casually, as if this whole thing was too routine to be interesting. 'And we do the same for them.'

'Impressive nevertheless. I could've come back here from any direction.'

Jorgenson chuckled. 'Not in the age of Google Maps.'

'Still shows commitment. Hanging round like that on an empty dual carriageway. Could've taken me all night to show up.'

'Cheers. Always appreciate it when my policework gets commended.'

'I imagine it doesn't happen very often. Seems like a small-time gig for a Cold Cases DI, though.'

David's words petered out as they headed down a narrow side road.

'It's a busy night,' Jorgenson replied. 'We all have to muck in.'

David glanced left and right. Black, silent fields lay on either side. 'Doesn't look busy.'

'Well, you're in the country. There's lots going on out here that no one ever sees.'

'I don't know if this'll make any difference,' David said, 'but when I left Mrs Bulstrode's company a few hours ago, it was on reasonable terms. If her husband made this complaint earlier today, it's likely been superseded by now.'

Jorgenson regarded him with amusement through the rear-view mirror. 'Surely you already know, Mr Crime Beat UK? We don't need a complainant to charge someone with assault.'

'It was self-defence … and minor stuff. A fracas.'

'We can give your excuses the minuscule attention they deserve when we get to the nick. In the meantime, stop talking.'

David gazed around again, seeing only darkness. By his estimation the closest police station with custody facilities was Chelmsford, the turn-off to which lay only a few miles from where he'd been pulled over. This was not the quickest route to it, if it was a route to anywhere.

In front of him, Jorgenson was a motionless, heavy-set form behind the wheel.

On first seeing the DI, David had instinctively knocked his phone down into the footwell, and backheeled it under his seat. The last thing he'd wanted was the bastard seeing that text from Norm. But now, denuding himself of communications felt like a big error.

'Isn't this a breach of protocol?' David said. 'Aren't there at least two of you required when it's a prisoner transport? Especially in a vehicle like this, which isn't designed for that purpose.'

Jorgenson laughed. It was a low, menacing rumble. 'It's usually the case that *one* of us is all *I* need.'

David began testing the cuffs. But his wrists were clamped.

'But speak of the devil,' the DI said.

David saw that they were approaching a small crossroads, on the right side of which a figure in dark clothing was waiting. He wasn't surprised when they pulled up, and the figure, which was wearing black running gear, black gloves and a black anorak, pulled its hood back to reveal the youthful features of DS Tim Bly. Jorgenson powered his window down and Bly leaned in, giving the prisoner a cursory glance.

'You get everything?' Jorgenson asked.

'Everything you asked for. It's in the car.'

David looked past them and saw that another vehicle, the make and model impossible to discern, was waiting by the kerb a dozen yards down the lane on the right.

'We've got miladdo bang to rights, as you can see,' Jorgenson said. 'But we're not done yet. It'd be pretty difficult secreting anything on his person, seeing as he's dressed for his hols an' all. I've had a look anyway, but there's nothing there. At the very least though, we need his phone and his dictation machine. He was driving a red Fiesta. It's locked up six miles down the A12, northbound carriageway.' He handed David's keys through the window. 'Scoot down there, Timmo. Seize anything of interest, but like I say, the phone and the Dictaphone are the main thing.'

'Illegal searches now, Inspector Jorgenson?' David said.

Jorgenson chuckled. 'Another dipshit who reads stuff online and thinks he knows the law.'

Bly snorted a smile, though he didn't look overjoyed. And that wasn't a good sign.

Jorgenson was an old-schooler, a heavyweight. He'd been in the job when the rules were routinely bent. On top of that, he was corrupt. Black bag stuff wouldn't bother him. But Bly was a relative newbie. Not long out of uniform, he'd have had the multiple regulations that modern-day cops lived by hammered into him. OK, he might be in awe of law-unto-themselves dinosaurs like Jorgenson, but how keen would he be to get his own hands dirty?

And if that was the reason for his unhappiness now, it hardly boded well.

'Norm...?' It was Anushka. She sounded shrill, panicky.

Norm had struggled to find the phone on his bedside table. Now he struggled to find the lamp. 'Erm... yeah.'

'What're you doing?'

'Anushka, it's the middle of the night. What do you think I'm doing?'

'Did you go to the Shed earlier? I mean when you got back from the prison?'

'Yes.' He found the lamp switch. 'For about five minutes. Why?'

'Did you take anything away with you? I mean like our laptops, that box of paperwork David got from Freddie Martindale?'

Norm knuckled the sleep from his eyes. 'I left everything as was.'

'In that case, I don't suppose I need to ask if you left the door open as well, with its lock smashed? And all the lights on?'

He sat up properly. 'What are you saying – the Shed's been burgled?'

'It looks like it. But I don't think it's a routine burglary.'

'How do you mean?'

'The petty cash is still in David's top drawer, even though they'd broken it open. Whoever it is, they've only taken stuff relating to the story.'

Norm swung his legs to the floor. 'If you're at the Shed, where's David?'

'That's the other thing.' Her voice almost broke. 'I don't know.'

'You've checked his house hasn't been broken into as well?'

'I've walked around and I can't see any sign of that. But there's an alarm on the house, isn't there?'

Norm paused. David's house was indeed alarmed, but the Shed wasn't. Not yet. 'This is probably a dumb question, but you've tried the doorbell?'

'Course I have, and no one bloody answered!' She sounded panicky, almost tearful. 'His car's not here anyway. Norm, he's not back – and he should have been. It was ages ago when I spoke to him.'

'Anushka, cool it.' Norm switched the phone to loud-speaker as he got dressed. 'Cornwall to Colchester's no quick jaunt. He could still be on the road. You've tried ringing him, I presume?'

'It keeps switching to voice-mail.'

'Could be out of power, been a long day ...'

'I spoke to him at roughly eleven. He said he was one hour away.'

'Could have run into traffic.'

'*Oh, come on, Norm! A break-in at the Shed and now this!*'

'All right.' Norm climbed into his shoes. 'Listen ... after your first visit to Keppel Hall, you taught us both to use the location-share on WhatsApp.'

'Oh God, yes. I also told you both to keep it on. I'll check.'

'Fine, you check. But in the meantime stay put. I'm coming over.'

'Norm ...' She sounded querulous. 'This thing's just got real, hasn't it?'

He understood why it made her nervous. It was easy to discuss crimes and criminals when it was playing out on a storyboard in a newspaper office. But there was always a moment when you suddenly came face to face with that dangerous breed, and it touched all kinds of deep, primal fears about predators and their capabilities.

'You don't think this means we're onto them, do you?' Anushka asked. 'The kidnappers?'

'Not necessarily. Stay put, like I say.'

'It's just that, if we are, I'm here on my *own*.'

Norm halted on the staircase, the full import of that striking him. When he continued down it was at speed. 'I'll be a few minutes. Secure the door if you can. Barricade yourself in if it makes you feel better.'

'Shouldn't we call the police?'

'Not this time.'

'Why not?'

'You're just going to have to trust me.'

'That's the sort of thing David would say.'

'Yeah.' He climbed into his Jaguar. 'And on this occasion, he'd be right.'

44

David was facing a difficult decision. But unlike previous tough calls, this one didn't involve weighing professional gain against basic human ethics as much as his chances of being jailed against his chances of being killed.

Ten minutes ago, they'd left Tim Bly climbing into his own vehicle, and now were pushing deeper into the night, following single-track farm lanes that David had never even known existed.

'You think no one'll notice I've gone?' David enquired.

Jorgenson made no reply.

'If nothing else, Jason Bulstrode might be interested to know how it all panned out? He's the one who lodged the complaint.'

Again, nothing.

David looked out of the window, straining his eyes to pierce the murk. And failing. They drove on, making turns seemingly at random.

'You know what a joke coppers like you are these days, Jorgenson?' David said.

The gaze that flickered his way through the rear-view mirror was baleful.

'You think you're the only ones who know what you're doing,' David added. 'In most cases, though, you're the ones who make mistakes, who give the job a bad name.'

'Just keep talking, Crime Beat.'

'You act as though these rules you're happy to break were imposed purely to make your lives difficult. Whereas, in reality, they were brought in to protect members of the public against blokes exactly like you. Just think, Jorgs – if *you* weren't there we wouldn't even need these rules you despise. It's no wonder coppers like you are a dying breed. You spent all your careers fitting people up and kicking their heads in, yet it made no difference to the crime stats, did it? You're not some tyrannosaur tearing your way through the underworld, Jorgenson. You're a fucking brontosaurus, all attitude and belly, waddling along at a snail's pace.'

Even in the darkness of the moving vehicle, he could see his captor's neck and shoulders stiffening, could sense the anger seething off him.

'Skiving, cutting corners,' David said. 'Locked in a bog somewhere when it turns nasty.'

The DI threw a furious half-glance at him.

The irony was that David's laundry list of contempt was more designed to work himself up than his opponent. His blood too was simmering, his whole body tensing.

'You were a laughing stock even when I was on Crime Beat. Especially after Lampwick Lane. I mean, you obviously conned someone to make it to DI.'

'I'm warning you, Kelman…' Again, the words were a dangerous rumble.

'Somehow, blokes like you have this ability to get through their careers fucking up and yet still get promoted, don't you? Is it that old mirage thing – when walking round the nick all day carrying a piece of paper makes it look like you're working? Or is it just that you've got stuff on people? That'd be more like it, wouldn't it? Easier finding shit to blackmail the bosses with than catching criminals, eh? *Criminals*, Tony ... you know? Your fucking mates.'

'You shut your—'

Jorgenson had half turned again, but hadn't completed the sentence before his mouth met the heel of David's left training shoe.

SMACK!

It was a stupendous kick.

The David of old wouldn't have been able to manage it. He wouldn't have been motivated for one thing. But more importantly, he wouldn't have been physically adept enough. The new David though, was lean, flexible and strong, and had easily been able to roll back, coil his body like a spring and then catapult his legs forward, packing enormous power as he did.

Jorgenson's head swung leftward across his shoulders, his hands slid from the wheel, and the Kuga veered sideways, jolting down into a ditch, its nearside bodywork ploughing along the hedgerow, before sputtering to a halt.

Breathing hard, David righted himself.

In front of him, Jorgenson hung sideways in his seat belt. He wasn't unconscious, but stunned and groaning, his head lolling.

David spun on his backside, drew his legs back and rammed both feet forward again, this time slamming the offside rear passenger window, the entire pane exploding outward.

He thrust his feet forward a third time, now in a genuinely athletic effort, knifing his legs and body out through the gap where the window had been, banging his lower back on the bottom of the frame, but gritting his teeth and riding it out as he wriggled free of the car.

He commenced running along the road, or rather stag-gering. With his hands still clamped behind his back, it was difficult. Plus, the road surface was unmade. In the glow of the headlights, it was more like a rutted track, muddy after the recent rain and sloping uphill. David stumbled and tripped. Behind him meanwhile, the Kuga's driver door banged open, Jorgenson swearing as he broke out into the night. Bound or not, David still felt that he could outrun the overweight, ale-guzzling bastard. The problem would come if Jorgenson realised that and opted to get his car out of the ditch instead, which he'd manage in a minute or two, all of which time David would be blundering along darkened, empty roads leading to who knew where.

And then … salvation. Of a sort.

A light had come into view about sixty yards ahead. It looked to be emanating from a single bulb located on the wall of a brick building standing to the left. David stumbled onward, panting but re-energised. Only as he drew closer did he realise that the light shone onto an open space covered with thorny scrub and bits of rusty farm machinery. What was more, the track appeared to lead into that space as if this was the end of the line. And there were several shadowy figures waiting there.

Waiting for him and Jorgenson maybe?

David tottered to a halt, the sweat chilling on his body.

He barely heard the hefty feet come thudding up behind, but cringed at the excruciating pain as a massive fist slammed into the back of his neck. He sagged downward, stupefied, hit the ground with his knees, and then was only half aware of being dragged back to his feet.

Jorgenson came round into view, fists twisted into David's

vest. The copper's face was spattered crimson, but written with an angry kind of glee.

'You fucking shithouse, Kelman!' he hissed. 'I love it when toerags give me all the reason I need. But fucking trust you to do it the one time I can't retaliate.' He swung David around and marched him one-handed up the track. 'Don't get me wrong. I'd be happy to do this myself, but why get any deeper in than I need to? You deserve the best kicking any bloke in Britain's ever had. Tonight though, we've got some experts to take care of it.'

David's blurry eyes focused again on the figures waiting just ahead.

There were three of them in total.

45

'Norman Harrington?' the female voice said. 'That name sounds familiar, though someone I know vaguely is not someone I appreciate phone calls from in the early hours of the morning.'

'I'm sorry, Ms Curzon,' Norm replied as he drove. 'Perhaps you can consider this an indirect phone call from David Kelman?'

'David . . . ? Ah, yes. You're the Norman Harrington who used to work with David on the *Essex Examiner.*' Her accent was posh, but her voice croaky, as if she smoked too many tabs and swilled too many coffees. 'I'd still like to know what you think you're playing at, daaahling?'

'I seriously need your help. Or rather, David does.'

Connie Curzon, editor of *Scandalous*, was about to reply but a male voice mumbled something in the bedroom alongside her.

'It's work-related,' she snapped at whoever it was.

'For God's sake,' Anushka asked from the front passenger seat. 'What's happening?'

'Who's that with you?' Connie demanded to know, her voice suspicious. No doubt there were many people who'd enjoy making her the butt end of a nasty joke. 'This had better not be some kind of stupid game.'

'It's no game, Ms Curzon,' Anushka spoke up. 'And we're

sorry for calling you at home. We got your number from a contacts database that David had me set up for him…'

'And you say you're not our techie genius,' Norm muttered.

'My name's Anushka Chawla,' Anushka added. 'I'm also ex-*Examiner* and I'm working with David and Norman on a story…'

'It's charming to learn that David has got some of his old friends back,' Connie cut in, 'but I would remind you of the hour. And as I'm now taking the trouble to go downstairs and put a pot of coffee on, it had better be worth more than that.'

'David's in trouble,' Norm said.

'And mysteriously,' Connie replied, 'the world hasn't stopped turning.'

'It's bad, Ms Curzon. At least, we think it is.'

A brief but profound silence greeted this, followed by what sounded like coffee bubbling in a percolator and then a gentle trickle as it was poured into a mug.

'Ms Curzon?' Norm asked.

'I'm here.'

'I know this is weird…'

'It's not weird, darling. It would be weird if David *didn't* get himself into trouble at some point. No one else on my books snoops the way he does. But before you look to apportion blame, he never OKs any of his projects with me beforehand. He's entirely his own man.'

'I know that.' Norm steered his Jaguar onto the A12. 'But I'm still wondering if I can ask you a couple of questions?'

'You can ask anything you wish. Whether I'll answer is another matter.'

'It's about someone you may know.'

'Someone I may know?'

'I should also congratulate you, by the way, on your helmsmanship of *Scandalous*. Two hundred thou a week is no small circulation in a digital age.'

'You can save the toadying for another time, Norman. I'm sure you hate what we do here. So, let's get to it, eh? I need my beauty sleep more than most.'

'First of all,' he said, 'I'm wondering if you've ever heard the name Lou Garoo?'

'Hmm.' She was clearly mulling it over. 'I'm sure I'd remember it if I had, so it's a no-go thus far.'

'In that case, I'd like to talk to you about Nick Thorogood.' A pregnant silence followed. Norm glanced at the screen glowing on Anushka's lap; it was her phone and it portrayed a sat nav-type road map. 'We on target?' he mouthed.

She nodded, but wasn't paying much attention to it. She awaited Connie's reply.

'You know who I'm talking about?' Norm asked.

'Of course,' Connie said.

'*What* do you know, Ms Curzon? I'm talking the real stuff, not the froth.'

Another silence; briefer this time.

'It sounds terribly intriguing, this thing you and David are working on.' Though in truth, Connie didn't sound intrigued. More like wary.

'We can bring you in if you help us out,' Norm said.

'Let's get one thing clear first. This trouble David's got himself into – it's definitely to do with Nick Thorogood?'

'Would that bother you?' Norm asked.

'David,' she sighed. 'David, David … how many times did I tell you no?'

That was the last response either had expected. Mainly

because it sounded heartfelt; in other words, it implied that the editor of *Scandalous*, one of the most cynical mags on the market, didn't just view David as a useful freelancer, but someone she cared about.

It also implied that investigating Nick Thorogood was genuinely a bad idea.

'Ms Curzon,' Norm persisted, 'there must be something you can tell us?'

'Nick Thorogood thinks he's a national treasure,' she replied.

'I get that.'

'He's not. In actual fact he's a nasty piece of work.'

'I get that too. You only have to look at his past...'

'I'm not talking about his past. So he was a chancer in the City. Wow. Idiots like that were ten-a-penny back then. Though I wouldn't deny that a willingness to play fast and loose with other people's money betrays a certain degree of immorality. Today, Nick has cultivated this image of likeable playboy, whose worst offence is that he enjoys his wealth in public. Ostensibly, he funds this lavish lifestyle by providing for every entertainment need the rich and famous have when they're visiting London. They sign on with Nick Thorogood and they'll never need to call a taxi or ride the Tube ... they'll never need to travel anywhere unless it's in one of his luxury limousines. He'll secure the best rooms for them in the best hotels, the best seats at all the best shows, the best tables in the best restaurants. And they never have to lift a finger themselves. It's all part of the one-stop service.'

'You said "ostensibly",' Norm said. 'So that's not the whole story?'

'Darling, even from the little you see of Nick Thorogood in the public arena, do you seriously think a man like that could ever be satisfied playing a glorified booking-agent? True, he performs that role and he performs it well, but the real money rolls in from different sources.'

'We're all ears.'

'I've already explained to you that the people he entertains are the topmost tier. We're not talking the local greengrocer who got lucky on the Lottery, or some middle-manager who sails on cruise ships and thinks it gold-plates him. Nick Thorogood's preferred customer base is the world's highest-rollers. Titans in their fields, the untouchables ... and, my dear, some of these people have the grossest appetites.'

'We're talking sex?' Norm said.

'Of course we're talking sex. And drugs. And a whole range of other bizarre, unedifying itches that people will pay to have scratched – so long as discretion is also part of the package.'

On reflection, it was perhaps obvious. Thorogood's company was even called London After Midnight. How much more in plain sight could he have hidden?

'If all this is true, how come someone like you gives Thorogood a pass?' Norm said. 'Others wouldn't get one. Their reputations would be mud.'

'My dear Norman, it's the nature of the beast. Look at the people he caters to. Each one has a thousand different ways to prevent his or her name being sullied. Thorogood himself doesn't have to do very much. But he's thorough too. And ruthless. If any of the press *do* get interested, and he can't fob them off with the laddishness of it all, he'll pay. The money on offer is usually eye-watering. And if that doesn't work, well, he can use other means.'

'You mean threats? He's dangerous?'

'Perhaps not Thorogood himself.' Connie paused, as

though wondering how best to articulate something she had clearly experienced for herself. 'Look, I don't wish to alarm you, but like many people operating in those elevated circles, Nick Thorogood has extensive nefarious contacts. One of his closer business associates is Vladimir Ivankov. Do you know that name?'

Norm didn't. He glanced at Anushka, who also shook her head. 'That's a negative.'

'It's no surprise,' Connie said. 'Ivankov's another of these staggeringly wealthy oligarchs who have now settled in the UK, though unlike many of the others, this one likes to keep a low profile. Back home he has massive stakes in a number of what were once publicly owned oil, gas and steel companies. You ever hear of the "loans for shares" scandal? Moscow, 1995?'

Norm had. He'd researched it during his Crime Beat days. In short, it was an attempt to raise cash reserves for the Russian government, but it was rigged in favour of government supporters, and it led to the privatisation of state assets at criminally low prices. The whole thing ended up creating a superpowered but super-corrupt upper class.

'Ivankov was up to his ears in it,' Connie said. 'On top of that, he also now controls a range of secretive international investment firms, among, shall we say, *other* things...'

'So basically,' Norm interrupted, 'David's got on the wrong side of the Russian Mafia?'

'You can't possibly write that,' Connie said, 'and certainly not with my name attached. But do the maths, Norman.'

'So this is the real reason you won't write the truth about Nick Thorogood?'

'It's not just me, I assure you. All of this adds up to make him less of a prospect where any news or features editor might be concerned, even if it's a lightweight story.'

'Ms Curzon!' Anushka put in. 'What David and we are looking into is a bit more serious than pimping for footballers and pop stars.'

'Oh dear.' Connie sounded worried. 'In that case it's better if you don't tell me any more.'

'On the basis that you can't help?' Norm asked. 'Or won't?'

'On the basis that what I don't know is less likely to get me killed.'

Norm appreciated the candour. 'In that case we'll leave it there.'

'No, wait!' Anushka blurted.

'*We'll leave it there*,' Norm reiterated. 'Thanks for all your help, Ms Curzon. If this story has a happy ending, I'll be sure to copy you in.'

'Don't bother. In fact, it's best if you never contact me regarding this matter again. OK?'

'As you wish.'

The line went dead.

Anushka snorted. 'Bloody drama queen!'

'Drama queen nothing,' he replied. 'Looks like we've poked a real hornets' nest here.'

She considered. 'Even if Nick Thorogood's dodgier than anyone thought, I don't suppose we actually *know* that he's Lou Garoo.'

It was David who'd made that link, of course. And he'd only passed it on by text. He hadn't discussed it with them in any detail yet.

'No,' Norm agreed. 'And I will admit to being a bit worried about the *Night Prowler* thing. I mean, yeah, Thorogood used to howl on live TV. But how would Oya Oyinola know that? Did they screen *Night Prowler* back in Ivory Coast?'

'They might have.' Anushka became thoughtful. 'And just suppose they did. And suppose she recognised Thorogood as the one at that party with Ralph and Jodie. That would explain why Jodie wanted to go and talk to her dad but ended up not doing; perhaps she was unsure how to broach such a delicate subject. Might also be the reason why Jodie isn't dead yet, Thorogood being an old family friend. But there's no damn proof.'

Norm mused. 'What was it Connie Curzon said? That it all adds up?'

'The police wouldn't even regard it as circumstantial.'

'The Russian connections are impressive.'

'Maybe we should just see what's happening with David?'

Norm nodded. 'How far are we?'

She glanced at her phone, a tiny icon indicating David's mobile sitting in the middle of a luminous road map. As promised, David had kept his location-share turned on.

'Very close,' she said. 'By the looks of it, he's parked up on the northbound... in fact, he's coming up now.'

The dual carriageway remained empty, but Norm decelerated from sixty to fifty. As he did, they sailed by a familiar red Ford Fiesta sitting alone on the hard shoulder on the opposite carriageway. There was no light on inside it and they spied no movement. Anushka pivoted in her seat, watching as they passed it by.

'Abandoned by the side of the road,' Norm said. 'That's never a good sign.'

'Wait a minute...' Anushka released her belt so that she could turn properly. 'A car's pulling up behind it.'

Norm decelerated again, glancing at the offside mirror. It

failed to give him a visual on the Fiesta, but he knew that a vehicle had just passed them, headed the opposite way.

'Can you get the number?' he asked.

'No, it's too far. But someone's getting out. Bloke on his own...' What little she could see passed from view as the road curved. 'Damn it! Norm, you've got to turn round.'

He accelerated, eyes peeled for the next turn-off.

'Hang on!' Anushka said. 'David's phone's on the move.'

Norm risked a glance at the screen, but it was difficult to see.

'It's left the main drag,' she said. 'Gone onto the back roads.'

Norm frowned.

'Could that have been David?' Anushka wondered. 'Getting out the other car?'

'Could've been.'

'I'll ring him.'

'Don't! Let's work on the basis it isn't David.'

'Who else was it, then? A car thief?'

He almost laughed. 'You mean like an opportunist? He just saw the car and went for it? Even we're not that unlucky.'

'So what do we do?'

'They're still on the move?'

She checked her screen. 'Yeah. Heading into the sticks.'

'Keep tracking them.' They'd reached the M25 round-about, Norm swinging around it at high speed. 'I'll keep driving.'

46

David remained groggy, but still made several mental notes. The grey van parked in the corner of the overgrown yard, next to a purple BMW X3, for example: in shape, it still resembled an ambulance. Then there were the three figures waiting close by. All wore dark clothing: leather jackets, black gloves and black knitted ski masks.

One was slighter than the others and shaped like a woman. The other two were clearly male, one of them squat and powerfully built, the other taller. The quiet menace exuding from the trio was sufficient even to make someone who'd just been punched in the base of the skull straighten up with fear.

'This is him,' Jorgenson said, frogmarching David forward. 'Do your fucking worst. You'll be doing the world a favour.'

The woman was the closest. She cocked her masked head to one side, regarding David with piercing green eyes. 'You don't look like much, Mr Kelman.' Her accent was Northern Irish. 'But it takes all sorts, doesn't it?'

Jorgenson unfastened the handcuffs, and pushed David. He tripped and would have fallen full length had he not landed on the squat, brawny male, who wrapped him in a bearhug, exerting only a little of his strength though even that felt as though it could crush someone's life out. There was clearly no point in struggling, though David's captor still turned him around, twisting his right wrist into a gooseneck.

David gasped; the slightest pressure and he was sure his lower arm would snap. If that wasn't enough, his assailant dug something hard, almost certainly a pistol, into his ribs.

From the corner of his vision, David watched the taller man hand over a wad of notes. Jorgenson skimmed through it, before looking up, irritated. 'What about the rest? This is less than half what we agreed.'

The woman stood unmoved. 'You've delivered less than half of what we were expecting.'

'For Christ's sake, Mara! I brought you Kelman ...'

Mara, David thought. If he hadn't been certain before that he was in the presence of Jodie Martindale's three kidnappers, he was now.

'What about his mates?' the taller man asked. He spoke with a West Midlands accent, which David thought he recognised.

Jorgenson shrugged. 'How much threat can they be?'

'Doesn't matter,' the woman said. 'That's not what we agreed.'

'Look, we've been watching them for a few days. One's a slip of a girl who'll go off the moment some Prince Charming arrives. The other's this old poof who's ready for the knacker's yard. What I *have* got is their laptops. I don't know how much they've written up, or if they've got any other database anywhere, but now you've got *him* ...' he nodded at David, 'you can find out, can't you? I've also brought you Freddie Martindale's bumph. The stuff they retrieved from the squat in Chatham. Did you find the blue-haired kid, by the way?'

'We found her,' the woman said.

'And?'

'She's been dealt with.'

'Clean?'

'Her dealer's in the frame. Wasn't hard.'

'What about the old priest?'

'No one'll even notice he's gone.'

Jorgenson nodded. 'Well, perhaps that should be it for the mo, yeah? Too many corpses leaves a trail all of its own. Best to leave the other journalists be, eh? Like I say, without Kelman, they couldn't find their own arseholes.'

The trio remained inscrutable behind their masks.

As well as terror, David now felt a dull sense of disbelief, not to mention failure. They'd been under observation all this time? And he'd never twigged...

And now there was a direct threat to the others. Not that *he* was going to walk away. Not if his abductors were happy to have this conversation in front of him, and use their real names.

He glanced at the nearby building. It might once have been part of a farm or an abandoned industrial unit, though all he could see of it now was old stone walls, gaping doorways, electric light shining through broken, grime-encrusted windows.

'Where are the laptops and the paperwork?' the woman asked.

'Tim's got them,' Jorgenson replied. 'He's on his way. He's also got this fella's phone – and his Dictaphone. You can check through it all. Just in case there's someone we've missed.' He paused. 'So, what about the money?' There was no reply. 'Look, if you're insisting on it, I can give you the other two's addresses. You can take it from there yourselves.'

The woman turned to her taller compatriot. 'Give him another quarter.'

Jorgenson grunted with dissatisfaction, but accepted the money.

'It won't be difficult finding *your* address either, Jorgenson,' the woman said. 'So be sure you've not fucked us in any way, even by accident.'

The cop eyed her as he slid the cash under his jacket. If he was about to respond, it was negated when an engine growled and a metallic brown Toyota Prius wallowed into the car park.

David shook his head at the sight of it. He'd even spotted the damn Toyota, but had failed to read genuine significance into it.

The car braked and Tim Bly clambered out. 'I've got the stuff,' he said, approaching.

The woman turned to the brute holding David. 'Take him inside.'

The brute wheeled David around and marched him towards the brick structure. David staggered once, twice, and then vomited.

His captor gave a low belly laugh. 'Is good. Get that bad shit out, uh?' He sounded Eastern European. 'We get you comfortable for long, long night.'

47

'OK, according to the map, we're now off-road,' Anushka said.

Norm nodded as he followed the dirt track. 'Where's David?'

'Not too far ahead of us. In fact, he's stopped.'

The truth was that they didn't know if it was David they were following. Once they'd swung around the roundabout and headed back, they'd passed his Fiesta, still parked on the shoulder. Had he left his phone in the car and did someone else now have it? Or, more alarmingly, did they have David? Either way, there'd been no choice but to follow the signal.

Norm slowed down. 'Can you estimate how far ahead he is?'

'Half a mile. Just left of the road.'

The route ascended gently. When they passed a gap in the hedgerow on the left, Norm hit the brake. 'Here?'

Anushka stared through the darkness. 'No. That's just a field. Minus a gate.'

They pressed on, but the road now curved, and suddenly was half blocked by a black Ford Kuga parked so hard to the left that its nearside wheels were down in the ditch, its bodywork meshed with the undergrowth.

Norm halted behind it. They sat motionless, engine rumbling.

Now that they looked closer, the Kuga's rear offside window had shattered outward.

They got out warily.

'This isn't the car from the A12,' Anushka said, 'but it looks familiar.'

'What do you mean?'

'Think I saw it parked the other day. Near David's house. I thought it belonged to one of his neighbours. Either that, or ...'

'Someone pretending to be a neighbour?' Norm suggested.

Anushka got out her phone. 'Time to call the cops, yeah?'

Norm moved back to his Jag. 'You think they'll get here in time?'

'In time for what?'

'In time to stop whatever's going to happen to David now that he's got to wherever he was being taken. We can't even give them directions because we're on unnamed roads ...'

From further along the track, an engine stuttered to life.

'In the car!' Norm said, jumping behind the wheel.

Anushka complied. 'We can't turn around here.'

'No, but we can get out of sight.'

He flipped the Jag into reverse and accelerated back along the track, spinning the wheel left and reversing through the entrance into the field, where he swung them through a three-point turn and then accelerated forward, sliding to a halt behind the hedgerow, so that they were out of sight of the road.

He switched the engine off and gestured for silence when Anushka tried to speak again.

'We can't just hide,' she whispered. 'We need to see who it is and what's going on.'

'Do it quietly then.'

She opened her door and slipped out. Norm did the same, not quite as lithely, though it didn't matter too much because the vehicle they'd heard coming was now negotiating its way noisily past the abandoned Kuga.

Anushka's dim form circled the Jag and padded up to the hedgerow. Norm followed.

The vegetation was in lush profusion. They couldn't see a thing when they tried to peer through it, and didn't dare attempt to push foliage aside because now the approaching vehicle had halted and even switched off its engine. They listened, eyes locked on each other as they heard car doors open.

'What'll they do to him?' someone asked. The voice was young and sounded nervous.

'What does it matter?' an older voice replied. 'He's threatened me with Lampwick Lane for the last fucking time.'

Even in the gloom, Norm could see Anushka mouthing: 'Jorgenson'.

'Do we really want to be connected to this?' the younger voice wondered.

'Bit fucking late to have second thoughts now,' the other replied.

'It's not too late to go back up there and stop it.'

'What's wrong with you, Timmo? Do you know how long we'll get? You any idea what it's like for a copper inside? I mean, yeah, we'd be in isolation, but who'd be making the food we'd eat? Ever had a broken glass omelette for your brekky? How about kippers dipped in diarrhea?'

'For fuck's sake!'

'Look, Jerry Corrigan brought me in on this because he's

a mate and it was an earner. Not because he thought we'd all go down.'

'And because he needed you onside. I mean, something to do with you running the investigation into the Martindale girl.'

'Yeah, so that's another good thing. They can't afford for us to get nicked.'

'So, after they've topped Kelman, what's to stop them doing the same to us?'

Jorgenson sounded thoughtful. 'They won't know when they'll next need us. Truth is it's more likely they'll go and top those other two journalists. Assuming they decide they need to. They'll find that out tonight by leaning on Kelman ...'

'Christ, Tony!'

'Told you at the start, Timmo – you come along with me, it won't be normal coppering.'

'Fuck.'

'Get in your Toyota and get fucking home. And when you're there, get your story straight for what you've been doing tonight, just in case.'

A car door banged closed, an engine revved to life, and a vehicle, presumably Tim Bly's Toyota, rumbled away, its lights flickering as it passed the entrance to the field.

The stillness after it had gone was ear-pummelling. Norm and Anushka stood rigid, the breath tight in their chests. The silence beyond the wall of vegetation was suddenly profound and protracted, as though Jorgenson was listening back to them. A footfall crunched on the other side of the hedgerow. And then another, and another.

Sweat trickled down Norm's face. Was Jorgenson coming to check in the field?

But then a car door opened, before slamming again. Anushka closed her eyes with relief, but Norm didn't because now another thought struck him. He glanced around at the field entrance. The Kuga would have to reverse in here to be able to turn around. Which meant that Jorgenson would spot the Jaguar in the glow of his lights.

He lurched forward, grabbing Anushka's forearm. Running seemed their sole option.

An engine roared to life, and there was a huge scrunching of mud and leaf mulch and then of vegetation ripping and tearing as the Kuga pulled itself free. But it was accelerating forward, not reversing, and the next they knew, it had rounded the bend in the road and the sound of it was dwindling.

Norm felt his shoulders sag. There must be a turning space up ahead. And indeed, less than a couple of minutes later, they heard the vehicle coming back, this time travelling at speed. It growled past the entrance to the field without slowing down.

The night fell silent.

Anushka turned to Norm. 'They're going to torture David.'

'I know.' He stumbled on foot towards the field entrance.

She followed. 'What're we going to do?'

'What do you think? Stop them.'

48

David was bundled into the building through a doorway underneath the exterior bulb. Initially, there was a tiny antechamber with hooks on the left side, various black waterproofs hanging there. Then he was shoved through a left-hand doorway into what appeared to be the main chamber. It was spacious, but again lit by a single bulb, its walls breezeblock, its floor basic cement. The only furnishing was what looked like an old school chair in the middle, alongside a crudely made table. Several other doorways led off into darkness and dust.

David was flung into the chair with such force that it almost tipped over backwards. His brawny captor walked around to the back, keeping his firearm, which looked like a Browning semi-automatic, trained on David's head.

'Hands!'

Cowed by continued prods to his skull from the steel muzzle, David thrust his hands behind his back. He sat awkwardly while his wrists were looped with a tight, sharp cord, which his captor, once he'd drawn them together, wove around the slats in the back of the chair. When the brawny guy came back into view, David's arms were pinioned behind him.

Whatever face lay behind that knitted mask, it chuckled.

'You need to piss pants?' the bastard asked. 'Go ahead. Is quite normal.'

'So you've done this before?' David said.

The chuckle became a hearty laugh, which was all the answer he needed.

The other two now came in. They'd removed their jackets, revealing a sweat-top in the woman's case, a T-shirt in the man's, though both were also wearing shoulder holsters with pistols inserted. The woman was checking through a phone that David recognised as his own, clearly taking note of the numbers recently logged, the man carrying a bulging sack so dirty it was almost black. Its hefty metallic contents clanked when he dumped it on the table. The woman regarded David for several long seconds, before tossing the phone onto the table, alongside the sack. She reached up and stripped off her ski mask.

He was taken aback by the handsome face underneath. She wasn't young, probably approaching fifty, but now that she'd unfurled it, her flame-red hair fell past her shoulders. Her eyes were an intense green, her cheekbones well defined. However, her mouth was cruel. Everything about her was cruel. Her eyes might be scintillating, but they were also hard as pebbles.

'So, Mr Kelman,' she said in her Ulster brogue, 'by all accounts, you have a habit of getting into trouble. But tonight, let me assure you, you've trumped anything that's happened before.'

David swallowed foul-tasting spittle. 'You know me but I don't know you. Bit of an unfair advantage, don't you think?'

'You can call me Mara. You already know that much.'

'And who do you think you've taken prisoner, Mara? Someone important? I'm no one.'

'You wouldn't be the first,' she replied.

The brawnier of the two men chuckled again.

'I'm serious,' David said. 'I'm just a journalist – and not a very good one. I fouled up once too often. I've been trying to find my way back in with a new story, a new angle. I thought I'd found one, but I clearly haven't.'

'The problem is you have,' the taller man replied.

Again, his voice and Brummie accent seemed familiar. David gazed up at him.

'Do … do I know you?' he asked.

There was a brief but intrigued silence. Mara glanced at the taller guy. 'Does he?'

The taller guy said nothing, but after a second of what seemed like reluctant hesitation, yanked off his own ski mask. David's heart sank when the face underneath was exposed.

'The situation's simple, Mr Kelman,' Mara said. 'We're going to ask you lots of questions and you're going to answer them.'

David hung his head. 'I can't tell you what I don't know.'

'What do you think's in that sack alongside you?'

'Dunno.'

'*Look at me!*' Her voice was a whipcrack.

David straightened up.

'Pray we don't need to go into the sack to show you,' she said, quieter. 'But just to prove from the outset that we mean what we say …'

She stepped up close, and for the next two minutes, David was subjected to the hardest non-stop face-slapping he had ever imagined.

Norm and Anushka had opted not to ascend the road. Whatever was happening a few hundred yards from where they'd left the car, it sounded too dangerous to simply walk in through the front door. They'd thus doubled back along the inside of the hedgerow, passing the Jag and keeping going until the ground tilted upward and they'd found themselves among thickets. From here on, they pushed their way through continuous leafage until they were deep inside the coppice and the vegetation thinned out. But it remained dark, and they were poked and clawed by branches as they blundered uphill.

'We should perhaps be quieter about this,' Anushka whispered, aware that they were threshing the undergrowth in their efforts to make haste.

'I agree,' Norm whispered back. 'But whatever's happening up there is happening *now*.'

They slogged on, puffing as the slope steepened.

'David was right about the police being in on it,' Anushka grunted.

'He was right about *some* of the police being in on it,' Norm replied. 'Jorgenson and Bly are a regular double-act. But Corrigan's name shouldn't be a surprise either.'

'He was one of the coppers sent to prison after Lampwick Lane, wasn't he?'

'Correct.'

'And he's out already? Lampwick Lane was only eight years ago.'

'I don't want to disillusion you about the strong arm of the law in twenty-first-century Britain, Nushka,' Norm said, 'but he was out in time to participate in the Martindale kidnapping, and that was six years ago.'

'Do you think he did?'

Norm paused, face sparkling in the slivered moonlight. 'We don't know yet. We don't know what's going on. As always, it's not just the proof we're lacking, it's the connective tissue. We don't know how all these parts fit together.

But Corrigan's just the sort to be involved. The Lampwick Lane trial was before you joined the *Examiner*, but Corrigan persuaded the CPS he was only muscle – that the actual dodgy dealing was done by Elgin and Pettigrew.'

'They believed that?' Anushka asked as they continued up.

'Only because it suited them to.'

'He turned evidence?'

'Yep.' Norm halted for another breather. 'It was David who lit the Lampwick Lane gunpowder, but Corrigan made sure it went bang.'

'Wouldn't that mean he'd have to go into witness protection?'

'Yes. As soon as he'd completed his ridiculously short sentence. I think he got a year and a half, which he served in Category C.'

'So how can he be part of this team?'

Norm shrugged as they clambered on. 'Obviously, he jumped ship. Whoever looks after the supergrasses of the world these days, they weren't going to publicise it.'

'And immediately he got involved in serious crime again?'

'Corrigan was a firearms commander and a personal protection expert. He'd always be a good guy to hire as an enforcer. On top of that, he was clever enough to keep Jorgenson's name out of his Lampwick Lane revelations, which meant he still had an insider in the cops, which all in all, would have made him quite an asset.'

'We're not dealing with the B team here, are we?' Anushka said.

Norm mopped his brow. 'No, we're not.'

'And you still don't want to call the police?'

'I'd give that another twenty minutes.'

'Why, for God's sake?'

'Because the message will go out over the force radio, and Tony Jorgenson will hear it, and he's probably still the closest unit. You think he won't volunteer to deal with it himself? Anyway…' he dropped to a crouch, 'from here on, we need to zip it.'

Taller than her by several inches, he'd just seen over the mass of rhododendron shrubs on the slope above. Anushka couldn't, so she crept forward on all fours. And saw lights.

'We're there,' she breathed.

Norm nodded. He didn't say it, but he was simply relieved that they weren't hearing screams.

49

'You of all people ought to have stayed well clear of this debacle, Jerry,' David said, addressing Corrigan.

Despite his blue-collar Brummie accent, Corrigan had a clipped, military appearance with a trim moustache and square jaw. He bared his teeth. 'You telling me how to live my life?'

'You didn't learn anything from last time?' David turned to Mara and her other henchman. 'You know this idiot thought he was onto a good thing eight years ago. Not only did he get nicked, he took his mates down too. In fact, he made sure they went down to save his own skin.'

David, though his head was still ringing from the slapping, both sides of his face red and raw, had managed to push his fear down deep. The awful but simple truth was that these people were here to do a job and would do it to the best of their ability, which was presumably considerable. And no amount of pleading was going to cut it. His best chance now, if it was any kind of chance, was to try to sow dissent.

David nodded at Corrigan. 'I don't know what kind of track record you've got, Mara, but the more *he* knows, the more chance there is *you'll* be answering for it.'

The woman remained indifferent. 'You don't need to worry about us, Mr Kelman. You should be more worried about yourself.'

'No, you should be worried about *your*self. This guy Corrigan's a rat.'

Corrigan was slowly turning pink with rage.

'It might not stop at the cops either,' David said. 'What are you, Mara? Ex-IRA, ex-UDA? Who one day gave up her ideals for megabucks? There could be a lot of people over there who'd love to know where you are now. Knowing this fella, he'll put you up for auction.'

David forced a smile, exuding a confidence he didn't feel.

'You finished?' she asked. 'If so, perhaps we can get down to it. We need to know two main things, Mr Kelman. How much you know. Every scrap of it. And who else knows it. Only when we're satisfied on both those counts will tonight's business conclude.'

David glanced from one to the other, his bravura diminishing.

'I get it,' Mara said. 'You've been watching too many movies where fast-talking smart-arses can blab their way out of anything.' She shook her head. 'No. That doesn't really happen. So, are you going to tell us?'

'Look …' David stuttered. 'You already know everything I know.'

'OK, let's start with some easy ones. We know how you came into possession of Freddie Martindale's mobile phone. But what we don't know is who else you played that message to. Who else you told. And whether there are any other recordings you might have made.'

'Look, come on. You heard what that bastard Jorgenson said. There's no need to get anyone else involved in this.'

Her right hand swept down, smacking him so hard across the face that he felt and heard his nose fracture.

'Who else knows about the phone?' she asked again. 'And where might we find them?'

David coughed as he inhaled fresh blood. 'For once, Jorgenson was talking sense ...'

'Never mind fucking Jorgenson!' she snapped. 'He's another loose end we'll have to tie up. *Look at me!*'

David glared at her. 'Nobody knows, OK! This was *my* story and I don't share. Ask anyone.'

'All right.' Mara stepped back. 'I'll ask Admir.' She turned to the brawny guy. 'What do you reckon?'

'We need to see,' Mr Brawn replied.

He took off his jacket first, to reveal another gun holster but also a black vest stretched over a hugely muscular physique. When he tugged his mask off, the head underneath was shaven, the face ordinary enough except for the thick, white scar tissue criss-crossing it in vivid streaks. David recalled the 'old facial scars' sported by the suspect at the petrol station on the A47. The guy grinned at David as he pulled off his black leather gloves, revealing a tattoo on the palm of his right hand, a brightly coloured rose nestling among vicious thorns, before pulling on a pair of latex disposables, and rummaging inside the sack on the table. Heavy tools clunked together.

'Admir was an Albanian commando,' Mara said. 'But he absconded during a training exercise here in the UK. He's been freelancing ever since. And he's particularly good at eliciting information.'

David eyed the grinning muscle man. He desperately did not want to mention Norm and Anushka's names. Even though his captors already knew who they were, they didn't know how much they knew. If he mentioned that Anushka had heard Jodie Martindale's message and had gone to

Chatham and interviewed prostitutes, she'd be the next one in this room.

Admir grinned all the more as he brought out a rusty steel pipe about thirty inches long.

Mara regarded David blankly. 'The question stands, Mr Kelman.'

'You can't make us all disappear,' he said. 'Someone's going to put two and two together.'

'That's what tonight's all about,' she replied. 'To make sure there's no someone left.'

She nodded at Admir, who swung the pipe hard, cracking it squarely across David's left shinbone.

'Did you hear something?' Anushka asked.

'Like what?' Norm replied.

'A cry ... or shout.'

Norm shook his head but in truth he wasn't sure. Had he heard it and was he kidding himself? He shuddered, unable to believe where he was and what he was engaged in.

The slope had levelled off and they were waiting just inside the cover of the woods. A structure stood fifteen or so yards in front of them surrounded by weeds, thorns and broken, corroded machine parts. It was impossible to tell what the building had once been. Its walls were bare brick, while the little they could see of its roof was corrugated metal. All the windows contained glass, but in shards. There were no lights behind any of the openings facing them.

They listened hard, and now realised that they could hear muffled voices.

A second passed before Norm was able to drive himself forward. Anushka followed, nervously eyeing the building's blind, black apertures.

They reached the outer wall and waited, breathing hard. Sidling to the left, they approached the first window. And heard the voices more clearly. Norm risked a peep, seeing a dirty, rubbish-cluttered room, though an internal door stood ajar at the back of it, and a small amount of light filtered through. The voices were even clearer.

'If you're just mercs, you're in it for the money, yeah?' It sounded like David, though his voice was strained, hoarse. 'I can get you money. Lots. All you've got to do is let me go.'

'You can get us money?' a woman with a Northern Irish accent replied. Even from this distance, she didn't sound as if she was being entirely serious. 'For real?'

They pressed on, coming to an open door. When they looked in, they saw that it was a small outhouse. Anushka activated the torch on her phone. A wall of shelves faced them, crammed with dusty bric-a-brac. They leaned closer, but aside from a large spider scampering out of sight, saw only rusted tools, tins caked with paint, bottles of spirit. But once close to the shelving, they could hear the voices inside with near-perfect clarity.

'I can sell my house,' David gasped. 'My car...'

A man barked with laughter.

'I can get it,' David insisted. 'Look, if you guys are just hired hands, you don't need to be around when the shit hits the fan. I know someone ... who can pay.'

'Even if that was true,' the woman replied, 'even if you had the readies to buy out this contract, what about our other contracts? You see, we know someone too ... and that someone keeps us very busy all year round. Will whatever you get for that shoebox house of yours compensate us for loss of earnings on that scale?'

'I suppose it might,' a man with a Birmingham accent said, chuckling. 'If he's genuinely prepared to chuck the car in too.'

'We already have car, no?' a second man put in, his accent Eastern European.

'Oh dear, that's true,' the woman said. 'Seems you're shit out of luck, Mr Kelman.'

There was a sharp, echoing thud, something heavy and metallic striking flesh and bone. A strangled gasp of agony followed it.

Anushka grabbed Norm's wrist. '*We have to do something now!*'

He nodded, sweating again. They went back outside, continuing to circle the building, thoughts whirling. They'd never been in a situation like this. They doubted there were many who had. But then they rounded a corner and stopped dead.

An open space lay in front of them, well lit by a single outdoor bulb. Again, it was overgrown with weeds. More pieces of discarded machinery were scattered. But on the far side, two vehicles were parked against a fence. One of them was a purple BMW, the other a grey van, though it wasn't so much the van's colour that struck them as much as its shape.

It was the dead-spit of an ambulance.

'It's *them*,' Anushka breathed. 'It's really *them*.'

Norm slid further along the wall. Underneath the bulb, there was another open doorway. He waited alongside it for several heartbeats, before peeking. Anushka watched from behind, hair creeping, but there was no explosion of noise, no shouts of anger. Norm sidled back.

His face was milk-pale, his eyes bright but blank. 'You're

going to have to trust me,' he whispered. 'Do you trust me, Anushka?'

She nodded. 'Of course.'

'Because I've got an idea. But we're going to need to be lucky. We're going to need to be very, very lucky.'

50

'Stage One is the limbs,' Mara said, strolling around the chair. 'Always the limbs. The idea is to inflict severe pain but not do so much damage that the subject sees no possibility of full recovery. A lot of people don't even get to Stage One.' She halted in front of David, who hung sideways in his bonds, hunched and drooling. 'They don't like pain, simple as. But others, like you maybe, who've got something to hide that they value, try to ride it out. I mean, they give in the end. They *all* give in the end. But that usually happens at Stage Two, when they realise the damage will be permanent.'

'Go ... go take your head for a shit, you bitch,' he stammered.

He knew it was over. That no matter how much he tried to reason, plead, beg, it would make no difference. He'd never crack this case. He'd never see Tabby and Tommy again. And now the bastards were hurting him, abominably so. He didn't even dare look at his lower left leg, which was exposed of course because he was wearing shorts, but he knew that it was fractured. There was no room left now for anything but anger and defiance.

'That's more like the David Kelman I was led to expect,' Mara said. 'Someone who doesn't like being bested, who hates coming second.'

'Did all those gelignite fumes fuck your head up,' he

snarled. 'I said piss off. And take your pantomime sidekicks with you.'

'My my, you really don't like it when others get on top, do you?'

He spat a bloody gobbet at her feet.

'Mind…' She cocked her head to one side. 'Everything we thought we'd learned about you implied you were selfishness personified. That if it would save *your* arse, you'd serve anyone to the hangman. And yet here you are, busted up and still refusing to drop your mates in the shit.' She squatted. 'What is it, Mr Kelman? You feel a responsibility to these people? Could you only fix your screwed-up life by dragging all these others in, and were you so focused on making yourself Number One again that you never even considered they might pay the price? I can see how guilt like that would make a man obstinate. But there we are again, you see.' She mopped back his sweat-soaked hair. 'Guilt. You're obviously learning…'

'And you obviously aren't,' he said through gritted teeth. 'Otherwise you'd go straight to Stage Three.'

'Oh, we'll get to Stage Three.' She stood up. 'That's definitely on today's itinerary. But we always save the best till last.' She turned to Admir.

He grinned. 'Same leg?'

'Enough with the legs,' she said. 'I don't want to be here all night. Stage Two.'

Admir guffawed, delighted. He tossed the pipe onto the table and rummaged anew in his sack of torture tools.

'We want that info, Mr Kelman,' Mara said. 'And we want it now.'

'There's nothing more to tell,' he replied, though he couldn't suppress a new thrill of terror when he saw what the Albanian had produced. A huge pair of heavy-duty seca-teurs, so big, their blades so glintingly sharp, that they looked more suitable for shearing industrial cables than plant stems.

Admir snapped them open and closed. 'First, I cut off bits you no need. Little piece at a time, huh?'

He placed his shears on the table alongside the pipe, grinned into David's face up close, and then grabbed his shorts by the waistband … and somewhere outside, an engine rumbled to life.

'What the fuck!' Corrigan said, spinning around.

Admir straightened up too; Mara pulled her pistol. There was a brief stunned silence, and then Corrigan blundered to the nearest window, peering out.

'Christ Jesus!' he shouted. 'It's the ambulance!' From out-side, they heard a crunch of grit as wheels swung in a wide circle. 'Someone's pinching it!'

Corrigan dashed for the door, Admir accompanying him, both with guns drawn.

Mara stood frozen, green eyes livid. The glare she directed at David could have burned him alive. Then she ran after them. She didn't even reach the door before Corrigan burst back in, shaking out his leather jacket.

'Bastards!' he growled. 'Must've lifted the keys from my pocket.'

She pushed past him, going outside herself, but returned quickly, dragging on her own leather. 'It's away down the hill! You left the keys in your fucking jacket?'

'For fuck's sake!' Corrigan retorted. 'No one knows about this place. Who'd be out here?'

Mara walked over to David, eyes still flaming. 'You're more resourceful than I anticipated.'

David could only shrug. He didn't know what was happening out there; he was too busy being thankful for it.

'Don't worry.' She backed away. 'I won't underestimate you again.'

Admir came inside, also coating up, but Mara pushed him towards the door.

'Get the BMW.' She pointed at Corrigan. 'Watch Kelman. Whatever happens, he doesn't leave here alive.'

Corrigan nodded. His pistol was still drawn, but he looked flustered. David wasn't sure whether this owed to his embarrassment at having left the ambulance keys where the thieves could find them, or indicated a more general worry. The ambulance was the vehicle they'd kidnapped Jodie Martindale and Rick Tamworth in, maybe other targets too. What would a forensic sweep of its interior reveal?

Mara went out after Admir, and David heard the BMW roar to life and then the skidding of its tyres as it reversed at speed out of its parking place.

'Who you going to cut a deal with to get yourself out of this one, Corrigan?' he asked.

Corrigan twirled from the window. 'You little shit. You're not so clever. You won't survive tonight, whatever happens.'

'Neither will you, by the looks of it.'

Corrigan was about to reply, but couldn't find the words. He glanced through the window again, and then walked to the door, his weapon dressed down as he stepped out through the small antechamber.

David slumped, exhausted. The white-noise pain that had filled his body when Admir battered his shin with the pipe had localised itself into a dull, repetitive throb just below his left knee. Not for the first time, he tried to wrestle his wrists loose, but the cord bit into him. His head drooped forward, sweat dripping from his brow.

'God help me,' he breathed.

A hand landed on his shoulder.

He jerked up, and was incredulous to see Anushka standing there. She was rigid as a flagpole, terrified, but her eyes bugged even more on sight of his bloodied face.

'Where did you come from?' he hissed.

She put a finger to her lips as she stared towards the front door.

'OK,' he whispered, 'but get me out of this.'

She dug into her anorak pocket, pulling out what looked like an old hacksaw blade, and hunkered down behind him. He felt her sawing at the cords, and sensed her frustration.

'Crap,' she muttered despairingly. 'Crap …'

'The hand-shears,' he said. 'Use the hand-shears … on the table.'

Anushka glanced up and spied the secateurs. She snatched them, dropped to her haunches again and began snipping.

'*What the fuck!*' a Brummie voice thundered across the room.

They looked up as Corrigan advanced from the doorway, his pistol trained on them.

'Get up, girlie!' he said. 'Get up and step away from him. And chuck those cutters. Do it now or I'll kill you both.'

Anushka obeyed, the secateurs clattering into a corner.

'I said step away.'

She complied.

'And who the fuck are you supposed to be?' Corrigan said. 'His Indian spirit guide?' He chuckled at his own pathetic joke, though his eyes remained hard. He was still alarmed by the turn of events. He didn't know what was going to happen next.

David remained slumped in the chair, but watched him intently. Corrigan approached until he was close, gun still aimed at Anushka.

'Hands!' he said. 'Let me see 'em!'

Scared as a rabbit, Anushka raised her hands.

Again the big guy chuckled. 'This the best you can do, Kelman?'

'No,' David said. '*This* is.'

And he lunged. Though he'd kept his hands behind his back, they'd both been freed and he used them to grab Corrigan's gun arm, dragging it downward. The Browning detonated, a slug screaming from the concrete floor, smashing a hole in the ceiling. As David jumped upright to grapple with him, agony lanced along his left leg, through his hip and into his torso, exploding in his head. He bore through it as they tussled, but even if he hadn't been injured, the journalist was a ragdoll tied to a bull. The bigger, brawnier Corrigan swung him furiously around. Anushka watched, frozen, only belatedly rooting in her pocket again.

'Nushka, get out!' David shouted, just as a massive left hook dropped him onto his side.

Corrigan turned to face his other opponent, and was hit clean in the eyes by the white spirit Anushka had found in the outhouse and poured into a small metal flask.

At first he was surprised rather than hurt, but then bellowed with pain. He threw his left arm up to try to wipe his face, at the same time pointing the Browning and pumping the trigger twice. But Anushka had already moved, scampering around him to help David back to his feet.

'You bitch!' Corrigan screamed. 'You goddamn ... *Jesus!*'

The ex-cop whirled like a dervish as he tried to clear the burning substance from his eyes. He fired another wild shot; it punched a hole in one of the few remaining panes of glass in the front windows.

The twosome ducked around him, David snatching his phone from the table before they crossed the room towards an internal doorway. But David was hobbling badly. Anushka had loaned him her shoulder to lean on, but she was neither tall nor strong.

She glanced back.

Corrigan had fallen against the table. He was still trying to clear his vision. But he'd heard them, and now pointed the gun in their general direction.

She pushed David sideways.

With an echoing *boom*, a chunk was blown out of the breezeblock wall behind them. Anushka wheeled them both around, and they passed through the doorway, tottering along a black corridor, night air breezing in from the far end.

'Nushka ... not saying you're not a genius,' David stammered, 'but where the hell are we going?'

'Norm's car's just through there ... *Wait*.'

They'd come out at the side of the building, a wall of trees and bushes some fifteen yards ahead, but to the left the passage joined the open space out front, and the figure of Mara was visible there. She'd emerged from the downhill road, pistol in hand.

'They didn't both go after the ambulance,' Anushka whispered, backing up.

'What you talking about?' David gasped.

She shushed him, leaning out again and looking. Mara had vanished. Presumably drawn back up here by the gunfire, she'd headed inside but through the front entrance.

'Hurry!' Anushka hauled David towards the trees.

They broke through the outer vegetation, and then were stumbling down a steepening slope, branches and twigs entwining them.

'What about the ambulance?' David asked, focusing on anything he could to blot out the pain of his leg.

'Norm's pinched it. We figured they wouldn't let it go. They'd have to chase it.'

'I hope for his sake he can outrun them ...'

'He should be able to. That bald-headed bastard's driving the BMW, but we've already slow-punctured its tyres. He won't get far. I hoped that bitch would've gone with him ...'

'She knows what she's doing,' David grunted. 'She'll be after us in no time.'

'If we can get to the car, they'll have nothing to chase us in.'

'Did you hear what they said back there? They're contractors – hired guns. They're not the main ones.'

'You saying they weren't the kidnappers?'

'No ...' He yelped as they jolted down a steeper section of slope. 'But they're working for someone else.'

'And we know who.' Ahead, the ground levelled out, moonlight filtering through the thinning trees. 'Don't we!'

'We still haven't got proof.'

'Worry about that later!' She pushed David onto the open field. 'At present, it's about staying alive.'

51

'Will you stop making a fuss!' Anushka snapped as she helped David across the field.

'I'm trying not to.'

'Try harder!'

It was difficult going. The field had been left fallow and was now more of a meadow, shin-deep in thick summer grass, the earth beneath it firm but wet on top. As they advanced towards Norm's Jaguar, David risked looking over his shoulder, but couldn't see anything in the darkness. Anushka assisted him into the front passenger seat. He still managed to jolt his leg, and yowled.

'*David!*'

'I'm sorry ...'

'Man up!' She circled around the vehicle and climbed behind the wheel.

'Listen to you,' he said. 'Thought you were Miss Politically Correct.'

'We've got bigger fish to fry today.' She turned the engine on, the headlights picking out the field's exit. 'If that lunatic woman's come down the road instead of trying to follow us through the trees, she could be waiting around that corner.'

'I know,' he said.

'So what do we do?'

'No choice. We go for it.'

Anushka threw the Jag into gear and rammed the pedal to

the metal. The car surged forward, fishtailing on the uneven surface before swerving out through the gap. No bullets struck them, and David, who'd sunk down in his seat, levered himself up again and glanced behind, seeing an empty road.

'We should be home and dry from here,' he said.

Anushka kept her foot down. He clung on as they spun around each blind bend.

'Except,' she said, 'that I don't know where I'm going.'

'Isn't there a sat nav?' He opened the glove compartment. There was a pair of driving gloves in there, alongside Norm's Dictaphone, two aerosols containing de-icer, and nothing else.

'Use WhatsApp!' Anushka said. 'Follow Norm. He's taking that ambulance somewhere safe.'

'Where?'

'I don't know. He said he'd find somewhere.'

'I see we're well organised...'

'Hey, we had about a minute to make this plan before they did something *really* horrible to you. Don't be so bloody ungrateful.'

With painful effort, David fished out his phone. Only for Anushka to shout and jam the brakes on. David was thrown against his belt, the device disappearing into the footwell.

About one hundred yards in front, a car was parked skew-whiff, blocking the road.

'Fuck!' Anushka breathed. In the cherry-red glow of the car's rear brake lights, they could see BMW insignia. 'It's that bald bastard – I thought he'd have got a bit farther than this.'

David squinted. A male silhouette was visible against the brake lights. It was Admir, some forty yards away, but advancing towards them. Already, they could see his broad, squat torso and apelike shoulders, even a glint of moonlight from his shaved bullet-head.

'Get us out of here, Nushka,' David said.

'I can't turn round, there's no room.'

'There was a left-hand turn about two dozen yards back. *Quick as you can!*'

Anushka glanced frontward again. The Albanian torturer was even closer. She knocked the Jag into reverse and accelerated backward. Admir halted, perhaps trying to work out what was going on and who this was. Maybe he'd thought it was some poor farm worker who he'd planned to carjack. But now the truth dawned on him. He drew his pistol.

'*Nushka, quickly!*' David shouted.

There was a flicker of light, a *crack* of gunfire, and a slug punched the middle of the windscreen, passing between them, exiting via the window at the back.

'Oh my God!' Anushka shrieked.

She hit the gas and they slid past the turn before slamming to a halt, then changed gear, swinging them forward around the corner. The route facing them was nothing more than a rutted cart-track. But there was no option. They ploughed on, slower and slower as ever-stickier mud clogged their wheels. David glanced back, just as Admir came cavorting around the corner. He fired again, the bullet careening off their upper nearside bodywork.

Anushka tromped the gas, the mud's glutinous grip broke, and they accelerated away. There was a third muzzle-flash, but far behind, no impact resulting.

'All right!' David hooted. 'All right! Fuck that slaphead bastard!'

'Yeah, but where the hell are we going?'

'Just keep driving. Even roads like these lead somewhere.'

'All this for a dead girl,' she muttered.

'If we genuinely thought she was dead, I doubt any of us would be here.'

'You need to get real, David. These people don't want to get caught. If she wasn't dead before, she probably is now.'

Ahead, the road promised little. It twisted and turned, its runnels deep in liquid filth. Thorn and weed rustled along the vehicle's sides. They lurched and jolted.

Anushka whimpered, but David urged her on. He fingered the bullet hole in the windscreen. It was jagged-edged but circular, about three inches in diameter. Cracks radiated out, but the shatter-proof window was holding. 'Norm's going to be pissed off,' he muttered.

'Shit, what's *that*?'

David glanced left, and at first couldn't tell what he was seeing, though it looked as if a light of some sort, a glowing orb, was crossing the field, bouncing because it was travelling at speed, looming steadily closer.

'David – what *is* that?'

He continued to stare, bewildered, and was shaken to his core when he realised that it wasn't a single orb, but two, and that they weren't orbs, but headlights. It was some kind of off-road vehicle. And it was intent on intercepting them.

'Gotta go faster,' he said. 'Much faster.'

'I can't on this surface!'

He glanced at the speed dial. They were only travelling at just over forty. He checked left again. The vehicle was even closer. It was large and ungainly, but coming at an angle, intent on hitting this road somewhere ahead of them.

A turn-off sped by on the right.

David had no chance to see where it led, and no time to suggest they go back and investigate. Twenty yards in front, their mechanical opponent exploded from the field, bringing fences and perimeter bushes along with it, clattering down the few yards of embankment into their path.

It was a tractor, nothing more than that. But of course it was much bigger than they were, and on a network of muddy lanes like these, far more manoeuvrable. What was more, they were already close enough for David to see that it was Mara in the driving cab.

She sat side-on as they skidded towards her, their brakes refusing to bite.

She pointed at them. And not with her finger.

'Down!' David shouted, ducking.

Anushka threw her body to the right.

A second slug hit the windscreen and then the backrest of Anushka's seat, punching a great wad of foam out through its rear.

Anushka threw the Jag into reverse.

'There was a right-hand turn,' David said.

'I saw it.'

In front of them, Mara worked the gears to bring her own vehicle round. Half a second later, though they were reversing at speed, she was powering towards them. She fired again, through her own windscreen, which completely shattered. She was off-target, but in no time had cleared what remained of the glass, striking it with the gun.

'Coming up!' David called, looking behind.

Anushka swung them right, rear-end first as she turned in a blind semi-circle – plunging them boot-first into a mountain of soft, dark sludge, the putrid stench of which assailed them even through the small hole in their rear window.

'Manure!' David choked. 'That's all we need!'

'Stop complaining!' Anushka fought the wheel and gears simultaneously.

The tractor ballooned into view on their right, just as Anushka spun the wheel left, the Jag cutting an arc as it leapt forward, a blizzard of cow crap spraying the air behind it.

And the tractor, which no longer had a windshield.

David roared with laughter.

'Who did you say was shit out of luck!' he yelled.

Anushka now steered them along a track they hadn't previously seen. It was mostly overgrown and appeared to lead into a wood. Glancing back again, David saw the tractor following, though it had lost ground. Its entire front, and presumably its driver, were caked in stinking, suppurating filth. The headlamps themselves barely shone through it. The hefty vehicle held the track, however, though they were now among trees, the route meandering, which meant that they repeatedly lost sight of it.

'This is good,' David said.

At which point the track ended.

Anushka rammed her anchors on, bringing them to a sliding halt at the edge of a sudden drop away.

'A track that leads to nowhere?' David said in disbelief. 'Unless there used to be a bridge here...'

'Used to be's no good to us,' Anushka said. 'What's below?'

He leaned across the dash. 'It's not too bad... shallow descent. Twenty yards.' He glanced left and right. 'Think it's an old railway cutting. Straight as an arrow, but no metals left.'

She gazed at him, eyes wide. 'What're you suggesting?'

Behind them, the tractor crashed into view.

'The bleeding obvious,' he replied.

She tromped the pedal. They jolted down the slope, turning left when they struck the bottom. Immediately, they were on a firmer surface: there were puddles and patches of vegetation, but it was mostly pebbles and grit and, as David had said, ran straight as a ribbon. This helped the tractor too, of course. It descended behind them and was still in pursuit. Its headlights brightened as it emerged from its shroud of muck.

It lacked the speed, though.

'We're getting ahead,' Anushka said, checking her rearview mirror.

But no sooner had they felt that first pang of relief than the track-bed became cluttered with greenery. Bushes and thickets sprang up. Wiry, fibrous branches crunched and snapped underneath them or tangled the wheels and axles. Rapidly, they lost speed again.

'Nooo,' Anushka moaned. 'Please no!'

The tractor was having less trouble, and gaining. A muzzle-flash split the darkness, a slug thudding into their bodywork, the entire car juddering.

Anushka hammered the gas, but the jungle deepened, and now they were struggling through at a snail's pace. To either side, the embankments vanished, the land falling away, and the next thing they were above the countryside, fenced in on either side as they traversed an elevated section of line. Behind them, the tractor crept closer. Another shot punched out the rear nearside window.

David peered forward, squinting. 'There has to be a way off here ... *hang on!*'

'What is it?' she asked, frantic.

'*Right turn! Right turn!*'

'Where?'

'Just ahead! *Right turn for Christ's sake!*'

Anushka wasn't sure which of the two gaps she saw first. The open gateway in the fence on their right-hand side or the point about five yards past that, where the vegetation abruptly ended, their improvised roadway dropping into blackness.

Hitting the turn at this speed was the hardest thing she'd ever done, the vehicle's nearside clattering a concrete gate-post, the pair of them flung sideways. But then they were limping down a dirt road, which curved steeply through a small wood, and at its lower end brought them out onto a real road again.

They were just in time to look up at the empty sky where the railway bridge had long ago collapsed, and see the tractor skid as it failed to complete the turn, spin on its axis, teeter and then topple, turning upside down as it fell eighteen feet or so, its cab crushed to scrap by its colossal impact with the road.

As the dust settled, David and Anushka stared agog at the twisted hunk of metal, its shattered innards hanging out on every side, its wheels still turning as they jutted upward.

'Oh my God,' Anushka breathed.

David didn't know what to say … until his eye caught a flicker of movement above. A human figure appeared, silhouetted on the broken parapet where the bridge had once been.

They knew it was her because she squeezed off two more shots. Anushka floored the gas, the Jag tearing away down the road, both rounds pinging the vehicle but failing to penetrate.

'I was about to say I hope she's not dead!' Anushka stuttered. 'Now, I'm not so sure.'

'Hold that thought.' David sank back into his seat. 'The night's not over yet.'

52

'I don't know what your insurance status is when it comes to gunfire,' David said, sitting sallow-faced on an upturned crate. 'But I can't see you having to pay for this one entirely out of your own pocket.'

Norm regarded his Jaguar in a daze. 'I suppose I should be grateful it's the car and not you two.' He glanced from David to Anushka, who leaned against the garage wall. He'd never seen either of them looking as dishevelled. David's nose was still a bloody mess and his lower left leg a knobbly mass of bruising. 'You're sure you don't want to go to hospital?'

David mopped moisture from his brow. It would be sensible to get his leg looked at. The pain was still localised, but it went deep, blazing fiercely whenever he put weight on it.

'Don't think we've got time,' he finally said.

'David ...' Anushka sounded concerned. 'That leg's obviously broken.'

'I'd be there all night, having to answer all kinds of dumb questions,' he said. 'Plus, who's to say our three nutty friends wouldn't find me there?'

'Come back to my place, then? Or Norm's. At least we can strap you up.'

'And what if Jorgenson and his cronies are watching your houses?'

She said nothing to that, because she recognised that he

was right. They hadn't returned to David's Fiesta for the same reason.

Norm sighed. He would always be the one who, even in extraordinary circumstances, would cleave to wisdom and logic, insisting they do things by the book and seek professional assistance. But at present that sensible man was still grappling with the notion that it was the middle of the night and he was enclosed in a lock-up garage in Colchester, sitting on a pair of vehicles, one of which was bullet-riddled, the other a spray-painted former ambulance that had been used in the commission of at least one serious crime.

The garage, which was double-sized and therefore could accommodate the Jaguar and the van, had belonged to his late mother. It was in close proximity to what had once been her city-centre townhouse, but was not actually connected to it. His mother had died twenty years ago now; he'd sold the house but had retained ownership of the garage, which was well located if he'd ever wanted to come into town himself.

'We need to do something, whatever it is,' he said. 'The longer we mess about, the more our opponents will regroup. Before we do that, though, we have to get our story straight. To try and establish in our own minds what exactly is going on here.'

It was David who broke the resulting silence.

'The way I see it – if this guy Lou Garoo is really Nick Thorogood, that means Ralph Martindale knew who was responsible for his daughter's abduction all along.'

'We can't be sure of that,' Anushka said.

'Ralph named him – as good as.'

'If that was Ralph naming him, why not just write "Nick Thorogood" instead of leaving a cryptic message linking to one of his business cards?'

David shrugged. 'Bit of extra insurance. Ralph didn't want to leave written evidence that he'd told us anything direct.'

'But if Ralph knew all along,' Anushka said, 'why leave it six years before mentioning it?'

'Most likely because he's at death's door,' Norm replied. 'All this time, the reward for his silence was Jodie's survival, albeit in captivity. But now he's ailing badly, and when he dies, they'll be able to kill her too. With impunity.'

'I'm sure it boils down to this Share Club that Thorogood and Martindale created,' David said.

He'd already briefly explained what he knew about it, but now he explained it again in greater detail: how a bunch of hotshot City guys, talented speculators all, had formed a syndicate, the members of which would throw their spare thousands into a central fund from which they would tactically invest, buying shares in promising up-and-coming ventures.

'Staggering wealth was generated,' David said, shaking his head at the simplicity of it. 'The problem was that this particular Share Club's central fund was corrupt from the start. Nick Thorogood wasn't just using it to launder the proceeds of fraud but to underwrite the British end of a sex trafficking ring. If news of that was to get out, there'd be massive ramifications for all those City firms that emerged from this wellspring – even the respectable ones. The scandal alone would ruin most of them even before the law got involved. And then there might be the matter of reparations for the victims. Jodie Martindale got a hint of this from Oya Oyinola at the Royal Wallasea. Oya spotted her at a high-society function in company with Thorogood and tracked her down, intent on warning her what he was really like. Jodie then went to tell her father. Ralph, in turn, went to

Thorogood, who responded by hiring three contract killers to abduct Jodie and hold her hostage ...'

'And just in time,' Norm said, 'if Jodie was about to share this info with her boyfriend.'

'We have to go to the police *now*,' Anushka said. 'Because time's up for Jodie.'

David sighed. 'I thought we'd already discussed that.'

'Tony Jorgenson and Tim Bly aren't the only boys in blue.'

'But they're heading up the Martindale enquiry. And even if they weren't, my name's still shit.' He rubbed at his aching forehead. 'This whole rigmarole of trying to get someone to listen, and then being passed up the chain until we reach someone who's actually authorised to make a response is a slow-motion nightmare. The glaciers would have melted first.'

'We can't sit around and wait for the answer to come down from heaven,' she said.

'We're not going to,' he replied. 'But the last thing we want to do is rush into this. There are possibilities here we may not have considered ...'

53

'For Christ's sake!' the angry voice said through the speaker. 'Do you know what time it is?'

'Mr Bulstrode,' David replied. 'It's David Kelman. I'm sorry for the lateness of the hour, but I need to talk to you. It's very important. Can I come up to the house?'

There was a profound and protracted silence. And then: 'Kelman!' The tone was one of utter disbelief. 'Are you actually serious?'

'I need to speak to you and your wife, Mr Bulstrode. Please. It's vital.'

Before Jason Bulstrode could reply, another voice filtered through the tannoy.

'Who is it?' It was Hannah Bulstrode.

'Mrs Bulstrode, it's David Kelman. You wanted me to keep you informed? Well, I have an important update, but it's for you and your husband's ears only.'

Another lengthy silence ensued, followed by an electronic hum and a metallic *clunk*, and the heavy gates at the foot of the drive to Rosehill House opened.

They proceeded up, David leaning on Norm.

'Forgot it was all uphill,' he winced.

'*Here.*' Anushka spied something in the rose bushes and lifted it out. 'Try this.'

It was a garden rake, but although it wasn't comfortable

to tuck its pronged head under his armpit, David used it and it helped a little.

At the top of the drive, they took the steps up to the front of the house. The huge front door was already open, lamplight spilling out. The Bulstrodes stood side by side in pyjamas and dressing gowns. Jason Bulstrode in particular looked vexed, his beady eyes fixed on them through his thick-lensed glasses.

'Are you out of your miniature mind?' he said, before David could even speak.

'I promise I'm not,' David panted, still leaning on his improvised crutch. 'These are my associates from the *Enquirer*, by the way. Anushka Chawla and Norman Harrington.'

The householders barely looked at the other two, Jason Bulstrode remaining visibly hostile, though Hannah seemed shocked by David's physical condition.

'You'd better come inside,' she said.

They were led down a wide, elegant hallway with oaken beams overhead, and antique weapons and suits of armour on either side. The main lounge was enormous, though at least half of it was an add-on, a conservatory. Its huge plate-glass windows looked out onto expansive rear gardens. Inside, what looked like a ninety-inch plasma screen TV occupied one whole wall, while a luxury sofa seemed to run on and on.

'You look like you've been dragged through a bush back-wards,' Hannah said.

'I've had a rough night,' David agreed.

'What in Christ's name are you doing here, Kelman?' her husband interrupted. 'We only got to bed a couple of hours ago. We were on the road all yesterday evening.'

'Mr Bulstrode, I'm sure your wife's told you that I'm trying to help ...'

'We all are,' Anushka put in. 'That's why we're here.'

Jason glanced at her, and then at Norm, appraising them for the first time.

'Sit down, Mr Kelman,' Hannah said.

'Before you fucking fall down,' Jason added, heading across the room to an open drinks cabinet.

David settled himself on the couch, laying the rake next to him. Feeling awkward, the other two remained standing.

'I'm sorry about what happened with your sister, Mr Bulstrode,' David said. 'It was my fault but it was unintended.'

'Seems like you specialise in having accidents.' Jason mixed himself what looked like a scotch and soda. His movements were short and stiff, as if he was still very annoyed.

'The thing is—'

'Just tell us why you're here. And it had better be good, because we're all sick of the bloody sight of you.'

David glanced at Hannah, who'd sat down a few feet away.

'Mrs Bulstrode, over the last few hours, I've been abducted, held at gunpoint, beaten up and have sustained what I suspect is a broken leg, which was done deliberately by the way, with a length of steel pipe.'

Again she looked shocked, but her husband chuckled.

'Who do we send our congratulations to?' he enquired.

'Mr Bulstrode, your wife and I went to see her father yesterday,' David explained.

'I know all about that – and I disapprove. Ralph is a weak, sickly man who doesn't need that kind of hassle. If I'd known Hannah was intending to take you there, I'd have stepped in.'

'I'm sure she told you everything that had happened up to that point, and what happened when we got there?'

Jason sipped his drink. 'She told me about this message you thought you heard on Freddie's phone. And about this murdered prostitute you say Jodie had a meeting with not long before she was kidnapped. Even though it doesn't sound as if there's a shred of evidence to prove that's what happened. She also mentioned this theory of yours that Freddie was murdered too. Which is something else I ought to consider suing you for – not just for stalking us, but for causing us extreme pain and distress.' His gaze swivelled across all three of them. 'Freddie committed suicide. It's a bitter pill for us to swallow, but there's no official suggestion that anything else happened.'

'Unfortunately there's no suggestion of anything now,' David said. 'Official or otherwise.'

Hannah frowned. 'I don't understand.'

'Squeaky, the girl who told me that Freddie was murdered . . . Freddie's partner for want of a better term, the one he was squatting with. We're pretty sure that she's now dead.'

'Good lord,' Hannah said slowly.

'Mrs Bulstrode,' Anushka butted in, '*anyone* who's been trying to find out what happened to Jodie is now dead. Freddie, his girlfriend. And tonight it was almost David.'

Hannah glanced from one to the other. 'What actually happened tonight?'

As hurriedly as he could, David described the events since he'd returned from Devon, including his reinterpretation of the message Ralph Martindale had scribbled for him, this time as an allegation against Nick Thorogood, his subsequent abduction by Jorgenson, his rescue, his escape, and their journey here.

Jason regarded David blankly. 'So, let me get this straight. Someone like you, who's brought nothing but misery to this family, is seriously expecting us to believe that the police were in on Jodie's kidnapping. And not only the police, Nick Thorogood as well – one of Ralph's long-standing business partners and an old close friend of this family. And that Ralph himself knew about it and never said anything at the time?'

'I know it's a lot to take in,' David replied.

'Really?' Jason swilled more scotch. 'You think?'

'You know, Mr Bulstrode,' Norm said, 'this talent you have for making everything seem ridiculous simply by using sarcasm … we're none of us gaining from that. Especially not your wife, who seven hours ago asked David to continue investigating her sister's disappearance. Which he has done, even though it nearly cost him his life. Now if you have genuine points to make, by all means make them, but mockery for mockery's sake is unhelpful at every level.'

He fixed Jason with a defiant stare, which Jason returned with thoughtful interest.

'You were the other one involved in that news story about Jodie, weren't you?' Jason said. '*Both* of you were responsible for what happened to her. So if all this tosh turns out to be true, *both* of you will be absolved.'

'Whatever your opinion of me,' Norm replied, 'let me assure you that Nick Thorogood is not the good old boy you seem to think.'

'He's not everyone's cup of tea,' Jason said. 'I get that. He lives the high life and shows off about it. But why would he risk all that by getting involved in a kidnapping? And a kidnapping of his friend's daughter? I mean why, for Christ's sake? What could possibly motivate him?'

'We're coming to that,' David said.

'To start with,' Norm replied, 'one of Thorogood's close friends is a Russian gangster called Vladimir Ivankov.'

Jason levelled a warning finger. 'You be careful, my friend. We happen to know Vladimir Ivankov, and he's a perfectly pleasant guy.'

'How well do you know him?' David asked.

Surprisingly, Jason hesitated to answer.

'We know him through Nick,' Hannah said. 'That's all.'

'So, he's a friend of a friend,' Norm said. 'That's no surprise. Look, I've no doubt that when he's over here in the UK, moving in polite circles, Ivankov's charming and well behaved. But you need to trust us, back home his reputation is somewhat different.'

'This is ridiculous,' Jason blurted. 'If there's some local police corruption involved in this, that's one thing. But Nick stands condemned because of someone he knows?'

'He's condemned because we've got evidence connecting him to sex trafficking,' Anushka asserted.

'Sex trafficking!' Jason's eyes literally bugged. 'How do you infer that from a scornful message that might, just *might*, reflect something written on a business card?'

'We don't just infer it from that,' she said, 'we infer it from the phrase *loup-garou*.'

The Bulstrodes looked at her, puzzled.

'That's what Oya Oyinola, the murdered prostitute who met with Jodie, called a certain Englishman,' Anushka explained. 'An Englishman who kept appearing at the house on the Isle of Sheppey where she was held prisoner after being trafficked into the UK with a lot of other women. Oya saw this same man again years later. He was in company with Jodie at a party in London. She didn't know his real name, so she gave him a nickname. Her first language was French, and in French, *loup-garou* means "werewolf" or "wolf-man". Didn't Nick Thorogood use a wolf's howl as his signature on *Night Prowler* – whenever he kissed a pretty girl?'

Spoken aloud, it sounded shaky even to Anushka's ears.

But the Bulstrodes continued to stare at her, not just with puzzlement now but with real surprise. Even Jason seemed startled.

'Good lord,' Hannah finally said. 'Are you serious? Wolf-man? Because Vladimir Ivankov used to call Nick "Wolf-man" or "Wolfie" as a kind of wind-up.'

'That was nothing to do with *Night Prowler*,' Jason retorted.

'It wasn't unconnected.' Hannah turned to the others. 'Vladimir said that whenever Nick slept with a woman, he would ... well, on reaching orgasm, he'd sign it with a wolf's howl.'

Anushka glanced at Norm. 'So Oya didn't even need to have seen that programme.'

'This still could be a coincidence,' Jason argued.

'There are an awful lot of coincidences here, Mr Bulstrode,' Anushka replied.

'I think so too,' Hannah added, watching her husband.

'If none of this convinces you,' David put in. 'We've also got what we believe is the vehicle Jodie was abducted in.'

The Bulstrodes looked so astonished that he had to repeat himself.

'How ... do you know it's the same one?' Hannah stammered.

'We can't be one hundred per cent sure, but if nothing else, it's the same vehicle that was seen near Keppel Hall in Chatham shortly before Freddie was killed there. It's also a former ambulance, which was something Freddie said about the van that took Jodie and Rick.'

'Where is it?' Jason asked.

'In a safe place,' David replied.

'So you haven't taken it to the police?'

'How can we?' Anushka said. 'Whoever we give it to, it'll end up with DI Jorgenson.'

'That's the obstacle we face continually,' David added. 'Look, Mrs Bulstrode, Jorgenson should have come to you by now with Freddie's phone. Or at least informed you about it. It's been two weeks. That's why I think the phone's a goner. We bring in that ambulance, it'll never make it to a forensics lab.' He turned to her husband. 'Mr Bulstrode, we're not just telling you that Tony Jorgenson is corrupt. We're telling you that he's colluding with and covering for dangerous criminals. Kidnappers, murderers. Do you think we'd make accusations like that just to play a joke on your family?'

The Bulstrodes looked at each other again, Hannah making a wordless plea.

'It's tenuous, Hannah,' her husband replied, though his tone was softer. 'I just don't want you to get your hopes up, not when they've been dashed so many times in the past.'

'We follow every lead, Jason,' she said. 'We agreed that all those years ago. No stone unturned.'

'These people are implicating Nick, who's been part of the furniture since the year dot. But not just Nick, your own father ...'

'We struggled with that too,' David said. 'But what else

could he do to keep his daughter alive apart from keep his mouth shut?'

'I'm sure there are lots of things he could have done,' Jason countered.

'Maybe if he'd kept a clear head,' Anushka said, 'but this whole thing has torn him apart ... brought him to his knees mentally and physically.'

Hannah looked at her husband again, pleadingly. He, in turn, glared at David.

'I swear to you, Kelman – if you're filling my wife's head with unfounded hope, when the reality is probably that Jodie's been lying in an unmarked grave for many years ...'

'But what if she's not?' Hannah said.

David shook his head. 'I'm not saying she's alive, Mr Bulstrode. I'm saying she was alive recently. And that we think we've uncovered evidence of an horrific conspiracy surrounding her abduction. Listen, I understand why you don't like me. But if you slam the door on us now, aren't you at the very least going to spend the rest of your life wondering what might have been?'

'Jason, please!' Hannah's tone had become urgent. 'We *have* to look into this.'

Jason placed his drink on a sideboard. 'So, the main reason you don't want the police involved is this DI Jorgenson?'

'As he's head of Cold Cases, we can't get around him,' David said.

'He'll be out there looking for us now,' Anushka added.

Jason pondered. 'So, what you need is to be speaking to a higher rank?'

'Someone *much* higher,' David said. 'Someone who can make things happen.'

Jason turned to his wife. 'I'll call Charles.'

Hannah nodded hopefully. 'Now?'

He clearly didn't like the idea, but indicated that he would, and she sagged with relief.

'Charles …?' David said.

'Charles Williford,' Hannah said. 'Deputy Chief Constable of Essex.'

'He'll take a call at this hour?' Norm asked.

Jason ignored that, heading out. 'I'll call from the study,' he told his wife.

'He'll take Jason's call any time,' Hannah said. 'They play golf together twice a week. But the rest of you should sit down. I imagine that even Jason will take a few minutes persuading Charles to get out of bed at this time of night. In the meantime, can I get anyone a drink?'

'I'm all right,' Norm said. 'Thanks for offering.'

'I'm OK too,' David added, increasingly troubled by his leg, which wasn't just worsening in terms of pain but stiffening too.

'I wouldn't mind a glass of water, if you've got one,' Anushka said.

'Of course.' Hannah left the room.

'What now?' Anushka asked.

'Now … we wait,' David grunted. 'Nothing else we can do.'

Hannah returned, carrying a water-filled glass on a tray.

'I'm sorry we came here so late, Mrs Bulstrode,' David said. 'The truth is, we didn't really know where any of us would be if we left it till morning.'

Hannah nodded non-committally. She must have believed him, he reasoned, or she must have *wanted* to believe him, to encourage her husband to do what he was now doing. But clearly there was some doubt in her mind. What was it her husband had said – that she'd had her hopes raised so many times? She herself had told David that they'd had to deal with opportunist investigators, conmen basically.

'Anything I can get for your leg, Mr Kelman?' she asked. 'A painkiller?'

David wiped more sweat away. 'That'd be kind, thank you.'

She disappeared through to her kitchen again.

'Nice lady,' Norm observed.

'Nicer than I deserve,' David replied. 'Before either of you says it.'

Hannah returned with the requisite pills and another glass of water. He downed them.

As he did, Jason came back in, hands in his dressing-gown pockets. He moved to the drinks cabinet to pour himself another scotch.

'Well?' Hannah asked.

'Charles was grouchy,' he said. 'Plus he didn't know what to make of all this.' He turned to face them again. 'But there are a couple of cars en route.'

'No one from the Cold Case Unit?' Anushka asked.

'No,' he confirmed. 'When the name Jorgenson came up, Charles didn't seem surprised. Which must say something. Instead, he's sending over officers from Major Crimes. They investigated the case originally, and he thinks they'll be delighted to have another crack at it now. Especially with new information.'

Hannah glanced at David. 'Maybe you should retrieve the ambulance? Is it close by?'

'It is,' he said, 'but I think it'll just be easier if I take them when they get here.'

'As you wish.'

Jason sipped his scotch again. It was a considerable measure compared to the first one.

Despite his refusing a drink earlier, David reflected that he wouldn't actually have minded one now. Because even after the tablets he'd taken, the throbbing in his leg was intensifying, and because he was wearied to his bones. Also because he was nervous.

Very nervous.

So nervous that the next few minutes dragged by.

And yet despite that, when a car horn tooted outside, he jerked upright so fast that he jarred his leg again and grimaced in agony.

Jason crossed the room. 'I'll open the gate.'

Hannah stood up, but remained with her guests. 'You just have to tell them everything you told us,' she advised. 'It'll be a relief, I expect? Knowing there's now someone involved who can take action.'

David nodded but didn't smile. Once the real police got hold of this thing, it would be out of his hands. Which meant the ability to write a news story based on the work he'd done would also be beyond his control. If the cops made arrests and it went to trial, it could be months before things progressed to that point. And that was if the police were successful.

It was a bitter realisation. Despite all his protestations to the contrary, hadn't this thing ultimately been about launching an online paper with a spanking big story?

From out in the hall, he heard a door opening and voices.

He got clumsily to his feet. Anushka came to assist. Hannah straightened herself out. Her husband re-entered.

'Here they are,' he said. 'They're all yours.'

David and the others stared silently at the three individuals who filed in after him.

Mara, Admir and Jerry Corrigan.

54

'Now, obviously,' Jason said, making his way back to the drinks cabinet, 'no one move.'

Instinctively, the three journalists backed away. Hannah Bulstrode stared in bemusement at the newcomers. She realised that they weren't police officers – something to do with their rugged leather garb and the guns they all sported, one of them, the one in Admir's hands, a Steyr submachine gun – but it still took an age for the penny to drop. Only when she saw David's face did she realise.

'Jason?' she said slowly. 'Jason, what—'

'Shut up, Hannah!' Jason returned with his refill. 'OK? Keep it zipped.'

'You're not telling us *you're* in on this?' Anushka blurted.

'Work it out,' David said wearily. 'Who has the most to lose if the MDS Group goes under – apart from the guy who'll likely inherit it in a few weeks' time.'

'*Jason?*' Hannah pinned her husband with a gaze that he didn't seem to want to meet.

'I'll explain everything in due course,' he told her. 'But you're going to have some hard thinking to do before morning.'

'The rest of you sit down!' Mara said harshly, indicating the couch with her pistol. She'd cleaned off most of the cow shit, though her hair was still clogged and a foul aroma hung over her. 'All of you! *Sit!*'

'I see your status in life is now reflected by your smell,' David said.

She struck the side of his head with her gun. It was a brutal blow, the metal clanking on bone. David toppled dizzily onto the couch.

'You sodding cow!' Anushka screamed, but the assassin ignored her.

'I'll enjoy saving you till last, Kelman,' she hissed through clenched teeth.

David was aware of hot stickiness on the left side of his face. Anushka lurched towards him, but Mara cocked her firearm and aimed it at her face.

'Stay where you are! Leave him!'

'You're not as clever as you think, Mr Kelman,' Jason said. 'I'm mildly impressed you got this far. But in reality it's not just MDS under threat.'

'It's every company that sprang from the Share Club, isn't it?' Norm said.

Jason threw him a glance. 'Quite correct, Mr Harrington. An awful lot of which are now power-broking investment firms at the heart of international finance, and though the majority of their CEOs could make a defence that they thought they were drawing their seed capital legitimately, that they didn't know about Nick Thorogood's very dubious sidelines, or that illicit money was being laundered through the Share Club ... Well, for any investment company to even be associated with sex trafficking would be catastrophic.'

'Jason?' Hannah stammered, her face white. 'You're not telling me you're involved in this? I mean, OK ... you'd want to protect MDS. I see that. It was misguided, but—'

'*Hannah!*' He still didn't look at her. 'Shut ... the ... fuck ... up!'

'Truth is,' David raised his head dazedly, 'your husband was involved from the start.'

'He wasn't around back then!' she snapped, voice thick. 'Jason was a child in the eighties ...'

'But not when your sister was kidnapped,' David said. 'He was MDS's chief accountant by then.'

Hannah looked too distraught to believe it. Her attention wavered from person to person.

'Who do you think these three people are?' Anushka asked, her face written with fear.

'I ...' Hannah's tearful eyes rolled to her husband.

'Do *you* want to tell her?' David asked him. 'Or shall I?'

The silence that followed seemed to elongate. Jason looked fleetingly guilty. Hannah's expression changed too, hardening, eyes narrowing. Perhaps a host of unanswered questions were flooding back to her: curious inconsistencies in things her husband had said and done over the years; odd, quirky moments when she'd felt he wasn't being straight with her; late-night phone calls he'd neglected to explain; meetings with people she didn't know.

Finally, he glanced around. 'Don't look at me like that, Hannah. We had something to protect.'

'We?' she asked coldly.

'It's never as simple as people think,' he said. 'The bankers are always at fault, aren't they! The bankers are driven by greed – they enjoy incalculable wealth, but they always want more. And yet you could put all these fat cats together, and all their holiday homes, and their limousines, and their yachts ... and weigh them against a single ordinary human life, some working man from the sticks, and they'd be found wanting. Well no, actually. That's as far from the truth as it gets. That's the voice of the ignorant peasant who tore down the establishment in Revolutionary France and finished up with the Terror. That's the voice of the naïve Russian student who ushered in Stalin. You know what contribution the financial sector makes to this country. What is it – fifteen per cent of GDP? You want to see it brought to its knees just because one of its founding fathers was a deviant?'

'That's quite a speech,' David said. 'And quite an exaggeration on every level, I'd say.'

'So would I.' Hannah glared at her husband. 'And my former question stands. Who's *we*?'

'Dear God!' Jason almost laughed. 'You think Ralph was being blackmailed? You think Ralph only found out what Nick and I were trying to protect after Jodie was abducted?'

Her expression faltered again. 'Jason, you're not telling me ...?'

'They were in it together,' David said. 'Why else, when Jodie made that panic-stricken phone call, didn't she call home?'

'You're saying Daddy knew Jodie was about to be kidnapped,' Hannah asked, 'and said nothing?'

'For Christ's sake!' Jason snorted. 'He *authorised* it.'

For a second, David thought their hostess's legs would buckle.

'Once Jodie knew about the sex trafficking, there was one option,' Jason said. 'She had to disappear.'

'My sister?' Hannah whispered. 'She couldn't have known about it. Not in any detail ... not from some bloody sex worker!'

'She had half an idea and that was enough. She was appalled, disgusted. She agonised for a few days, and then went to see Ralph ... and she wouldn't let it drop, wouldn't let him fob her off.'

Tears coursed down Hannah's cheeks. 'Daddy did *not* know about this sex-trafficking ring, he did *not* have his own daughter abducted ...'

'It was that or have her killed.'

The matter-of-factness of Jason's tone shocked even David.

'Only he couldn't bring himself to do the latter.' Jason shrugged. 'Obviously, he couldn't. It was his own daughter. So he hired a team to abduct her and make it look like a real kidnapping – a kidnapping that had gone wrong.' He glanced at David. 'In that regard, this narcissistic idiot over here played right into our hands. Oh, don't worry, Hannah, your father's paid for it. It's tortured him these last six years. You've seen what he's become. Freddie's death was the final straw.'

'And ... and was Freddie murdered too?' she whispered.

'He was already dead, let's face it.' Jason swilled more scotch. 'He was a loser, a druggie.'

'But Jodie's alive at least?'

'As of now, yes.'

'But ... you're telling me she's been a prisoner these last six years?'

'Don't panic, we didn't chain her in a dungeon. She's been living in comfort.' He frowned. 'But I must admit, it's getting expensive.'

'And that's an expense they won't keep meeting when your father dies,' David said.

Hannah glanced at him wet-eyed, and then back at her husband, who made no denial.

'How ...' Hannah struggled to compose herself. 'How did all this come about?'

Jason put his empty glass down. 'When Nick started London After Midnight. It soon became clear that it wasn't going to earn him the fortune he'd been used to, but one of the people who hired him to provide a good time was our Russian businessman pal, Vladimir Ivankov.'

'"Russian businessman" being a euphemism in this case for mob boss,' David interrupted.

Jason shrugged. 'It seems that London After Midnight surpassed itself on that occasion. Of course, Nick wasn't just showing him the sights and treating him to the best steaks. Ivankov had more exotic tastes. And Nick ... well, he knew every dive and shithole in London, didn't he? He'd been a customer in most of them. Our Ruskie pal couldn't have hooked up with anyone better. It wasn't long before they were mates, before they were talking business, the kind of business Ivankov and his people did in other European countries and now wanted to do in the UK. When Nick saw the sort of money involved, he never looked back.'

'And the Share Club was the cover?'

'And the springboard.'

Hannah was calmer now, strangely detached. 'And that's the point where Daddy got involved?'

Jason shook his head. 'Hannah ... Ralph and Nick went way back. They were thick as thieves, literally. Your father was just as guilty of the fraud that saw Nick sacked from Morgan Stanley – it was just that he didn't get caught. And Nick never blew the gaff on him, so they remained close. Scratching each other's backs, doing deals.'

She shook her head. 'You're not telling me Daddy was *part* of this sex trafficking ring?'

'No, but he knew all about it, and the money coming in from it was so huge ... I mean, it flooded the Share Club with funds, all of which went back to the City clean. He wasn't complaining, was he?'

'And when did *you* get involved?' She wasn't so much calm now as cold.

'You said it yourself. I was only a kid then. I joined MDS in '99. Me and you hadn't even met.'

'I asked *when* you got involved.'

'Not long after I first got there.'

'How?'

'For Christ's sake, woman!' He made a dismissive gesture. 'The same way Jodie did. It's the City. It's a hive of indiscretion. People get drunk or coked-up. And then they talk.'

'But unlike Jodie, *you* weren't abducted.'

'Because unlike Jodie, *he* could be bought,' David said. 'What was it you wanted, Jase? The top job … oh, and the hand of the boss's daughter?'

'Don't listen to Captain Lucky Guess here,' Jason told her. 'He's shortly to depart this world, and no one'll care. But you and me are solid, Hannah. Whatever you think about me now, I'm sure our relationship is strong enough to get through this …'

She stared at him as if he were someone she didn't know.

'But we'll discuss our future later on,' he said. 'In private.'

'Our *future*?'

'Hannah, if we don't clean this up, you can forget the five-star lifestyle you've become accustomed to. All that'll be over. They might even have doubts about *your* innocence. Isn't that what people say? That no one could be so close to a criminal and not know what he was up to? Anyway, I'll give you a couple of hours to think it through. Don't waste them.' He turned to his henchmen. 'There's a spare bedroom upstairs, first on the left. You'll know it because the key's in the door and there's no furniture inside. Lock her in. Search her first – make sure she hasn't got a phone.'

Hannah listened to this incredulously, but only began screaming and cursing when Corrigan, eyes still reddish and sore, grabbed her arm and lugged her out into the hall.

'Anything happens to her, it won't be quite so easy for you to inherit MDS,' David said.

Jason smiled. 'It'd be a problem, for sure. Less of a problem, though, is what to do with you people. Especially as now, very conveniently, I've got you all under one roof.'

'And all three of us will be missed. You need to think about that very carefully.'

Jason pulled a face. 'Please don't regurgitate that crap you hear on TV thrillers. Of course you'll be missed. Everyone who disappears is missed. In most cases, the police look for them. In some, no trace is ever found ... and yet the majority of us learn to live with it.'

'You think we haven't told people what we're working on?' David said.

'I *know* you haven't. Because like all sociopathically ambitious newsmen, you won't have wanted any other outlet stealing your story ... so no, your tongues haven't been wagging about this. The little you've gathered we now have anyway, having raided that outside toilet you call an HQ.' Jason's smile broadened. 'Just to be on the safe side, though, Mara and her guys are going to take you away somewhere nice and quiet, and ... how was it they used to put it in olden times? Subject you to the question. And this time there'll be no one coming to help.'

Mara stepped forward. 'On your feet!'

The journalists did as instructed, Norm and Anushka supporting David, Mara and Admir jabbing and prodding them across the lounge and along the hall towards the front door. As they did, Corrigan descended a staircase on the right, throwing a key onto a shelf. 'What about the ambulance?' he asked.

'Yes,' Jason said, bringing up the rear. 'That's one thing you can tell us first, Kelman. Where is it?'

David remained silent.

Jason's smile thinned. 'I'd start the way I mean to go on, if I was you. Quick answers will save Mara and her boys a lot of time and irritation, and you and your friends a lot of pain.'

David glanced at the other two. They stared back, pale-faced.

'If we're going to die anyway …' he said.

'There are different ways to die,' Mara replied.

David's shoulders slumped. 'It's down in the layby.'

'Just across the road?' Jason said. '*That's* your hiding place?'

'It's as good as any.'

Jason shook his head. 'I said I was mildly impressed by you. I take that back. You're just a lucky bastard.'

He opened the front door, Admir backing out, his Steyr levelled on the prisoners.

Immediately, he was bathed in the glare of several giant spotlights.

'So it seems,' David said.

'Armed police!' came a voice through a loudhailer. 'Drop your weapons!'

Mara shrieked, dragging Norm and Anushka back, elbowing David out the way and pouring gunfire through the doorway.

Admir ducked in past her, shooting backward. Wildly, thunderously.

A spotlight imploded as the front door slammed closed.

55

There were two narrow windows, one to either side of the front door. Admir and Corrigan claimed one each, Admir on the right near the foot of the staircase, Corrigan on the left, both knocking out the frosted glass panes with the grips of their weapons before unleashing fire. Admir blazed with his submachine gun, the noise and fury so startling that the prisoners, who were fleetingly forgotten, could only back away, stunned.

Mara leaned around the half-open door, pumping the trigger of her pistol until it was empty. Digging out a fresh magazine and slotting it in place, she charged down the hall, buffeting David with such force that his injured leg gave way and he fell, landing against the base of the staircase newel post. She reached the triangular door to an under-stair closet, opened it, leaned inside, and the entire house was plunged into blackness. The shooting meanwhile went on, and with a detonation they heard indoors, a second police spotlight shattered.

'Jerry!' Mara snapped, joining Corrigan at the left-hand window. 'Get topside, cover the back. See if there's an exit through the garden. They can't have surrounded this whole place. There aren't enough firearms cops in the whole of Essex.'

Corrigan clumped his way upstairs.

Again, she took pot-shots at whoever was outside. Whether she was targeting opponents or it was just a wild fusillade was unclear. But now, Jason Bulstrode, who'd been standing with eyes goggling, came urgently forward, grabbing at Mara's shoulder.

'For Christ's sake! Don't be shooting at the police! Jesus God, what the hell are you doing?'

She shrugged him off and kept firing.

In the staccato light of repeated muzzle flashes, David saw the householder's face drenched with sweat. Even in his most convoluted plans, he'd clearly never bargained for this.

Jason snatched Mara's leather jacket. 'At least take me with you! If you're getting out of here, you've got to take me with you!'

This time she spun round.

And fired.

Clean into Jason's midriff.

He clenched up, his body folding over, and went down.

'Consider yourself taken,' she said.

Admir broke off shooting to register what she'd done.

'No witnesses,' she said.

He nodded, and ducked as what appeared to be a return shot glanced from the window-frame. Bobbing back up, he resumed firing.

'Jerry!' Mara called upstairs as she reloaded. 'Kill the woman!'

She then turned left, to where Norm had been taking cover against an internal door. And raised her pistol. He twirled, trying to force his way through the door. It opened. But not before she'd shot him in the back, punching him through into the darkness beyond. Next, she swung to where

434

David lay watching her, smiling as she took careful aim at him. But she'd forgotten about Anushka, who'd been sheltering alongside a suit of medieval armour, and now grabbed the spiked mace from the suit's articulated steel gauntlet and rushed forward.

It packed massive impact as she arced it down onto the back of the gunwoman's skull.

Mara's head jolted downward. She sagged silently to her knees, and fell face-first to the floor. Anushka backed away, gasping, wondering what she'd done. Only when Mara groaned and moved slightly, not just alive but not even unconscious, did she release the mace, which fell with a clatter, and cavort towards David, who was trying to get upright.

'No!' He waved her away. 'Check on Norm!'

She wheeled about, disappearing through the internal door. David glanced at Admir, so busy engaging the besieging forces that he hadn't noticed his partner's injury. Mara grunted again, her hands flat on the floor as she attempted to lever herself up, but her head hung limp and blood was sopping through her hair and pooling on the carpet.

Overhead meanwhile, David could hear a hammering and crashing of woodwork. Accompanying it were muffled screams of terror.

He was torn with indecision. Friends and colleagues should be his priority, but Hannah Bulstrode was a crucial witness.

Mara was now on all fours but still groggy, while Admir remained distracted.

It was a chance David couldn't waste. He hopped around the newel post, in the process spying the key thrown onto the shelf. Grabbing it, he commenced the ascent, though the pain in his leg was unbearable. He ended up flat on his belly, scaling the stair like a crocodile, but he was less than halfway when he heard Mara's voice.

'Admir ... *get that bastard!*'

He glanced behind him and down. Mara, back on her feet and gun in hand, was stumbling towards the internal door. Admir, though, was gazing up the stairway, and clicking a fresh magazine into his submachine gun.

David rolled onto his back as the weapon was trained up at him.

Admir grinned. And squeezed the trigger.

But nothing happened.

With no other option, David launched himself out and down, landing on top of the Albanian with his entire body-weight. Even Admir, squat and strong, was knocked from his feet.

David punched and clawed at the figure beneath him like an animal. To no avail. An elbow impacted under his chin, a forearm smashed into the side of his neck, and then he was the one underneath and Admir on top. A succession of savage blows, delivered by gloved but clublike fists, struck his head and body. The Albanian swayed back to his feet, hissing with glee as he drove in with his military-style boots three or four times before stepping back and fiddling with his submachine gun.

David peered up through blurred, bloodied eyes. Fixated by the sudden appearance of a cherry-red dot on the side of Admir's chest. The assassin didn't notice it; he was confused when David flung himself over, wrapping his hands around his ringing skull.

The *BOOM* of the police rifle was concussive even over the racket upstairs.

Admir hit the wall with such force that he was catapulted back across the hall, before coming to rest alongside Jason Bulstrode.

Even in these circumstances, to actually see someone die was a shock, but David fought to retain control. The submachine gun lay at his feet. If Admir couldn't fix the damn thing, he certainly couldn't. But appearances might be everything. He grabbed it, looped its strap over his shoulder and lumbered back up the stairs, dizzied with agony, but trying to focus.

There's a spare bedroom upstairs, Hannah's husband had said. *First on the left.*

At the top, he again heard the smashing and banging of timber under assault; it drew his attention left, along the carpeted passage. Corrigan was there, giving it everything he had to a locked door – shoulder, knees, feet – though the lock was holding.

David reared onto his knees and levelled the submachine gun. 'Corrigan!'

The ex-cop jerked around. He still had his Browning. Why he hadn't used that to shoot the lock off the door bewildered David, but maybe the guy really was as dumb as he appeared.

'Drop it!' David shouted. 'Do it now or you're dead!'

Corrigan stood rigid. He'd let this fool get the better of him before, of course. Did he really want to do that again?

'Don't think about it!' David warned him, hoping the useless gun wasn't shaking too visibly.

Corrigan tore away down the passage, diving out of sight through a door on the left.

'Shit!' David lurched up onto his one good leg.

The locked door, which was cracked and splintered but

still upright, was about five yards in front on the right. The other door, behind which the ex-cop was now lurking, was another ten yards beyond that. David could make it to the locked door without crossing Corrigan's line of vision. But if Corrigan was lying in wait, listening...?

There was another crash of woodwork, but now from downstairs. Could it be the police forcing entry? Or was it Mara closing in on wherever Anushka was hiding? And what state was Norm in? David swallowed bile. He could only contemplate one problem at a time.

Venturing forward, he kept the weapon trained on Corrigan's doorway.

'I'm warning you, Jezzer!' he said, opting again for bravado rather than stealth. 'Chuck that weapon out where I can see it or I'm coming, and I'll turn you to Swiss fucking cheese!'

There was no reply from the black rectangle. At any second, Corrigan could appear there, Browning blazing, and David wouldn't have a chance. Breathless, he reached the locked door. Still watching the other entrance, he slipped the key into the lock. The door opened.

'Hannah, it's me!' He thrust himself through, bringing the key with him and banging the door closed. 'Don't hit me!'

It wasn't much of a hiding place, but there'd only been so much Anushka could do.

The moment she'd barged into the small, dark room, she'd found herself in a study, where Norm was leaning forward over a desk, head dangling.

'Norm,' she'd breathed.

He'd mumbled something incoherent, and then she'd seen the glitter of a wet stain down the left side of his back. He was wearing a dark anorak so the full extent of it hadn't at first been visible. But then she'd made a quick inspection and, perhaps to her relief, had seen that it was issuing from a wound at the rear of his shoulder rather than some central point.

Galvanised by the chaos in the hall, she'd wrapped an arm around his body, put his arm over her shoulders, and attempted to steer him across the study and through an open door on the far side. He'd moved stiffly and clumsily, hobbling rather than walking.

'I've got to get you out of here,' she'd panted.

When Norm hadn't replied, she'd glanced at his face and been shaken to see that even in the semi-darkness it was stark white and that his eyes were closed.

The next few minutes had been a nightmare of uncertainty as they'd turned left and right through a succession of ground-floor reception rooms. All were low-ceilinged and sported heavy black beams, all displayed ornaments and were furnished with leather armchairs, fireside settles and the like. They were also decked with antique weapons. But though Anushka grabbed a couple, none felt even vaguely as useful as the spiked mace: a firelock pistol that fell apart in her hand; a poniard that looked lethal but was actually more rust than steel.

Instead, she'd searched for a refuge, finding none until they entered a fifth chamber, which was larger and longer than the others. It had grand panoramic windows, but also a lengthy central table with elegantly carved chairs ranged down either side, and its top laid with a white cloth and much silver and glassware.

It was around now when she heard the first sound of

pursuit: a door banging open and a de-muffling of the racket that still filled other parts of the house.

'Under the table!' Anushka had whispered. 'Under the table! There's nothing else for it!'

Norm had gone down without arguing, but she'd still had to push and shove to get him out of sight underneath it, where there was just sufficient room for her to climb in alongside him, and sit with knees against chest, sweat beading her brow. She'd been unsure if there was sufficient overhang from the tablecloth to cover them, but they were where they were.

At which point, a pair of feet came into the dining room.

Anushka glanced at Norm, but his head hung low and she couldn't see his face.

She held her breath as whoever it was stomped around the room, circling the table. She bit on a scream when the feet halted alongside her.

There was heavy, hoarse breathing. Whoever it was, they'd been hurt. Anushka risked turning her head, and saw the legs and feet standing side-on. The clothing comprised dark trousers and combat boots, but the build seemed relatively slight.

Mara …

The legs moved on, but only a few feet before there was a splintering, echoing *CRASH* as polished woodwork exploded. Anushka clamped her hands to her ears, but they didn't block out a deep, reverberating jangle. There'd been a grandfather clock in the corner. But why in God's name had Mara smashed it?

Unless …

It seemed incredible, but could the maniac have been looking inside? To see if one of them had hidden there?

There was another *CRASH* as more delicate woodwork exploded.

Anushka almost sobbed.

The gun-toting bitch was searching the whole damn room.

56

The room was a typical spare, small and boxy, and as Jason Bulstrode had said, empty and unfurnished. No curtain hung on the window, so it was filled with moonlight, which revealed Hannah Bulstrode balled up in a corner, hair in disarray.

It took an age for her to lower her hands. The eyes and cheeks below were wet with weeping.

'Kelman!' she said, relieved.

David gestured for quiet as he cocked an ear to the corridor outside. There was a further smashing of woodwork downstairs, but upstairs it was suddenly quiet. He limped across to the window.

'Jason ...' Hannah shook her head. 'He *can't* be the one behind this.'

'If it's any consolation, he's not the main man.' David took a position to one side of the aperture. Directly below, by about ten feet, was a sloped but transparent roof.

'He couldn't have been coerced?' she wondered in a small but hopeless voice.

'Didn't sound like it, I'm afraid.'

She relapsed into a thoughtful, accepting silence.

David didn't have the heart to update her on the latest disaster. Whoever the main man was, Nick Thorogood most likely, he'd evidently instructed his trio of killers to clean house if it all went wrong. But Hannah was under enough stress already without being told that this had included lesser underlings like her husband.

'Is that the police out there?' she asked, standing.

'I presume so.' David squinted, peering beyond the roof below and the other extremities of the house. But the night hid all.

'Thank God,' she said.

'Don't celebrate too soon. They're not inside yet.'

'But how can they be here?'

He crossed back to the door and listened. 'No time to explain.'

'You?' she asked. 'Did *you* plan this?'

'I didn't exactly plan it. I made a phone call on the way over here.'

'But how did you know my father was involved?'

David hobbled to the window again. 'The moment I connected Nick Thorogood to the trafficking ring, it became a strong possibility.' He glanced around at her. 'Why would Thorogood try to blackmail your father by keeping Jodie alive? It would have been much easier just to kill the pair of them. In light of that, it seemed obvious that Jodie was being held on her father's orders. It *had* to be that. He couldn't bring himself to have her killed, and the conflict of loyalties wore him down over the next few years.'

'But you also knew about Jason?'

'That was an easier call, though I had no reason to suspect him until Tony Jorgenson arrested me for assaulting your security men in Cornwall. A Cold Cases DI like Jorgenson would never have been allocated a job like that. In addition, he knew about my Dictaphone. He couldn't have possessed any of that info, either about the Dictaphone or your security guys, unless Jason had contacted him personally. And given that Jorgenson was in on it, it thus went that Jason was too.'

A floorboard creaked outside.

They listened.

Another creak. Just behind the door.

'What's down there?' David hissed, nodding at the window.

'The indoor swimming pool,' she whispered.

'Is the roof glass or PVC?'

'PVC, I think ...'

'Good.'

Her eyes widened. 'Are you serious?'

On the other side of the door, a metallic click signified the cocking of Corrigan's Browning.

'What do *you* think?' he asked her.

Anushka cringed as Mara swept around the dining room. Destroying everything: vases, statuettes, cupboards. Her growing fury did not bode well for the duo she was hunting.

When an ear-splitting silence fell, Anushka knew their time had come. The booted feet were alongside her again, standing amid wreckage. A hand streaked with dried blood reached down and grabbed the edge of the tablecloth, preparing to yank it away – when there was a colossal impact from somewhere outside.

The hand jerked away and the feet moved quickly, circling the table again, coming to a halt in front of one of the panoramic windows. Half a second later, Mara was gone. She'd run from the dining room at full speed.

Anushka hardly dared breathe. She told herself that she'd count to a hundred before she so much as twitched. But it was long before then when she reached forward and nudged at Norm, who slumped sideways.

'Oh my God... *no!*' She fumbled at his neck, searching for the carotid.

His pulse was weak. She had to get him out of here, she realised.

She clambered from under the table, looking aghast at the destruction around her. And then made her way to the panoramic window, from the corner of which she could see some kind of glazed annex to the main building. Was it a greenhouse or another conservatory? Either way, she was certain that there should not be a huge, jagged hole in the middle of its upwardly sloped roof.

57

Fortunately, the swimming pool was deep enough for both David and Hannah to land in from on high without striking the bottom. But now they were enmeshed in splintered sections of PVC, and it was a struggle to fight their way to the side.

Somewhere overhead, beyond the semi-demolished roof, they knew that Jerry Corrigan would be staring down. He'd finally kicked in the bedroom door just as they'd leapt from the windowsill. He'd have known where they'd gone because the window was left open. Whether he could see them now was another matter, but it wasn't unfeasible. Whether he was mad enough to open fire anyway, simply hoping to hit something, was also a possibility.

'Quickly.' David hauled himself up a steel ladder, lugging Hannah behind him.

He was still riddled with pain. He'd thumped his leg on impact with the roof, but adrenaline was taking care of the worst of it, at least for the moment. They were now on the side, where sufficient moonlight shafted in to show that the pool itself was rectangular, thirty or so feet in length and about fifteen wide. At the house end, he saw a solid, log-built structure with a single, small window in the door, a sauna no doubt, and next to that, an ordinary door standing open on a darkened, tiled corridor with the aura of a changing area or shower. To the right of that was a wall of tall rubber plants, and then a short flight of stairs leading down to a lower corridor, which presumably led into the main building.

Hannah sat on the edge of the pool, coughing.

David seized her elbow and lifted her to her feet. 'Is there an exit?'

She pointed to the top of the stairway. 'There's a fire-door before you get back to the house.'

They moved in that direction, David stepping gingerly.

And then stopping abruptly, signalling for silence.

They stood dripping, listening intently. Hearing nothing.

But smelling something.

Manure.

David grabbed her hand and stumbled towards the sauna. 'In here.'

'What do you mean?'

'Get in and keep down.'

She did so, just as a pair of feet entered the corridor beyond the rubber plants. Along with the stink, now in all its eye-watering glory.

David's heart thudded as he backed into the changing area, knocking over an aluminium pole with a net at one end. He caught it before it fell and clattered.

Booted feet clomped up the short stairway and onto the poolside.

Large sections of ceiling were still floating on the surface, but the water had calmed sufficiently to show that nobody was lying submerged.

'Bastards!' David heard Mara whisper.

The feet drew closer, but sounded heavy, almost dragging. She'd taken a crack on the skull and clearly hadn't recovered fully. But she was still armed with a pistol, while all he had was this pool net. Before he could even think about shrinking into the darkness behind him, she lumbered into view from his left, gun trained in front of her. This close, he was chilled to recognise the distinctive triangular barrel of a Desert Eagle. One of the largest-calibre semi-automatics in circulation, this thing would stop a bull elephant.

By instinct rather than design, he lunged out with the net, and though he didn't manage to snare the deadly weapon, he whacked it out of her grasp.

It flew across the pool, landing on the far side, where it skittered and bounced along the tiles.

Mara swung about, turning a face of blood-streaked rage on him.

David hopped forward, the pole horizontal, trying to drive her back towards the pool. She deflected it and caught him with a karate blow. He lost his footing, but she grabbed him before he hit the ground, both hands hooked into his sodden vest, flinging him along the poolside.

The tiles were rubbery and soft, but thin and clearly laid over concrete or asphalt, and when he rolled to a halt against the far wall, he felt as though he'd been kicked by several horses. His entire leg had gone numb.

Mara walked after him, smiling as she pulled into view the kind of knife that only Rambo would have used: twelve inches at least, one gleaming edge curved and serrated. She didn't speak as she stood over him, but with all that congealed blood, a grin that split her ear to ear, and hair hanging in a gluey, straggling mat, she was like some demonic scarecrow. David lay frozen. She raised the blade, delighted by his terror ... so delighted that she failed to notice Hannah close behind with the pool net. When she did, it was too late. She spun, but for the second time that night was dealt a stinging blow to the cranium. However, it was a lightweight implement. She kept her feet, parried the second blow and struck Hannah on the chin with the pommel of her knife.

Hannah tottered backwards, Mara following, landing a roundhouse kick in her side, which pitched her full length into the water. David, still dazed, lurched up and tried to grapple with the assassin from behind, but he was badly weakened. When she rammed her elbow back into his solar plexus, he toppled away, landing against the tiled wall and sliding down it. This time when she approached, she kicked his ribs a couple of times, before planting her boot-sole on his left shin, and pressing it hard.

David convulsed with pain, burying his teeth in his lip. After what seemed like minutes but was probably only seconds, she grew bored, stepping back and raising the knife again, its blade angled downward...

And jolted as the first echoing shot tore through her body.

She remained standing.

Even when the second one hit her.

Though not the third or the fourth, the latter two spinning her like a top as she fell twitching and jerking into the pool, where she sank from view beneath a spreading cloud of crimson.

Bewildered, David gazed across the water – to where Hannah, her own mouth running with blood, clung to the ladder with her right hand, and with her left still pointed the Desert Eagle, smoke trailing from its muzzle.

Upstairs, Jerry Corrigan still had half a clip for his Browning. On top of that, he'd found Admir's submachine gun next to the open window. It had amused him in a not particularly funny way that its magazine hadn't been fitted properly, which meant that Kelman wouldn't even have been able to fire the damn thing.

He snicked it into place and was tempted to lean out and spray what remained of the pool-house roof. But they'd have ducked back into the main building by now, and he couldn't afford to waste ammo. He moved to the bedroom door and listened.

An eerie silence pervaded the building.

As a former SFO, he knew what that would mean. Whoever was commanding the team outside wouldn't yet consider that they had enough info to make an assault. They'd have snipers in place, complete with night-vision and telescopic sighting, but though they'd returned fire earlier, now that things had gone quiet, they were biding their time. Most likely they'd want to talk and would be waiting for a negotiator to arrive. Of course, if it all kicked off again, they'd have no option but to come in.

He moved onto the landing, both firearms cocked and ready, one in each hand.

At the top of the stairs, he waited. Again, he heard nothing from below. Peeking down, he could see the two smashed windows. For some reason, there was no sign of either Mara or Admir, and that was a worry, because at least one of them had needed to guard the front of the building.

He descended a few steps, before slinging the Steyr over his shoulder, slipping his Browning into its holster and clambering over an upper section of banister. He hung by his hands and dropped into the hall. He landed lithely, but was distracted by the sight of two bodies. The first was Jason Bulstrode, which was no surprise – they'd come here with orders to dispose of the expendables if necessary. The other, though, was Admir.

Cursing silently, Corrigan unslung his Steyr, drew his Browning, and proceeded along the hall towards the rear of the house, scanning every darkened doorway. And froze ... as four loud shots rang out.

Somewhere not too far from where he was now.

He dropped to a crouch, icy sweat swamping his entire body, knowing without needing to be told that word would already be rushing along the chain of command.

'Shiiit ...' he stammered.

And then he heard it. That familiar smashing, banging and shouting. The tell-tale sounds of cops making rapid entry.

He galloped forward. He was heavily armed, probably better-armed than most of the assaulters he'd be facing. Maybe he could blast his way out into the garden, make a run for it.

He burst into the lounge.

Where he never even saw the heavy wooden shaft that struck him in the face with such force that his head spun on its axis, his feet flew from under him, and the plush carpet hit his back so hard that both his weapons bounced away into the darkness.

A second passed before David limped from the shadows, staring in fascination at the half a garden rake still quivering in his fist. Then he became aware of the exploding glass and woodwork, and the intense beams of light spearing inward.

'*Armed police!*' a gruff voice called. '*Weapon down ... On your knees!*'

David tossed the broken shaft and sank painfully down.

'*Don't you fucking move!*'

'No worries, mate.'

'*Hands! Let me see them!*'

David stuck his mitts in the air, dazzled by torchlight but

conscious of dark figures encroaching on all sides. 'Don't shoot,' he said.

'Stay put.' The cop sounded calmer. One of the torch beams roved the floor and halted on Corrigan, who was semi-conscious and groaning. 'What's wrong with him?'

'It's only his head,' David said. 'So probably not much.'

58

Though Rosehill House was officially a crime scene, the pinkish glow of dawn found its gravelled parking areas thronging with first-responders, paramedics from the two ambulances mingling with the firearms officers, local uniforms and plain clothes.

David, stitched and covered in Elastoplast, and leaning thankfully on a proper crutch, limped through it all until he found the person he wanted.

Detective Sergeant Lynda Hagen stood in conflab with a couple of older male colleagues. He only approached when the men had gone. Considering the earliness of the hour, she looked remarkably unfrazzled, wearing a blouse and jeans under a light summer jacket. He stood alongside her, staring back at the house, which was now taped off and ablaze with light.

'How did you get my private number?' she asked, not looking at him.

'I've still got *some* friends inside your ranks.'

'I'd love to know who they are.'

'I'll bet you would, but we magicians must keep some secrets. Anyway, I'm glad you came.'

She glanced sidelong at him. 'When you rang me at silly o'clock in the morning, laid it on the line what you thought you knew, and said that you were coming here even if I wasn't, you didn't leave me much choice.'

'You didn't have to bring the entire Essex Police just for that.'

She glanced back to the house. 'A couple of days ago, we pulled the body of a young woman off a woodland bonfire.'

'Shit...'

'It was late yesterday when we managed to ID her. She was a known drug addict.'

David swallowed. He knew what was coming.

'The evidence pointed to one of her dealers,' Hagen said. 'But there were problems with that. Then I remembered that name you gave me the other day. Yvonne.'

'Blue hair?'

'Yes. Her full name was Yvonne Matthews. Runaway from Manchester. Nineteen.'

'Jesus...'

'I went to bed last night seriously wondering what you were into, Mr Kelman. Then, after you called, well... the Jag in the Colchester lock-up checked out. Fresh bullet damage is never a sign that all's well.'

'So what about Jodie Martindale?' he asked.

She shrugged. 'Jason Bulstrode's no gangster. He should sing like the proverbial – assuming he survives the night.'

'I'm amazed he's still alive.'

'Even if he makes it, he'll spend the rest of his life pooping in a bag. Still, at least that'll be unattractive to the prison butches.' She shrugged. 'If it doesn't work with Bulstrode, we've always got Corrigan. He's squealed in the past. With luck he'll squeal again.'

'You're not going to offer him another deal?' David said.

'That'll be out of my hands. We're in Major Investigations territory now. But he's almost certainly going down for life. Whether the judge imposes a minimum tariff might be up to Corrigan. Of course, until we speak to him, we'll just have to search the premises, see what we can find and hope we get lucky.'

'Well,' he offered her a small electronic device, 'this ought to help.'

Hagen regarded it warily. 'What is it?'

'In case Bulstrode doesn't make it, call it his last testament.'

'What do you mean?'

David hit playback.

'There's a spare bedroom upstairs, first on the left,' came Jason Bulstrode's voice. *'You'll know it because the key's in the door and there's no furniture inside. Lock her in. Search her first – make sure she hasn't got a phone.'*

'Anything happens to her, it won't be quite so easy for you to inherit MDS,' David's voice said.

David clicked it off. 'It worked. Thank God.'

'That's a Dictaphone?' Hagen asked slowly.

'Belongs to Norm Harrington. I took it from his car earlier. Once inside, it was just a matter of switching it on and sliding it under the couch.'

She regarded him with astonishment. 'You recorded stuff?'

'I recorded everything.' He offered it again. 'That was one of the main reasons for coming here tonight. Along with trying to force your hand, of course. Quite a performance we all put on in there, if I say so myself. We had to get Jason to talk somehow.'

She still didn't take it from him. It was almost as though she couldn't believe it. 'This amounts to a confession?'

'In full. It also implicates Nick Thorogood.'

Hagen dug urgently into her jacket pocket, pulled on a pair of disposable gloves and opened a sterile evidence sack. And halted. 'What's the catch?'

'Don't get you?'

'You don't want to make use of this yourself? For your latest exclusive?'

David mused. 'Not till you guys have done with it. Once burned and all that.' Seeing she was still hesitant, he slipped it into the bag for her. 'Will that be enough?'

'If you've got a voice recording of Jason Bulstrode coughing to the offence, then yes, probably. We can find a way to work this into evidence.' She pondered. 'Even if he names Nick Thorogood as an accomplice, it'll amount to no more than an accusation. But that's a start. And if Thorogood was unwise enough to show his face at this halfway house where the trafficked women were being kept, maybe he was also unwise enough to show it at wherever Jodie Martindale's being held. So that's another reason to find her alive.'

David nodded. 'What about Jorgenson?'

'Professional Standards are on it. They'll nail him and his sidekick to the wall. Which reminds me – you given your statement yet?'

'Not yet. That's why I'm still here and not in Casualty.'

She glanced down. 'Leg bad?'

'I'm not Long John Silver, but I don't think I'm far off.'

'Stick around if you can. If not, let us know where you'll be.' She made to move off, but then turned again. 'Mr Kelman ... I'm not saying I misread you all those years ago. But anyone tells me again that leopards can't change their spots, I'll call them a liar.'

And she moved away to find the SIO.

David half-smiled. Damn, but she was gorgeous. He wondered if she was happily married. Speaking of someone who wasn't, his eyes now fell on Anushka, seated on a garden bench about fifteen yards away, wrapped in foil.

He hobbled over there.

'Norm's been taken to Colchester General,' she said in a weepy voice.

'I know.'

'They say it doesn't look too bad. The bullet went clean through his shoulder.' She shuddered. 'It's mainly soft tissue.'

'He'll be OK. He's a tough old coot.'

'God almighty, David...' She gazed at him with harrowed eyes. 'How can you be so blasé?'

'All right, I'm sorry.' He sat down next to her, nudging her along with his hips. 'Suppose it's a form of self-defence. But look at the positives. A battle wound is nothing to be ashamed of. Far from it.'

'Where's Mrs Bulstrode?'

'She's gone to hospital too.'

'Was she hurt?'

'Hard to say. Not physically.'

Anushka shuddered again. 'She must be in a wretched state.'

'She's had her fair share of crap to deal with, there's no denying that.'

'Please tell me it's not always going to be like this.'

'It's not always going to be like this.'

'Say it like you mean it!'

'Nushka, I can't. But, you know, this is not a road *you* have to take. You've got a good job already.'

'Yeah, I stack shelves all day or supervise other people doing it.'

'That makes you even more awesome then, doesn't it?'

She stared at him, puzzled. 'Awesome?'

'What you've done this last couple of weeks. You've been amazing. Look what we've achieved together.'

She seemed incredulous. 'Are you *enjoying* all this?'

'Well, apart from the broken leg.'

'I'm serious.'

'What do you want me to say? I'm sorry that shit happens. Of course I am. But the bastards responsible are being brought to book. And we did our bit.'

Sometimes David wondered if behaving as if this kind of thing didn't trouble him – being objective rather than emotional, as that old sweat copper had advised – did more harm than good, maybe damaged him as a person. But he wasn't going to pretend that he didn't feel proud.

'It's deceptively easy, isn't it,' she sniffled. 'When you're in the newsroom, and it's all just words and photos?'

'Easy was never in the job description.' He watched as an undertaker's van reversed along the drive, its back doors opening to reveal a neat stack of temporary coffins. 'If it was easy … they'd all be out here doing it.'

Epilogue

'Incredible,' Norm said. 'All this time they were holding her in an everyday suburban house? And none of the neighbours suspected a thing?'

Though his left arm was fixed in a sling, he sat upright in his chair in the Shed, regarding the front page of the first edition of the *Essex Enquirer* emblazoned on his screen.

JODIE MARTINDALE FOUND

The strapline over the top added:

Heiress released alive after six-year subterranean captivity in Braintree basement

The colour photograph accompanying it, one of several that Anushka had been on hand to take after the police had tipped the *Enquirer* off that they were about to raid the premises, depicted a detached house sitting on a street so ordinary that it could have graced any estate agent's window. You wouldn't have looked at it twice were it not for the presence of an armoured police troop-carrier and a phalanx of gun-toting coppers.

'Her jailers had the appearance of an ordinary family,' Anushka replied. She was in her supermarket uniform, but had popped over during her lunchbreak. 'Kept themselves to themselves. As for Jodie, no one saw or heard a thing. The cellar was sound-proofed. I mean, it was comfy enough. Carpets, wallpaper, toilet, shower … clean as a whistle, ventilated. Even had its own kitchen. Everything she could want.'

'Except her freedom,' David said, coming through the door awkwardly, still not used to his heavy hospital boot.

'How'd it go with the Martindales' solicitor?' Norm asked.

David eased himself onto his chair. 'Considering the last time I met Mr Whelks was at that infamous press conference all those years ago, reasonably well.'

'Was he forthcoming?' Norm asked.

'It was interesting, for sure.'

Anushka pulled her chair closer. 'The police got any leads on this weird family who were keeping Jodie?'

'Nope.'

'I can't believe they'd just done a runner,' she said. 'That Jodie was the only person in that house when the law arrived.'

David shrugged. 'I'd be surprised if they're even in the UK now, given that they were all foreign nationals.'

The hunt for Jodie Martindale's jailers had been widely publicised, their descriptions circulated. But clearly they'd been informed well in advance of the police coming to call.

'Did Whelks say how Jodie got that phone call out a few weeks ago?' Norm asked.

'He did actually.' David adjusted his position in a futile quest for comfort. 'This family … they weren't a real family. The eldest *son*, for want of a better term, was Russian.'

Norm rolled his eyes. 'Ivankov's people again …'

'If so, this one was on his best behaviour. Probably under orders to be. But he obviously liked Jodie because he couldn't do enough for her. Ran errands, bought her books, DVDs, magazines, that kind of thing. When she complained about headaches, he went out to get painkillers. This was over a period of several weeks. She didn't take them, of course. She saved them up. When she had enough, she invited him in for a cup of coffee. He was suspicious but she said she was desperate for some company. He accepted – and she drugged him. Not properly. He wasn't completely out, but he was sufficiently drowsy for her to get his phone off him. Seems like all her jailers carried a burner, which they were under orders not to use unless it was an emergency. She was able to make a call on it, but off the top of her head, there were only three numbers she could remember. Home and two mobiles, her father's and Freddie's. The first two were a no-no because her jailers had been specifically instructed to let her know that she was being held under her father's authority.'

'Why?' Anushka looked puzzled. 'So she'd know she was in no danger of being killed?'

'I think it's more likely the instruction came from Nick Thorogood,' David said. 'And it was probably for Ralph's benefit.'

Norm nodded. 'If he knew that his daughter was aware he was involved, he'd be much less likely to change his mind and try to persuade his allies to let her go.'

'So why not call 999?' Anushka asked.

David shrugged. 'She knew from the magazines her jailer had brought her that there'd been hoax calls. She reckoned she didn't have much time on the line and that she'd only be believed if she could speak to someone she knew.'

'Which only left Freddie,' Norm said.

'It was the longest shot imaginable,' David replied. 'And

even then her jailer was able to overpower her before she could leave a coherent message.'

'And yet that was the call that saved her life,' Anushka said.

Again, David looked thoughtful. 'She was owed a bit of luck. Sounds as if she'd never wanted to get Rick Tamworth involved, but eventually realised there was no one else she could speak to about it. Young Freddie had been foisted on them that night, though, hence his pointless trip to the chip shop. Incredible misfortune she finally chose to confide in her boyfriend just as the kidnappers were about to strike.'

'One day earlier and it could all have been so different,' Anushka said.

David shrugged.

Norm flipped a few pages on screen, checking out more of Anushka's photos: an ambulance on the drive alongside the house; a carpeted stairway leading down from a doorway at the back of a kitchen closet; the central passage in a mysterious underground complex.

'Whatever,' he said, 'this'll be quite a story when we're allowed to write it in full. The only question is whether we turn it into a book.'

'Any more offers?' David asked.

'You could say that. Percy's phone never stops ringing.' Percy Hodges was Norm's literary agent, though now they'd signed contracts so that he was representing all of them.

'Well, there's more to tell now than we ever could through the *Enquirer*,' David said. 'And the case isn't even closed.'

That latter point was true, and it remained sore.

Both Ralph Martindale and Jason Bulstrode were beyond prosecution, the latter having survived his gunshot wound but now lying in a coma. Vladimir Ivankov, meanwhile, was somewhere in Eastern Europe and unreachable. Even though the police had spoken to the sex workers in Chatham, they hadn't found any trace of the alleged trafficking ring, and certainly no house on the Isle of Sheppey that was being used as a staging post for captive women. Still no evidence had come to light that was adequate to overturn the Coroner's verdict that Freddie Martindale had committed suicide, while James Lynch's legal team were not convinced the statements provided by Brian Fairclough and Chris Jaycox (both of whom had been drinking heavily on the night in question) would be adequate to disprove their client's guilt in the murder of Oya Oyinola. That said, Jerry Corrigan had been remanded in custody on charges of kidnapping David Kelman and criminal use of firearms. There was heavier stuff that could be brought against him yet, which indicated that some kind of discussion was under way. He'd already had several meetings in his cell with representatives of the Crown Prosecution Service and officers from Essex Police's Major Investigations Team. The assumption could only be that Corrigan was the one who'd revealed the whereabouts of Jodie Martindale, and that he'd probably be testifying against Tony Jorgenson and Tim Bly, both of whom had been arrested and charged with a range of offences, including tampering with evidence, bribery, burglary, kidnapping and conspiracy to commit murder.

This still felt insufficient, though, when the real prize proved elusive.

Nick Thorogood had already given several well-publicised interviews, damning the 'scurrilous rumours, stemming from some rather indiscreet police activity' that had connected him to an 'allegedly very serious criminal enterprise', and assuring the public that he would 'fight these outrageous accusations to the fullest extent'. In the most recent one, which he'd given at the ornate front gate of his Hertfordshire mansion, he appeared in vintage Thorogood style, looking relaxed and confident in a lilac suit and pink and blue Paisley shirt and tie, advising the world that he would be 'undertaking this fight with the full support and backing of some very considerable people in the entertainment world and the business communities of this country and others…many of whom are enraged that, simply by association with me, their own good names may be wrongly tarnished'.

To conclude, he'd fixed the TV camera with a cool and angry gaze.

It wouldn't be untrue to say that they'd all been a little unnerved by that. Not that this part of the investigation was in their hands.

'The main question,' Norm said, 'is when do we get our exclusive with Jodie?'

David pondered that. This would be their ultimate reward.

Long before the full details of Jodie's kidnapping and unlawful imprisonment ceased to be *sub judice*, other news organisations would have wheedled out the incredible facts of the case, and would be ready to go with it the moment they were allowed to. The one advantage the *Enquirer* team had, aside from being able to tell their own inside version of events, was the loose arrangement David had made with Hannah Bulstrode that, in return for their successful efforts, the *Enquirer* would have sole access to Jodie and thus be the only news outlet to print the tale from her perspective too.

'Well?' Norm asked again.

'Now that Hannah knows she'll not be facing a murder charge for Mara's death, she's taken Jodie abroad,' David replied. 'I don't know where – a private hospital somewhere in Switzerland or Germany. It's going to be a long road to recovery.'

Norm shrugged. 'None of us thought it was going to happen soon.'

David produced an envelope. 'In lieu of all that, Hannah wrote this letter. Whelks gave it to me earlier.' He passed it around, so that Norm and Anushka could both read it.

Dear Mr Kelman,

I hope you can forgive this impersonal form of contact. But Jodie is far from well, and I felt the best thing I could do was take her away for a long holiday. And when I say away, I mean away from the UK.

She is in such a fragile state that she needs ongoing professional care, but also peace, quiet and, above all, privacy.

As you'll probably understand, I too am going through a difficult time. Not to put too fine a point on it, our lives have been destroyed. In business terms alone, I am left presiding over a complex web of catastrophe, and must rely on the help and advice of others, many of whom I am not even closely acquainted with. The legal ramifications of these recent incidents are also indescribably huge, and all this is before we even consider the personal and domestic disasters that have befallen us. I would like to say we will see it through, Jodie and I, but alas I cannot be certain.

I am under no illusion that neither of us would have survived had it not been for your intervention. For this reason alone, not to mention the safe return of my beloved sister, I remain permanently grateful to you ...

Even if you'd had any responsibility for creating this terrible saga, which we now know you do not, you and your colleagues would have done more than enough to expunge that guilt a hundred times over. Unfortunately, though, and I do hope you can forgive me for this and not consider it some kind of double-cross, after long reflection I cannot permit you to interview Jodie at any time soon, or even at all.

Her ordeal was beyond imagining, and according to the doctors who have assessed her, she might never recover fully. In that light, forcing her to relive the circumstances of her kidnapping and incarceration, not to mention the bombshell revelation that her own father was behind it, would be too great a risk to countenance. Jodie sends her heartfelt thanks, however, and begs you not to feel deceived or mistrusted.

No doubt you'll consider this a cruel blow. But please try to understand our reasons.

Your friend forever,
Hannah Bulstrode

'Well, we've still got *our* part of the story,' Norm said. 'We'll still sell millions of copies when the book gets published.'

David nodded. 'I was half expecting this, to be honest.'

'But do you feel deceived?' Anushka wondered.

'Kind of. Not sure it matters that much. What *does* matter is that your lunchbreak's ended.'

Anushka leapt to her feet. 'Oh hell!' She glanced at her watch, grabbed her bag and rushed for the door. 'Shit, I've got to run. I'll call you guys later.'

They wandered out onto the drive, David leaning on his crutch as Anushka's Fiat reversed at speed onto the road, swinging through a quick three-point turn and accelerating away. Aside from that, it was a pleasant, peaceful day, the late August sun mellow but warm, the cheery sounds of children filtering through the trees bordering the park.

'You're taking this rather well, if you don't mind me saying,' Norm remarked.

'These things happen. Nothing to be gained by making a fuss.'

'You sure? We lost the main villains, and now we've lost the heroine too.'

'Yeah, but we got the result.' David hobbled back to the Shed. 'Trust me, mate, I can live with that.'

Credits

Paul Finch and Orion Fiction would like to thank everyone at Orion who worked on the publication of *Never Seen Again*.

Editorial
Emad Akhtar
Celia Killen

Copy-editor
Clare Wallis

Proofreader
Linda Joyce

Audio
Paul Stark
Jake Alderson
Georgina Cutler

Marketing
Helena Fouracre

Editorial Management
Jane Hughes
Charlie Panayiotou
Tamara Morriss
Claire Boyle

Contracts
Anne Goddard
Ellie Bowker
Humayra Ahmed

Design
Nick Shah
Nick May
Joanna Ridley
Helen Ewing

Finance
Nick Gibson
Jasdip Nandra
Elizabeth Beaumont
Ibukun Ademefun
Afeera Ahmed
Sue Baker
Tom Costello

Inventory
Jo Jacobs
Dan Stevens

Production
Ruth Sharvell
Fiona McIntosh

Publicity
Alainna Hadjigeorgiou

Sales
Jen Wilson
Victoria Laws
Esther Waters
Frances Doyle
Ben Goddard
Jack Hallam
Anna Egelstaff
Inês Figueira
Barbara Ronan
Andrew Hally
Dominic Smith
Deborah Deyong
Lauren Buck
Maggy Park
Linda McGregor

Sinead White
Jemimah James
Rachael Jones
Jack Dennison
Nigel Andrews
Ian Williamson
Julia Benson
Declan Kyle
Robert Mackenzie
Megan Smith
Charlotte Clay
Rebecca Cobbold

Operations
Sharon Willis

Rights
Susan Howe
Krystyna Kujawinska
Jessica Purdue
Ayesha Kinley
Louise Henderson